NIVEOUS
WAR

WOLFSTAR 02

NIVEOUS WAR

The Uncharted Horizon Serial

Jason Diamond | C. R. Buchanan

4 Horsemen
Publications, Inc.

Niveous War: The Uncharted Horizon Serial
Copyright © 2026 CR Buchanan and Jason Diamond. All rights reserved.

Published By: 4 Horsemen Publications, Inc.

4 Horsemen Publications, Inc.
PO Box 419
Sylva, NC 28779
4horsemenpublications.com
info@4horsemenpublications.com

Cover Illustration by CD Corrigan
Typesetting by Autumn Skye
Edited by Jen Paquette

All rights to the work within are reserved to the author and publisher. No part of this publication may be reproduced, stored in a retrieval system, or transmitted in any form or by any means, electronic, mechanical, photocopying, recording, scanning, or otherwise, except as permitted under Section 107 or 108 of the 1976 International Copyright Act, without prior written permission except in brief quotations embodied in critical articles and reviews. Please contact either the Publisher or Author to gain permission.

All characters, organizations, and events portrayed in this novel are either products of the author's imagination or are used fictitiously.

All brands, quotes, and cited work respectfully belongs to the original rights holders and bear no affiliation to the authors or publisher.

WolfStar is a work of fiction. Any names, characters, businesses, events, incidents, and anything else in this work of fiction are products of the author/s' imagination/s. Any resemblance to actual people, alive, dead, or soon-to-be-born, is purely coincidental.

Library of Congress Control Number: 2025941874

Paperback ISBN-13: 979-8-8232-0952-6
Hardcover ISBN-13: 979-8-8232-0953-3
Audiobook ISBN-13: 979-8-8232-0955-7
Ebook ISBN-13: 979-8-8232-0954-0

TABLE OF CONTENTS

Introduction	ix
Chapter 1	1
Chapter 2	14
Chapter 3	23
Chapter 4	30
Chapter 5	42
Chapter 6	61
Chapter 7	71
Chapter 8	83
Chapter 9	89
Chapter 10	101
Chapter 11	107
Chapter 12	121
Chapter 13	125
Chapter 14	133
Chapter 15	138
Chapter 16	147
Chapter 17	155
Chapter 18	159
Chapter 19	176
Chapter 20	200
Chapter 21	211
Chapter 22	228

Chapter 23	237
Chapter 24	245
Chapter 25	254
Chapter 26	262
Chapter 27	272
Chapter 28	283
Chapter 29	288
Chapter 30	296
Chapter 31	312
Language translations	319
Book Club Questions	331
Author Bios	333

INTRODUCTION

Humanity's newfound sanctuary beckons with unparalleled beauty and the promise of life beyond imagination. The Dah'Sel accepted our presence with open arms, but a worry looms. Uprisers are wreaking havoc on Kepler 442b.

Interstellar vessels await to transport a selected few to the new world. Hope, unprecedented in 100 aionas, dawns on civilization's future, but those who survived fear for loved ones still to come. Most fear the worst.

The unyielding Upriser war against the Armada allows crime to run rampant, leaving civilians with a grim choice: join them in rebellion or confront the brutal consequences of remaining loyal to their neutral state. Killers... Sadists... Torturers... Their plan is unknown.

Doom is Dolofónos.

CHAPTER 1
Waterfall

Dolofónos sits in a clear, cube-shaped maximum-security cell reserved for those in line to be executed, with an eye patch over his left eye. His face is a tangle of scars—soul, a figment of the imagination. Burn scars cover patches on top of his head where hair refuses to grow.

His cell door, its seams, handles, roof, and all things inside it are comprised of translucent, hollow lead. There is nothing on his clear bed for comfort. A vacuum toilet keeps him company with a button on the wall he can push once a tak for the four ounces of water he will have to drink from a clear spigot. Mental torture, courtesy of the Armada for those who deserve it.

The floor he inhabits contains 15 evenly spaced, translucent, cube-shaped cells. A single captive moves about in all but one. Some exercise. Others sleep. One stares blankly from his chamber, as if watching an unseen halo-projection.

Drops of water sporadically hit the top of all cells. It runs slowly down their clear sides as a constant reminder of what looms overhead. Water is the deterrent that prevents any attempts to escape.

Three guards enter with a new prisoner in escort. They guide him across the white floor to the empty cell. The new arrival nods to another prisoner in one of the cubical cells. The captive does not acknowledge him.

A sharp blow from the stock of an onium rifle to the back of the new prisoner's head knocks him unconscious.

"No communication allowed amongst prisoners," shouts the guard for the others to hear. "No eye contact." He studies his inmates while the other two guards drag the man into his cell. "And no talking. Keep your eyes on the ground."

They toss the sleeping prisoner in without care, then shut and lock the cell door behind him. His chest rises and falls as he lies on the ground.

"Welcome to C.H.I.," says the guard.

It is normal for prisoners to communicate when locked up in most places. Not here. C.H.I. (the Chimark Holding Institute) is the only place designed to hold people like Dolofónos. No one may speak when confined to this level of security. Trying is futile. Hollow lead cancels sound waves, and the facility forbids hand signals or prolonged eye contact.

Visual feed recorders line its besmite walls, ceiling, and floor. It is the hardest known substance on Kep Four. A single guard stands beside each prisoner cell flanking the walls and main entrance. Workstations are present next to each of them. Their jobs are simple.

Watch. Control. Shoot.

At the top center of the back wall is the maximum-security overlook station. From there, guards can see wall-to-wall across the 300-pace prisoner hold. Only those in the overlook have the power to open and close all cell doors with a series of old-world manual switches. With them is an always-watchful pair of snipers ready to fire. They stand stoically in expression and wait for a reason to shoot.

WATERFALL

"Best we monitor the new prisoner when he wakes," says the first sniper.

"I get first shot," says the second.

"Not a chance," says the other guard. "I haven't bagged an Upriser in cycles."

Above the overlook station are two additional guard towers. A male and female Armada official pace in each. Separating glass divides them from the cell block below.

All 14 guards at floor level watch beneath covered guard stations as water drips from the ceiling. Sprinkles of makeshift rain fill the area, drizzle over clear cubical cell walls, and wash away into small drains throughout the floor. Prisoners inside their cells have a water-blurred view of surrounding faces.

Schematics of the dripping water source are electro-stenciled on the floor of each cell. Prisoners have it alone to look at. The design is simple: A large chamber between the upper outer walls of the prison wraps the facility and takes up two stories of the floor's volume overhead—three times the amount of water needed to fill the level Dolofónos is on. Each sniper in the overlook room has a flood switch mounted next to them. When thrown, water pours in from overhead inlets until it fills the area from cells to ceiling. What remains in the chamber after flood activation is enough for a second downpour. It is a last-ditch effort set in place to guarantee a drowning death for both prisoners and guards alike, should a bad enough situation arise to activate it.

Administration shows halo-projector videos of the water system's first use 31 cycles ago to prisoners. They must watch it every 19 rotations. There were no survivors. No prisoner has challenged it since.

NIVEOUS WAR

All is quiet on the maximum-security level. Time passes. Guards and prisoners do much of nothing—boredom on the faces of all.

The intercom clicks to life.

"Guard rotation," says an overhead worker. "Seventeen teks. Complete your rotation logs."

Guards working the floor step to their stations and make their inputs. An alarm rings out. Visual input sensors high in the security hold's corners go red. Guards on the floor scramble to tactical positions.

Faint gunshots echo from an unknown location. Onium rifles in the backdrop grow louder by the tik. Prisoners stand in their cubes and hit the sides of them as if someone can hear them.

Dolofónos rises slowly, stretches, and smiles. Scars on his face pull tight around his lips, cheeks, and right eye.

"It's about time," he says.

The outburst of firearms grows louder. An unknown explosion rocks the maximum-security unit guards. Soldiers and inmates alike recoil away and duck for cover. Dolofónos does not flinch.

Inmates stay low. Debris rolls across the floor as guards take battle positions. Smoke takes its time to clear.

A group of Uprisers breach the main door and push through the cloud with bad intentions. The guards open fire, but adversaries bleed into the scene. They are great in numbers and swarm like the locus of Shremba. Fearless red-and-black-suited murderers attack without apprehensions of death or being the first to die at the front of the line.

One by one they fall, yet the swarm continues.

"For Dolofónos!" shouts a female Upriser with long, wild hair unkept for many rotations.

WATERFALL

Others echo her words as snipers reload in the overlook station. They hit their marks. Upriser after Upriser goes down, but it is of no use. Too many red-and-black invaders pour into the area.

"Flood it," says the overlook guard.

A high-positioned sniper looks at his Armada colleagues below.

"The guards are still fighting down there," says the sniper. "If we—"

"Flood it," shouts the overlook guard. "Flood it, or we're dying with them."

The sniper eyes her and moves his wrist over a bio-scanner. His DNA rotates over his hand for a half tik and disappears. The security casing lifts from the flood switch, setting off a siren to pierce delicate eardrums of all in range.

A magno-barrier rises where the Uprisers breach the floor. Dozens of black-and-red-suited savages are stuck on the other side of it and can no longer enter. Twelve eight-pace gates rise from overhead to release a torrential flush of water and rinse evil from the floor.

"Nooo," whispers a hopeless guard.

Uprisers beat against the magno-barrier as shadowy water sweeps their comrades off their feet. Their shouts go unheard. All they can do is watch their fellow guards get beaten against walls, cells, and stations under the power of crashing water and its intense waves.

Screams of mercy and fearful cries for help cannot penetrate the water's reverberating tone. Less than 10 tiks of flow submerge Dolofónos's cell along with the others. Small breathing holes in each provide them with their last shower. The floodwater is dark and brown from cycles of sitting stagnate. Prisoners disappear from sight when it rises past their clear holds.

Guards in the overlook lower the separating glass and take aim to shoot the swimming Upriser's arms and legs as they come up for air. They are helpless. Drowned, shot, or both are their last moments alongside their Armada enemies.

Dolofónos may not survive long enough for the 12 waterfalls to finish their freefall from the floating prison and to the Sigma Green district three clicks below. He does not appear worried about it. The man is terrible news. People on Kep Four would be better off if he died, but it could also spark heavy backlash from the Uprisers if he dies in C.H.I.

Gloomy liquid closes in on the top of the hold. Uprisers in the sniper overlook raise the separating glass back up. They watch as water rises above it. Bleeding guards and Uprisers bang against its glass, silently begging for the water to be drained.

Internal pressure triples with the rise in water and air pressure as the level fills. It bursts the eardrums of those holding their breath for an additional moment of pain before they drown. They grab the sides of their heads and sink for a tek before swimming back to the surface. Blood floats from their ears to merge with their liquid executioner.

There is only one breath of air left before the water rises its last pace to reach the ceiling. Prisoners reach for the tops of their cells in vain after being submerged beneath guards that swim above them. Dolofónos sits calmly in his clear cell with his legs locked onto the bed's hard corner.

The overlook station's door blows from its fasteners with a short-lived rush of flames. It impacts an Armada guard and sniper. They are dead before hitting the ground. More Uprisers enter and drop fast as gunfire between them and the guards unfolds. Three Uprisers drop from multiple gunshot wounds to their chests and heads.

WATERFALL

A trio of Uprisers breach the high overlook station as water presses against its separating glass. A fishbowl of guards struggle behind it. All three Uprisers throw T-Blades (electrically charged knives) at the guards. Two bury into Armada chests. One hits a guard's shoulder. All three Armada defenders drop from the electrical charges, and invasive Uprisers take back their blades to finish the job with a single drag across each jugular.

Three more enter and stab the downed guards, two of which are clutching their necks with a red rush overtaking their fingers. Dying guards fight back with flailing arms until they are too weak to defend themselves and succumb to the damage inflicted upon their bodies. The last guard on his back in the overlook tower tries to speak before he is gone, but his words are a gurgle of blood.

Their attackers stand, wipe their blades, and step over the guards' bodies to flip a pair of levers at each end of the room.

"Three..." says an Upriser. "Two ... One ... Go."

They raise the levers in sync. The eight-pace panels that were letting the water in close to stop its flow. A tek passes. Twelve similar panels open and drain the floor at a rate slower than it filled.

An air-raid siren wails to warn the Sigma Green district below C.H.I. of an incoming downpour. They must take cover. Lives ended in the past from the falling torrent's power.

Old water from above will ensure the cleanest spot-on Kep Four becomes the Sigma Green district under the floating maximum-security facility next to the capital of Chimark. The Uprisers shot most of the guards before it drained. The water will leave a blood-red tint on the district of poverty as a reminder of the consequences that follow actions taken against the Armada.

Grates over outflowing water channels prevent anyone left breathing from getting pushed out. Guards and Uprisers are stuck against them until the last drop of water drains. Four remaining guards and three Uprisers stand to gasp for air. Several are dead with lungs full of H_2O.

The magno-barrier drops where the enemy blew out the wall to breach the cell floor Dolofónos is on. Uprisers surge in and overpower C.H.I.'s water-logged guards with gunfire. The white floor of murky water turns into splotches and swirls of deep red.

Dolofónos is lying in his cell. He is not breathing. His door opens along with the other cells on the floor.

1-2
Extract

A pair of Uprisers drag Dolofónos from his cell. They place a rusted metallic box at his side and activate it. The box reacts and targets Dolofónos, opening from the top like a flower to lie flat and extend an oxygen-purging unit over his mouth. A cylindrical drone emerges from the metallic box to read Dolofónos's vitals. It hovers over its target with two telescoping arms capped with flat pads to perform rapid compressions at 43 to every breath.

Dolofónos's chest rises and falls with heart-shocks from each pad's administration of electricity. His body twitches with each compression. The fight to revive him is crucial for their cause.

The outdated unit supplies a slight shock per compression once thought to be overkill. It mimics a life rack's functionality, though primitive by current standards. They either stole or purchased it from the underground.

WATERFALL

The process goes on for 20 or 30 tiks before Dolofónos takes his first breath. A celebration ensues from the Uprisers that revived him. Other Uprisers are lying unconscious, unresponsive, and not breathing in their cells.

Dolofónos gasps and rolls to his side as those around him cheer. The two that drug him from the cell assist him to his feet. He embraces them for saving his life and raises his arms high overhead in celebration. More cheers follow. Their leader is evil but has them blinded in a fight for the so-called better good.

A few guards stir from the floor in the background. An Upriser moves in for the kill.

"Stop," orders Dolofónos. "We're taking them with us."

Uprisers surround the remaining guards and lead them toward the breached wall. One kicks a guard's legs out from under him and laughs as he gets back to his feet. The palm-width symbol on their uniform of a human pelvic bone is in the perfect place. It rests over where their hearts would be, if they had any.

1-3
Takeover

Uprisers lead Dolofónos through the C.H.I. compound. Armada bodies are strewn about in their own blood. They must have taken over the section and wiped out all Armada personnel and security feeds before jail-breaking their leader. Armada military would be all over them and leave little chance of their escape otherwise. It is a well-planned extraction and most likely involves someone assisting from the inside.

A tall female Upriser with coal black hair and a missing right arm replaced with robotics meets Dolofónos in the hall to take point with him.

"Saddee," whispers one Armada hostage to another.

A single gunshot rips through his head. He falls limp to the floor.

"It's pronounced *sad eye*," says the female Upriser.

She steps to her rescued leader, makes momentary eye contact with him, and smiles.

"Saddi," says Dolofónos. "Glad you could make it."

"Eight cycles together and you think I'm missing a party now?" asks Saddi.

"Any alarms?"

"None."

"How many are left in the building?" asks Dolofónos.

"Few," answers Saddi.

They force the captive guards into a jog as she hands him a sidearm. He halts everyone and slides it over his right hand to examine it.

"A VR3?" he asks. "How?"

"From the corpse of a capital leader," answers Saddi. "You don't know him."

The VR3 (Voltage Reaction 3rd burst) is a smart hand and wrist-mounted sidearm that sits on the back of the user's hand when gripped in a natural firing stance. A short, modular barrel housed in a custom-fit gauntlet ... the weapon wraps snugly around the back of the user's wrist. The barrel is low-profile, no longer than the back of his palm when not extended.

Dolofónos extends his right arm with his fingers open wide and stops. A pistol grip flips around his hand into his palm, and a barrel extends from the back of his hand. Holographic sights that only he can see pop up with the amount of rounds remaining in the weapon, wind speed, and temperature. Only our capital leader's guards were intended to carry this slick and deadly auto-targeting weapon.

He grabs its handle and activates it. The weapon buzzes.

"Thank you," says Dolofónos, deactivating the VR3 and collapsing it again. "Let's move. Kill anything not wearing red-and-black."

Dolofónos leads his Uprisers to the only door on the maximum-security floor with barrels trained on their captive's skulls. His bare feet slip on the floor, and he almost falls.

"Stop," orders Dolofónos.

His Uprisers come to a halt. He looks down at the nearest guard's feet to eye his terra boots.

"I need that guard's boots," says Dolofónos.

Saddi shoots the guard in the head. He crumbles where he stands to lie in a red rush that pools from his head. She removes his terra boots and hands them to her leader.

Dolofónos kneels to secure his terra boots.

"I changed my mind," says Dolofónos. "We don't need the extra weight."

His men pull triggers. Point blank onium blasts wrap the guards' heads. Their bodies fall. Dolofónos straps the terra boots to his feet and stands.

"Ask every inmate in here if they'd like to become an Upriser," says Dolofónos. "Bring those that do with you. Kill the ones that don't in their cells."

"You heard him," says Saddi.

The Uprisers split up and head into the various levels of C.H.I.

1–4
Falling

Dolofónos and his Uprisers are taking to the air in dozens of stolen Armada cargo vessels painted red-and-black with thousands of freed prisoners on board.

"Vessels two, six, and seven," says Saddi. "Collide with the west city flier and take it out."

"What?" asks a pilot.

"Do it," says Saddi.

Three vessels take a path toward the outer perimeter of the floating prison. They head toward the black, cone-peeked, ferromagnetic city flyers that hold the prison high in the brown.

They move toward it without hesitation and slam into the west city flier in sync. The city lifts cannot maintain their grip on the prison, which drops on its west side before it slips into a free fall. It will reach and decimate the Sigma Green district and its population below in less than a tek. An entire city gone, wiped from existence.

The rest take toward an unknown location as Armada patrol vessels move into intercept. The distance between them and the enemy is vast, but they are closing fast. Blasts of fire stream from Armada patrol units. A Bomba class 1 intercepts from the opposite direction from below.

"Hit the brown," says Saddi. "Everyone surface-side, get ready."

The slower Bomba-Class Armada misses several shots. It strikes down only one Upriser vessel as they juke left, right, high, and low with hard air-braking and acceleration. The modified cargo vessels litter the brown with rapid waves of onium shots. Several hit Chimark's distant energy dome to ripple its exterior.

WATERFALL

The Bomba fires a scat-shot, releasing a single burst of 51 antimatter balls from a large barrel. The Uprisers maneuver with aggression to escape the oversized shotgun blast of death headed in their direction. All but Dolofónos and Saddi's vessel are hit.

Each struck vessel continues its already doomed flight into obscurity as it disappears from existence. The Bomba pays them no mind and moves for Dolofónos and Saddi's craft.

"Give me feeds on the other ships," says Dolofónos.

"Incoming," says Saddi.

The rear visual feed pane powers up to show what lies in their wake. His comrades' ships turn into nothing—like metallic flash-paper reverse-sintering in slow motion. The damage is done. Antimatter has given its kiss of death. Pilots and passengers alike burn from existence with their vessels.

Dolofónos and Saddi's craft slips into the brown with the freed prisoners on board. His working eye holds two emotions: anger with hateful tension and a vengeful spirit for the vessels he lost, each battling for position behind scars; Najasa is ahead of him, the Bomba behind him.

Patrol units move in behind the larger Bomba for backup, but it is too late.

"Now," says Saddi.

Weapons blasting from hundreds of unseen sources rain upward from below to beat incoming Armada ships into surrender and force them to pull up. Chasing Armada units make small warp jumps from the attack and escape, but Dolofónos is gone, and there is nothing anyone can do about it but wish Kep Four Syndrome's cellular lung decay will claim him.

CHAPTER 2
Internal Thoughts

My head spins with the room around me as I fall from the bed. I jump when my body jolts me from slumber and reach to catch myself at the last tik before spilling onto the tele-tent floor. My sheets slip from the corners as I use them to pull myself up.

I stir to open my eyes and sit up with a naked question. "Was that a...?"

What I witnessed baffles me. I am unsure if it was a vision or a dream. It was one or the other. Hopefully, it was just a bad dream.

The whole thing is stuck in my mind as I stand to get dressed. I was not in a cell like I saw Dolofónos in during my incarceration. Not even once. I cannot imagine the need to empty my bowels in a clear cube on a toilet of the same make.

I wish the Uprisers to see the truth about all the suffering they cause in time, but another part of me realizes they never will. It is a testament to the fact we are all products of our environment and, had I been in the right circumstances during my upbringing and left behind for dead, I might have followed Dolofónos as well. Instead, I chose the A.R.S. to satisfy a vengeance over my brother Comilo.

INTERNAL THOUGHTS

Neither route is what one would call admirable. I try not to think about it. Such are the consequences of living in a torn world.

I dream like everybody else, but I have never had one so vivid and in line with what might be happening back on Kep Four. If odds are in my favor, it was not a vision. I doubt it was. Those have only happened while I was awake since my arrival on Wah'Lor.

"Okay, Mason," I say to myself, "you need to talk to the doctors and get your lesson plan in order for the Dah'Sel and Armada youths' educational programs."

I grab my filing scroll and sit back on the tele-tent's firm bed to place my palms against its cylindrical sides with my fingers parted.

"Open Mason educational file," I say. "Lesson three."

A clear pane rolls out like paper and becomes stiff, which allows me to operate it by touch. There are no projections or holographic capabilities within it. Filing scrolls are touch and work systems, designed to feel retro and give a more hands-on experience. Most find them primitive, and they are, but that makes them extraordinary.

I scroll through lesson three. My plan is to implement it with our youth once the last section of their edu-center is complete, which is a specialized learning center designed to house all ages of Dah'Sel and humanity to learn the other races' lifestyles and languages. It is being built with Armada technology using Dah'Sel resources in a blend of two civilizations at different stages of development.

Our Armada team is building a system of advanced technological learning in the center for them to grow accustomed to some of our devices. On another note, the Dah'Sel have nearly completed their section of the edu-center, for children of Kep Four to learn the ways of Wah'Lor before venturing into it.

The theory behind the first stage of our integrated learning process is to immerse Kep Four's children in a Dah'Sel environment and vice versa. Wete'Uza is not only an elder but a teacher amongst their youth. She will focus on language through the earlier cycles of human children's lives. The same will go for me teaching Dah'Sel youth, and those I teach will no doubt have the same dumbfounded expressions on their faces Pru'Cet had when I first freed him on *Athanasios*.

"Now," I ask myself, "what order to go with? Grason's method or something more subtle?"

No. I will devise my own system. Grason's method of education is too Armada-driven. Its intent is to educate while grooming youth with a predisposition to hold the Armada and its governing system as absolute. I do not agree with it.

My tele-tent beeps. Ten to one tells me it is Sargeant Bentley.

"Go ahead," I say.

"Mason," says Sergeant Bentley. "Can I come in?"

"I'm not dressed yet."

"Never mind," he says. "Listen. I need you to help set up some edu-center programs for the Dah'Sel on basic and advanced technology for their adults. Armada laborers can learn more about the seasons and how to live off the land from Din'Mos while that's underway."

"Yes, Sergeant Major," I say.

"Think you'll have time after you get back with Pru'Cet and Dr. Sellers later?" he asks.

"Yes, Sergeant Major," I answer. "Has Pru'Cet been working on his end of things?"

INTERNAL THOUGHTS

"That's what he asked about you," answers Sergeant Bentley.

I stand to stretch. My shoulder hurts, but it is not bad. I must have slept wrong on it.

"Sounds like Pru'Cet," I answer through a yawn. "I'll get on it as soon as I can."

"Thanks, Mason," says Sergeant Bentley. "No rush. We're still in the early stages of talking about it now. I'll catch up with you later."

"Aye aye, Sergeant Major," I say.

Sergeant Bentley ends the comm link.

Alone-time used to be something I considered a prized position, but after six cycles of incarceration, I grew close to my squad and got to know the Dah'Sel. My opinion on the subject has changed. I have grown to enjoy being around others and do not feel as awkward as I did about it seven cycles ago. There is love for them within me and warmth in the air when around the Dah'Sel, especially Pru'Cet, whom I am going to join in exploring a region called Zasaza that Dr. Sellers wants to check out.

I am busy, but understand Sergeant Bentley's mental urgency. Armada vessels did not bring a never-ending supply of nutrition with the interstellar ships that have made it here so far. The first of the vessels to arrive was more about getting higher-ranking people and those with specialized trade skills off Kep Four.

All will do their part to ensure a good life here. Our survival necessitates this. The old saying is that hard work breeds good mental health. I will look forward to it when the planet warms.

We must learn to live off the land, which is something humanity has zero hands-on experience doing. Knowledge of Ancient Earth farming techniques is in our records, but we have never had fertile land available to put it into practice. The coming summer will be our chance to learn firsthand about the crop's seasonal fauna phases here.

All ships still to come are larger than *Athanasios*. The next interstellar jump ship, known as the *Lifeboat*, will carry the rest of humanity to come at its full capacity of 140,000 strong. Although the Ein-Rosen bridge makes the trip short, those onboard will experience overcrowding.

The *Armada's Ark* will arrive after that. While it is the same size as the one that will haul 140,000 people, there will only be 55,000 onboard. The rest of the ship's space is for everything Kep Four offers as far as nutrition is concerned. It will also carry DNA and stem cells for human life along with the few animal species saved for the last 432 cycles—most of which are extinct.

Dr. Sellers is against introducing Kep Four's extinct flora and fauna to Wah'Lor. I stand with him on the thought. There is no way to know how it will affect the ecosystem here.

The Armada saved DNA and seeds to guarantee our future. Everyone knew Kep Four was dying. I found out during my first rotation of school at four cycles of age. It has been the long-standing proposal, even more so with the Dah'Sel only having crops tilled to feed their own upon our arrival.

A third ship to cross the interstellar boundary will also only haul 20,000 selected Armada members, but there is good reason for it. The Planetary Sovereign has dubbed it the *Dwarf*. It is the largest offered by the Armada and its only purpose is destruction. Most of its interior is being reserved for Armada ground transport vessels, several smaller fighters, construction equipment, and whatever else they thought of for combative purposes on the one-way trip. I did not investigate its fine details.

INTERNAL THOUGHTS

I need to get out of my head to focus on what Sergeant Bentley needs me to do and wish to talk with Mother in the memory files. There is so much work ahead of me and everyone else, but we must work diligently to stay the course.

"Unmentionables," I say, sliding into undergarments that leave little to the imagination.

Sleek clothes the Dah'Sel provided for me and the rest of my squad go on first. They are silky in comfort, but I do not know what their composition is.

"Boots, hoodie, gloves, and sanity," I say while dressing. "Check."

I pause about the rotation to come, in thought of further upsetting the Vee'Sal once the rest of humanity arrives. We thought the Vee'Sal would wage a civil war with the Dah'Sel for accepting us into their lives with open arms. They despise the fact humanity cured the Dah'Sel of the Klaz'Dra. They believe the historical lineage of the *kook elo jipwa—black-sky transformation*—is something special that should always be.

Power in my tele-tent flashes white lights. A long-toned series of beeps follows three final red and white flashes. A planetary update is incoming. This will be the first since the Sovereign's arrival on Wah'Lor.

2-2
Broadcast

The viewing pane in my tele-tent activates. The Planetary Sovereign's image renders. He waits a few tiks before speaking.

"If I can have everyone's attention," he says. "This is mainly for new arrivals still in orbit and those to come, but I feel an update is important. Wah'Lor is snow-covered. Water still waves in its oceans, but smaller lakes have frozen since our arrival. The Langaea is white. The ground is hard.

Nights are unpleasantly cold. This is new to all of us, but the Dah'Sel handle it well. We're blessed to have them at our side as we tackle adapting to the new world. It is going to be hard, but the brown is behind us. A fair trade. Armada members making the trip bring only necessities. Coming to Wah'Lor was not a jump of comfort. It was an act of desperation. An act of survival. And I believe it is paying off so far."

The Planetary Sovereign catches a breath and nods with confidence. His face has aged. A few more wrinkles adorn his eyes than before my imprisonment. It is to be understood. He is a man under unimaginable stress.

"The other Kla'Wah sect on Wah'Lor, the Vee'Sal, keep to themselves," he continues. "Humans have seen little of them. They are unhappy about our arrival and even more so that we treated the Dah'Sel to rid them of their albatross. It is a crime and blasphemy in their eyes that we stopped its ravaging, more so that the Dah'Sel accepted the Exhibition Anchor squad after bloodshed fell on both sides. As far as the Vee'Sal are concerned ... humanity forced the cure upon the Dah'Sel, causing them to think unclearly and accept human friendship with hoodwinked minds. They are to be avoided. On another note, there is no sovereign over this planet. It is neither mine nor any others to control. It does not need our protection; we need it to protect us. Nonetheless, I appreciate the respect everyone has shown me."

The Planetary Sovereign pulls up a filing scroll and opens it to read.

"I have issued a guideline to avoid further burdening the Dah'Sel sect of Kla'Wah," he continues. "Kep Four transplants are to reserve replication and manufacturing generators for simple tool creation, water, food, and heating for the one-hundred forty thousand plus Kep Four transplants coming to live on this planet, only forty thousand of which

INTERNAL THOUGHTS

have arrived. We're still awaiting the arrival of the *Lifeboat*, *Dwarf*, and the *Ark*. Of the five interstellar vessels that have made it, only four remain in orbit: Dr. Wright's *Athanasios*, Captain Selk's *Barrows*, Captain Menjay's *Flemlace*, and Captain Balter's *Uno*, which arrived just two rotations ago. The other two, *Columbas* and *Wurrukatte*, rest on the surface of Wah'Lor—now dubbed housing units one and two. It took sixty-two rotations to convert them into housing units for incoming transplants to live in. Armada workers moved their engines to the ship's exterior to make room for living quarters. I have scheduled three more vessels to make the interstellar leap over the next several rotations. Of the people on Kep Four, over a million now know they are destined to die on the planet. Prisoners and civilians in districts of poverty like the Sigma Green District and Najasa will not live another five cycles. This is something we must all accept."

"What?" I ask.

"Captain Menjay," continues the Planetary Sovereign, "he brought bad news when *Flemlace* arrived a few rotations ago. The Uprisers grow in numbers by the tek, and there are few Armada personnel left to stand against them. Dolofónos's persuasion is clear among his followers. That's why I moved up the last interstellar ships to reach Wah'Lor's orbit within a few dozen rotations, if there is anyone left to pilot them. Kep Four's inhabitants face an uncertain fate. The Armada is taking a beating from attacking Uprisers, and many lives are being lost on both sides, but Dolofónos and his minions are gaining members faster than they are losing them. Nobody can go back to help them, and they are being referred to as *The Left Behind*. Some will make it; some will perish. Those that have made it to Wah'Lor with family remaining on Kepler 442b, my spirit is with them. It's with all of you. We will hope, but let's make the best of it, Armada strong. My final note: what the Dah'Sel call the Fak sa pasho will take place on the evening of this rotation. I am asking all of you to abide by the Dah'Sel's wishes. The only members of humanity permitted to join their celebration … are members of the *Athanasios* exploration crew. Led by Sergeant Major Bentley and the late Dr. Wright, they were the first of us to arrive alongside the Wah'Lor originals. They have spent more time with the Dah'Sel than any of us and have been trusted to join them in Fak sa pasho. Our time will come to join in this celebration when we are as trusted as they are. Thank you for your time. Sovereign out."

My thoughts are stuck between the beauty of this world and people with family back on that dying brown rock. Sergeant Bentley cleared my memory files to be picked up by carriers and brought here. It was nice of him, and something I did not think he would grant me. Not after all I had done to cause him and the Armada stress.

"Open to exit," I say.

The tele-tent door lock rotates. I slide it open and step into a white world with a wince, squinting to shield my eyes as they adjust to the power of Wah'Lor's two stars beaming off the white. The scent in the air is clean when the bitter wind hits me with snow covering abundant vegetation. I shiver and take it into my lungs through my mouth for its cooling sensation to invade my chest and smile.

CHAPTER 3
Escapade

I exit my tele-tent, stretch my arms overhead, and bend my spine from left to right and front to back to stretch out. I look at HU-1 and HU-2, the housing units 600 paces from my tele-tent. Families and workers move about it. They are helping fresh arrivals settle into their new homes and showing them the layout while running OVER the rules and guidelines of Wah'Lor with them.

Beyond them, at double the distance away from me, is the makeshift airfield we set up to stage vessels not currently in use, which is almost all of them. It houses my squad's Argos with a few others like it, Bomba Class 1s, medical transports, hoppers, rendezvous shuttles, and more. There are almost 30 crafts parked there, but my Beltric Class Six is not among them. It is still engaged as *Athanasios*'s cockpit.

I study Armada personnel walking the airfield while Dah'Sel youth stand at its perimeter. They look and point while admiring the vessels with juvenile curiosity. As long as it has been, the vessels still draw their attention, especially the ones they have not seen in operation yet.

Dr. Sellers pulls up on an A.A.T.V. with four small tracks reminding me of a miniature Argos without the cover. He is pulling two others behind it like a short magna rail train. I take a step back as he comes to a stop at my feet.

"Trying to run me over or what?" I ask.

"Got a full load here," answers Dr. Sellers. "Going is easier than stopping."

"Where's Pru'Cet?" I ask.

"Looks like he's coming now," answers Dr. Sellers, hopping off the A.A.T.V. to unhook the other two.

"McKayla," calls Pru'Cet, running across the field from behind me with a satchel. "Pru'Cet ready."

"Good to know," I say, pointing to the satchel. "What's that?"

"Keep safe in Zasaza cold time," he answers, patting the satchel.

"All right," says Dr. Sellers. "Ready to ride?"

He presses a button on each of the A.A.T.V.s. Their handlebars light up as they start and run silently on zero-point energy. Pru'Cet walks over to one, hops on, and smiles.

"You're letting him drive one of these?" I ask.

"You taught him, Mason," says Dr. Sellers. "Didn't you?"

"No," I answer with a slow shake of my head.

"But you took him out on one about twenty rotations ago," says Dr. Sellers

"Yeah," I say, "but I didn't let him drive. That's why he was on the back."

Pru'Cet fiddles with the controls as we walk over.

"Pru—"

The A.A.T.V. jumps forward and knocks Dr. Sellers to the ground. I hop back and watch as Pru'Cet stops, starts, and stops again in repeating, jerky movements.

"Hold on a tik there, Pru'Cet," says Dr. Sellers, getting up from the ground.

We jog behind him with others in the field staring. He comes to a stop and looks our way with ample eyes and a mouth partially agape.

"*Ma,*" says Pru'Cet, shaking his head with a nervous chuckle. "*Ma. Ma. Ma.*"

"No is right," I say. "Get down before you kill yourself."

"Or one of us," says Dr. Sellers.

I grab Pru'Cet by the hand as he steps to get off and accidentally hits, opens, and locks the throttle position hold in a single stroke. The A.A.T.V.'s tracks spin, and it takes off toward the woods past Lesdelop ti'it renasa, snatching him to the ground and me face-first into the snow. I look up with a mouth full of icy slush to see it tearing across the field.

"Dr. Sellers to everyone on comms in the field," says Dr. Sellers. "Take cover." He cups his hands over his mouth and shouts downfield toward Lesdelop. "Watch out!"

Din'Mos and a few Dah'Sel youths playing next to the building look his way. The A.A.T.V heads right for them. They scurry to round the structure's corner, but the smaller of the youths trips. Din'Mos dives toward her, grabs her hand from the ground, and snatches her into him as she pulls in her legs. It passes right next to them.

"That was too close," says Dr. Sellers.

"What's going on, Sellers?" asks Sergeant Bentley over comms.

"Runaway A.A.T.V., Sergeant Major," answers Dr. Sellers. "Everyone's fine. It's in the clear. We're going after it now."

"Keep me informed," says Sergeant Bentley.

I stand and spit the mouthful of slush to the ground. The A.A.T.V. passes the Dah'Sel's animal hold next to Lesdelop and narrowly misses a few trees before reaching the clearing beyond them and continuing.

"It's going to hit something eventually," I say.

"*Blight o hempa,*" says Pru'Cet. "*Blight o hempa.*"

"It's okay," I say. "I mean, it wouldn't be if someone got hurt."

"Come on," says Dr. Sellers. "Let's go chase it down."

I climb on the free A.A.T.V. and motion Pru'Cet to crowd onto its single seat design behind me. Dr. Sellers climbs on the other. We take off.

3-2
Chase

Lesdelop is behind us. We have made our way into the four-click wide clearing beyond the trees and can see the other A.A.T.V. just over two clicks ahead of us. I am unsure if we can catch it before it reaches the Zasaza area of Wah'Lor.

"Let's open them up," says Dr. Sellers.

We throttle up to full speed and rip across the white field. A stiff wind beats against my eyes, forcing me to squint. I should have brought my sunbans but didn't think we would be driving this fast. At least cloud cover is keeping me from getting snow-blinded.

I depress the small lever next to my right thumb and slide it right to lock in the throttle position hold. The A.A.T.V. continues forward. It almost got Pru'Cet and others hurt but makes it easier on the wrist and keeps your forearm from fatiguing over long runs with bumpy terrain. The harder you squeeze the right grip, the faster you go. My forearms and wrist would fatigue overtime without it.

Nature's white powder rises from each side of our A.A.T.V.s with each bump and arches out steadily behind us as we go. We are gaining on the one ahead and going twice as fast as it is, but the unmanned off-road vessel is nearing Zasaza. I think we can catch it.

The vehicle's arc of snow hits us as we move in beside it—Dr. Sellers on the right and me on the left. We slow to match its speed. He stretches for its throttle hold button but cannot reach it. He tries again. A bump sends him from his seat. He almost falls under its tracks before catching and pulling himself back into the driver's seat. Dr. Sellers's tracks touch the unmanned A.A.T.V.'s tracks and lifts him to an angle.

"Mason," he calls. "One of you is going to have to get on it to stop it."

I think for a tik. Pru'Cet is far more agile than me, but he might hurt himself before he can figure out how to release the hold. It is going to have to be me.

"Pru'Cet," I say, turning back in glances to face him. "*Ama icci hueton, ne pes gingo vasika fadada. Pes ama golos cea?*"

"*Lipfa,*" answers Pru'Cet. "*Lipfa.*"

I check to ensure my throttle hold is disengaged and stand on the seat for a brief tik.

"Careful, Mason," says Dr. Sellers.

I release the throttle, look at Dr. Sellers for a smidge of gallantry, turn my attention back to the unmanned A.A.T.V., and leap. My right knee lands on the seat. Momentum carries me over the other sides of it, but a hard shove from Dr. Sellers keeps me on it long enough to upright myself. My eyes go unconsciously up to see Zasaza less than 100 paces ahead.

"Stop it, Mason," says Dr. Sellers, slowing as I pull ahead of him. "Stop it or bail."

I disengage the throttle hold and lock in its brakes with my left foot. The A.A.T.V. slides sideways with its tracks locked in position but does not slow on the icy surface. The outskirts of Zasaza's trees are upon me.

"*Wubeno,*" I say, jumping from the A.A.T.V.'s left side away from the trees.

My body hits the snow and rolls a few times. Maybe two or three. I am unsure and glad the snow is thick enough to separate my impact from the frozen ground.

I come to a stop and sit up, checking my arms and legs. They are unbroken. I am fine.

Dr. Sellers eases my way and stops without looking at me. My A.A.T.V. has come to a stop. Pru'Cet is off it and running my way. He winces.

The loud crash and clatter behind me tell me the off-road vehicle is damaged. I sigh and stand.

"Anything broken?" asks Dr. Sellers.

"Besides the A.A.T.V. and my pride?" I ask in return. "So much for me being heroic without being airborne."

"Could be worse," he says. "Might as well head back and let Sergeant Bentley know why we're down a unit. He may want to go ahead and send out a recovery team to drag it back."

I turn to look, against better judgment. The A.A.T.V. is barely visible at about 40 paces into Zasaza. I can only see part of it. The front left side ... I think. It is not upright, and a track is missing from it.

Pru'Cet reaches us. We turn to face him, but he does not talk. He stands in place with a guilty expression while avoiding eye contact.

"Seeing that I'm not going to get to explore Zasaza anymore..." says Dr. Sellers, pointing at Pru'Cet's satchel. "What's in the bag?"

"Heal after poison bite," answers Pru'Cet.

"Poison bite?" asks Dr. Sellers.

"Zasaza poison danger in cold time to go," he answers, pulling out an unknown root to show us. "This sometime keep life after tyce bite when eat."

"Tyce?" asks Dr. Sellers.

"Crawl no legs," answers Pru'Cet, moving his hand and arm like a snake and hanging two curved fingers from his mouth like fangs.

"Well," says Dr. Sellers, cutting me a look of relief with a deep breath. "Now I'm kind of glad we didn't go."

"Could have told us that before we left, Pru'Cet," I say, climbing on the A.A.T.V. seat in front of him to drive.

Dr. Sellers shakes his head as we take off for Lesdelop. It was an adventure, albeit a short-lived one. I, for one, am just happy that I can still walk after bailing off that thing.

CHAPTER 4
Taxi

The ride back was peaceful and uneventful. All I could do besides think about how magnificent life is here was wonder if we were going to get scolded for the A.A.T.V. incident. Sergeant Bentley was surprisingly easy on us. Wah'Lor has affected us all for the best.

I turn toward Lesdelop ti'it renasa to see James Algash. Part of me will always feel guilty about the rotation the poor guy worked Hangar 9's Beltric Class Six Starfighter station when I stole it. We have not talked about it since.

He climbs from calf-deep snow into a Hopper—a small four-person rendezvous shuttle shaped like a spherical BlazeBall designed for taking people from a planet's surface, into orbit, and back. My strides are long as I jog across the field through thick fallen white powder.

"Algash," I shout to catch his attention as he lowers the door.

He did not hear me.

"Algash," I repeat with faster steps.

"McKayla," calls Pru'Cet.

I give him a wave but do not break stride. He is in no more garments than when we first arrived, and snow is bunching up in his fur like an ungroomed animal of wool. He must have gotten wet, but a loincloth, fur, and bare feet are all he needs to stay warm with his naturally elevated body temperature.

"*Blight uptru ledasno nest,*" I say.

"*Tump,*" says Pru'Cet. "McKayla."

"*Blight uptru ledasno nest,*" I repeat. "*Blight o hempa.*"

It does not feel good to blow off Pru'Cet. He has become my best friend. One of the best I have had since the little girl my brother and I played with during our younger cycles in Najasa. It rarely happens though. Pru'Cet will understand, and I told him I would return soon.

I make it to the hopper's rendezvous point as it fires up.

"Hold on," I say, beating against the pilot's door with my palms.

"Algash," I say. "Algash."

He slides the door up.

"Are you skyjacking me again?" he asks.

"Hilarious," I answer. "Which jump-ship are you headed to?"

"*Barrows,*" he answers.

"Any chance you can swing me to *Athanasios* on your way?"

"Get in," answers Algash, snickering the words through his teeth. "It beats you taking it from me."

"Oh," I say. "Now you want to talk about it?"

"No," he answers. "You're just going to catch flak about it every time you need a lift now that I'm assigned to transports."

I shake my head. It was a running joke when people started arriving here. He is the only one that still gives me a hard time about it.

"Never going to live that down now, am I?" I ask.

Algash lowers the door.

"Probably not," he answers.

I move to the other side of the hopper, enter, and close the door behind me. We sit in silence for a moment while I examine the craft's white interior and controls. They blend with the snow.

"Give me a few teks to wait and see if I get a lift request from anyone," he says. "This isn't a scheduled run."

"That's fine," I answer, studying the landscape and staring into a distant tree line.

Edible plants grow and thrive in the harshest of winters here. I have never heard of anything like it. Dr. Sellers learned small summer plants retreat into the ground and remain dormant during the winters to spring back up when the planet warms. Winter flora is the opposite. It hides from summer's heat to return when the planet chills.

Larger, blue-leafed trees called blez'nez have a warm-blooded nature. Snow will not settle upon them. It melts tiks after contact, and their vibrant colors transition to a slightly brighter existence through chilly times. It has something to do with the tree's DNA, soil on Wah'Lor, and thermogenic photosynthesis, but I am not interested enough in the subject to have an educational conversation with Dr. Sellers about it.

I am not as comfortable as the blez'nez trees are. My wardrobe has gone from comfortable to bulky and restrictive, but I am safe and warm. The view is something to marvel: white fields cover everything for as far as the eye can see, small summer vegetation has retreated into the soil, winter sprouts are half-grown, and the icy planetary ring system contests it all for dominance over the scene. Those who have made the leap are in awe when they reach the surface.

I watch Pru'Cet walk back to the Lesdelop ti'it renasa structure where his family is waiting. Like Pru'Cet, the rest of the Dah'Sel wear little more than when we landed. Their flowy, silk-like hair keeps them warmer than us during the frost but cooler through summer. It is gorgeous on them and the reason their body temperatures developed to run 8 degrees warmer than ours. Different shades and colors add to their individualism, unlike humanity, with our slowly unifying look beyond height and weight—excluding the fact that our hair has steadily grown since we got here. Still, I wish to have their natural wintertime covering.

Dah'Sel elder and leader, Wat'Uza, has taken a liking to our original squad. He is wise with a kind demeanor. His mate, Wete'Uza, is every bit as kind as he is. They make a great pairing, and I am glad they lead through kindness.

Pru'Cet is better than ever. His Mother, Nala'Cet, accepted me and the rest of us with open arms. His sister, Tila'Cet, is gorgeous until the end of what the word could describe. Her body is what I wish mine could be: tall, slender, curvy, and with faultless blue eyes. She glides when she walks and speaks with a voice angelic in nature. I am captivated by her silky silver three-inch coat of flowing perfection, its white highlights, and everything else about her.

"Ready?" asks Algash.

"What?" I ask. "Sorry. I was in my own head."

"Always are," he scuffs. "Ready to ascend?"

"Yes, sir. Let's go."

He powers up the hopper as I turn to examine HU-1. We rise from the cold ground. Conversion is almost complete. I could stay there if I asked, but, like the rest of those from my original squad and a few others, we have already adjusted and are comfortable in the tele-tents.

Transplant priority has gone to Armada members and individuals who helped or supported them through secondary channels, such as donating A.R.O. (Artifact Recovery

Operation) investors and the vile scientists I spent six cycles of my life incarcerated over.

Hopefully, those still left to depart can make it without incident. I wish everybody could come, but that is an impossibility. People in the position my family was in before I joined the Armada will not make it.

I am grateful to be on Wah'Lor. It beats the nasal worms out of breathing toxic air, wondering if I will survive a conflict between the now warring Armada and Uprisers, and longing to be on an interstellar ship I would probably never be getting on. On a positive note, Dr. Wright appointed me the unofficial ambassador to bridge the gap that links humans and Dah'Sel.

There has been no conflict over it yet, but I do not think the Armada and Vee'Sal will become friends. Not in my lifetime. They will reconcile their differences between themselves and the Dah'Sel long before that happens. We are not high on the list of positivity and avoid wandering far from Lesdelop at night to prevent unintentional encounters with Vee'Sal exposing themselves to the night's shine. It was a hard-learned lesson.

I look toward the wooded region between the Dah'Sel and Vee'Sal as we rise farther, toward puffy light gray clouds. It is where we lost them. Nine new Armada arrivals celebrated their successful trips to the new world and ventured too far on the eve of one rotation.

They were in two groups of five and four. One went north, the other east past the lassabax. None of them returned.

We must be cautious here. The air is clean. Food and water are abundant, and there are no Uprisers to worry about, but curiosity ends lives on Wah'Lor.

There are animals here that follow the smaller plants' seasonal hibernation cycles. I saw but a few before winter enveloped the planet. There is no wildlife beyond flyers and what the Dah'Sel keep here as livestock during the transitional period between seasons, which I find interesting.

I am positive the Vee'Sal have livestock, but I am unsure about their methods to maintain them. A click-wide river beyond the woodland separates their region from this one. I have never seen it. Pru'Cet says they live in vast structures carved into the sides of a great plateau. *Athanasios* confirmed its location 80 clicks from here. They call it Lesdelop ti'it ratim-zis, which translates to *Home to generations*.

The Vee'Sal home reads like a hollow maze on *Athanasios*'s sonographic imaging projections. The complex infrastructure has an empiric internal design with an abundance of decor. From what the Dah'Sel have said about it, it must be impressive.

I know we will settle our differences with the Vee'Sal in time, and their opinions about us will change if humanity does nothing foolish. Our former Kep Four ruler is doing well at accepting the fact that he no longer holds the position of Planetary Sovereign.

As he stated, this is not his world to rule. As a hierarchy, he is still over the Armada and is considered by most of humanity to be their leader. Some feel differently about it, but no one is at anyone's throat over it. I will have to wait and see how it unfolds as time progresses to form my own opinion.

"Getting close," says Algash.

I nod but keep my eyes on Wah'Lor as the light fades to darkness. We will surpass the upper atmosphere any tik. I have not been into the black since our arrival, had forgotten how beautiful Wah'Lor is from orbit, and will soon look down upon this niveous world from *Athanasios* once again.

Armada scientists have not figured out exactly why yet, but intergalactic jumps are burning our vessels' exterior hulls. No electro-stenciling remains on them after a jump. Hulls are spider-webbed with cracks like drying paint when they exit the Ein-Rosen bridge.

The outermost components in *Athanasios* fried when we exited the Ein-Rosen bridge, which left us momentarily without power and nearly caused us to spiral into Wah'Lor for a fiery end. Ships that arrived after us have had extra shield systems added to compensate, but their Alcubierre drive system rings continue to fail after the jump. We do not have the resources to repair them. Dr. Wright's initial thought was to reinforce them, but they cannot be shielded without losing proper function.

My body rocks. I jump and grab the harness and strap myself in with Algash laughing at me as we touchdown in the *Athanasios* docking bay.

"You could have warned me," I say.

"I did," he says. "Twice. You were dreaming awake."

He powers down the hopper. I slide up the door and exit.

"Thanks, Algash," I say.

"Not a problem, bandit," he says.

I smile and reach to lower the door.

"Hey," he says. "You think I'm giving you a hard time? Wait until Kuzio sees you."

"The reaper's here?" I ask. "Since when?"

"Since two rotations ago."

Algash gives me a wink and powers the hopper back up. I release a sigh and lower the door. He will no doubt laugh about Kuzio confronting me on his way to *Barrows*.

I remove my warmer outer garments with just under two taks remaining before I must return to the surface. Pru'Cet is meeting me there to prepare for Fak sa pasho. I can only hope he brings Tila'Cet with him. I would like to get to know her better.

Mother's opinion on my thoughts for Tila'Cet is needed, but I must word it so she can understand. She does not know this world and would not believe me anyhow. I look forward to talking to her and kissing her forehead again.

4-2
The Walk

Docking went smoother than I thought it would. Algash has made good strides in improvement as a pilot since the last time I saw him fly. He was rough around the edges at one point. I smile about his *'skyjacking'* remark while walking *Athanasios*'s corridors. He is a good kid, though not my cup of tea to hang out with regularly. Algash is forever Armada-dry, but I think he is coming around.

"Mason," says Dr. Wright. "I'm surprised to see you without Wah'Lor soil under your boots. Memory file?"

"Yes, sir," I answer. "How'd you know?"

"Can't think of another reason for you to board *Athanasios*, since everything that happened up here."

My face sinks. That was the last thing I wanted to think about when I came up here. Anything but that. Morris, Dr. Utley, Rhigas, Skedelski ... they are gone.

"I shouldn't have mentioned it," says Dr. Wright.

"It's..." I say, pausing for my lie. "It's fine. I'm okay."

An awkward moment of silence stiffens the air.

I exit and turn into the main corridor that leads to personal quarters without another word. Two workers pass me with hover carts full of tools as I step beyond a repair worker soldering the entrance to an open baker-channel. I give them a nod as I press forward.

A chill ripples through my skin. It is either from the temperature Dr. Wright has the level programmed at or from being here. I would guess both. Each step feels heavy. I still get anxiety and feel uneasy on this vessel.

Skedelski died to save our lives from that thing that was once Rhigas in this corridor. This is where it chased me. That moment sent a terror through me like nothing before. I can feel it returning now. I must get out of here.

Time between steps shortens as I quicken my pace. I make a left and grab the first ascension ladder I see.

"Down," I say.

It lowers me a few levels. I exit for my quarters. My name comes into view:

'MASON'

The door receiver reads my palm until a small strand of DNA spins above my wrist in a three-dimensional holographic fashion. The door breaks down into smaller and smaller cubes. They twist from bottom to top and come to rest against the ceiling.

My eyes, like always, stay glued to them as I enter and back away.

"Close door."

4-3
Mother

I watch the door reform, seal, and become solid. The memory of my first time entering it... I will never get used to these colors. I would rather sleep in the tele-tent most nights, especially when I want to be alone. A quiet party is what it feels like on the surface of Wah'Lor with all the bonfires, singing, and dancing. Summer was so vibrant down there before the season changed.

"Open memory file eight sixty-seven," I say.

I press my left finger to my ear's tragus and hold it there for five tiks. My recall chip activates. They are not standard issue, linked to nothing externally, and given to Armada personal with high ranking and/or special abilities that benefit their cause.

My eyes close in wait for the memory file to take over. It is not as interactive as the one I had back on Kep Four. I have not programmed an expanding frame on the wall to imagine walking into Mother's home yet. I may eventually, but I just need to talk to someone right now, and I have not spoken to her since I settled on the planet below.

The memory file is certainly at work. I can feel it taking over and smile in wait. A tingle in my temples follows. I open my eyes to find myself back on Kep Four in the Infinidome—a stadium where onium-cycles race on an infinity-symbol-shaped track.

I can already smell high-revving onium-cycles, like it happened the previous rotation. They were ground-based vessels consisting of nothing more than two wheels, an engine, and a seat. The handlebars controlled both wheels, and the cycles could pivot through 25 percent of its mounting system for lateral movements. They were also fast and could turn on the tip of a finger, but dangerous.

I look at the course I did a handful of races on while still a recruit in the Armada. No one is on it. The race has ended, and Mother is approaching me.

"Run memory file," I say.

Mother unfreezes in the Infinidome racer's pit and grabs my competition jacket as I take it off. The onium cycle track is deafening with cheers as Delgado, long before she lost her legs and when I was just a cadet, takes the podium. She is tall, slender, and looks good up there. Jealous sweeps over me.

"You can't win them all," says Mother.

"She kicked the side of my cycle," I say. "I couldn't catch her after I recovered."

"Everyone battles on that track," says Mother.

"I know," I say. "She's long-legged and foot-dragging in the corners. I couldn't. I'm short. I accept it, but it doesn't make her a better racer than me."

"Doesn't it?" asks Mother.

"She might as well have cheated," I say.

I turn to walk off. Mother grabs me by the shoulder and spins me around.

"You think you're invincible?" she asks.

Delgado walks from the podium and approaches us.

"Good moves, kid," says Delgado. "You got promise."

"Thanks," I say with disdain. "Rematch?"

"No," answers Delgado. "I'm done for the season. Already scored enough points to win. No need for the last few races on the circuit. Have fun with the rest of the season and keep it up though."

She walks away. I watch her with full knowledge that I will not have a chance at redemption. My skin boils.

"You're mad," says Mother.

"Am not," I say.

Dolofónos and his gang scrap out a research facility for parts. A homeless man in torn civilian garb left behind by the Armada tries to steal food from his men, but they see him, sneak up behind him, and club him behind the head. The man folds to the floor, unconscious.

The image shifts. It is choppy, quick, and blurry, but I can see the homeless man on his knees with his back to Dolofónos. The Upriser leader raises a steel projectile-based sidearm from his hip. His movements are slow. It feels like a tak passes before he has its barrel at the back of the man's head.

"Please..." says the homeless man. "I'm just hungry. My kids are hungry. That's all. I didn't mean—"

Dolofónos fires. The homeless man's head rattles with the gunshot.

The gunshot's boom jolts me from the vision and back to reality. My eyes come into focus. Mother bids for my attention.

"Are you feeling well?" she asks.

Dolofónos is stuck in my head. It was not a dream. It was something different. Real. It happened. I know it did.

"Another envisioning," I whisper.

"What?" asks Mother.

She would not understand hypnagogic hallucinations paired with H-SAM, as Dr. Sellers once called them, and I am not bothering to explain it.

"I have to leave," I say.

"What was that all about?" she asks.

"Nothing," I answer, leaning in to kiss her forehead. "Sorry. Love you."

"But I don't—"

"Pause memory file," I interrupt.

I stop for everything to become motionless in my head.

"Exit memory file," I say.

She is gone. I am back in my quarters, and mental gymnastics are at play in my head, but the doctors will have to hear about the vision later. If it happened, there is nothing anyone can do about it.

Fak Sa Pasho will start tonight. It will be the first time any of us have experienced it, and the first time the Dah'Sel ever held the event under the moon. I grab my dark-tinted sunbans from the counter to protect my eyes from snow blindness and exit.

CHAPTER 5
Fak Sa Pasho

I exit my *Athanasios* living quarters and make my way to the externally mounted drop pods. Perhaps I should have had one sent down to grab me instead of running across the field with Dah'Sel and humans alike staring at me to catch Algash before he departed, but I did not think about them. Mother was on my mind.

I turn through corridor after corridor until reaching the nearest drop pod past Med Bay.

"McKayla Mason for drop pod clearance," I say.

The door's four-way seam activates to brighten into a large red cross.

"Headed back down already?" asks Dr. Wright over comms.

"What are you still doing up here?" I ask in return. "Fak sa pasho is later this rotation. In fact, why don't you hit the surface more often?"

"My home's here," he answers. "I helped design it, supervised its construction, and this is where I feel the most comfortable. Didn't I already ask you about being on the surface all the time?"

"Touché," I say.

"All right," says Dr. Wright. "You're clear."

The plus-shaped door seam turns red. Each of the four panels moves away from the center on a diagonal path, like teeth from some alien animal I have yet to discover on Wah'Lor.

I glance inside.

"Looks like the Armada's stepping up their game," I say.

"It's the small things," says Dr. Wright. "Isn't it?"

Its interior is plush with soft padded walls, and its overall shape reminds me of the gaznote eggs I ate growing up in Najasa with that slight indention near its center. Armada green and black line it. There are no controls. A single seat is available for me and nothing more, but it looks comfortable.

I take a seat. My body sinks into it like a cloud, and there is not much room in here to move. Good thing I am not claustrophobic.

"Surface-side," I say. "Armada transplant location."

The doors close in reverse order from how they opened. A spider harness encases me, and I jump. I was not ready for it. It has been a long time since I saw one of these.

The name *spider harness* is fitting. Thousands of spider-web-sized fibers emerge from each side of the backrest and seat to lock me in place. It is the type of high-tech sensation I have missed since I left Kep Four. I am glad they added it to the drop pods and close my eyes to relax before it drops me from *Athanasios*. Spider harnesses are made for pilots with my mindset. A grin creeps across my face like it is my first sip of Jerleanian all over again.

Its door opens.

"You've got to be kidding me," I say in disbelief.

I am already on the surface. I felt nothing, not even the drop pod dislodging itself from its holding position on *Athanasios*. Inertial dampers within it must be upgraded Armada tech integrated from newly arriving vessels emerging from the Ein-Rosen bridge.

I should have been more specific about where I wanted to go. It set me down half a click from where I needed to be. The new Armada airfield is 50 paces to my left and full of vessels and random workers I have not met.

A man in E.S.D. (Electro-Static Dissipative) gloves works on one of only two other Beltric Class Six's on the planet besides my cockpit-docked Beltric still up on *Athanasios*. One may be his, but he may be nothing more than an Armada mechanic. I wish to see what he is doing and make my way over.

The man working at an open panel on its underbelly is a tad taller than me and thin.

"You know," he says without turning to face me, "they used to call the front command portion of ships a bridge aionas ago."

It is a random statement, but I will play along.

"What do you think sparked the change?" I ask.

"Makes more sense," he answers. "The command center is the forwardmost part of vessels. Now we call sections for crew and cargo the bridge because it bridges the bow to the aft … which used to be called the stern."

"Didn't know I was such an aficionado," he says. "Did you?"

"How could I," I answer. "I don't think we've ever met."

He does not respond. The moment is awkward. I speak just to break the odd tension.

"Nice to see one of these up close again," I say as I approach. "Haven't seen the exterior of one in a long time."

The man stops, sets his tools on the tray next to him, and turns to face me.

"Cadet Mason," he says.

"Kuzio?" I ask.

He laughs.

"Bet you didn't think you'd ever see the reaper again in person," he says.

"I..." I say with a pause. "Algash said you were here. I figured our paths would cross ... eventually."

He removes the E.S.D. gloves and steps in to bump boots with me.

"I'm not a cadet anymore," I say.

"I figured that seven cycles ago," he says. "You went from thief, Armada traitor, ARS sympathizer, and someone that not only assaulted an Armada scientist but destroyed Armada property and disrupted experiments to cure Kep Four syndrome ... to becoming a hero of sorts. How the haze did you pull that off?"

"Well," I answer, unsure how to respond.

His words bother me. They are true, but these things are long behind me and something I have not thought about since reaching orbit here. I do not know what to say.

"Relax, Mason," says Kuzio. "Everyone has a past. Even me. I've heard about everything you've done and what you've been through. You've earned your redemption."

"Thank you," I say. "But now I'm curious."

"About what?" asks Kuzio

"You said everyone has a past like you were self-reflecting. What'd you do?"

"My father was a sergeant," he answers. "I was born into the Armada and sometimes he would tell me stories of things that happened in the field when the Upriser rebellion first started some thirty cycles ago."

"Around the time I was born?" I ask.

"Yes," he answers. "One rotation, news feeds covered a battle taking place in the Sigma Green District, where my father was sent to patrol with his squad. It was a bad scene for someone seventeen cycles of age to watch."

"Weren't you a cadet then?" I ask.

"I was," answers Kuzio, "and, like you, I stole an Argos being lowered from Chimark above the district and moved in to help my father's squad. He made it out and only lost one member of his team, but I left with this."

He holds up his right arm and pulls down his shirt sleeve. The meat on his forearm has two sections missing from it, where the skin rests flat on the bone.

"So, Mason," he says, "we are not so dissimilar."

"Except for the fact that I was imprisoned, and you weren't," I say.

"Well," he says. "Your list of infractions was excessive … unless I was fed disinformation."

"No," I say with a shake of my head. "It was. I wouldn't change a thing if I had to do it again."

Kuzio smiles.

"I bet you wouldn't," he says, eyes going up over my shoulder. "Looks like they're starting runs already."

I look back to see a hopper lowering to the surface.

"That's my cue," I say. "I need to catch the next run."

"Better hurry," says Kuzio.

I cut him a half-smile and take off across the field.

"Mason," calls Kuzio, "you're a hell of a pilot."

"Thanks," I say without looking back.

I do not need to catch another lift into orbit. I just got back. It was a ruse to return to the others and end the conversation. I do not feel comfortable contemplating my past.

Interstellar transport vessels converted to housing units are a few paces away and staggering in size when sitting flush on a planetary surface like this. It is humbling.

The crew has positioned HU-2's mighty engine off the port side. They have carved new entrances and exit points into lower portions of its hull at the front and back of the former vessel. Civilians are moving in and out of its rear exit with their children to play in the snow. The fun will not last forever. Once they settle in on this world, each of them will receive assignments.

Armada personnel are entering and exiting a new door carved in the vessel's nose. They must have the civilians of wealth and Armada personnel separated into two different sides of a ship. I stop to look around.

My breath is floating in front of me. My skin is burning from the frigid air. I am shaking.

"Great," I say through shaking words. "I can't tell where I am with these two things in front of me at ground level, and I did not grab my jacket from the docking bay before I left with the enthusiasm of Fak sa pasho in mind. Good job, Mason."

Pru'Cet's uncle Bah'Cet comes into view as I make my way across the snow-covered field. His flowing coat of fine hair is silver, primarily like the rest of the 'Cet family, but black on his hands and neck. The *Cet* in Bah'Cet is their family marker and lets others in their sect immediately identify them as part of a particular bloodline. Like with Pru'Cet, the *Bah* in the first half of his name comprises three letters—as we would spell it out in our language. It is always a single syllable at the front of any family marker for males. Women have two syllables at the front of their family marker comprising four characters.

Bah'Cet is the leading engineer for the Dah'Sel sect on Wah'Lor. He is brilliant. Without modern tools and technology, what he has accomplished would be a daunting task for most humans to achieve. Nobody else in the sect knows how to manipulate the planet's elements, combine resources, and build stability and structures the way he does.

I speed up to catch him.

"Bah'Cet," I call.

He stops and turns.

"McKayla," says Bah'Cet. "*Tret'tret ka ama?*"

"Good," I answer, knowing, like many others, he understands our language better than he speaks it.

"*Tret'tret ot e sawez Armada greh jesen-zic?*" I ask.

"Kuzsoec," he says, motioning me to follow. "*E greh ot qua ulapra-zim.*"

"Great," I say with an ear-to-ear beam of inspiration. "*Topcal ot yapo-zic.* I'm excited. I can't wait to work with your children when you finish it."

"*Ne e Dah'Sel bea ver fit-zis,*" he says.

And the Dah'Sel with your children. I could not have hoped for a better reply. It sounds nice rolling across his lips, and my heart is ecstatic to know they are glad to have us.

A hand on my back... I jump and turn to see Pru'Cet. He is pointing at me. Glad he found it amusing.

"Pru'Cet," I say. "How many times have I told you not to do that over the last half of a cycle?"

"I quiet," answers Pru'Cet.

"I know you are," I say. "But say something, would you?"

"Sorry," he says.

Pru'Cet gets excited to talk in our language when he is around Armada personnel. It is not perfect, but he speaks our words better than anyone else in the Dah'Sel sect and has become a decent translator for the Kla'Wah. He is my assistant ambassador.

"Night here soon," says Pru'Cet.

The last sun is setting. The rotation went by fast. I failed to notice. It sometimes happens here with everything going on and what we are trying to accomplish. There is a positive aspect—it means we stay busy and productive enough not to be standing around scratching our foreheads.

The final blue star sets faster than the first in winter because of its position in binary orbit with the other star and rotation of the Wah'Lor planetary horizon in relation to the planetary tilt. It should take only 20 teks from where it is now until nightfall. Bonfires will blaze soon after to melt away cold falling flakes.

"I'm cold," I say.

Bah'Cet looks my way, steps in front of me, and squats down ... pulling me in for a piggyback ride. I hop on and bury myself into him. His body radiates heat into my chest, face, arms, and inner thighs. My shaking slows. I relax and sink further into him.

"*Hueton ama ka*," says Bah'Cet.

I look up. He has brought me to my tele-tent door, but he is too cozy to release.

"McKayla," says Bah'Cet, bouncing up and down.

I hop off.

"*Dada ama*," I say.

Bah'Cet stands there for a good seven tiks and gives me a slow, uncoordinated wink and walks away. I nod. He must be trying to pick up on human traits in social settings.

I study the field between my tele-tent and Lesdelop ti'it renasa. The Dah'Sel are setting up multiple tinder piles for bonfires in the snowy fields while civilians and Armada members alike are unloading boxes of liquor and beer cubes from hover carts for the party. There will be a big celebration at the Fak sa pasho—*Rotation of reflection*. This is when they celebrate the spirit and lives of fallen loved ones, those that fell since creation, and bless Kla'Wah spirits lost to the Klaz'Dra.

In the black of this rotation, we will be the first outsiders joining them since life began on Wah'Lor. We will remember Morris, Dr. Utley, Skedelski, and Rhigas, who fell to the Klaz'Dra. And we will do it with Kla'Wah honor.

5-2
Getting ready

My tele-tent is free of snow. Its geothermal-powered heating and cooling system is a technological blessing to have right now. A pace-wide patch of grass they call *zibot* outlines my tiny home. It is too warm for snow to settle near it.

"Mason," calls Dr. Sellers, stopping me before I enter and tossing me a brown jacket. "I saw you coming and thought you might need that. Why are you dressed down?"

"Because I can't focus on anything but that awful rotation when I'm on *Athanasios*," I answer.

"That, I believe," says Dr. Sellers. "I'm thinking about trying to brew something similar to Mez and Jerleanian here on Wah'Lor. Think you want to sample some in a few rotations?"

"I've been dry since the N.C.O. Pub night," I answer, putting on the jacket. "Count me in. I don't want my liver to start thinking I care about it. But I am about to freeze here."

"Your liver will never think that," says Dr. Sellers. "I'll let you know when it's ready."

"Dr. Sellers," calls Sergeant Bentley. "We're ready for you."

I cut my eyes across the field. Sergeant Bentley is waving him over.

"Catch you later, Mason," says Dr. Sellers. "I'll see you in the field when the moon rises, no?"

"Yeah," I answer. "I'll be there."

He gives me a pat on the shoulder and departs with Sergeant Bentley. I think they are planning for this evening's session. I finish working with younger Dah'Sel most rotations and venture to the fields a few clicks toward the second sunset. It is there we meet Din'Mos—the top Dah'Sel farmer with a scar across his face that once held Fister hostage. He has become a good friend of Sergeant Bentley's and is who we learn how to survive in a world partially unfamiliar to us from.

I turn back toward my tele-tent in thought over Sergeant Bentley and how he was once concerned about me being in the presence of Pru'Cet, only to turn good friends with one of the Dah'Sel himself. Even more so, one that held a blade across Fister's throat. It is funny how half a cycle can change mentalities.

I approach my tele-tent.

"Open," I say.

Its lock rotates. I open it to enter.

Its inside is the usual three paces wide, six paces, extended Armada configuration, but there is only a half-pace worth of headspace between the top of my head and the ceiling. Tele-tents reconfigure themselves to match their assigned owners while conserving heat and energy output. Skedelski would have never fit in here if they did not auto-configure for those entering.

My reflection catches in the bathroom area's sink mirror. This jacket looks great on Dr. Sellers, but it is ugly on me. It may balance the dark hair on my head now grown out to a palm's width in length, but I cannot see my hands in these long sleeves.

"Yeah," I say. "Not me."

I remove the jacket along with my pants. The Dah'Sel's cotton-textured undergarments are coming off next. My skin breathes when I drop them to the floor, and I feel free. This is the only way to sleep.

My head hits the pillow on my small cot next to an Armada-issued cooking station. I did not eat meat before I came here, and I certainly am not about to start. The fruits and vegetables of Wah'Lor are the most flavorful things humanity has tasted in a natural state for aionas.

My favorite is slezbrez fruit. Its appearance resembles a jellyfish, and it squishes in your mouth. Still, when you bite into it, a tightening happens within its fibers until its firmness reminds you of Kep Four's dela pear fruit: firm, crunchy, juicy, and rushes of organic sugar moving across your pallet. It is addicting in all the best ways.

A high percentage of humanity no longer eats meat. Less than 50 percent back on Kep Four ate it, and obesity was non-existent. That number is probably down to somewhere around 10 percent now. I close my eyes thinking about it. My smile is not going away, but that is okay. I do not want it to leave me.

I curl into the blanket and close my eyes. Never has sleep been as good as it is on Wah'Lor. This is home. I have a few teks to nap before Fak Sa Pasho is at full force, and I get to try rench-snech for the first time.

5-3
Smoke

Two taks pass before I wake and slide into traditional two-piece Kla'Wah loincloths with brown and white patterns for the night's event. It is far more revealing than anything I am used to wearing in public. I might as well be a ceiling dancer at the N.C.O. pub back on Kep Four. My rear is almost showing, and I do not fill out its top well, but it is comfortable. I cannot wait to see my original squad mates' reactions to each other in this type of attire.

This evening should be a good time and an interesting one. I am unsure what to expect other than my feet being warmer than my skin. This footwear is leather lined with a thick fluff of down feathers and compliments the rest of what little I am wearing.

A blistering breeze hits me when I open my tele-tent's door.

"Holy Armada," I say with shivers.

The door closes behind me. I march toward Lesdelop ti'it renasa. Bonfires reach for the night sky past falling snowflakes over a white, moon-glistened ground. They burn a bright orange with occasional traces of green in their tails. It must be the wood they are burning.

Comilo would have loved it here. We never enjoyed such a thing together. It was impossible in Kep Four's air.

I walk through the snow toward an event that others are already dancing to in force. Sergeant Bentley emerges from his tele-tent on my right as I pass it by.

"This is ridiculous," he says.

Laughter seeps from me like steam from the top of a hot teakettle. His physique is lean, muscular, and nice, but I hope he is wearing something under it. The man has no room for wardrobe malfunctions.

"Keep laughing, Mason," he says. "Don't act like you're not showing a little back there."

"I know," I say. "But what are we going to do about it?"

He shakes his head and walks at my side.

"Nothing that won't offend their tradition," he says.

The Dah'Sel smoke rench-snech from wooden pipes and wrapped yellow leaves as we approach the nearest bonfire from a quarter click out. Laughing... Dancing... Stumbling over each other... Looks fun.

"You ready for this?" asks Sergeant Bentley.

"Dying for it," I answer.

We have seen them smoking it in small amounts before. The Planetary Sovereign issued explicit orders for humanity not to try it when he first arrived. Tonight is a different night altogether. In honor of myself and other *Athanasios* crewmembers, troubles we faced upon arrival, what we risked, saving humanity, and those we lost to the Klaz'Dra, he has asked us to join with the Dah'Sel in their ways.

Dr. Sellers is ahead of us with his homemade mez/Jerleanian station up and running, passing Armada issued drinking cups out to Dah'Sel. I am unsure how they are going to handle it. They must feel the same about us and rench-snech.

"How do you think this is going to go over?" asks Sergeant Bentley.

"I'll let you know when the suns rise," I answer.

Pru'Cet has a beer in one hand. I do not know what kind it is. Neither does he, but my hairy little buddy already has permagrin from it and the stem of rench-snech in his other hand. I have not seen him smoke it before. He had not reached that age until recently. It will be fascinating to see how he handles himself.

His mother, Nala'Cet, watches him through smiles, proud he is coming of age. She is a sweet lady. I still remember the look on her face when she was chasing after the Argos with Pru'Cet caged in the back of it. Her love for him is fierce, and I have grown to cherish her. I never want to see that kind of fear or pain in her eyes again.

A group of youth and adults alike are playing a game I have yet to see in the snow beside Lesdelop ti'it renasa. They are in a circle tossing one of the four-legged chicken-looking birds called *yeena* into the snow and letting it sink beneath it. A few tiks after it lands, the yeena pops up from a different location and they try to catch it before it drops beneath the snow again. It is a challenging game because the yeena blends well with the snow since its feathers turn white as winter approaches.

We reach the bonfire, and I take a seat five paces from the pit of flame's base. My exposed face, stomach, and legs warm in front of it. The rest of my original squad ... Fister, Sapp, Bell, Delgado, Dr. Sellers, and so forth ... they are all here.

"Better late than never," says Dr. Wright, approaching from a drop pod.

The group cheers. His planet-side appearances are rare. I am glad to see him.

"Silence," shouts Wat'Uza.

Everyone grows quiet. Youth stop playing with the yeena. Music dies.

"*Plama pisip trestaluk crez sawez blenya-zis ti'it Fak sa pasho,*" continues Wat'Uza.

"Welcome friends, Fak sa pasho," translates Pru'Cet.

"*Bea siwbe, ohrap ka. Bea pisip, saisay ka,*" continues Wat'Uza. "*Po ot ledram ti'it volna saftic ohrap wabuki faxi, ne ti'it t e grinsapes bea disen human verallto-zis.*"

The rest of my squad and I look to Pru'Cet for further translation, but he is running the words through his head. My eyes widen with an internal giggle over Pru'Cet's shorthand translations. He is trying, if nothing else.

"*E kipoa-zis licea nebes gwan conan su e siju,*" continues Wat'Uza. "*Fesnop ot tom meldu sa ricath reema pisip renasa.*"

"Together, we one," Translates Pru'Cet. "Now we remember. Share with these human friends. New humans need earn Fak sa pasho. We proud."

Sergeant Bentley leans in to steal my attention. His shoulders shrug and his palms go up to insinuate he does not understand Pru'Cet's shorthand translations.

I raise up a finger to say, '*give me a tik,*' and wave him off. Wat'Uza stops to lock eyes with me. I hope we did not break his concentration, because I am in high regard with the Dah'Sel and proud of it. I love them.

"*Ama muto-zim pisip,*" continues Wat'Uza with a prideful pause. "*Ohrap uptru muto ama ena jasros prakanto.*" He holds up his arms at a forty-degree angle. "*Rot, plama pisip inhala rench-snech ne glakef ver sopet.*"

Surrounding Dah'Sel cheer, rejoin the party, and return to playing their instruments. Their youth return to play with the yeena. My squad mates look at Pru'Cet.

"You save us," translates Pru'Cet, raising his arms as Wat'Uza did. "We save you, no starve. We rench-snech and sopet."

My squad and I cheer and clap as Dah'Sel cheers fade.

"Mason," says Sergeant Bentley.

"Pru'Cet..." I say, looking into the corners of my eyes for a nice way to put it. "He did his best. It was good enough for you to get the point.

A bump at my left side... I cut an eye that direction. Tila'Cet sat next to me. My heart races. I cannot help but wonder why she has not paired up yet. Those in the Dah'Sel sect pair up at an early age, not much older than Pru'Cet is now.

She cuts me a few looks that I catch from the corner of my eye, but I am trying to be cool about it. I do not think it is working. I smile every time she makes eye contact with me. She does the same.

We have caught each other staring from time to time, more so over the last 20 or 30 rotations, but we look away as if it were unintentional. The first to make me nervous was her, and I can feel it now. It is as addictive as it is unbearable.

I should try to ignore her for now, but I doubt I will be able to. She is Beautiful—*friveka*, as they say on Wah'Lor, and I do not want to cross any lines. Perhaps, in time. I do not know.

"What's on your mind, Mason?" asks Dr. Sellers.

"Nothing," I answer, shaking my head with wide eyes.

He looks past me to see Tila'Cet sitting at my side and chuckles under his breath.

"Tila'Cet," he says.

I open my eyes and throw him the most serious expression I can muster with cheeks flushing red, mouthing him a single word. '*No.*'

"Never mind," he says, waving her off.

I do not know if she looked his way or even heard him, but I was not about to be thrown under the transport. He means well, but not a chance. I would die if he outed me to Tila'Cet.

The others glance between us. They do not have a clue. I have mentioned nothing about Tila'Cet to anyone but Dr. Sellers, who smirks and extends a glass with a three-finger pour of his version of Jerleanian to Nala'Cet.

"Let's see you handle it like a pro," says Fister.

"More pro than you," says Bell. "I bet she slams it."

"A third of a rotation's worth of work says she doesn't," says Sapp.

"I'll second that," says Fister.

"Bet," says Bell. "You guys are on."

"All three of you are horrible," says Delgado. "But I'm in with Sapp."

Nala'Cet is looking back and forth between everyone as they talk. She turns to me with a single brow raised and parted lips. I motion for her to drink, but she shakes her head.

"Mason," says Dr. Sellers.

I glance his way. He eyes me for a tik and motions to Tila'Cet, but I follow Nala'Cet's suit and shake my head through further blushing cheeks. My resistance goes ignored.

Dr. Sellers hands me a pair of glasses with three-finger pours, all but forcing me to hand one to Tila'Cet. I take a sip. It is not spot-on, but it is not bad either. I would even say he hit the mark.

Tila'Cet takes a sip and exhales sharply, wincing her head back with her eyes shut tight. Her mother watches her and stares at her own glass with uncertainty.

"*Sopet,*" I say, hoping she will drink.

"*Ma,*" she says.

"*Sopet,*" I urge.

Nala'Cet hands me the rench-snech she is smoking and stares me down.

"Okay," I say, looking at her mother. "*Tigeth.*"

"*Sopet,*" says Pru'Cet and Tila'Cet, joining in my peer pressure.

"*Sopet,*" chants my squad with Din'Mos as he approaches. "*Sopet. Sopet. Sopet.*"

Nala'Cet looks at us and laughs while shaking her head as we gang up on her—as if she is not curious to try it. I take a long puff of rench-snech, inhale until my lungs are full, and exhale without breaking eye-contact with her.

"See," says Bell. "I told you she wasn't—"

Nala'Cet takes the glass and throws it back like water.

"Sip," I shout, smoke exhaling with the word as I tear into a cough.

I hit the rench-snech too hard. She downed her drink too fast. We are both coughing.

Pru'Cet nor his sister try to help. They are cheering and laughing. Everyone is. I fall backward off my seat with my lung's last heave. Hysteria surrounds me.

My back meets the snow. Rench-snech hits hard and fast. I feel light, like I am floating, and my head is fuzzy. My thoughts are clear, but I feel high. Giggles take over me for a few teks while the party around me slips away.

A hand... I take it and am pulled up to return to my seat. It is Tila'Cet. Her hand on my back... My skin feels sensitive to the touch. It is a love drug. Peace drug. Whatever it is, I accept it with an open mind as its sensations shift.

Delgado is underneath Sergeant Bentley in flickering firelight, kissing softly with him when she spots me and points. They both look my way, chuckle, and go back to making out.

"Need a hand?" asks a familiar voice.

I look up. Bell reaches down for me with Sapp and Fister at his side.

"What the haze?" I ask. "Tila'Cet just helped me up."

"Yeah," says Fister, sitting on a tree stump to my right. "That didn't happen."

"You've been there for," says Sapp with a pause. "I don't know. I'm too messed up to tell."

"Five or six teks," says Bell.

"You want help up or not?" asks Sapp, hand still extended.

"Thanks," I say, taking another puff of rench-snech. "You want some?"

"Not me," says Sapp. "I am spun right now."

"I'll take some," says Bell.

"Me too," says Fister. "Smoke."

I take two heavy pulls from my back, release thick clouds of auburn smoke, and hand it to Bell as I inhale a third into my lungs. He takes a few puffs and passes it to Fister. Everything around me blurs. It is getting hard to focus, but all is simultaneously clearer than it was after the first hit.

Sapp pulls me up, and they help me sit. Sergeant Bentley and Delgado are gone. Music is still going. Dah'Sel dance and sing in unison.

"What is in that stuff?" I ask.

"*Dit ama gav reema cea?*" asks Tila'Cet.

I turn to face her on a log bench. Lost in her eyes, the words do not come.

"*Dit ama?*" she asks again.

"No," I say. "I mean, I would have. I just thought you already helped me up. And you have no idea what I'm saying."

She brushes snow from my back and stops her hand for a moment when she notices how cold my skin is.

"I'm okay," I say through subtle shivers.

Tila'Cet smiles, turns me, and pulls my back into her delicate chest to wrap her arms around me. Warmth penetrates. I relax. The smoke, the touch of Tila'Cet, whatever the reason, it feels nice.

I look up through my brows long enough to see Pru'Cet and Nala'Cet, who I find to be a wonderful Mother, smile as I brush the hairs on Tila'Cet's arm, pull them between my fingers, and battle against weighted eyes lost to the power of rench-snech and her comforting embrace. Everything fades until the fire is gone. My consciousness disappears with it to a place more secure than sleep itself.

CHAPTER 6
The Gift

The red-and-black StarBird jail-breaking Uprisers and Saddi brought for Dolofónos's escape upon rescue coasts low through the air over Kep Four's Denta fields. The area forms a thin ring with less pollution around The Suicide Fields. Between it and the fatal fields where so many took their last breath is a regular zone of the planet's brown. The Suicide Fields are bulls-eyed at its center. The vessel creeps over them as if someone on board is remembering the rotations were tolerable.

I remember them as if my terra boots were still trudging its soil. The Denta fields of Kep Four are still toxic, but not like the rest of the planet was in my youth. We used to take our respirators off there for a full 30 tiks—though there was nothing to admire when we did. Thirty tiks is not much, but it was the only place I could pretend the world was right after my brother Comilo passed, even if just for a moment.

A few Uprisers move about in the StarBird's hold and stack plastic boxes with unknown content from floor to ceiling. Two of them open a box. Each removes a hand-sized red-and-black object wrapped tightly bound in layers of thin filament. Their fingers pry them open.

"Think they could have made these any harder to open?" asks one of the Uprisers.

"Only if they wrapped it in molten metal and let it harden," answers the other.

The wraps give way. They remove its contents. A full red-and-black uniform comprising a top and bottom that are full of wrinkles from being compressed unfolds.

"These are for the new recruits," says the first Upriser.

The door behind them opens as he lays the garment on the box he got it from. Saddi enters.

"Where's Dolofónos's uniform," asks Saddi.

The first Upriser walks to a sleek container the size of a fully laid-out suit. The second carries one similar but shorter to his side and stacks it on the first box.

"And the third?" asks Saddi.

"Beside you," answers the first Upriser. "Against the wall."

Saddi looks to her right across her robotic arm. A cuboid box taller than her stands leaning on the bulkhead a few paces away. She picks it up and smiles.

"He's going to love this," she says, motioning to the others. "Follow me. Grab the rest."

The Uprisers pick up the other two boxes and follow her from the hold.

6-2
Leaves

Dolofónos is in the StarBirds's ready room. He studies the planet's surface on a viewing pane highlighting capital cities. Digital circles highlighting population numbers and current happenings encircle some cities but not all. He moves the image to display Najasa and the Sigma Green District and taps the terminal in thought before marking them with red circles and a matching 'X' over them.

"Change population count," says Dolofónos.

THE GIFT

"*Designated population indicators are currently—*"

"Override," says Dolofónos, interrupting the A.I. system. "Set population to nothing."

"*Confirmed,*" says A.I.

The system resets the numbers around Najasa and the Sigma Green District to read:

'POPULATION ZERO.'

The ready room door beeps.

"Who is it?" asks Dolofónos.

"Saddi," she answers over comms.

"Enter," he says.

The door opens and Saddi walks in with the cuboid box. Her accompanying Uprisers carry in two more boxes and place them on the table in the middle of the room. They exit without uttering a word.

"What's this?" asks Dolofónos.

"Open them and find out," she answers.

Dolofónos adjusts his eye patch and cuts her a curious look with a squinted right eye over a partial grin.

He grabs the smaller of the business suit-sized boxes.

"Not that one," says Saddi. "Open the other one first."

"Okay," he says, swapping the top box for the one underneath it.

He opens it and removes a neatly folded red-and-black uniform.

"Oh," he says, trying to hold back a smile as he holds it up and unfolds it. "This is... Really?"

"Thought you needed a change of pace," says Saddi. "Something to make you feel like the world-conquering leader you're destined to be."

He removes the pants and lays them across the table under the long-sleeved top. Wild black leaves cover to overwhelm the red backdropped uniform and form a camouflage layout.

"Can't say I don't like it," says Dolofónos.

He grabs the other box and opens it. His head cocks as he reaches in with an increased smirk. The same black leaves over red fill the box like a folded sheet of silk. He pulls it out by the collar and holds it up, letting the rest of it drop to his waist.

"A cape?" he asks.

"For a ruler," says Saddi. "It's going to look great on you with what's next."

Dolofónos lays it over the uniform and moves the cuboid box she is holding up. She passes it to him as he approaches. He takes it and eyes her for a moment,

"Well?" asks Saddi.

He carries it to his new uniform, sets it down, and opens it with a full smile he can no longer contain. In the box is a metallic red-and-black staff with solid gold-outlined hardened bones that form four tips at its end. He pulls it out to examine it, standing it next to himself. The staff is a full head taller than he is.

He wraps his hands around its lower metallic hand grip, raises it, lowers its tip, and grabs the upper grip with his free hand. The bones at its tip spark with currents of electrical like a taser built to take down dyoggs.

"Squeeze both grips tight and it will charge," says Saddi. "Squeeze them long enough and it overloads with a forward discharge."

"Does it work?" asks Dolofónos.

"Of course, it works," answers Saddi.

"We'll see," he says, setting the staff on the uniform and walking to Saddi. "Devilishly marvelous. That's what you are."

He lifts her chin to kiss her bottom lip.

"Then put it on," says Saddi, lip still in his mouth. "People are waiting on you."

She winks and turns to take a step toward the door.

"Saddi," says Dolofónos.

She turns to face him. Dolofónos is turned halfway through a spinning back fist when she sees him. His face grimaces with hate and power as he guides the hammer side of his fist toward her face.

Her robotic right arm moves quick. She catches him by the wrist and stops him in his tracks. They lock one eye to two for a moment. She squeezes a little. His teeth show as he sucks air through them to ignore the pain.

"Good girl," he says.

"Thought I lost my edge," she says. "Didn't you?"

"Had to check," answers Dolofónos.

She smiles, releases her grip, and lowers her arm before turning to exit without looking back.

"You weren't locked up that long," she says.

Dolofónos cocks a half smile and watches her until the door closes, and she is gone. He moves to the table with a deep breath of pride and freedom, then removes his shirt. His eye patch slides up with it. The socket behind it is empty. He rubs the void in his head and puts the eye patch back in place before reaching for his new uniform.

6-3
Declaration

I see only the tip of a staff in the ready room Dolofónos got dressed in. Saddi enters.

"We've touched down," she says. "Tell me you're eager."

"I've spent cycles waiting for this," says Dolofónos.

They walk to the corner of the ready room and punch in a series of codes on a nearby panel. A round seal opens in the side of the wall. Its upper and lower right and lefts sides continue to expand until they step through the now square opening to a mass of cheering predators.

Thousands of Uprisers surround the red-and-black graffiti-laden fallen Rushmore monuments outside The Suicide Fields. They face their sire's StarBird as he steps onto Kep Four's tainted soil for the first time since his incarceration.

They chant with fists and weapons raised in the air.

"Uprisers ready for war," they shout. "Uprisers ready for war."

Dolofónos's steps forward. The cape hangs over his shoulders and down his sides until he raises his arms overhead to silence the crowd. Twenty tiks in time slip by before chants become whispers, then quietness.

He and Saddi march forward into the crowd. They part a path to the fallen monuments for their highest-standing member to walk. Dolofónos's working eye turns in its socket to follow a small animal.

A short, thin Upriser to his left looks toward brown soil as his leader passes him. Dolofónos stops and stares at the top of his follower's head. He flips the staff up and sticks it to the man's chest, surging electricity into him until he falls, then discharges its remaining energy into the flagert.

Dolofónos continues to the fallen monuments. The flagert lies on the ground behind him like a charred bag of black meat. Stench drifts through the crowd to wrinkle noses.

"Told you it worked," says Saddi, "but that was our scientist from the capital of Galhet."

"The Upriser or the flagert," he asks, handing the staff to Saddi.

Dolofónos climbs upon an ascension ladder that carries him to the top of George Washington's head. She tosses the staff up to him. He holds it at his side with its butt on the stone carving's temple. Its hardened bone tips point to a heaven beyond the brown that awaits none of them. His cape blows in Kep Four's fatal winds as he overlooks the awaiting crowd.

Uprisers are in their traditional black with thin red lightning bolt pinstripes and a human pelvic bone on their upper right chests.

Saddi holds a scrap-made pane encased in a small metal pan. Three finger-sized antennas protrude from it. She pulls up a list of city feeds and inputs codes with the black Upriser flag with a human pelvic bone at its center flying with the Butchers behind her. Like the scouting spheres on the Argo vessels, visual input relay drones hover around Dolofónos at various heights to transmit signals across Kep Four.

"Planetary update panes intercepted," says Saddi.

Dolofónos places an amplator to his neck on the left side of his vocal cords. A sea of followers listens as he speaks. They are vast in numbers and cover dust-obscured surroundings a half-click in any direction.

His image plays on video panes lining capital cities and civilian territories once reserved for the Planetary Sovereign's updates. They broadcast it everywhere. Thousands in Najasa and the Sigma Greed District, along with their underground markets, clutch every word uttered by the madman.

Onlookers shout and cheer when he stops speaking to look over his followers. Hardcore and devout Uprisers of old are the only ones physically present for his speech.

"And as new world leader…" says Dolofónos. "As your sire and sovereign, I'll ensure we claim what's ours to rebuild the lives of those falsely imprisoned for the crime of hunger or stealing to feed families and gain clothing for warmth. The Armada has abandoned us. I know that. You know that, but our time is here and now. We will find our way. They no longer have the numbers to resist Upriser pressure. Those that used to hold power have all but given Kep Four to us, and we will do with it what we want."

The crowd of Uprisers, Butchers, new recruits marked as Uprisers by a red cloth tied around their right biceps alone, and freed prisoners with shifting civilians celebrate his words in districts by chanting his name, jumping up and down, and bouncing shoulders off one another. He is a savage Messiah to the freed, hope for the new, and leader of a failing world.

"We will find a way to survive the Armada's death sentence," continues Dolofónos. "Join me, if you have not already, and build a new life. Join me and survive."

His voice raises to rally spirits.

"Join me," shouts Dolofónos, staff held high in the air, "and we will find our way off this dying rock by building our own ships, if need be, but be warned. Those who oppose us … those that do not join the Upriser movement … we will use them to paint surface-side streets red. If you stand against us, you and your families will either die on Kep Four or at the hands of the Uprisers."

More cheers supporting violence reverberate into the air. The crowd is bloodthirsty and blind in allegiance to him.

"If you do not stand with us," says Dolofónos, "you stand against everything you should be fighting for. Worse, more you stand against me, and you might as well be walking into The Suicide Fields yourself. If not..." Dolofónos smiles. "I'll walk you naked into them myself."

He looks down at the fallen George Washington monument beneath his feet.

"All great empires fall," he continues, "but not us, not this rotation. This rotation, we take back. Heed this message as a foreshadowing of your future and choose your destiny."

"Saddi," says Dolofónos, motioning to the visual input relay drones. "Kill feeds to city panes."

Saddi kills the feed. Surrounding drones shift from green to red, then silver, and hover away from him. Najasa and the Sigma Green District lose their pane update feeds. Anything else he says will be from his mouth and only to Upriser ears. He steps to the edge of a once-strong Rushmore Monument to approach an ascension ladder.

Dolofónos tosses the staff down to Saddi. She catches it as he glides down the ladder where Uprisers meet him with hugs, pats on the back, cheers, and overall heavy support, muffled through protective gear and old Farcas. A sea of criminals surrounds him as Saddi tosses the staff back to him. He catches it and walks through the crowd.

"Now that audio and visual relays have ended," says Dolofónos. "Let me tell you, the Uprisers of old, those that have been forever loyal, what we're really going to do."

He walks through the crowd. They part a wide path for him to pace. All watch with proud admiration to be what they are.

"Our plan is to build only one ship," says Dolofónos. "Everyone else on this planet can suck its atmosphere until their lungs are full. We'll build a vessel large enough for all sixty-two thousand Uprisers."

Dolofónos pauses in what I can only assume to be an evil thought.

"Better yet..." he continues through a twisted grin, "I know how we can leave a mark that'll burn the word 'Uprisers' into the hearts of Kep Four. Now go. Enjoy the last of our time on this wretched planet and prepare your minds for the fact we'll soon be off this world."

The Upriser crowd cheers. People like them do not need to know his blueprint or final conceptual idea. They need only know he is Dolofónos and lords over an unidentified future.

Cheers fade. The imagery around them blurs into blackness. I can no longer tell what is happening or hear them. A sensory deprivation of unknown origin has taken over me. I am no longer privy.

CHAPTER 7
Trading Places

I wake up and struggle to distinguish my surroundings through foggy eyes. My eyes are not adapting quickly. I pop my neck—three cracks to the left, one to the right—and stretch my back like a small, red-tailed firecat.

It comes into focus.

"My tele-tent?" I ask. "How am I in my tele-tent?"

I am unsure how I got here. Maybe I walked. I guess somebody could have carried me. Regardless of the two possibilities, I am sure plenty will tease me about it this rotation. Whatever the case may be, I need to wake up more.

"Power up cooking station," I say.

A headache pounds against my skull while I wait. The cooking station comes to life.

"Generate stimulant five," I say. "Add nutritional supplement one-thirty-one to the mix."

I have lived off the land with the Dah'Sel for the last 200-plus rotations since our acceptance on Wah'Lor. I have drunk nothing but fresh water from the nearby river, except for stimulant five. It is my weakness.

The automated atomic generator processes my usual waking drink and brings it to life in its cylindrical center hold. I love the first sip. The sensation of dirty ice water inside my cheeks amps me up every time.

A tap at my door grabs my attention.

I sit on the edge of my little bed to wipe sleep and morning horror from my face. There is nothing I can do about the breath.

"Open," I say.

Its door slides open to reveal the last and first person I wanted to see. Pru'Cet being the latter, because I want to ask him what happened to me last night without being teased by the rest of my squad. Tila'Cet would be the former. Do not get me wrong. I am glad to be in her presence, but not while I look like this with my head hurting.

"*Specap*," says Tila'Cet.

I sip stimulant five and swish it around my mouth to cleanse the stench before speaking. It will not work, but I must try. I refuse to have her think of me as the human with bad breath.

"*Specap*," I return her greeting.

"*Pizta gwan kela-zis*," urges Pru'Cet.

Tila'Cet takes me in her eyes and smiles with embarrassment. Our language gives her trouble, but Pru'Cet has helped her learn some of our words. She holds her hands cupped together in front of her. I would be nervous not knowing a language if I were her too, especially when she is around someone like me who is fluent in theirs.

"I sleep you," says Tila'Cet.

I turn my head down and smile with capillaries flushing my cheeks with fresh blood. She is looking at Pru'Cet when I look up again. Perhaps I jumped the gun on my thoughts. I think she is awaiting him to give her the proper words.

"Tele-tent," he says.

She returns her attention to me.

"Tell ... a ... tent?" she asks.

"You?" I ask, pointing to my bed. "Sleep here?"

"Yes," she answers.

My eyes widen.

"With me?"

Tila'Cet giggles and turns away for a tik. I bet she is blushing under the short layer of light silver hair covering her face. I know I am. Pru'Cet has his usual, broad, ear-to-ear grin on his. He finds humor in just about everything.

"Trade," she continues.

"Oh," I say. "You mean, you want to sleep in here for a night, and I sleep in Lesdelop?"

"Trade," she repeats.

"Yeah. Okay. When?"

Her head tilts.

"*Jappa?*" I ask.

"This..." she answers. "Ro ... rot ... ate."

"Rotation," I say.

"This ... ro ... tation," she repeats.

"Evening rotation," says Pru'Cet. "She say black sky."

"Yes." Tila'Cet nods.

"Of course," I answer with a fast and excited nod. "Yes."

She claps her hands together, which is a mannerism she got from Pru'Cet, who got it from me, and moves in to raise her arms for a traditional Kla'Wah embrace. The tele-tent ceiling rises to make room for her arms. I move in to place our palms together, but she is too tall.

"*Blight crelo hitto ver aryan-zis,*" I say.

Tila'Cet bends her elbows a little. I move in on tippy toes to reach them but turn my head in fear of my breath. My eyes close on instinct, our palms touch, and our foreheads lower until she reaches mine for contact. A moment passes. I lower my hands with hers for a hug. Tila'Cet's body is warm and soft, like a blanket hiding delicate curves beneath its sheets.

She releases me and backs from my tele-tent to walk away. Pru'Cet watches me.

"What are you staring at?" I ask.

I am unsure what he has said to her behind closed doors over rotations past, but I would not put trying to help get us closer beyond him.

"Kuzsoec, McKayla," he says. "Come."

"If you have any idea what I feel like right now," I say. "That rench-snech might not be as bad as randy-root, but I need to take it slower if I do that again."

"Rany-root?" he asks.

"Randy-root," I answer. "It is like rench-snech; only it makes you feel much worse the following rotation."

I down my stimulant five as Pru'Cet exits the tele-tent.

"All right," I say. "Let's go."

I exit to applause. My squad and several Dah'Sel clap at the fact that I am up and about. My jaw just dropped a little. Pru'Cet has a smirk on his face. I hope I did nothing stupid during Fak sa pasho. I was out of it by the time it ended. Though I cannot remember how it concluded.

"Pru'Cet," I say. "You could have warned me."

"Warned you?" asks Delgado. "It was his idea."

I reach for Pru'Cet, but he is too quick and evades my grasp.

"Come here, you little..."

"Still feeling the rench effect?" asks Sergeant Bentley.

"Rench effect?" I ask.

"That's what we're calling the hangover," he answers.

"Oh," I say and stop to force a sarcastic smile. "Yeah. Even better now that I have a field of people clapping for me."

"What'd you expect, lightweight?" asks Bell.

"Got to learn to hold that liquor," says Sapp.

"To haze with the liquor," says Fister. "It's that rench-snech she needs to be careful with. I know it hit me hard at some point last night. That stuff will pin you down and put you to sleep sore."

"Glad I am not the only one," I say.

"Most of us just woke within the last two-forty," says Sergeant Bentley. "At least you got some sleep."

"Yes and no," I say. "What are we doing this rotation again?"

"Nothing," answers Sergeant Bentley. "The rotations after Fak sa pasho are rotations of rest. We'll be the only Kep Four transplants in the field for a bit. Remember?"

"That's right," I answer. "I just need a bit more time for that stuff to leave my system's all."

Forgetting things is not something I am used to. I rub my head. It is cold and clammy.

"We're all headed down to the lassabax for a swim," says Bell. "Are you coming with us?"

"In this cold," I answer, rubbing my head. "No. Have fun freezing to death."

"All right," says Sergeant Bentley. "Sleep it off and catch up with us when you feel better." He turns to the others. "Let's go."

The Dah'Sel, Pru'Cet, and my squad of friends leave for the river. Delgado is arm-in-arm with Sergeant Bentley.

"Well," I say, watching Sergeant Bentley and Delgado. "I guess that's happening now?" I turn to Dr. Sellers. "You're not going with them?"

"I was," answers Dr. Sellers.

"What changed your mind?"

"You did," he answers.

"Me?" I ask.

"Rench-snech effects wore off everyone already," he says. "What's really going on with you? I don't think you slept."

"I slept like a rock," I say.

"Are you still having those visions?" he asks with worry in his voice. "Are they getting worse?"

"Ah, man," I say through a sigh. "This again?"

"Talk to me, Mason," says Dr. Sellers.

"Yes, and I don't know," I answer. "I'm not sure."

"How can you not know?" he asks.

"I can't tell if what I'm having sometimes are visions or dreams."

"Okay then," he says, placing his hands on my shoulder to guide me. "Sounds like you're coming with me."

"I'm fine," I say. "I don't need—"

"Doctor's prerogative," interrupts Dr. Sellers, turning me and patting me on the back as we walk to the clearing and stop. "Dr. Sellers requesting drop pod clearance for myself and Mason."

"Request granted," answers a familiar voice.

"Was that Algash?" I ask.

"It was," answers Dr. Sellers. "They're trying him out in a few unique positions."

A pair of drop pods touch down a few paces from us. The doors slide open.

Dr. Sellers climbs in the first one.

"Meet you on *Athanasios*," he says.

The door closes, and it takes off.

"I should have stayed in bed," I say, climbing into the other drop pod.

I look across the field of white beyond the tele-tents and bengas the Dah'Sel erected for us. Fister is almost out of sight and not going with the others to swim. Sad-looking dofabe trees in the distance ahead of him with long drooping branches and leaves do not await him. That is where Dr. Morris, Utley, and Skedelski were buried. His fallen cousin is not with them.

Fister veers off to his left on his way to visit Rhigas, a full click away from them at the field's furthest edge. He is not buried alone there. He lies in the ground with Dah'Sel of the past who died while transformed to keep evil away from those beneath the dofabe trees. Fister will be there with him for at least the night. This is his moment after the Fak sa pasho to remember the one he was closest to in life, and one we all know he wishes to be back with us.

It takes a moment to turn away from him. I long to offer Fister support but do not want to smother him, not in a moment so personal. He needs this, and he needs to do it with him and his cousin alone together.

7-2
Dark Memories

We get onboard *Athanasios* and head straight for the Med Lab. Memories impose themselves upon me when I walk these corridors. I keep my head down and eye the floor until we reach the Med Lab.

Dr. Sellers is awaiting me with the door open when I arrive. They have repaired the Med Lab, but all I see is the blood-laden floor with the door bent and repeatedly trying to close. *Athanasios* is not haunted; I am haunted by it.

"So..." I say, sitting on the bed. "What now?"

"Lie down," says Dr. Sellers.

"Why do I have to lie down?" I ask.

"I want to map what's going on when you sleep," he answers.

"But I'm not sleepy right now."

"You will be in a moment," he says.

Dr. Sellers grabs a tubular injector and steps to the bed beside me.

"I don't want to sleep," I say. "Seriously. Like, not going to happen."

"Mason, you need to let me—"

"No," I interrupt and stand.

"Why not?" asks Dr. Sellers, setting down the tubular injector. "And be honest with me here."

"I've been having crazy dreams is all," I answer. "I don't feel like dreaming right now."

"More visions?" asks Dr. Sellers.

"I've only had one vision the last few rotations," I answer, "but my dreams are the same things the visions are about."

"Elaborate," says Dr. Sellers.

"One vision I had," I say, "there was this homeless man stealing food from Dolofónos. One of his Uprisers saw it happening and apprehended him. Dolofónos executed him for it."

"And the dreams are the same?" he asks.

"Yes and no," I answer, while pacing. "They're all on Kep Four and surround Dolofónos."

"What happened in them?" he asks.

"Why does it matter?" I ask in return.

"Because your visions when we first arrived were accurate from what you told me," he says. "If you would have mentioned it to someone before—"

"What are you about to say?" I ask with a raised voice. "I think about it all the time. How do you think I feel? Do you think anyone would have believed me? You thought they were hypnagogic hallucinations."

"Okay," says Dr. Sellers with a slow nod. "You're right. I'm sorry. Doesn't matter anymore. I believe you now. Our whole squad does. What anyone else here thinks is irrelevant."

"In my first dream," I say. "The Uprisers were breaking Dolofónos from a maximum-security flood hold. They just came in, started killing people, and took him. In another dream, he was giving a speech about taking over Kep Four and getting off it. It played on city and district panes for all to see."

"Did it feel like a vision?" asks Dr. Sellers.

"It felt like a dream," I answer. "But it's like I was there, just as I am in my visions. Not as an active participant but as someone watching and unable to interfere."

Dr. Sellers moves to an inlaid medicator with claw marks surrounding its mounting hold. The hover beds and other equipment are new, but marks of what took place here remain. A bitter reminder of the dangers we once faced.

"Wasn't the I.M. damaged when that Rhigas monster thing tore up the Med Bay?" I ask.

"They just installed this one," answers Dr. Sellers. "Armada brought one for each ship in orbit and two for each on the surface. This is the replacement."

He directs his attention back to the I.M.

"Sperprazidoneri," he says. "Time release tablets for McKayla Mason. Coordinate the dosage with her medical records. Total release duration, thirty-one taks."

I love the inlaid medicator's design. It prompts me to think about the engineering rings that almost ruined Expedition Anchor's departure. An outer I.M. ring rests flat against the wall. The center one insets a quarter pace into it. An unknown amount of chemicals mix to make small, chewy, medicated tablets.

Dr. Sellers hands me a small vial of the newly infused meds.

"Here you are," he says. "Sperprazidoneri. One a rotation. It should help you get a good night's rest."

"Thanks," I say. "When do I take them?"

"Nighttime only," answers Dr. Sellers. "And only before you're going to fall asleep."

"What happens if I take one now?"

"Better lie on that gurney before you do that."

"Wait," I say. "This is a sedative?"

"It has some mixed into it," he answers. "You need sleep, Mason. And you need it with your brain resting while you get it. I suggest taking it when you get to your tele. It'll wear off in a few taks before suns set."

"Do me a favor?" I ask.

"What's that?" asks Dr. Sellers.

"Keep this between us."

"Done."

The med door slides open, and I step through it.

"Mason," says Dr. Sellers.

I stop.

"Yeah?"

"I'll double-check your dreams with Kep Four when they open the next micro-Rosen," he answers. "I'll get a probe through with the message."

A half-hearted Armada salute is all he gets as I exit. I am glad Armada scientists back on Kep Four found a way to open the smaller micro-Rosen wormholes. They are not large enough to get anything beyond signals and messages through, but two-way communication can now be established from time to time. Updates are rare because of the power it consumes opening them while we are rationing energy usage. It is better than nothing.

7-3
Sleep

Athanasios is not home for me, but I do not want to go planetside with everyone down at lassabax. Not if I am about to take this Sperprazidoneri, as Dr. Sellers called it. The feeling hits me hard as I stop outside the Med Lab door.

"Don't want to be explaining this to everyone if I sleep too long," I say aloud. "Personal quarters it is."

I make my way through *Athanasios* and wish the lightheadedness to be gone when I wake. Maybe that is not correct. It is more of a groggy feeling and hard to explain. My thoughts are not 100 percent right now. I even forgot this rotation was a rotation of rest for the Dah'Sel's Fak sa pasho.

My personal quarters come into view when I round a corner halfway through the corridor. I will prepare myself for dreamland in 20 more paces. Or, should I say, a land of sleep where dreams dare not visit.

The usual halo projection of DNA spins for a tik as the door receiver reads my palm. It breaks down for me. My room greets me with no warm welcome. It should have been Algash's room, but it is mine. Beats a jail cell.

I open the bottle, grab stimulant five I did not finish the other rotation, and gather the nerve to chew this tablet of Sperprazidoneri up.

"Wait," I tell myself. "Stimulant five's probably not helping with my sleep or dreams."

It is true. That stuff gets your mind going. It speeds mine up like an Alterninian racer on the last lap for victory. I think it is best to set it down.

"Power up cooking station," I say.

It buzzes with life.

"Generate H2O."

I wait for it to finish its... Ah; it is done. Good. I am getting cranky from lack of sleep. Dr. Sellers might be onto something. Those dreams have not let my mind count sleep as needed rest.

I grab the water and pop what Dr. Sellers gave me into my mouth for a good chew. It has a tough jelly texture, and its flavor reminds me oddly of brickfield stalks found under capital cities in the underground market on Kep Four: sweet, chalky, and moist. I swallow it and follow with the entire glass of water.

"This better work," I mumble.

My clothes come off until nothing separates flesh from air. A good stretch relieves built tension. A yawn joins the sensation.

I slither between the covers and pull them over my head to hide from life.

"*Athanasios*," I say. "Power off lights."

Darkness comforts me. The darker, the better. I like to wake up as if I am blind. It heightens the other senses to create deprivation. I feel the Sperprazidoneri. It is already at work. Thoughts become hard to form. Muscles relax to near numbness.

Armada medications absorb through the lips, cheeks, teeth, tongue, palate, salivatory glands, and periodontium parts of the mouth. They are fast, effective, and send me to sleep. In about 10 more, I think I will be...

CHAPTER 8
Vengeance

Kep Four is burning.

The poverty-stricken district of Najasa is up in flames with violence as Dolofónos's minions launch an onslaught on its air filtration unit. Uprisers by the thousands aim weapons at the structure's base and darken the brown above as they fire. The saturated bombardment of weapons tearing into the air filtration unit echoes the district with sharp cracks of gunfire from automatic onium rifles and flamethrowers. Its base crumples and it leans for a moment.

They stop firing and wait for it to fall, but the mighty structure holds its position in an ominously tipping fashion. The quarter-click-wide unit reaching for the sky topples and spills across bridges, failed businesses, and the remnants of housing structures that should have been condemned cycles ago. It lands with a thunderous crash and crushes everything in its path like an overwhelming force of nature driven by a disease known as human hatred and the madness of one man's revolution.

The city trembles as the impact's shockwave moves through the streets of Najasa and destroys the underground market and traps the unlucky beneath it. Uprisers on foot too slow to run are crushed in its wake and left under the massive weight of twisted metal and debris in their permanent graves. A dark gray cloud swirls upward with sparks. Sporadic flames roll vertically into the brown and turn a dark shade of taupe, looming overhead for a tek before sinking to the surface and smothering hope until nothing remains but suffocating silence—followed by the sound of choking breaths as those surface side struggle to breathe behind failing respirators.

I watch helplessly, unable to intervene and bound to the confines of my own mind as those caught in the crossfire are left to either betray their own morals or fall victim to Dolofónos's demands to join him. It is an agonizing spectacle to take in. There is no escape, nowhere to run, and nowhere to hide. I cannot look away and am forced to bear witness to his acts of lunacy.

The district I once called home is unrecognizable.

A single plume of smoke and ash rises from Galhet. It is one of the last two capital cities remaining in the sky, but its protective dome has long since fallen. Buildings that once defined the capital cities as strong and proud metropolises are no more. What remains is a wasteland to remind all left on Kep Four of the downward spirals to come. I have never been there. It no longer matters. They have all fallen to the Uprisers—crushed by the weight of their hubris. No one is untouchable.

People die by the thousands under other floating capital cities as they fall through the brown to join the poor beneath them. Surface-side populations are wiped out—bodies vaporized by catastrophic forces. Those beyond the impact radius burn as radioactive isotopes seep from the damaged power cores running the capitals invade their flesh. Fires rage through the streets. Intense heat consumes anything organic.

VENGEANCE

People outside the blast ring are left to suffocate in further polluting air without filtration systems. This is what Dolofónos wants—complete and utter destruction with a scoop of chaos for civilians who do not join his fight. Death to Armada resistance... He tolerates no hope. There will be no redemption.

I scream unheard words for it to stop but am shackled as an observer while violence tears apart families. A disinclined subconscious keeps my eyes open as any hope I had for those on Kep Four dies alongside them. My core bleeds with its civilians.

The blackest hearts kick in a front door and open fire on a father and husband.

"No," shouts a father. "Please no. Don't shoot my—"

He crashes from the front door of his run-down living space that is barely held together by a smattering of homemade walls and doors made from scrap and sealed together with hardened mud and ropes. He lands hard with an Upriser exiting behind him.

"Not my husband," shouts a woman inside. "We need him. Not their father."

She is tossed into the street next to her husband. Uprisers throw their children into the road next to them to watch in tears as their parents are beaten and murdered for refusing to join Dolofónos: a single gunshot for the father, five stabs to the back for their mother.

"Run," I plead in thought. "Run or fight back. Anything."

I would help if I could, but all I can do is wish a child's cry to be loud enough to drown out a mother's last gurgling scream. The freshly orphaned children cry over their parents in the streets, remove their masks to hold their faces, and kiss their cheeks while crying. Coughing ensues as their little lungs meet atmospheric toxicity, and they die next to the very people who gave them life.

Bodies and parentless youth fill the streets of Najasa. Children in another area hold their mothers' and fathers' cold, lifeless faces as they weep with tiny hands too weak to drag them inside. Solace for them fled the scene before the attack began and comfort left with it. One by one, their respirators fail until they succumb. If there is an afterlife, only they will know.

Dolofónos's voice booms through the city's comms system to echo Kep Four's airwaves mixed with promises of salvation and threats of violence.

"Witness punishments that are now taking place for the crime of treason against the Uprisers," says Dolofónos from Galhet as mayhem reigns below. "Join us and avoid this fate. Join us to live on. There will be no shelter from death for those too stubborn to accept their fate. Save yourself. Save your children. Become part of a new Armada, a better Armada, and eat until your stomach is full. Make love to your wives and husbands until your minds are full, knowing they are safe. Join us, and I will love you as my own, protect you with my life, and surround you with unfathomable luxuries. Resist, and meet a fate worse than death. This is my time, your time, and our time to rule the world with power you would never find otherwise. Uprisers are the new power. Let us be your family. Let me be your salvation. Say it with me: The Armada forces suffering. We are no longer condemned. No more Armada leaving us behind. We are not forgotten."

His speech continues as the suffering continues, but not everybody is resisting. Much of the civilian population gathers in masses in overthrown districts.

"No more Armada leaving us behind," shouts Uprisers in Galhet. "We are not forgotten."

"We are no longer condemned," chants a crowd in Najasa. "Armada forces suffering," chants the masses in Mona.

8-2
Food and Love

Hopeful recruits line up in droves to join Dolofónos outside of a former Armada hanger fallen to the hands of evil. The smell of food drifts through the air. Tables are laden with delicacies for them to gaze upon, but only those in red-and-black may partake in the feast. It is a tactic of control to brainwash potential recruits into believing they are making the right choice. Promising them protection, comfort, and a future that may never come is intoxicating, and none without families in the lower districts can resist the call.

I cannot judge desperation. They are waiting in desolation for Dolofónos ... for anyone to save them. Perhaps I would do the same in their position. I do not know.

Dozens of linen generators power up in Najasa to create a mass supply of red-and-black Upriser uniforms for those joining. New member uniforms differ from those the original Uprisers are wearing. The long-sleeved portion of their jackets is solid red and matches the pants that come with it. The center of the overcoat is black, along with their boots.

This creates a robust visual separation between Dolofónos's newer recruits and the others. He promises they can earn the right to wear stylish black and red seam-lined uniforms in time, but they will not. Dolofónos is incapable of maintaining a promise that does not benefit him.

Linen areas stretching over a click long fill with people joining him for power, food, to protect their families, and other reasons I probably could not understand. I do not think I would have ever joined them, not even in a situation so full of gloom, but I am not a "left behind" feeling the pressure of an unpleasant death approaching. I can only speculate how long my moral resistance would hold up in such a setting.

Dozens of tables full of food and beverages outline the reflective, six-story, heavily armored former Armada hanger's exterior. Many in civilian clothing are entering to become Uprisers. Only those who join them and exit in proper recruit attire can eat. Uprisers of old—as Dolofónos calls his long-standing members—have security regarding their futures. The newer recruits will have to do something unholy to capture a spot as a full-fledged Upriser.

New recruits are exiting the building and going to a feast as those soon to enter watch on with rumbling abdomens. Uprisers have cleared out food storage facilities, eateries, and all things surrounding healthy indulgences in the city. They have not only taken it over but turned it into a desperate region full of families willing to do anything instead of watching their children or spouses die of starvation.

Capital city Galhet has officially become the first captured by Dolofónos.

CHAPTER 9
Snow Hot

I wake with lightheadedness replaced by a headache. "So much for Sperprazidoneri stopping the dreams," I say.

I throw my clothes back on and ready myself for winter's chill. There are supposed to be steady winds in a few rotations, and it is going to be snowing this evening. I have faith in Pru'Cet's uncle Bah'Cet, and I am not worried about it. He is a brilliant engineer from what I have seen and heard. I believe the schooling structure he designed for the Armada's education of Wah'Lor and the Kla'Wah language will be adequate once complete.

My most significant concern is how well I will teach children and adults in the Dah'Sel community. It is not because of their disposition; I have never taught our language to anyone before. There is only one language on Kep Four, so there was never a need. Sure, I have studied languages of Ancient Earth with heavy fascination and diligence over the cycles. I have even learned a few from others, but I have never been one to teach.

The closest I ever came to being a teacher, besides when I deciphered remnants of 850,000 cycle old structures and advanced artifacts unearthed back on Kep Four, was when I worked with Pru'Cet on *Athanasios*.

"This should be fun," I say with nervous sarcasm. "Exit and lock."

My door does its dance to let me out. I make my way to the drop pod in a jog. I want to get off this ship.

"Mason requesting drop pod clearance," I say.

"All clear, Mason," says Algash over comms.

"Where's Dr. Wright?" I ask, breathing through my jog.

"On the surface for the rotations of rest fallowing Fak sa pasho," he answers.

"I haven't seen him since the end of its observance," I say.

"Good," says Algash. "He needs to live for once in his life."

The drop pod opens as I arrive. I enter with wonder of what it will be like to spend an entire evening inside Lesdelop ti'it renasa. Wat'Uza has granted no one else to enter since our arrival but me. My first time was nine rotations ago, thanks to Tila'Cet and Pru'Cet. I grin about it as the door closes.

9-2
New Words

The first of Wah'Lor's twin blue stars is soon to set over a niveous horizon carpeted with white-topped trees. I have been teaching a few Dah'Sel parents our words for a quarter of a rotation on this world. That is three-quarters of a rotation back on Kep Four, and I am exhausted. It was not on my agenda. Word got around about Pru'Cet teaching what he knows to humans with Wat'Uza, and Dah'Sel were awaiting me when I landed.

What unexpectedly became my first lesson with them ended moments ago, and I have a few more hands to shake, hugs to give, or arms to raise so I can touch palms and foreheads together with my new students in their customary embrace. Almost ... just a few more to go.

They were grateful to learn some of our language. It is a lesson we can learn from them. Many who have transplanted from Kep Four refuse to learn the Dah'Sel language. As someone dedicated to languages, I find it a closed-minded mentality. Some are not ready, but we moved to their planet, not the other way around. They forgave us for our mistakes and took time to teach us how to survive here.

My students are departing. I feel fulfilled this rotation. Not because what I did was some marvelous thing, but because I have experienced recent psychological health issues. I know now that I am desired amongst them beyond any doubt.

Tila'Cet, Nala'Cet, and Bah'Cet lingered and are the last to speak with me. It is nice to have them so close to me with no blood relatives alive. The 'Cets, along with my squad, are family.

"My new family," I whisper to myself.

"*Ama polasa utlu?*" asks Tila'Cet.

"Did I say that out loud?" I ask. "It was nothing. Just a deep thought."

"Deep thought?" she asks.

"*Lipfa,*" I answer.

"Okay," says Tila'Cet, with a lean, to kiss me on the cheek.

She walks away with picturesque steps, swaying a delightful loincloth with henna-style designs on it behind her and my spirit in her hands. She has enraptured me. As soon as she is ready, I am all in. There will be some on both sides that will not accept it, but most will. Minus the hair that covers their bodies, the Dah'Sel are not so different from us genetically. We are the same.

"That reminds me," I say to myself. "I need to talk with Sergeant Bentley and the others."

My squad walks toward me from across the field.

"Dr. Wright," I say. "I asked Algash where you were earlier."

"Hiding from work for a change," says Dr. Wright.

"Good for you," says Delgado.

Sergeant Bentley pats him on the back and turns to me.

"How'd class go?" asks Sergeant Bentley.

"Well," I answer. "It went well. I want to show you guys something."

I take Pru'Cet by the wrist and drag him with me.

"Looks like we're following Mason," says Sergeant Bentley.

It is nice to have their confidence. It was hard-earned, and I think this will surprise them as much as it did me. I will know soon.

9-3
Lesdelop

I lead my squad to the large Lesdelop ti'it renasa structure. The Dah'Sel held Fister captive in it. There is irony in the fact they held a prisoner in a structure that's name translates as *Home to all*. I have never brought it up, but it is drearily memorable.

Sergeant Bentley slows as we approach and stops. The others stop with him. I turn back to face them.

"What are you doing?" I ask.

"We can't go in there," says Sergeant Bentley.

"It's okay," I say. "They let me almost ten rotations ago for the first time and have a look around. I spent a couple of rotations studying the walls and asked them if it'd be okay to bring others in after Fak sa Pasho."

"And they said yes?" asks Sergeant Bentley.

"Only you guys," I answer. "Our squad, that is. They've known us for half a cycle now, but I think it'll be quite some time before they trust new arrivals. There are so many of them. I doubt they'll ever be comfortable turning this place into a mosh pit of humanity."

"I'll wait out here," says Fister. "You understand?"

"I do," I answer, motioning to the sky.

Fister has not gotten over how they held him hostage. They were unjust in what they did, but Lesdelop ti'it renasa reminds him of the moment he lost Rhigas over our initial misunderstanding with the Dah'Sel. To him, it harbors more than troublesome memories. It is emotional. His Lesdelop is my *Athanasios*.

"Well," says Dr. Sellers. "Let's go."

We approach a pair of Dah'Sel guards always at the main entrance. I give them a nod, and they part ways for me.

I place my hands together with interlocked fingers in prayer fashion and nod as I pass by.

"*Dada ama reema fesnop*," I say.

They nod in return but remain stoic. They are protectors and are not here to make friends. These guards are loyalists of an old-fashioned Dah'Sel lifestyle I have yet to educate myself about.

9–4
Inscription

My squad follows me inside.

"I see they took down the ivory transformation horns," says Sapp.

"They don't need them anymore," I say. "Listen, you guys can't leave the main hall."

"Everyone hear and understand what Mason just said?" asks Sergeant Bentley.

My squad confirms. We move forward and stop after 15 paces when I point to the reflective walls lined with hieroglyphics.

"Remember these?" I ask.

"What about them?" asks Sergeant Bentley.

"They correspond directly to what I deciphered from the artifacts found buried beneath Mount Ragat on Kep Four."

"What are you saying?" asks Dr. Wright. "You're saying it's from the same civilization that left that stuff on Kep Four?"

"If not," says Dr. Sellers, "it's a pretty big haze of a coincidence."

"That's not possible," says Bell.

"That's what everyone said about an eight hundred-and-fifty thousand-cycle-old artifact having more technology than our own," I say.

"Can you read it?" asks Delgado.

"I can," I answer, "but it doesn't make any sense. It's nonsensical when I put it all together. Pru'Cet can read it, but what Pru'Cet reads to me doesn't line up with what I get when I read it."

"What do you mean?" asks Sergeant Bentley.

"I talked to Pru'Cet here along with Wete and Wat'Uza," I answer. "About twenty generations ago, before the Dah'Sel and Vee'Sal separated to form their sects, they were in the process of developing a written structure for their language. Lore here says a system of underground caves led to discovering what's only referred to as shiny, light-emitting rocks that look like buildings. Some of the other things they described line up with what I saw on Kep Four."

"Okay," says Sergeant Bentley. "Let me wrap my head around this, and excuse me for repeating Dr. Wright here, but you think the same civilization was once here that was on Kep Four before us?"

I nod.

"No way," says Bell. "Then why can't you read it, or why doesn't it make sense when you do."

"The Kla'Wah, both Dah'Sel and Vee'Sal, decided to use the symbols on the artifacts here on Wah'Lor as words and characters for the written portion of their language. What's written on the walls where you're standing now tells a story of their history, the struggles they faced over the cycles, and shares memoirs of elders who once led them. It makes perfect sense in correlation with how they applied the symbols to their language, but it's still gibberish to me."

"Where are the Wah'Lor artifacts located?" asks Dr. Wright.

"I'm not saying," I say, shaking my head. "I swore to Wat'Uza I wouldn't. It's considered a forbidden zone. They call it E Plako Helkla—*The forbidden region*. I think, because it's where they got the symbols for the written language, but none of us have any idea who put it there."

"McKayla good Dah'Sel friend," says Pru'Cet.

I throw him a smile and return my attention to the squad.

"It'll be a great disrespect to locate it without their permission," I continue. "Besides, if it's truly from the same civilization, you won't be able to locate it anyway. The ones on Kep Four couldn't be detected. They were only discovered by accident during a mining operation, according to historical records. Not even Armada technology could figure out why they couldn't be picked up on scans. So, if you want to see it, they're going to have to tell you where they're at themselves."

"What does it say according to translations from Kep Four?" asks Sergeant Bentley.

"Same," I answer. "I promised them I wouldn't say after telling him I could read it."

"Does he know about the artifacts on Kep Four?" asks Dr. Wright.

"No," I answer.

"She's right," says Dr. Sellers. "She shouldn't say anything yet."

The others look at their squad mates with questions in their eyes.

"They may have been on Kep Four 850,000 cycles before we arrived," continues Dr. Sellers, "but their technology was already beyond our understanding nearly a million cycles ago. If they're still around and active here, we might not recognize their technology if we saw it or even know that we were looking at it in the first place."

"The walls here in Lessdelop ti'it renasa are a history lesson in their own right," I say. "Their words dictate rule, peace, and land treaties between the Dah'Sel and Vee'Sal along with other stuff I mentioned. There's nothing here you won't be able to learn in the new edu-centers."

"*Ledram ot gomee,*" says a Dah'Sel guard.

"Time's up," I say, leading the others from Lesdelop ti'it renasa.

I am always polite when it comes to the Dah'Sel, their beliefs, and their traditions. It pays to be cordial. I am not alone in this belief.

9-5
Permission

The final sun sets as we make our way across the field, and my head hurts. Sharp pain at each temple and the base of my skull stabs in random places, each a flickering of pain resembling a pinprick. I interlock my fingers behind my head and wrap my elbows forward to press my forearms into my temples as I step with Fister approaching.

"You okay?" asks Fister.

"Yeah," I answer.

Dr. Wright grabs my shoulder to stop me.

"What's wrong?" he asks.

The others stop in the snow with me. They are worried about my health. I can see it all over their faces—eyes locked onto me, awaiting an answer I will not give them. I appreciate it, but we have more important things to discuss.

"I'm fine," I say, letting go of my head and pretending the pain is gone.

"Don't lie to us, Mason," says Sergeant Bentley. "We're family here."

"Been hurting worse the last few rotations or so," I say.

"Didn't you say you started going into Lessdelop and deciphering the walls?"

"Yeah, but that doesn't have anything to do with it."

"How do you know?" asks Bell.

"It's just words," I answer. "I've been focusing hard on it and thinking a lot about the artifacts on Kep Four is all."

"That's when your visions of Kep Four started?" asks Dr. Sellers.

"You're having more visions?" asks Sergeant Bentley.

"Why didn't you tell me about this, Dr. Sellers?" asks Dr. Wright.

"Armada classified one point fifteen," answers Dr. Sellers.

"Noted," says Dr. Wright.

"After Mason's latest incident..." says Dr. Sellers. "I downloaded the last probe sent through the micro-Rosen from Kep Four earlier this rotation and asked for an update on Dolofónos."

"Dolofónos?" asks everyone.

"That's who she's been seeing when she has them," answers Dr. Sellers. "But they've mostly been taking place in her sleep. We're not sure if they're dreams or the same kind of thing that she was having during our initial conflict with the Dah'Sel."

"They've never really stopped," I say. "But they were happy, peaceful moments until a while back. Things like Armada members forming unions, children being born, and things like that. They were nice, and I was awake when they happened."

"And now?" asks Delgado.

"Now," I say, not wanting to. "I only see Uprisers, war, death, Dolo in C.H.I, and worse."

"What about them?" asks Sapp. "And Dolofónos was imprisoned."

"She said she saw the Uprisers taking over the maximum flood unit he's in," says Dr. Sellers.

"I think they're trying to overthrow the Armada," I answer. "I keep seeing all these violent images. And the capitals ... they've dropped some of them."

"You mean..." says Sergeant Bentley, pausing in disbelief. "You mean dropped them onto Kep Four?"

I nod.

"Onto the districts below," I say.

"And Chimark?" asks Fister.

I shake my head for his answer and squint my eyes as the pain in my head ramps up.

"I don't even know if it's real," I say.

We stand in silence, lost in our thoughts for a moment. Though I did not tell them about them at the time, they know the last images I saw of conflict came to be true. None of us want to say it, but things must be bad back on Kep Four. I would not see such images otherwise.

"How long until we get a probe back with an answer?" asks Dr. Wright.

"Three rotations," answers Dr. Sellers, "and the last three ships are set to arrive in six."

"I don't want to talk about it anymore if that's okay," I say. "I do think the rench-snech made them worse though."

"Could be," says Dr. Wright. "But I told you guys not to try it."

"I think you missed out," says Fister. "Beats condensed liquid cubes."

Delgado eyes Sergeant Bentley.

"I agree," she says.

Sergeant Bentley takes a step back from her.

Dr. Wright shakes his head.

"Why would you guys listen to me about inhaling an alien substance?" he asks. "What do I know?"

"How about this?" asks Fister. "It's cold, dark, snowing, and I'm ready for a run to sweat some of this out after the other night. Who's with me?"

"I'll go," says Sapp.

"With you," says Bell.

"Not this soldier," says Delgado, tapping her legs.

"Maybe later," answers Dr. Wright. "I want to take Dr. Sellers with me and look over Mason's scans."

"Looks like I'm not having that run," says Dr. Sellers.

I give Pru'Cet a friendly nudge and walk across the field.

"We'll catch you hard-working doctors when you're done," says Fister.

"Mason," calls Dr. Wright.

I turn Pru'Cet and myself to face him.

"When we get up there," he continues. "We'll start with—"

I lose my balance and drop into a 1/4 pace of snow. My hands hit the packed powder beneath it, and I fall face-first into it over my shoulders. The doctors move to my side and grab me with Pru'Cet.

I try to stand with their help, only to fall again. They catch me. The pounding in my head … it is too much to bear. My vision is no longer clear. A blur, at best, is all I see.

"Lie on your back," says Dr. Sellers.

"What's happening to me?" I ask.

"We'll figure it out," answers Dr. Wright.

Dr. Sellers pulls a small piece of equipment from his coat, but I cannot make out what it is.

"Just lie in the snow for a bit," he says. "You're burning up."

"Dr. Wright to *Athanasios* medical unit one-fourteen.".

"Go ahead, Dr. Wright," answers an unknown responder.

"I need a stocked unit to grid five of field three. Code one."

"On our way," says the responder.

Code one is better than code five, which is life or death with the clock ticking.

"You could've been contaminated by something on Wah'Lor," says Dr. Sellers. "Or it could be the specifics of your H-SAM. You certainly have a fever."

"How high is it?" asks Dr. Wright.

"It's well over where it…"

The snow-covered world around me fades to black with their voices. A labored breath… Something is…

CHAPTER 10
Soulless

The district of Mona is in peril. Dolofónos's Uprisers have ransacked the immense area of deprivation—one building and housing structure at a time. Many in the area know what is coming and await the vandals outside building entrances in respirators to join the movement instead of falling to the waste side. Not all are so willing.

Barricaded doors secured by steel beams in some regions tell a story of resistance. Uprisers place explosives on a door and detonate them. The door and wall around it break apart. Debris falls into the building. Dolofónos's followers waste no time throwing in dozens of neurotoxic gas grenades with further explosives. They take cover. Gas flows from the opening and a series of explosions take place within its walls, each reverberating their own concussion into the area outside the building. Dust settles and they move in. Quietude follows.

Uprisers that entered the home emerge only three teks later. A female Upriser in the group waiting outside steps forward.

"Where are they?" she asks. "How many were there?"

"There's nothing left of whoever was in there," says an Upriser. "Just pieces. Looks like it was a family of five."

A stolen Argos flying Armada logos and colors is parked outside of a multi-story housing complex with an Upriser mounted on its turret. Next to it is a battering ram mounted on a cargo cube in the process of firing up its core. The Cube charges forward. Its batter pushes through the entrance and the rest of the vehicle takes down its wall as it smashes its way fully into the building. Someone inside opens fire on it.

Uprisers surge into the structure and return fire. Gunshots from more of its residents hold back the invading Uprisers. Onium bursts strobe-light its interior. No one inside wants any part of Dolofónos or what he is doing.

Two Armada patrol units turn in from down the street as the battle inside wages. The stolen Argos-mounted Upriser turns the turret their way and mows down the first patrol car. It bursts into flames. The second patrol turns down an alleyway to avoid his partner's fate and is hit with a flurry of rounds. Armada patrol personnel lose control of the vehicle. It slides into an alleyway corner to evade the ambush. The Argos shoots until the patrol unit has flames swirling around it. Its driver exits with charred skin, takes a few steps, and collapses without catching himself.

All unopened or barricaded housing units across the District of Mona are rewarded by having their doors kicked in. At 60,000 strong, black-and-red numbers are growing by the tak and waste no time taking supplies, food, protective clothing, and respirators from those unwilling to join. Execution follows the bandits' actions.

Several citizens rush from an alleyway between two housing units armed with pipes and sticks. Dozens of Uprisers swarm them from all directions with Armada issued T-Blades. Two of Dolofónos's men are struck in the head and go down, but their stolen Armada issued military blades stun the resisters. Three are killed where they lie—stabbed to death like dyogg meat on a chopping block in The Sigma Green District's market section of the Underground. The rest are held down and skinned alive to hear their final screams before they succumb to blood loss.

High-yield explosives reduce Armada contracted companies and civilian homes to piles of smoldering rubbish. Those working within company walls have their respirators stolen at gunpoint, leaving their workers unable to venture into Kep Four's toxic atmosphere. The air around them becomes an atmospheric jail cell in buildings that once provided income for their families.

Private residences that are the closest thing to a middle-class city on Kep Four are broken into. The same vile acts happen inside them all. Dolofónos and his minions continue altering the atmosphere into a weapon of persuasion and entrapment, but it does not stop there. Homeless civilians and good people who walk the sidewalks are targets. In a bloody echo of what is happening in other districts, they join the crooked crusade or die on the spot.

Firearms, blades, and metal bars bring deadly reigns upon the flesh of resistors. They will not stop until all have joined or perished. Dolofónos's code and new call-to-arms is a song composed of cruelty, and Mona is the symphony of his misery.

Pedestrians making their way home from work are attacked before they reach their personal transport vessels or are dragged from them and struck down. Some are killed where they lie, others tortured. Respirators pulled from faces leave the innocent to die on the street or search desperately for shelters they will not find.

Damage to air filtration systems is critical. The goal is clear: suffocate all non-Uprisers. No remorse is given to young or old. I hurt for them, but none more than the children. Rotations to come for them are unpromising.

Nutrition storages are minimally stocked in districts of poverty, but that stopped 45 rotations ago when the Armada's focus switched to getting off Kep Four. Uprisers are clearing out what remains and leaving Mona to starve—physical, mental, and environmental torture.

Uprisers on the other side of Mona disrupt water supplies with controlled explosives and leave them unrepairable. Three to six rotations without water will leave even the most hardened civilians weakened to Upriser demands.

"Relieve pressure from yourselves." Dolofónos's voice echoes Mona's streets. "Let us lift the weight of demise from your shoulders and carry you to a new life."

His tyrannical speech continues to pierce victims' ears as they start the final phase of Mona's downfall. I try to ignore his words, but as an unwilling listener. I cannot.

Dolofónos is a suitable name for what he has done to Mona's people and who knows where else. His name is of Ancient Earth Greek origin—translated from δολοφόνος. It is fitting. I doubt it is his real name, but the fact he chose it as a title speaks of his nature.

He lives up to the definition of the word Dolofónos and makes his last move on a crippled district. His Uprisers cut all power to leave civilians in a district black as pitch during the nights. Light will be a deep brown dusk during the rotations as Kep Four's sun strains to pierce polluted skies. Without lights, fuel will have to be burned for visibility in districts of the poor who cannot afford wrist lights. When they run out, their lives will fade with the rest of the planet.

SOULLESS

10-2
Stolen Schematics

Dolofónos walks underground in a concrete reinforcement unit I am unfamiliar with. It must be far from districts his men shut down. There is light, which means there is heat and electricity. He has routed district power supplies to his Uprisers. The man would not leave portions of a power grid for civilians and risk hope arising in them. At least, I do not think he would. He is far too sadistic for me to accept the possibility.

A short, heavy-set man with a bald spot and limp approaches him.

"We got the files," says the man.

"When can I see them?" asks Dolofónos.

"Now," answers the man. "Later. Whenever you want."

"Now," says Dolofónos.

"This way," says the man, motioning Dolofónos to follow.

He leads his leader to their left through cracked concrete corridors under low ceilings until they come to a rusted iron door that has seen better rotations.

"In here," says the man.

The door creaks as they open it. The entry is old and rusted, but it is commonplace in underground bunkers throughout unwealthy districts of Kep Four. Whether they would hold up under a cataclysm has yet to be tested. They would have had to fail and cost the lives of their crooked scientists before Armada practices could justify an offer to update them.

They turn left into another corridor. A series of Upriser slogans and slander against their oppressors line the walls as they walk:

NIVEOUS WAR

'We are not forgotten'

'Assassinate the Sovereign'

'The Armada is not in control'

'Die an Upriser'

The man grabs three integration jewels from an iron table in worse shape than the door they entered.

"Here," he says.

The rusty table wobbles when he pulls his hand from it.

"Why are you handing me integration jewels?" asks Dolofónos.

"They're not integration jewels anymore," the man answers. "We used the cases to build memory file units in them and reworked that with layout schematics Uprisers intercepted from Armada's interstellar jump ships."

"Interesting," says Dolofónos.

"In a moment," says the man, "we'll be walking the most important of the three ships they're building for their survival. They call it, the *Ark*."

He sticks one to the base of Dolofónos's skull and one to each of his temples.

"Ready?" he asks.

Dolofónos stretches a twisted smile across his scarred face.

"Yes," he answers.

The man presses his index finger to the integration jewel at the base of Dolofónos's skull, then to the ones on his temples. Dolofónos closes his eye, and he is on the *Ark* just as I was in Mother's room during my memory file visits. He walks, explores, and memorizes the *Ark*'s layout and design.

CHAPTER 11
Wat'Uza's Words

I awaken with Elder Wat'Uza and the others standing over me. They come slowly into focus as my blurred eyes adjust. A hard reflective overhead ceiling flickers with light. I look to my left and right.

"I'm in Lessdelop," I say. "This is the room they kept Fister in."

"Don't have to remind me," says Fister.

I whip my head to the room's entrance. He is here.

"You came in Lesdelop?" I ask.

"I was worried about you," says Fister. "Still am."

"We all are," says Sergeant Bentley.

I roll to my side to sit up.

Dr. Sellers stops me.

"Don't sit up too fast," he says. "Dr. Wright had someone bring you down some Mizophile."

"No fears," says Dr. Wright. "I only gave you a micro dose."

"*Ama wabuki crez kiskil-zic-zis*, McKayla" says Wat'Uza.

You have our blessings—it is nice to hear him say it. His strength in leadership is undeniable. That leadership paired with Wete'Uza's standing with the sect's mothers and children makes them an irreplaceable asset for their culture.

"Wait a tik," I say. "Something's different. My head is clear. Really clear."

"That's the point of treatment," says Dr. Wright.

"My headache's gone," I continue, "but I feel a little lazy now."

"It's the Mizophile," says Dr. Wright.

"Off the rench," I say, "and on the Mizo."

"Not quite," says Dr. Wright. "It won't stop you from having visions, but it will keep your headaches away."

"Doesn't mean go doing backflips on us or anything," says Dr. Sellers. "Dr. Wright found a fraction of brain swelling when he examined you. It went down with the Mizophile he gave you, but we think it's related to how active your visions have been."

"There may be a correlation with the intensity of the visions," interjects Dr. Wright. "He said the ones you've been having recently are longer and more detailed?"

"Yeah," I answer. "They're detailed, but jump from location to location, shifting time frames every now and then."

"*Blight licea jesen,*" says Wat'Uza, "*orsplap topcal ama wabuki crez gratalua.*"

Wat'Uza exits. I cannot help but wonder why he told me I had his permission. I have asked for nothing.

"What was he talking about?" I ask.

"I didn't really understand it all," answers Bell.

"Same," says Delgado. "All I got from it was *you* and *our*."

"What did he say?" asks Sergeant Bentley.

"He said," I answer, "*know that you have our permission.* But permission for what?"

"We're going to grab some of your things," says Sergeant Bentley.

"Am I being exiled?"

"Yes," he says with a smirk, pointing to the Wah'Lor mountain of Misdela. "Wah'Lor's suicide fields are just beyond that peak if you need them."

"Very funny," I say. "Wah'Lor doesn't have suicide fields. I'm not that drugged up."

My squad laughs, none more than Pru'Cet. I love that little nutcase, even though he is not so short anymore.

"You're staying in Lessdelop ti'it renasa tonight," says Sergeant Bentley.

I turn to the immense structure as a gust of wind blows snow from its top to rain upon us.

"In there?" I ask.

"Oladi Wat'Uza give permoson for McKayla," says Pru'Cet. "Remember? Tila'Cet say stay you tele."

"Permission," I correct him.

"Per ... miss ... eon."

"No," I say. "Per..."

"Per..."

"Mish..."

"Mish..."

"Un..." I say, stressing the pronunciation.

"Un..." Pru'Cet matches me.

"Great. Now put it together."

"Permisseon," he says, smiling as if he conquered the world.

My squad snickers and shakes their heads.

"Okay," I say. "Close enough. Am I really sleeping in here tonight?"

"We could all use a change of scenery," says Dr. Sellers. "You get to go first."

I am about to spend my first night in Lesdelop ti'it renasa and will do it under the sedative powers of Mizophile. I want to enjoy the stay as long as possible. There is no way to tell when I will have the chance again.

11-2
mtDNA

I have settled in with some of the belongings from my tele-tent—a night's worth brought over by friends. Laughter echoes from deep within Lesdelop's passageways. Somebody is having fun, and they are doing it without me. This shall not be the case for long.

It is surprisingly warm here. The beautiful, lantern-style carved stone surrounding the candles might be the reason it is so warm. They flicker yellow off reflective walls. Maybe it is a source of heat. Perhaps it is the Dah'Sel's natural body heat at a solid eight degrees warmer than ours. Feasibly, it is the Mizophile in my system.

We were perplexed to find we share much DNA with the Dah'Sel yet look quite different. *Athanasios* read mtDNA when Dr. Sellers ran the program against Pru'Cet's DNA. More mtDNA remains with us as we evolve than nuclear DNA. When comparing nuclear DNA in Dah'Sel like we did in Pru'Cet, we get vast differences that say we have grown to become separate species. However, we would look identical if we had not developed on different worlds and in other galaxies. Reversing the clock on each of our DNA sequences has proven we started out the same.

"The things I think about when I'm getting dressed," I say to myself.

This room is small but comfortable. They were nice enough to make an unusually soft spot for me to sleep on the ground beneath three tiki candles. They knew I would need more warmth than they do.

There is no door in my little room. The Dah'Sel do not care much for that type of security. Words like *hate* and *enemy* are not present in the language. They are a peaceful culture, a respectful one.

I take off my coat and thick environmental pants to fold them neatly in the corner of my temporary room.

"McKayla," says Pru'Cet.

I jump and turn to face him.

"What is up with you always sneaking up on people?"

"*Elopfas gwampa ti'it jasros,*" he answers. "Me still like McKayla jump."

"That makes one of us," I say with a shake of my head. "What is that?"

I motion to the garments he has folded in his arms. He looks down at them.

"Tila'Cet give you," he says. "Speak me bring you."

Pru'Cet outstretches his arms with eyes motioning me to grab them. I take the clothes without studying their design.

"Hmph," I say. "Tell her I said thank you."

"*Jelq,*" says Pru'Cet, pausing in thought. "How say *Jelq*. No remember."

"*Jelq* is *okay* in our words," I answer.

"Okay," he says. "You accept?"

"I do."

Pru'Cet stands tall and mimics the Armada salute.

"Sheesh," I say. "These are magnificent."

I turn to the three tiki-candle lights in examination as I unfold what Tila'Cet has sent me.

"Wow," I say. "This is ... uhmmmm."

The garments are a far cry from what I have worn rotation-to-rotation in the past. My standard undergarments are long-sleeved and full-length in covering. These are the opposite. They are Dah'Sel loincloths, but smaller and far sexier than anything I have seen them in.

"Must be night clothes," I say.

I am shy about it. If I put them on and parade around in the Lessdelop ti'it renasa structure in front of everybody with an exposed hairless body, I do not want to offend their culture. I certainly would not want to put off Tila'Cet. Or the 'Cet family at all, for that matter.

"And..." I say, holding up the garments. "It looks like I'm doing this."

I peek my head back out the entrance and scan the halls to ensure nobody can walk up on me unexpectedly while I am changing. The coast is clear.

"Okay," I encourage myself. "I can do this."

I strip to put on Tila'Cet's gift. Bare is not a strong enough word to describe how I feel in Lesdelop amongst the Dah'Sel right now. Unlike those that dwell here, I am entirely hairless. It sounds odd to most, but I found using sonic shavers every couple of rotations a waste of time. I had my follicles from the neck down rendered inactive when I was 17 cycles old.

I slide the bottom portion of the garments on. They move silk-like over my hips. A single attachment around my waist holds them in place. My privates are now covered under the loincloth by a snug section of material that tapers into a thin string. It settles itself between my cheeks and attaches at the back waistband to form a thong-like design under the loincloth.

A change in candlelight outside my room catches my attention. Someone passed between its sources. A shadow follows.

"No sense in being shy now," I say. "But no sense in being exposed, either."

I cover my chest with an arm and check myself out on the reflective walls. Another shadow—Tila'Cet steps into the doorway with examining eyes. There is a sparkle in them—a flutter.

"*Blight...*" she says, taking a step forward.

Her eyes call me, and I am unsure she knows it. It has been many cycles since I felt an attraction to somebody but never has one passed where I felt such a tug.

"*Blight,*" she continues with a halted breath, "*o hempa.*"

She swallows and eases back to reach for a small, braided string of blue cloth hanging next to the entrance. She pulls it as she backs across the threshold. A curtain mounted over the door that I failed to notice drops as she exits. Her arm is the last thing to pull beyond the curtain as she leaves.

Her shadow stares from beyond the curtain. She knows I watch her silhouette as well. She must. A moment passes before she walks away, and I take my first breath since she entered my reflective stone room. Air fills my lungs to wash out unexpected sensations of desire.

"Blue-eyed haze's fire," I say with a few more breaths.

A couple more tiks and I will finish getting dressed. I need to center myself. At least she is supposed to stay in my tele-tent this evening's rotation. I do not want things to get weird.

I slide the top she gave me on and examine myself in the reflective walls. Clothes like these are high-end fashion reserved for those of significant wealth on Kep Four, and it is seductive. The top and bottom loincloths go together as if handmade to entice.

Laughter in the back of the structure echoes into my temporary room. I need to finish getting ready. A small, Armada green and black box rests next to the end of my bed. I open it.

"Delgado," I whisper.

She brought me her makeup for the evening. I appreciate her gesture and will not let it go to waste.

"Why not?" I ask myself. "Blood-red under a deep blue overlay? Delgado, where did you go at night on Kep Four?"

I apply it and move through shades of flickering candlelight to watch it change tones. It blends in with the multicolored cloth braids hanging far enough at a hand-width wide to cover my front parts and center rear.

11-3
Dōnah

I sneak out to the smell of burning rench-snech. Several Dah'Sel laugh in their large, reflective stone hall at the back of the structure. They are sitting on small wooden tree stumps around a low burning fire with three different sides of flames: green, orange, and blue. It is time to find out how they spend their free time.

Two Dah'Sel play instruments made of dark wood with thin, purple strands of silk twisted tightly into strings. Their sound is high-pitched and graceful when plucked. Another plays a drum shaped like a flower. The fourth has a series of small drums wrapped around her waist like a belt, with several places to tap for percussion. The last plays a drum half the size he is, which releases deep bass tones.

Beautiful notes fill the air with beats and rhythms similar to the music I fly to. I wish Mother and Comilo could have seen this, known of Wah'Lor's existence, and were around to experience it with me. They would have enjoyed life here.

A Dah'Sel notices me. It is Pru'Cet's uncle Bah'Cet. He waves me to his side. I smile and nervously rub my hands together as I make my way toward him to have a seat. Not a tik later, somebody passes me a quarter-pace long, hollowed-out stick of burning rench-snech packed to the brim with its flower.

"Oh, boy," I say, shaking my head. "I don't know if I should."

"*Po ot gingo ki dwaloc ki e gazno ama loilcim-zim,*" he assures me.

"And you're sure about that?" I ask for confirmation. "You're sure it's not as strong as the last time? *Po ot gingo ki dwaloc ki e gazno blight loilcim-zim?*"

He shakes his head as those around him laugh. I take it with reluctance and raise it to my mouth. Bah'Cet reaches to stop me as Wat'Uza and Wete'Uza enter to sit with the rest of us.

"*Niss,*" says Bah'Cet.

Tila'Cet enters and sits on an empty stool less than a few palms across from me. Her eyes lock onto mine. The others watch intently. I can feel it and try to act as if I am not mesmerized by her presence. Juju. Sorcery. I once thought they were words reserved only to tell stories of fantasy, but I am second-guessing their place in the universe.

Tila'Cet leans forward with an arm extended over the low burning firepit between us and takes the pipe from me and turns the mouthpiece to herself. The fire's heat lifts hairs on her arms to match its dance as she places it in her mouth and inhales. Her head tilts into the air, and she blows a trail of auburn smoke to hover over my head.

She turns the pipe around one and a half times and places the mouthpiece to my lips. I watch her intently and pull in a breath of its smoke as she motions her eyes upward. Just as she does, I exhale the smoke over her head and follow suit, rotating it one and a half times and placing the mouthpiece to her lips. She inhales and exhales.

"*Dada ama*," I say. "Aren't you staying in my tele-tent tonight?"

"Are..." she pauses to ponder its pronunciation. "Aren't?"

"*Ka ama beena-zic ya en ubido lessdelop fesnop troqfel?*" I repeat.

"*Blight ledad*," says Tila'Cet.

Male and female alike, the Dah'Sel hoot, nudge each other and stare as she smiles. I look around in confusion. She said, *Blight ledad*. Meaning, *I was*. But why are they celebrating, and why is she not staying in my tele now?

Pru'Cet rubs my back.

"We happy have you family," he says.

"Yeah," I say. "Same. Am I missing..." I look around to see all eyes on me. "Do I not know something?"

"*Ama frex-zim?*" says Pru'Cet, pointing at my loincloth, then to his sister. "Tila'Cet offer? Yes?"

I nod.

"Yes. Of course."

Tila'Cet and Bah'Cet pull me in to raise our palms together. Pru'Cet joins us, and the entire room moves in until I am surrounded.

"Pru'Cet," I say. "Do I not know something about what I'm wearing?"

"You accept Tila'Cet's offer," he answers.

"You," says Tila'Cet, motioning between us. "Me."

"*Rarge*," says Wat'Uza.

"Wait," I say. "You mean I formed a union when I accepted this?"

The others in Lesdelop ti'it renasa stare. Music stops.

"Union?" I ask. "Like partners? Mates? Forever?"

Pru'Cet nods, points a finger on each hand at Tila'Cet and me, then brings them together to interlock them.

WAT'UZA'S WORDS

I do not know how to respond. Flabbergasted is the emotion I am experiencing. Shocked would also be an appropriate description. It was unknown to me that a union was formed when I accepted these loincloths and smoked with her.

No Dah'Sel would accept an offering, especially one of such caliber, and go back on it. They are neither liars nor play with one's emotions. It would be a great disrespect to them if I gave it back, and I refuse to break the bond between them, myself, my squad, and humanity—or create further rifts between them and us.

I look to Tila'Cet. Piercing eyes stab without being slowed by the effects of rench-snech. Perhaps it is fate that it happened this way. I do not know, but I will ride this wave to Wah'Lor's shores and see where it curls.

"Tila'Cet and I are together as partners?" I ask again.

Pru'Cet gets choked up over our union but tells the others what I asked crudely in their native tongue.

"You McKa'Cet now," says Pru'Cet. "No McKayla. McKa'Cet."

"I thought..." I say, stopping to think.

"*Ya ledram,*" says Tila'Cet.

Ya ledram—in time. She said it regarding our future. The others grow quiet.

"Twena..." Pru'Cet squints his eyes. "Tweny?"

"Twenty?" I ask.

He sighs and gives me a defeated look with a forced, emotionless expression. He has picked up our language better than most but still has moments of frustration.

"*Qe-toop heeza-zis licea prajet ola ama ka whattka,*" says Pru'Cet, motioning his arm toward the sky from left to right. "*Jazaxe ama ne Tila'Cet t bela ne suetrow tigeth bea ma kipoa-zis.*"

As short and simply put as the letter itself, the sound *'t'* means *share*. *'Beat ma kipoa-zis'* translates to *'With no others.'* The whole thing says Tila'Cet and I are soon to become one until our deaths. While it is official, nothing is set in stone. We have 20 rotations to change our minds while getting to know each other better. We can break this off before that, but not after. It is a lot to process, but she is worth getting to know.

"*Pes ama frex?*" asks Wat'Uza.

My eyes dance back and forth to Tila'Cet's in rhythm with a song unsung. There is only one answer in my mind. I already know how I am going to respond, doubts and being sucker-punched with this ceremony be damned.

"Yes," I say, looking back at Tila'Cet. "I do. *Blight frex.*"

Music starts back up when the performers return to their instruments. I was wrong in my assumption about what was going on tonight. This is why Wat'Uza said I could stay here. They are not partying. It is a celebration of me becoming a 'Cet. I am both nervous and excited enough to have a stroke over it.

I have not had a family for cycles and miss it. This means everything to me. My eyes water. This is a happy place.

11-4
Rapid Pulse

The night passes quickly, and I find myself with Tila'Cet. She guides me by hand and back to my room. My heart beats 130 clicks a tek as she pushes through the curtain with me in tow. I am ready, but not...

She turns to face me, lowers her forehead to mine, and raises my arms over our heads by the wrist. Our palms come together. I could float from the floor with her and not notice.

WAT'UZA'S WORDS

Her fingers interlock mine as she backs me into the stone wall with just enough height over me that when our foreheads meet, we could kiss.

A moment pushing forever passes. She gives me a proper human hug. Her breath on my neck... Hairs on her back and sides weave between my fingers. I kiss her gently on her upper jaw. Wait. She just pulled away from me and took a step back. *Did I offend her?*

"*Ma,*" says Tila'Cet.

"No?" I ask. "Why? *Wazme?*"

"*Qe-toop heeza-zis ne tom rarge licea prajet ola suetrow armona,*" she answers.

Twenty suns and a union must pass before body love? I accept it and know forming a union is an affirmation that two have become partners for life. It is beautiful to think as they do. With any luck, their way of life will bleed into humanity.

"Okay," I say with an impatient nod. "*Qe-toop heeza-zis.*"

She smiles and backs from my room to leave me with a hopeful heart. I could not be happier to get to know her on a deeper level, nor have I been so terrified of something. I need to be hurt as much as I need to hurt another. It is why I have avoided the possibility throughout my life, and it is all I will think about when I lie down.

Twenty suns will take time on this world to pass, but I can wait; maybe. I have liked her for a while, but it could also be rench-snech and Mizophile coursing through my veins. I doubt it. She is fantastic, but this is not something to rush.

Fleeting hands crush beautiful moments.

The Dah'Sel believe in taking somebody into their family before a union can solidify. I thought it was the reason they brought me in as one of them, but I was wrong. The 'Cets legitimately want me to be part of their family. It is an honor. It just so happens that those twenty suns must pass before it is official. At that moment, should I and Tila'Cet wish to explore the future between us, it will be set in besmite.

I will be ready when the time comes and can only hope for the same from Tila'Cet. I think we are on the same wavelength here. Twenty rotations shall tell, but for now, sleep is in order.

My eyes close, lost in a sea of chances. It feels good. Relaxing. I should fall asleep like this more often.

CHAPTER 12
Butcher Five

Dolofónos paces in an unknown underground structure with the staff in his left hand. They could have made it custom for him. I do not think so. That would require vast amounts of resources and a team with the knowledge of how to do so. Then again, I do not know who they have taken, who has joined as recruits—be it at force or otherwise—or what they have stolen while waging their never-ending war against the Armada.

Dolofónos clutches his fists and clinches his jaw as he walks back and forth within it. He stops and jabs the staff's bottom portion into the concrete at his left. Dust drops around him. He paces again.

"Butcher Five," shouts Dolofónos.

A man enters.

"Yes, sir?" asks Butcher Five.

Dolofónos walks to the far side of the room, places his right hand on his hip, and stares at black-and-red painted walls. There are no instrument panels or workstations. A meeting table painted in Upriser pelvic bones rests in its center with a dozen chairs made of bone around it.

Butcher Five watches him in wait. That is what Dolofónos called him. Butcher Five. He must be one of what the Armada referred to as his resistance leaders. If I am right, there is also a Butcher one, two, three, and four somewhere in his flock of death. Five is the highest ranking, one is the least, and all are above any other Uprisers other than Dolofónos or Saddi.

"I fear I may have overshot the number of new members I recruited," says Dolofónos.

"Talking about resources, sir?" asks Butcher Five.

"Afraid so," answers Dolofónos.

He turns to face Butcher Five and walks around the room's tables and chairs while he talks.

"We've brought in nearly thirty thousand new recruits," says Dolofónos. "I don't think half of them are worth the energy surplus it would take to kill them."

"What do you suggest?" asks Butcher Five.

"I'm either going to have to speed things up or cut some extra mouths," answers Dolofónos. "I thought we were going to get all the energy reserves and nutritional holds, but the Armada's already cleaned them out. How are things looking topside?"

"As you said," answers Butcher Five. "Resources are getting low. There's just not enough food. These new recruits are eating like there's tenfold what we have."

Dolofónos pulls a chair forcefully from the table. It slides into the wall behind him and bounces off it. A small bone from its backrest falls to the floor and spins for a tik before he steps on it and takes a seat.

"Ration them," he says.

"Me and the other four Butchers put the word out several rotations ago," says Butcher Five. "But there's too many of them. Our numbers have grown more than anticipated. We're playing a delicate balance between keeping them complacent with our promise to have them living like kings and having them revolt."

"Exactly how bad is the recruit situation?" asks Dolofónos.

"Bad," answers Butcher Five. "They're eating infected flagerts from the brown just so there's enough food to go around. Getting sick because of it. A few have died."

"Good," says Dolofónos. "Then we won't have to worry about them."

"I was referring to your Uprisers of old," says Butcher Five. "They're trying to keep the recruits happy until we make our move and leave them behind. They're the ones eating those animals, not the new recruits. Anything to keep their bellies full."

Dolofónos grabs a chair and throws it against the wall with no anger in his expression.

"Well, that has to stop then, doesn't it?" he asks. "Get the other Butchers together."

Dolofónos takes a seat, pulls out a cigar and a copper metallic heat stick, and presses a button on it. It produces no flame. Nor does it contact the stogie before he takes a thick inhalation of smoke. He closes his eyes to relax and exhales a billow of purple smoke that dissipates into nothing.

"Tell the other Butchers I said to put together a one-hundred-man unit with ten Argos vessels and select twenty-thousand recruits for each," says Dolofónos. "Arm the recruits with High-V sticks. Tell them they're going to lead imprisoned civilians into The Suicide Fields."

He takes another puff and taps the butt of his cigar onto the tabletop in thought. He exhales.

"If..." continues Dolofónos. "If they ask why, tell them they're carrying High-V sticks instead of rifles to prod captives into The Suicide Fields. Tell them it will entertain me."

I think about what he is saying. When a High-V stick is cranked up, its shock can be anything from mild to strong enough to shut down the cardiovascular system or melt neural pathways in the brain.

"Have everyone readied and selected within two rotations from now," continues Dolofónos. "Get any captive civilians we were planning on using as bartering chips against the Armada ready within three rotations."

"That's nearly a hundred thousand civilians," says Butcher Five. "We'd need a couple more rotations to organize everything and—"

"You have three to get everything in order," interrupts Dolofónos. "Split the civilians you'll be leading into the fields amongst the Butchers, their units, and their selected recruits. Twenty thousand for each unit."

Butcher Five nods with hesitation and exits. Dolofónos takes another puff of the cigar and smiles as he exits. His eyes never leave the door, and his thoughts fire in directions I am glad not to see. I do not know what he is planning, but I know it is not a ploy to save Kep Four.

CHAPTER 13
Awakening in the Field

I come around in the field with Pru'Cet and my squad hovering over me. I am scared. My heart races like I ran for 30 taks and did not stop to catch my breath.

"Mason?" asks Sergeant Bentley.

I take a moment to respond. I must admit that it is nice to have Sergeant Bentley fearfully concerned about me. Technically, and with no conflict on Wah'Lor, we are not a squad anymore. We have, however, stayed together. The Armada has recognized the fact that we have a bond and belong together. It makes sense.

"Mason?" repeats Sergeant Bentley.

"Huh?" I ask, still waking.

"How are you feeling?"

"I think," I answer with a pause. "I think I'm okay."

Pru'Cet pats my forehead to comfort me. Not that I have an injury, mind you, but he must have been significantly upset by my condition. He loves me like that, and I feel the same.

I take Sergeant Bentley's offered hand to help me up.

"You, okay?" asks Dr. Sellers.

"Yeah," I answer. "I just said that, and I'm getting used to these kinds of things."

"You shouldn't be having them enough to get used to them," says Dr. Wright. "Get her to HU-1's REM lab for observation."

"Come with me," says Dr. Wright. "And Dr. Sellers, come with us?"

"Great," I say, "but Pru'Cet's coming with me."

"I'd normally not keep him at bay," says Dr. Wright. "But we can only have a few people in the room when running REM cycle projections. Too many neural pathways in the vicinity at once can convolute readings."

I cut my eyes to the ground and swallow in thought. Being tested every time something happens to me that has become commonplace is tiresome. One more round of tests won't hurt, and it will put the doctors' minds at ease. At least, that's what I keep telling myself.

13-2
REM

We make our way to HU-1, which has become more than just a housing unit. Its operating center is now a production hub for the Klaz'Dra counter agent serum in case humans contract it from the Vee'Sal for unseen reasons. There are lots of scientists here I am unfamiliar with. Armada higher-ups have reassigned everybody to positions they feel are best for the current situation here on Wah'Lor.

I speak to no one as I pass by random Armada faces in the snowy field. Half of these people are unknown to me, and I cannot take the time to become their friend. There are too many people in the Armada to bother with learning who they are as individuals. My focus is on my peers, what is happening to me, and maintaining a peaceful coexistence with the Dah'Sel. It will not be an easy job with so many still to come from Kep Four.

The Armada is aggressive when faced with resistance. The Dah'Sel may not be a violent culture, but they will not accept a slow Armada takeover of land. I fear that the Planetary Sovereign secretly believes they can come here and claim whatever land they want as cycles go by, but that would not end peacefully.

I am a go-between for both, more so now that the 'Cet family took me in with Tila'Cet under the blessings of Wat'Uza. The Armada once rejected me, but I have become a vital link between peaceful coalition. The Dah'Sel expect only honesty and for me to look out for their best interests. As Kuzio said, I have earned my redemption.

Burden's weight is heavy on my shoulders as I make my way to HU-1 with Dr. Sellers and Dr. Wright. I do not know their overall game plan, but I know they want to help me with the difficulties I am facing.

The daunting size of the housing unit matches immense worry. It expands through my thoughts as I approach. The bigger the housing unit appears, the more it feels to grow within me. These visions ... wondering if they are real is not helping my angst. Neither is the thought of having my head investigated again.

13-3
REM

We enter HU-1 from the southern aft end. There are so many people here: workers, soldiers, and families with children running about. I envy their naivety to what may come, but it is not my place to tell them on speculation alone. To do such could cause unwarranted panic. Telling them is up to the doctors or Sergeant Bentley to decide.

Another doctor or scientist works at the station to my left. I do now know him and am unsure of his position in HU-1's Med Lab, but will find out soon.

"Dr. Klinroy," says Dr. Wright. "This is Mason, the woman I was telling you about."

Dr. Klinroy turns to face me. He is thick in the middle but not overweight, with an overall stature that reminds me of Sapp's—minus the beard and much older. I study him as he looks me over.

"Pleasure to meet you," he says, staring as if he knows me. "McKayla Mason ... I've heard a lot about you. You're quite infamous."

"Do we have to talk about it?" I ask.

"We don't," answers Dr. Klinroy.

I do not mind when people talk about me or my past. I know what I have done, but I have no desire to be part of the conversation. He can talk about it with Dr. Wright when I leave.

"I assume you know why you're here," says Dr. Klinroy. "I hope."

"Is that supposed to be a joke?" I ask with a put-off tone.

He cuts me what I believe to be a hint of a smile. It is hard to tell, but I find nothing about this funny. His sense of humor is dry. He and Dr. Utley would have gotten along fine.

"I know why I'm here," I answer.

"Good," says Dr. Klinroy. "Let's get you laid down." He steps away from the gurney area of HU-1's Med Lab. "Activate bed two."

A section on the floor slides open. A retracted hover gurney rises from it. The floor beneath it closes to create a solid surface. It locks into place.

"Why'd you have the gurneys lowered?" I ask.

"I had him retract them," interjects Dr. Wright. "We're trying to conserve as much energy as possible. While it's a minute savings, they continue relaying information to the Med Lab when they're up, and their magnetic field still draws power."

"Makes sense," I say.

"Lie down," says Dr. Sellers.

I take a shallow breath and move to the gurney. The rail system folds out of the way as I near it and climb on. The back of my head comes to rest as it expands and molds to match my neck, shoulders, and head.

"You got the dots?" asks Dr. Klinroy.

"Right here," answers Dr. Sellers.

"Say the word," says Dr. Wright. "And we'll get this show underway."

Dr. Sellers moves to my side with a small container of sticky dots, as Dr. Klinroy was so nice to call them. They are scan relays used to take readings at the biological level and return the information to HU-1's Med Lab mainframe. They are taking this more seriously than I thought they were going to. Sure, they are doctors, but I assumed the new guy here would think me to be as much a liability as other Armada personnel once did.

"When did you start working in HU-1?" I ask.

"I'm not," answers Dr. Klinroy.

"He's here for you," interjects Dr. Sellers. "I had him come over to read these tests with us."

He covers my forehead, face, and neck with them in total circumference. They are cold to the touch and feel sappy. I no doubt look like I am covered in reflective purple pimples.

"Looks good on you," says Dr. Sellers.

"Yeah, right," I say. "I probably look like a womosa bat."

Dr. Sellers smirks.

"You're not that cute," he says.

"Thanks," I say and close my eyes.

"Activate link," says Dr. Wright.

Dr. Klinroy eases to the Med Lab control panel. I study his motions. His movements are deliberate. He is a thinker, one who considers all avenues before proceeding with actions or decisions. His hair is gray, high and tight, and great for his age. If I had to guess, I would say he is around 123 cycles of age.

"Activating now," he says.

My head shivers. It feels like thousands of microscopic insects are crawling through my brain, but not on the outside. They are exploring the inside of its soft, fatty tissue.

"Okay," I say. "This is weird. How long this is going to—"

I wince when the insect sensation's intensity ramps up to cut me short. Those proverbial bugs in my skull sting like their feet have transformed into needles. I hope this is not the case for the duration of testing.

"Is starting to hurt," I say. "Isn't unbearable, but I wouldn't exactly call this a good time."

"We're going to be activating REM in a moment," says Dr. Klinroy.

I rub my fingertips anxiously together. Nervousness sets in, and I already want this test to be over. I want them all to be over with.

"I don't know if this is a good idea," I say.

"You'll be fine," says Dr. Sellers. "They're going to be displaying anything you see in your dreams on a three-dimensional projection at the center of the Med Lab. If you see it, we'll see it. If you're there, we'll be there. You just won't see us."

"At the same time," says Dr. Wright, "Dr. Klinroy will be mapping any and everything going on with that psyche of yours. Don't worry. He's the Armada's top scientist in the field of neurological disorders. I brought him here for a reason."

"Disorders?" I ask. "It's not a disorder. Everybody here knows that. It's because of my H-SAM and the fact that I went through the Ein-Rosen bridge in an inadequately protected ship. No offense, Dr. Wright."

"None taken," says Dr. Wright. "None of us could have predicted what was going to happen once inside the Ein-Rosen. There's always a first, and that first happened to be us. At least we learned information to inform other vessels so they can protect themselves during the jump. I'd say that's a good thing and something to be proud of. Wouldn't you?"

"I guess so," I answer.

I squint my eyes tightly through pain. An itch I cannot scratch ... a bad one. I am about to lose my mind here.

"Can you get this over with before my head explodes?" I ask.

"Activating REM now," says Dr. Klinroy. "Sweet dreams, Mason."

"Somehow," I say, "I doubt that, but how long will it take for me to—"

Those around me slip into obscurity, but I am not entirely gone. My body warms with the sense of a thick heated liquid pouring onto the top of my skull. It flows between the hairs on my head and over my ears to envelop my forehead and make its way behind my ears and run sluggishly over my face. While I can breathe, it feels like I am suffocating. It makes no sense. Unease rears its ugly head within my subconscious, but there is nothing I can do about it.

Its gooey sensation continues until my neck is covered. It makes its way over my shoulders. The feeling swallows my arms with my torso. A constriction of unknown origin squeezes my body tight and allows only enough room for shallow breaths.

My hips, thighs, knees, and calves are all swathed in it as I struggle to ignore the way it feels to drown in my body. It rolls over my ankles and heels. Another tik or two, and the sticky sensation will wrap my toes.

It takes everything I have not to freak out. I am not conscious. *Or am I?* I am somewhere in between.

My toes are gone. I can feel myself disappearing in the opposite order that the sensation flowed over me. Little pieces of my physical self no longer exist. My waist ... my hands and arms disappear with my chest. *How am I to take a breath of air with my lungs gone?*

I must keep my composure. Just a little more. It will be over soon. My neck, jaw, and face feel like they are physically vanishing from my body and over my forehead. It is getting harder to think. It steals the front half of my brain.

Fading thoughts are getting hard to...

CHAPTER 14
Red, Black, and Red

Nineteen empty cargo carriers sit a click from The Suicide Fields' point of no return. Twenty thousand Upriser recruits lead an equal number of civilians toward their deaths 3/4 of a click beyond them. The once residents of Mona have only torn clothes to cover their noses and mouths as improvised filters against Kep Four's toxic atmosphere. Most are coughing. They have no organic cuffs on to bind their wrists behind their backs the way mine did when they pulled me from imprisonment. There is no need.

Ten Argos ground vehicles roll behind the 20,000 Upriser recruits, leading civilians to their deaths. They roll at a glacial pace behind them, with only a driver and a man at the top turrets for each. Uprisers of old are on foot at the rear.

"Remove your outer layers of clothing," says Butcher Five. "All of you."

Their captives stop and stare at him as if his words are but a nightmare they are soon to wake from.

Butcher Five shoots six dead where they stand. The others remove the outer layers of their clothing. The brown sends most of them to itch at their arms and legs, but they will face more than an itch if they reach The Suicide Fields.

Butcher Five walks at point, as the march continues until they near the field's event horizon of mortality. Their captives slow and come to a stop. I fear for them. Their skin must be burning. More and more of them rub their eyes and cough as life drains from their steps.

"Keep walking," echoes Butcher Five's voice from an Argos comm speaker.

Captives take a few more steps and stop.

"Last warning," says Butcher Five.

They refuse to move. Some turn to shout at their abductors, but I do not know what they are saying. There are too many of them. Their words mutter together. I understand only their revolt against the march.

"Upriser recruits," says Butcher Five. "Push them in."

New recruits power up their High-V sticks at 20,000 strong. An electrical buzz fills polluted airwaves to blend in with civilians shouting requests for freedom. Dolofónos will not grant it to them. Death will be the freedom he provides.

"Move," shouts Butcher Five. "Highest possible High-V setting."

The recruits push forward. Several civilians hold their ground against them. The first few hit with the High-V sticks drop like felled trees before their masks and respirators are torn from their bodies while they are unconscious. Others scurry into The Suicide Fields. They can die at the hands of Upriser recruits or take their chances in the fields, neither of which is promising. I would take the High-V sticks as my way out.

They are 18 paces past the life-or-death event horizon when the air around them changes in color. Captives scream in agony. Many choose to come back and face the recruits and die at the ends of electrified weapons.

Those who run into the fields continue until they collapse. Their skin softens and disfigures slowly upon their arms, legs, and faces like melting butter to blisters and

RED, BLACK, AND RED

dissolve into Kep Four and become future dust in its winds. Tens of thousands meet a useless fate. The few hundred still alive in the fields wish otherwise.

Upriser recruits walk upon downed bodies as if tromping the wings of fallen angels to shoot the dead and living alike to ensure no survivors. It is a district genocide. This is all the red-and-black know for survival.

"Halt," says Butcher Five.

Upriser recruits stop in the field.

"Remove your mask and filtration systems," continues Butcher Five.

The command confuses them. They look to one another for answers they will not find.

"We're not captives," says an Upriser recruit.

"We're one of you now," shouts another.

"You have less than nothing to comply," continues Butcher Five. "Three ... two ... one..."

Each of the 80 Uprisers of old fire onium rifles alongside Butcher Five. Turrets atop the Argos units plug The Suicide Fields with fire to create bulk homicide leading to a new, small red river of blood. Civilian traitors lie in their final resting place amongst the very people they betrayed.

14-2
Repeat

Four other zones of The Suicide Fields mirror a similar fate. Mass executions of new recruits and civilians alike, spread 15 clicks apart along the event horizon, spells the downfall of a once-promising empire. On this rotation, 200,000 people are dying: 100,000 civilians; 100,000 new recruits. How people like Dolofónos continue to exist is something I will never grasp.

The most disturbing group of executioners is Butcher Two's unit. She commands her recruits to usher civilians into The Suicide Fields and shoots them in the legs when they turn back but not to remove their respirators. Butcher Two needs to see them suffer. She wants slow deaths to watch from the comfort of an Argos turret.

    "Cease fire," says Butcher Two.

    "But there are twenty or more still walking," says an Upriser.

    Butcher Two's eyes are vacant as she climbs into the nearest Argos.

    "Everyone, return to headquarters," she says.

    "Butcher Two?" asks an Upriser over Argos comms.

    "I said go."

    The other vessels and spared recruits march from The Suicide Fields toward unknown headquarters. None of them are safe. They never will be. Mortality comes with no shelter from it under the wing of Dolofónos, his Butchers, and Uprisers of old.

    Civilians under Butcher Two continue walking. Beeps of failure sound from their respirators.

    "Keep walking," shouts Butcher Two.

    Failure of several respirators... Their wearers collapse and writhe on the ground. Three on their last march turn back toward Mona in desperation. Butcher Two shoots them in the chest with three-round bursts from the turret. Their bodies come apart. Legs, arms, and the rest fly in multiple directions.

    "No turning back," shouts Butcher Two.

    Respirators on civilians and recruits lose their ability to protect their wearers. The Suicide Field's corrosiveness has broken them down. Take a breath and die or run for it and get shot. Those are their options. All choose the latter.

Butcher Two mows them down to Kep Four with an onslaught of rapid fire. One remains when she stops. His suit and respirator are torn. The brown crawls into it with him. The pain ... he screams. His skin festers behind the Farka.

"Make it stop," he begs. "Kill me. I don't care. End the pain."

Butcher Two watches from the turret. She does not move but watches until the man collapses.

"I have kids," says the man.

"You had kids," says Butcher Two.

The man crawls three paces on his hands and knees, then collapses dead. Butcher Two takes time to admire her work before she drops into the Argos and pulls away. The brown swallows her until she is out of sight.

CHAPTER 15
Klinroy's Feedback

I gasp and open my eyes. I am no longer in HU-1's Med Lab but on a flat stone of some kind. Something is on my face. I reach up to feel it. A respirator... I am in full protective gear. Dolofónos walks past me with his Butchers in tow. I move to get up and fall startled by the stone. Kep Four's tainted soil smacks hard into my cheek when I fall.

Pollution is high. Vision is 20 clicks at best. The fallen monuments ... *What has happened to me? Why am I back on Kep Four near The Suicide Fields?*

A sea of Uprisers is gathering around me. I make a break for it, but a Butcher grabs me.

"Ahhhh," I scream. "Get off of me. Let me go. Help!"

Another one grabs me as I struggle. Punches and kicks do no good. I am not a fighter.

"Kill her," chants the Uprisers. "Kill her. Kill her."

I cannot break free from the man holding me from behind. His grip is fast. A backward head butt to the face leaves him stumbling off me to clutch his nose in pain.

"Calm down," says Dolofónos. "We're not going to hurt you." He approaches me with lingering steps. "Your death will be painlessly spread across video panes lining cities and districts. The next planetary update will be an act of war contract against the Armada written in your blood."

"No..." I say, still struggling. "Let me..."

I fight until the air clears around me. The clothes my attackers are wearing shift to that of a doctor's garb. I am engulfed in panic as my new visual reveals Dr. Sellers. He holds me tight with my arms at my side so I cannot move.

"It's okay," he says. "The dream you were having kept playing out in here for a tek after you woke up. Your dreams hadn't subsided yet."

"Dolofónos," I say. "Dolofónos and the Butchers. They were—"

"They were nowhere, Mason," says Dr. Wright. "You were still in REM for about one tek when you awoke. Lucid dreams overlapped with what we have running out here."

"You're safe," says Dr. Sellers. "You see me?"

He grabs my shoulders. I nod.

"You're safe," he repeats.

I look from left to right and top to bottom to scan HU-1's Med Lab in search of an enemy. Nothing. There are only the Doctors here.

"The feedback stopped," says Dr. Klinroy, washing blood from his nose with a rag. "You should be okay."

I take a bit to gather myself and pull from Dr. Sellers' arms while closing my eyes to relax for a tik.

"That was—"

"Scary?" interrupts Dr. Klinroy. "I'd say so. It was certainly unsettling ... and painful."

I stop to study the bloody rag he is holding over his nose.

"Did I do that?" I ask. "I'm sorry."

"Wasn't your fault," says Dr. Klinroy. "You thought I was Dolofónos. No permanent harm done. I won't take it personally." He walks to the other side of the Med Lab to read the results. "It was an interesting first meeting, Mason."

"How are you feeling now?" asks Dr. Sellers.

"Fine," I answer. "A bit shook up, but I think I'm okay."

"Glad to hear it," he says. "The others were starting to worry about you."

"Others?" I ask.

"Your squad and a few Dah'Sel," answers Dr. Sellers. "They came by a few taks ago. You were out for eight."

"Eight taks?" I ask. "What did you guys get?"

"Everything," answers Dr. Wright. "We saw everything that you did."

"And?" I ask.

"I'm not sure just yet," answers Dr. Klinroy. "Your basic brainwaves? Your neuro and synaptic...? I don't know where to start."

"Summarize," says Dr. Wright.

"Mason..." says Dr. Klinroy with a bloody cloth still on his face from my headbutt. "Your readings are off the pane. It's unbelievable, even when compared to what you did with Dr. Utley during testing at the Armada. I don't know what to make of it yet. That's the truth. You're an enigma."

"Speculate further," says Dr. Wright.

"While it's possible that they're nothing more than dreams," says Dr. Klinroy, "her subconscious was too detailed. I say that because there's always something that's impossible in the real world or that doesn't fit that we can see watching from the outside. This was different. I've seen nothing like it." He scratches his jaw to think. "It could be you're somehow catching glimpses of the near future. Unheard of, I know, but ten cycles ago, we couldn't imagine being here."

"Or it could be glimpses of the past," interjects Dr. Sellers. "We still haven't gotten feedback from the last probe I sent, and I don't expect one anytime soon. They aren't scheduled for another six rotations."

KLINROY'S FEEDBACK

"I'd say it's interesting enough," says Dr. Klinroy, "at least interesting enough to issue a warning when you get a chance to communicate with them again. If what she's seeing is happening or soon to ... which you stated has been the case in the past with the Dah'Sel when you first arrived ... Kep Four's not looking like the place to be."

"Get that done as soon as you can, Dr. Sellers," says Dr. Wright.

"Yes, sir," says Dr. Sellers.

"How's your head feeling, Mason?" asks Dr. Klinroy.

"Better than it did before," I answer.

"Good," says Dr. Klinroy. "I put a time-release micropellet of Mizophile under your skin at your wrist. It's programmed to ramp up its release by a small fraction every tak. I'm not sure if it's going to be too much or too little with the time-released Sperprazidoneri already in your system, Dr. Sellers. With only this one test being done so far, I have nothing to compare it to and gauge exactly how fast this is progressing in intensity. If you feel yourself getting sleepy any more than normal, I'll lower it. If they get worse, I'll reprogram the rate of release."

"Okay," I say. "Thank you. Am I okay to go now?"

"You are, if Doctors Sellers and Wright agree to clear you."

I glance at Dr. Sellers to receive a nod.

"Consider yourself cleared," says Dr. Wright. "Just keep us updated."

I study their eyes. They are as unsure as I am. I turn and leave without a word.

The doctors watch me exit and hide their concerns. None are as concerned as me. A million questions battle for position in my mind. *What if they cannot stop it from happening? What if it gets worse?*

I was in so much pain last time. It is too much to go through again. I need a mental break. There is an exit in HU-1 with my name, and I am taking it.

15-2
Moonlight

I reach the door leading from HU-1 to nature and stop.

"Don't open the door yet," I command.

I am not ready to talk about any of this yet, but people will ask questions. It is human nature. Inquisitiveness lies within us all.

It is unpleasant to know I have both time-released Mizophile and Sperprazidoneri embedded under my skin. At its core, the Mez is an organic nano-bot-based chemical used in the medical field with many applications that include sleep aid, coma inducement, pain treatment, heightened senses, adrenalizing, and rendering many diseases inactive.

Each dose has a mixture of thousands of different nano-bots carrying heavy concentrations of various chemicals. They analyze the human body with parameters given by doctors and communicate amongst themselves to release the proper mixtures needed for correction.

The nano-bots turn solid, like a hardened pea, and form a protective shell around any remaining chemicals they may have. Once attaining the desired balance within the body, they exit via the urethra. It is what it is. I cannot stand here forever thinking about things beyond my control.

"Open door," I say.

The door opens, and I step out. Pru'Cet jogs up and gives me a quick hug as my squad comes into view behind him. They must have been on their way to check up on me.

"You, okay?" asks Pru'Cet.

KLINROY'S FEEDBACK

"Fine," I answer. "Why?"

"What do you mean why?" asks Fister. "I was worried about you. I mean, I did go into Lesdelop to see if you were alright."

"Dr. Klinroy said I'm fine," I lie.

"Dr. Klinroy?" asks Sergeant Bentley. "They moved him from HU-2 medical to HU-1?"

"No," I answer. "He was only there to examine me. I don't want to think about it right now. I'm going for a walk to clear my head."

My squad nods and gives me a group boot bump. I went from no family to multiple here between my squad and the 'Cets. It has been a welcome change.

"Don't be afraid to reach out if you want to talk," says Delgado. "You hear me?"

Bell and Sapp second her notion, and I leave the group to walk.

"See there," calls Sergeant Bentley from behind me. "You have an entire squad at your disposal. And if you want the haze kicked out of somebody, we're pretty good at that too."

I appreciate it but do not look back or respond. Pru'Cet stays at my side as I move across the open field of snow and shrubbery that melts spots of it away to form poke-a-dots of peeking of life around us.

"What do you want?" I ask.

He furrows his brows and rolls his eyes at me.

"You want speak now?" he asks, stopping to look right. "Okay. I leave now."

He walks off without warning. My eyebrows ruffle in curiosity as I watch him.

"Pru," I say. "Why did you ask me a question and walk away? Pru'Cet, I'm talking to—"

"*Specap*," says Tila'Cet.

I do a 180 to see Tila'Cet heading my way and walk backward. A blush from me gets a smile in return. No wonder Pru'Cet took off so fast.

"Hi," I say. "*Utlu ka ama pes-zic yetia hueton?* What are you doing out here?"

I try to keep conversations with Tila'Cet in both their words and ours, with compound words omitted for faster language acquisition. It will help her learn the language faster, and she has thanked me more than once. I am positive she desires to understand what Kep Four transplants are saying when around them.

She catches up to me. I turn and walk shoulder-to-shoulder with her.

"I…" she says, tapping her ear.

"Ear?" I ask.

"I ear you back—"

"Hear," I interrupt. "I'm sorry. Heard. I heard you're back."

"I," she continues, "heard you back. Pru'Cet say you … *yaw tralama ti'it jo hueton.*"

"*Blight yaw tralama.* I feel good." I smile. "*Blight o jelq.* I am okay."

"*Blight o loudac reema fasnop,*" she says.

"We're both happy," I say, motioning my hand between us.

Tila'Cet wants to ask me about what I am going through. I can feel it, but she deserves to know something far more important. They all do.

"Tila'Cet," I say, "evil humans might come to Wah'Lor."

She keeps at my side with every step with eyes locked onto me for a translation I do not want to tell her.

"*Baklee humans ofdrec kuzsoec ti'it Wah'Lor,*" I say.

She stops. Breaths halt. Her eyes waltz back and forth between mine in concern.

"*Utlu?*" she asks.

KLINROY'S FEEDBACK

"*Blight pes gingo orsplap.* I don't know." I say, turning my head to the moon, stars, and drifting snowflakes. "*Polasa fesnop ti'it trensapa.* Speak this to nobody."

"*Wazme gingo?*" she asks.

"*Plett blight ofdrec jo vasa,*" I say. "Because I might be wrong."

She pulls me in for a hug from behind and holds me. I look down at her arms and hold hers as well. My eyes close.

"*Cre ama polasa bea e Vee'Sal?*" I ask. "Can you speak with the Vee'Sal?"

"*Vee'Sal...*" Tila'Cet answers. "*Vee'Sal hueton pes gingo frex humans su Wah'Lor.*"

The Vee'Sal do not accept our presence. She is right. We have kept our agreement to stay away from them. They are understandably upset with the Dah'Sel because we hurt so many upon our arrival. Not even Wat'Uza may visit their place of Wah'Lor. The divide is great.

I hear they were on their way across the land to join the fight against us when Elder Wat'Uza called them off. They do not understand how Pru'Cet and the others of this sect allowed us to stay. I shall win them over some rotation.

I look back into the moonlight as Tila'Cet holds me.

"*Wazme pes ama grenas baklee humans ofdrec kuzsoec?*" asks Tila'Cet.

"Did Pru'Cet talk to you about my dreams?" I ask. "*Dit Pru'Cet polasa ti'it ama dase en heltno-zis?*"

"*Lipfa,*" she answers.

I turn to face her.

"*Blight matao-zim siwbe kuzsoec-zic,*" I say. "I saw them coming."

Tila'Cet looks toward our distant tele-tents and their Lessdelop ti'it renasa far across the snowy fields. She stares for a moment and looks to the Misdela mountain. I know what she is thinking. At least, I think I do. That mountain's far side is home to the Vee'Sal.

She looks back at me.

"*Blight uptru ikkida,*" she says.

"*Dada ama,*" I say with a smile. "Thank you."

Tila'Cet turns my body, wraps her arms around me, and sits in the snow with her legs crossed and me in her lap to keep me warm. I look up at the stars with her, still amazed at the fact I can see them from the surface of the planet. I went my whole life without such a thing before Wah'Lor. It is a boon, as is her warmth.

"I could stare at this all night," I say. "Forgotten in your arms."

"*Utlu ot fesnop ama polasa?*" asks Tila'Cet.

"*Blight grenas blight uptru pacala topcal tom nosaj,*" I answer.

I close my eyes to take in her warm embrace. This is a moment much needed to de-stress and get my mind off everything. Words like comfort will not suffice. This is where I am meant to be. I relax further into her. Tila'Cet's wrap on me tightens. I can feel her heart beating against my upper back and would not trade it for another 1,000 cycles of life.

CHAPTER 16
Planetary Downfall

The district I was born in is gone. Kep Four has swallowed Najasa into its belly like a starving thief in the night seeking a loaf of bread. My home world is officially on the last leg of its dim life. Everyone I grew up with is gone.

A fissure from the planetary quake and its aftershocks cuts the district in half and will forever remain where buildings once stood. It runs from south to north 3/4 across the district and cuts northeast at its center to continue over 50 clicks out into no-life's-land. The housing structure that Mother raised me in no longer exists. A planet that refuses to die without taking life has consumed it.

Najasa is not alone in its demise. Between the planet's opening tectonic plates and the Upriser rampage, few districts remain unscathed by the vengeful two-sided blade of anarchy, shaking Kep Four and its citizens to its core. Capital cities positioned high above the surface were safe places before the Uprisers' latest assaults. That has changed. Dolofónos destroyed what held most of them aloft. Only Chimark remains skyward.

The capital city of Galhet has crashed into the Denta fields. Radioactive pollution from the shattered capital city's power cores renders it no longer the least toxic place on Kep Four. What little life may have existed there before its collapse is gone. In the form of ashes rising with smoke and fumes, it mixes with the brown, one atom at a time.

All Armada members left on Kep Four have relocated to the capital of Chimark to make a stand before the last interstellar ships leave for Wah'Lor. There is strength in numbers. It must be taken advantage of.

Our Planetary Sovereign's right hand, once in charge of Armada military engagements controlling Dolofónos and his Uprisers, Commander Helmwoke, now runs the Armada on Kep Four and sits for a meeting in the Planetary conference hall. Hundreds below and around her await her words. She is the lone person left in command of Kep Four and all they have for global guidance.

"As many of you know," says Commander Helmwoke, "the micro-Rosen we opened between Kep Four and our brothers and sisters on our new home world has collapsed. The last three or four rotations have rendered us unable to communicate with those who have already made the trip, but our plan remains the same. We will have the *Dwarf* fully loaded with Armada military weapons and vessels and follow the Armada *Ark* into the Ein-Rosen bridge. We don't expect to run into any issues during departure, but with everything going on with the Uprisers right now, we aren't taking any chances. Most of us are making the trip in the *Lifeboat,* and the *Dwarf* will be in the air as overwatch until we make the jump. Only then will it follow."

"Commander Helmwoke," asks a lady in the crowd, "how many rotations until—"

The Planetary Conference Hall shakes violently with the planet. Several in attendance fall to the ground or from their seats. All eyes widen.

People reach frantically for grips on anything they can get their hands on to stabilize themselves. The violent shake intensifies and rocks the hall back and forth three or four paces at a time. The overhead halo-projection system my squad and I once watched lay out our trajectory path from the Milky Way to Andromeda during the Expedition Anchor briefing falls from above. Several Armada soldiers look up. It is freefalling directly toward them. They jump for safety in all directions like opening flower petals and land belly down on the hall's floor as is smashes near their feet. Sparks spring into the air behind them as they stand.

The building settles and ceases its angry shake. Chatter is high and difficult to make out as people panic and call to each other, looking for answers. Commander Helmwoke taps her small gavel on the marble surface in front of her. A loud rumble with deep pulsations fills the hall. It grows silent.

Those in attendance gather composure. Armada personnel stand and look at each other without an answer for what has happened. Dozens need medical attention. Blood drips from arms and foreheads, but all are alive.

"What was that?" asks Commander Helmwoke. "A quake couldn't have caused that. Not this many clicks above the surface."

The overseer on her and other capital leaders' wrists activate.

"Are we under attack?" asks the former capital leader of Galhet.

"Unlikely," says Commander Helmwoke. "Chimark's heavily guarded. I have every patrol ship left on Kep Four focused on us until we leave."

"It wasn't an attack," answers the tall capital leader. "The planet's surface is giving way. Eruptions are rampant." He studies his overseer's readings. "It was some sort of shockwave."

"What's causing them?" asks Commander Helmwoke.

"No way to tell," he answers, "but it's not coming from Kep Four by itself."

"Visual feed relays?"

"Nothing," answers the tall capital leader. "Districts below were ransacked by Uprisers before the quakes took them or destroyed by fallen capital cities."

The hall rocks again.

"Find out what's causing this," says Commander Helmwoke.

"Yes, Ma'am," says the tall capital leader.

He and several others move to the exit and stumble to the ground as the shaking subsides. They look back at Commander Helmwoke for a moment, share internal concerns and exit.

Another violent shake sends all inside to their knees and out of their seats. Commander Helmwoke reaches to stabilize herself but falls to the floor and tumbles down steps leading up to her seating area. She reaches for anything to stop herself. Nothing works. She is battered head over heels until her tumble stops at the bottom of the steps.

A man crawls to her aid. His face is covered in dust. His voice spikes with panic.

"Commander," he says. "Let me get you out of here."

He reaches down for her and pulls her to her knees.

"Thank you," she says. "We need to get out of here."

"I got you," he says. "I'll—"

A piece of marble debris hits him on the head, and he collapses at Commander Helmwoke's side. She reaches to check his pulse. She cannot. The shaking is violent, and she drops to her side to see a pool of blood puddling around his face—eyes open and staring into nothing.

The seating wall on her left across the Planetary Conference Hall collapses. Screams fill the room as it falls. Hundreds are crushed, killed, and injured as the hall's flooring, walls, and ceiling of polished marble with hints of fluctuating tans, greens, and whites swirling through them intended for beauty become terrifying. A grand structure designed for crucial meetings is a scene of chaos. The polished metallic floor they entered on and need as an escape route is a proverbial battleground for their survival. The very foundation they are crawling to safety on cracks.

Screams intensify as it ripples beneath them like water on a pond in heavy rain. Armada personnel are bounced in all directions into the seating, walls, floor, and each other. Heads collide.

Commander Helmwoke reaches to stabilize herself again and grabs for the steps next to her. It splinters under shakes of furious magnitude. She is thrown to her back—equilibrium lost. She looks up and knows she is not alone in the chaos.

The doors on the opposite side of the hall from where she sits are still clear. She pushes herself up to a piece of larger debris and holds on for a moment. Another jolt shakes the building, but she does not fall.

It subsides. She limps for the exit, but the shaking continues with lighter rumbles as she walks. Her path is staggered at best as others make the drunken walk to freedom. Some crawl. Others drag the injured their way. Many make it out. Several are smashed beneath fallen marble when half of the exit collapses.

She reaches the exit as the shaking stops again. Fresh air hits her dust-covered body, and she turns to look back with hundreds of others, 70 paces from the hall. Everyone on the floating capital city of Chimark that could make it out of a building has done so. Most are still intact, but the conference hall, made internally of stone, has fallen.

NIVEOUS WAR

16-2
Geo-Manipulation

Dolofónos laughs with a few of his Butchers and several Uprisers in his concrete underground reinforcement. They raise several glasses and spill an unknown liquor when they clank them together.

"That'll get their attention," says Dolofónos, with a psychotic laugh. "Don't you think?"

"Another toast to that," says Butcher Five.

They touch cigars together and take a puff.

"Saddi," says Dolofónos. "Do we have enough energy left to rock Chimark again?"

"We do," answers Saddi. "But my advice is to conserve until we know we can get off Kep Four."

Dolofónos takes a few puffs from his cigar in thought.

"I'll trust you on that," he says, turning to his Butchers. "How much longer until the next charges are in place?"

"Less than a rotation," answers Butcher Two. "They're half a click down with another quarter click to go before charges are close enough to another volcanic vein to generate an eruption."

"Status on jump vessels?" asks Dolofónos.

"They'll be loaded within three rotations," answers Butcher Two. "They'll most likely begin boarding the rotation after that."

"Keep all eyes on them," says Dolofónos.

He snuffs out his cigar and hands the Butchers some as he lights another.

"We're going to hit them with everything we got the moment the last one's completed. And when I say everything, I mean our tanks, energy reserves, and armaments are to be dry before we stop attacking. I want those ships."

"We all do," says Butcher One. "How else are we getting off this death rock?"

"How are our numbers looking?" asks Dolofónos.

"We're going to be packing twenty thousand into the *Dwarf* and another thirty into the *Ark*," says Butcher Three. "That is, of course, providing we can take them."

Dolofónos smirks.

"We'll take the jump ships or destroy them," says Dolofónos. "If we don't get off Kep Four, nobody does. Just make sure Chimark stays in the sky until we find out which it's going to be."

A scientist in an Upriser colored lab coat enters the room. He is slender and looks half-starved, with a sunken face and rail-thin arms. I assume him to be an Armada outcast. Perhaps a family member of his once served and had him housed before they died, and he was cast back to the streets. It is not unheard of for someone to betray the Armada when thrown to the brown.

"Dr. Tangin," says Dolofónos. "How can we help our newest and most welcomed addition?"

"Thank you for that," says the bookish Dr. Tangin. "And excuse the intrusion, sire. I have the data you were asking for."

"Good," says Dolofónos. "Let's hear it."

"Now," asks Tangin, looking at the others in the room.

"There are no secrets here with myself, my Butchers, or any of my long-standing Uprisers," says Dolofónos. "You'll learn this in time."

"Of course not," says Dr. Tangin, giving Dolofónos a quick bow. "I've retraced the Ein-Rosen trail left behind by the Armada vessels that have already made the jump."

"Well..." says Dolofónos, taking another puff of his cigar. "Where'd they go?"

"There's no way to tell exactly where they went," answers Dr. Tangin. "We can only see traces and trajectories from what we've put together on our end. I can tell you, however, that they went somewhere into the outer regions of the Andromeda galaxy."

"Good enough for me," says Dolofónos. "Check the region and do the math. Hack the Armada mainframe and find out which planet they thought was the most habitable. That'll be our target."

"Yes, sir," he says, standing in wait for something.

"Something else we can do for you?" asks Dolofónos.

"I want to let you know I am a loyalist," Dr. Tangin answers. "I know what it is like to be thrown to the firecats by the Armada. I was loyal to them and—"

"You have a place here now," says Dolofónos as he stands, embraces him, pats him on the back, and looks him in the eyes. "Are we the Armada, ladies and gentlemen?"

"No, sir," shouts all in the room.

"What are we?" continues Dolofónos.

"Blood," they shout.

"Did you hear that?" asks Dolofónos. "Blood. That's what you are now. You do right by us, we'll do right by you, and you won't get a personal visit from the Butchers."

CHAPTER 17
Anguish

A curdled scream from my throat and pain lighting up every nerve ending in my body like hot coals poured upon my skin and bones snatches me from slumber. I am no longer in Tila'Cet's arms on the ground outside of Lesdelop. Someone loads me into a standard transport shuttle, an Argos, or something. My hands are clutched around my temples as I wake. I cannot focus.

What are they putting me in? What's happening to my mind?

Another scream wrenches from my gut as agony sears through every fiber of my existence from betraying neurotransmitters. My skin feels like it is peeling off my body. I cannot...

"Make it stop," I beg. "Make it stop."

"We're trying," says Dr. Wright. "We're getting you to *Athanasios* now. Dr. Klinroy's already prepping."

"Increase the Mizophile," I say. "Anything."

"I can't interact with your implant from here," says Dr. Wright. "I don't think it's recognizing what's happening to you, regardless. We need to get you up to the Med Lab. It's the only one set up for your particular condition, which we're still trying to figure out, and the only place currently linked to your implant."

Delgado and a few others are with me. I cannot make them out or tell what they are saying. Panic is in the air. I will have to thank them if...

A wild scream seeps from me without warning. Someone takes my hand. Hair... It is Tila'Cet.

"*Blight o hueton bea ama,* McKayla," she says. "*Blight o hueton bea ama.*"

It comforts to know she is there with me, but it does not help the pain. I want it to stop. They can club me over the head with a dofabe branch and knock me out for all I care. I will accept anything that makes it go away.

I thrash without control. The pain is increasing. It is too much.

"MAKE IT STOP!" I scream.

"Hold still for a moment," says Dr. Sellers, placing me on a hover gurney.

"MAKE IT STOP!"

Dr. Sellers helps Dr. Wright bind me to it with electro straps. I struggle to get free, though I know why they are doing it. They are afraid I will hurt myself. I do not plan on hurting myself. Not yet, but if this pain keeps up, I do not know.

My squad and the 'Cets are here on the surface in support to keep me calm, but my mind is not correct. I cannot make out all they are saying. It is a jumble of slurs.

I cannot control my actions. My body wants to fight back, with or without my permission. Fight-or-flight instincts take over.

"Ahhhh... I can't—"

The words will not come out. My breaths are nothing but tiny gasps at best. The air is too thick to breathe. Suffocation...

A medical transport unit lowers itself to the Wah'Lor surface. Its loading door opens. It is bright inside. My eyes cannot adjust. My body is failing.

"Get her in," shouts Sergeant Bentley.

Doctors Sellers and Wright climb in as my squad loads me up. They are... The door shuts. I am already in.

Everything is... A breath of air is barely caught as I try to breathe.

"Ahhhhhhh..." I scream, thrashing beneath the restraints.

"Med-Vac three zero one confirming clearance for—"

"Get this damn thing moving," interrupts Dr. Wright with a shout.

Convulsions... The vessel jumps up and down. Faster and faster, until...

17-2
Stupor

I must have blacked out. They are moving me into *Athanasios*'s Med Lab on the hover gurney. I remember nothing between now and being loaded onto the transport from the surface of Wah'Lor.

"Whaaa happen?" I slur.

"I hit you with a half-life dose of Mezi-tranq," answers Dr. Wright.

"Is dat why my heeed doen't hurt as muuuch?"

"Yes," he answers. "Now stop talking and try to relax."

"I'll set up her neurological parameters," says Dr. Sellers.

They float me into position over the spot pop-up gurneys would typically rise from, and it locks into place with the Med Lab's artificially generated magnetic operating field. They are in a hurry that echoes the time we rushed Rhigas and Skedelski to surgery. It unsettles me to sense panic from doctors so seasoned in their trades.

"I'm ready," says Dr. Klinroy.

"Give me another tek here," says Dr. Wright, stepping away from me. "Done."

I reach to feel my face as he steps away, but I am still strapped to the gurney. I can feel the scan relay's sticky dots all over me. They are cold.

"What are you—"

"Relax, Mason," says Dr. Klinroy. "We're inducing coma in three..."

"Wha?" I ask.

"Two..."

"Wai," I strain.

"One..."

CHAPTER 18
Phase One

Dolofónos is in a large multi-tier stadium once reserved for championship Blaze-Ball events. A sea of red-and-black surrounds him—50,000 Uprisers of old comprising 40,000 men and 10,000 women. He walks the center of its field next to Saddi and his five Butchers with an amplator next to his vocal cords.

"Our time of retribution is upon us," says Dolofónos, voice resonating throughout the stadium.

The crowd of Uprisers cheer. He smiles and waits for it to thin. A tek passes. They are not stopping. He motions his hands toward the ground, and they grow quiet.

"This rotation," he continues, "is a moment we should all be proud of. It's what so many of us have fought so long and so hard to achieve. The 40,000 men and 10,000 women seated in the surrounding tiers here are the best of the worst I can throw at the Armada. We've already informed the remaining new recruits that Uprisers of old have seniority and will be leaving first, but we're coming back for everyone. They are ready to fight alongside us. Tomorrow, we will gather them for an ambitious strike at the heart of our oppressors. The Armada will have no shelter from the storm we bring. They will not see us coming; they will not be prepared; they will not stop us from taking those ships."

The crowd goes into an uproar.

"Alas..." he continues, pausing for the crowd to silence itself. "Alas, they will fall as they willingly watched and forced so many others to fall before them. The Armada enjoyed throwing the unfortunate into predicaments where they knew Kep Four would take their lives. Tomorrow, we return the favor."

He takes Saddi by the arm and circles the Butchers with her.

"This lovely lady, Saddi," he continues, "is the Butcher's go-to when I am not available. The Butchers are otherwise always in command, and they will be leading secondary attacks once the recruits are fully engaged in justified combat against our enemy."

More applause. Dolofónos motions to Butcher Five and hands him the amplator from his neck. Butcher Five places it next to his vocal cords and dusts off the red 'V' on each of his shoulders. 'I', 'II', 'III', and 'IV' mark the other Butchers.

Butcher Five steps forward.

"Attacking units will be the standard assignment," he says. "If you're normally with Butcher one, you'll be with Butcher one. If you're normally with me, you'll be with me, and so forth. As Dolofónos said, the blow we are about to strike the Armada with will not just be a crippling one. We're going there to dig graves. They are not leaving Kep Four without us. If we don't make it out with those ships, we all die here tomorrow, but we do it together. The Armada is condemning us to death, regardless. Let's take them with us."

The stadium erupts with claps, cheers, and shouts of taking down the Armada once and for all. Butcher Five waves his arms up and down to rally them into further hysteria and pulls the amplator from his neck.

Butcher Two grabs the amplator and places it on her neck as she steps forward.

PHASE ONE

"Uprisers ready for war?" she asks.

"Uprisers ready for war," chants the red-and-black-suited stadium. "Uprisers ready for war."

Another outbreak of cheers with weapons raised overhead takes place. Thousands of blasts from their onium rifles surge into the brown night sky. Chants continue and another volley is fired as teks of chants pass before the crowd settles.

"Good," says Butcher Two as she paces. "One rotation from the one currently upon us will be filled with a three-hundred-and-sixty-degree attack by new recruits. It happens on my mark and my mark alone. We're coming in from directly over Chimark's head and entering from the black into the brown. They'll not know we're there until it's too late."

She walks to a stadium section where Uprisers have a white '*TU II*' on their shoulders, representing their position as members of the troop unit under Butcher Two's command.

"Are we together on this?" she asks.

Pandemonium continues.

"That's what I want to hear from my wicked deuces," continues Butcher Two. "Now get out of here and get laid or something so I don't have to look at you."

18-2
Staging

The empty region of space above Chimark is no longer black over brown. It is red-and-black. Hundreds of vessels spanning a dozen classes and sizes orbit above it. Most are Bomba Class 1 Fighter Vessels. Fifty-one balls of antimatter reconfigured to affect selected targets face nose down toward Chimark from the black above.

"Recruits check-in." Dolofónos's voice echoes their comms.

"Recruit unit One-North is a go," says a recruit leader.

"Recruit unit Two-East is a go," says another.

"Recruit unit Three-West is three out."

"Recruit unit Four-South is a go."

"Recruit unit Five-Underside is a go."

Their signals are not being intercepted. Dolofónos must have their transmissions masked.

"Recruit unit Three-West is ready to go," says Butcher Three.

"Complete on all ends," answers an Upriser recruit. "Lowering high-yields now."

Dolofónos is in the ship forward's pilot seat of what appears to be a StarBird with Saddi standing behind him with her left arm on his shoulder. Her right robotic hand pinned to the ceiling to stabilize herself from unexpected incoming fire. A black upriser flag with a human pelvic bone centering it hangs on the wall at its rear. It could not have been too difficult to gain. Uprisers stole Armada city defense weapons before crashing capitals down to Kep Four.

"Let me know when the yields are ready to go," says Dolofónos.

"Yes, sire," says Saddi.

Dolofónos moves to the ship's interactive network.

"Overlay drilling progress with overhead views of Chimark," says Dolofónos.

"Overlaying now," says the StarBird's A.I.

A small, three-dimensional, holographic image pops up to rotate in front of him as other Uprisers tend to their duties in the ship's fuselage. It shows Chimark encased by its protective dome with six red dots forming a ring around it on the surface. 'YIELD 1', 'YIELD 2', and so forth are displayed

PHASE ONE

above them to represent each of the six high-yield explosives Dolofónos had Upriser recruits drill into Kep Four.

"Now," continues Dolofónos, "overlay positions of all vessels in ground-based recruit units."

Thousands of yellow dots appear on the projection to form a larger ring around Chimark at 600 clicks out. A portion of the dot to the south is denser in numbers than the rest of the ring. Recruits zoning in on the bottom part of Chimark are awaiting orders to attack alongside another squadron, hence the higher concentration of yellow markers in the area.

"Overlay orbiting units," says Dolofónos.

An array of blue dots appears on the projection to cover the capital city.

"High-Yields in position, charged, and ready," says a recruit.

"Anti-filtration in position?" asks Dolofónos.

"Yes, sir," answers another recruit.

"Then we are a go in ten," says Dolofónos, easing his way to Saddi. "Projections?"

"I don't think they're going to give us half the fuss you think they are," answers Saddi. "Between the initial high-yield geothermal attack, divers, a five-sided attack, and us coming in from topside, we shouldn't have any problem at all taking those ships."

"Then what are we waiting for?" he asks.

"For seven more to pass," answers Saddi. "This will put high-yields to a charging point only moments from failure, releasing the highest energy displacement possible when you activate them."

Dolofónos stands and walks to the main viewing pane to gaze upon Kep Four. Saddi moves to his side and places her hand on the small of his back. A smile creeps its way across her face until it is full. She cuts her eyes to Dolofónos without moving her head.

"And your time is upon you," she says. "Don't get impatient now."

Dolofónos snickers, cuts his eye to her, and returns his gaze to the forward view.

"I want every air and water filtration system within a thousand clicks taken out the moment those yields release their payload."

"It's already done," says Saddi.

"And the Geo-Incinerator?" asks Dolofónos.

"It's in position on the opposite side of the planet, sixteen clicks beneath the surface."

Dolofónos turns to Dr. Tangin.

"Is that deep enough?" he asks.

"Let's just say we better not be around when it goes off," answers Dr. Tangin.

"Perfect," says Dolofónos. "Route the six high-yields and Geo-Incinerator controls to me on the viewing pane here."

Dr. Tangin moves to its station, inputs a few commands, and turns back to Dolofónos.

"Done," he says.

"Then let's shake things up a bit," says Dolofónos.

"In three," says Dr. Tangin.

Dolofónos takes a deep breath to remain patient and gazes from the forward. Saddi walks in front of him and sits on the console to face him, swinging her legs and smiling as she watches him wait. She says nothing and enjoys the building tension of what is coming.

PHASE ONE

18-3
Acts of Savagery

The Bomba Class 1 fighter vessels in orbit above Chimark have spread out to form a massive circle 400 clicks wide.

"Initiate stage one assault," says Dolofónos.

Upriser vessels that surround the capital city take off from Kep Four's surface. Most fly on a straight vertical ascension, but one takes off on a sloped trajectory toward the capital city's belly. All operate on E-Drive to reduce the chances of losing their mask and being exposed to Chimark's ground and airborne identification and defense systems.

"All units one-click off the surface," says an Upriser recruit.

"Initiate stage two," says Dolofónos.

All six high-yield explosives buried into Kep Four's surface around Chimark detonate simultaneously. The ground around them bubbles into a large mound before building pressure breaks loose to produce six mushroom clouds containing planetary debris, smoke, and magma from cracked tectonic plates. The shockwave rises until it nears the recruit vessels.

"Sync micro jumps now," says Saddi. "Five ... four ... three ... two ... one ... engage."

Those attacking Chimark on vertical trajectories make a small micro-jump just as the mushroom cloud below reaches their vessels' afts. They jump and snatch rising matter from the cloud with them. It dissipates in their wake as they come out of warp.

They reach a level position with the floating capital and stop. Several continue another quarter click up and hit another micro-jump, stopping to use regular propulsion over the capital's energy dome. Upriser recruits leap from dozens of ships in X-Wing suits and dive through the dome.

Vessels they jumped from pull up as the recruits freefall through the energy dome and deploy parachutes. Each jumper unhooks a neutron explosive launcher from their sides, takes aim at Chimark's three dome generators, and fires. The RPG-like devices' subsonic neutron grenade produces substantial destruction upon impact and releases a field of lasting radiation.

Their explosions take out the energy dome. It disappears from Chimark. The brown bleeds slowly down upon the capital as fighting ensues. Debris rains upon the city and sends it into a state of chaos.

Corners of the main building come down and land behind several Armada personnel running for cover. A skywalk bridge connection from the capital museum to the Planetary Conference Hall's housing building comes down with a single explosion. Dozens of Armada members fall with pieces of the bridge and splat into the steel surface street side.

An air-raid siren echoes out to raise and lower in intensity with high-pitched chirps. Armada soldiers scramble for battle stations. Automated turrets rise from Chimark's floor and open fire.

"Battle stations," calls the A.I. *"All personnel are to report to battle stations immediately. Repeat. All personnel are to—"*

A heavy blast ripples through the top center of Armada Alliance Headquarters and the warning stops. More rubble rains from above. A series of several pace wide chunks of stone land on a transport rushing into the building for cover. They crush the vessel's front half flat with its driver inside.

Upriser recruits attack the capital's underside with a brief burst of fire and stop to lock their vessels into position while hanging upside down from its baseplate. Kep Four's

PHASE ONE

planetary debris and magma impact them. The collision rocks their ships. Chimark trembles.

Three of the vessels docked against the capital's underside detach. They topple along its ferromagnetic baseplate and explode. One bounces off its side and regains control before heading toward the black to escape.

The capital city's topside shakes violently. Armada members run to vessels and defensive positions; further sections of buildings break off with the tremble. Soldiers lose their footing in the vibrations and fall to the ground. One rushes to help a soldier clutching a missing leg but gets flattened by the Armada's billboard-sized three-planet emblem when it falls from the building and lands on him.

It is dark irony. The first planet in the emblem is a blue and green Ancient Earth. The second is a brown Kepler 442-b, and the third is a round empty space representing optimistic things to come. Those things are upon us, and it does not look promising.

Recruit vessels invading on horizontal attack trajectories take a heavy blow from the shockwave and struggle to regain control. Not all are lucky. Four of them smash into each other and explode in domino fashion. Uprisers that do not lose control in the shockwave open fire on Chimark, minus one location: Grid 9 of the staging pad where the *Dwarf,* the *Ark,* and the *Lifeboat* are prepping to launch.

"All personnel to defensive posture," calls Commander Helmwoke over comms. "Bottom side launch."

Dozens of Armada attack vessels drop from small openings beneath the capital city, only to be obliterated by Uprisers on their way out. They pour from Chimark's underside like broken pottery and fall in fragments to Kep Four's now fiery surface like trash. The Upriser's Underside-Five unit ceases fire but holds position.

A dogfight involving over 50 vessels coats the city in a spherical fashion. Overhead, weapon blasts and laser fire lights the sky and capital's surface like an outraged sun trying to burn all below. Some vessels fall to boom into buildings. Others fall to Kep Four. Most are Armada.

The vastly outnumbered Armada is holding its own, but many of their ships, buildings, and personnel succumb to the initial attack. Debris from destroyed Armada and Upriser recruit vessels continues to rain a fiery metal meteor shower upon Chimark.

"Initiate stage three assault," says Dolofónos.

Uprisers of old leave lower orbit in Bomba Class 1s and enter the upper atmosphere. Dolofónos behind them in the stolen StarBird. They are in a nosedive toward Chimark and fire scat-shots the entire way. The sky drips with swirling blasts of death upon all in their way. The blasts tear apart Armada and Upriser recruit vessels alike, but the enemy does not care. They continue firing. Their plan is to decimate.

"Release neural concussion charges," says Dolofónos.

Hail of small spheres freefall from the Bomba Class 1s to impact the city's surface. All on Chimark are knocked unconscious within a one-click radius. Armada and recruit vessels within the blast zone temporarily lose control when their pilots black out, but autopilot takes over and the vessels land themselves.

"Initiate stage four assault," says Dolofónos. "Maximum penetration."

The others fall to the rear as he takes the lead in the stolen StarBird and discharges a downward EMP; friendly and foe vessels alike lose power and plummet. Upriser recruit vessels clinging to the underside of the capital city power down when the EMP pushes through the city and reaches them. Their grip on the capital underbelly slips. They fall like the rest.

Dolofónos lands with Saddi and his high-ranking Uprisers.

"Initiate stage five assault," says Dolofónos, exiting the StarBird.

"Listen up," says Saddi. "Earn your keep if you don't want to end up dead like the new recruits did."

Dolofónos followers shout and charge across Chimark, moving once again like the locus of Shremba through the city to execute unconscious Armada members in their sleep. Those inside will meet the same fate. Dolofónos, his Butchers, and a few thousand others head directly to the *Dwarf*, the *Ark*, and the *Lifeboat*.

18-4
Highjack

Butchers Two and Five enter the *Dwarf*. Dolofónos and Saddi enter the back of the *Ark*. Butcher Three enters the front to assist them as Butcher One enters the *Lifeboat*. Thousands upon thousands of Uprisers enter before each of their unit's Butcher leader.

Butcher One's unit pushes through the *Lifeboat*. The Upriser walking point stops in his tracks when he rounds a bulkhead. A syringe has been jabbed into his neck by an Armada scientist.

"All stop," says the Upriser, frozen in fear with a needle in his neck.

Another Upriser behind him raises a fist for all behind him to halt their advance.

"Too late for that," says the Armada scientist.

He depresses its flange to force the barrel's contents into the Upriser's bloodstream. The point-man falls to the ground, and the scientist steps behind the wall with onium rounds flying his direction.

"Thought you were just going to walk in here and take it?" shouts the scientist.

Armada soldiers and personnel in the *Lifeboat* and Uprisers alike take cover and return fire. Two Armada scientists try to shut the vessel's rear entrance as the bandits press in. The one closest to the corridor gets shot and dies on the floor with a portion of his shoulder seared to the bone. The scientist that injected the first Upriser leans his back against the sealed door.

"They're almost to the forward," shouts the scientist into the vessel's depths.

Armada guards enter the area and take positions to hold back any invaders that may make it through the sealed entrance. They aim their weapons at the door. No one speaks. No one moves.

Uprisers are no doubt on the other side of it, surprised at the resistance and planning a way to power through it. They were caught off guard. Interstellar jump ship hulls were designed to protect them from the Ein-Rosen bridge's detrimental effects. The EMP and neural concussion charges did not affect their interiors, equipment, or personnel; and the Armada is ready for a fight in the *Lifeboat*. Many are there, prepping it as the last vessel to be completed

"We're taking this vessel under Dolofónos," shouts the muffled words of an Upriser behind the door.

"Fall back and get the next one sealed," says an Armada soldier.

They move toward the forward and enter it. The first door blows with shrapnel from its hold. Metal fragments jet down the corridor and kill two Armada soldiers. Another

PHASE ONE

opens fire on the Uprisers as the scientists shut the next door and seal him out.

Guards on the *Lifeboat* move in from the ship's bridge to protect the precious vessel armed with only sidearms. A few rounds rip through red-and-black uniforms. Their wearers drop to the ground and bleed out, but the Uprisers open fire to remove Armada guards with onium rifles.

A door in the corridor ahead of them shuts and locks.

"Take it down," says Butcher One.

A pair of Uprisers roll homemade cylinders resembling pipe bombs across the floor. They come to rest against a bulkhead. Butcher One and his Uprisers take cover.

Explosions shake the floor beneath their feet. Smoke clears. The Uprisers stand and peer through the cloud to see the door fall in their direction and clank to the floor with no walls at either side of it. Four Armada guards lie motionless on the other side of it.

"Move in," shouts Butcher One. "Move in."

His subordinates raise their rifles and press forward, double taping the fallen guards while stepping over them. Another guard enters from a back door on their right, only to be eliminated with shots that end his life. Uprisers secure the first area of the ship and continue their advance.

The Armada answers the call to battle, but it is futile. Upriser numbers are too great. They do not have the firepower or tactical advantage that the Butchers of Dolofónos have the luxury of bringing to the fight.

A blanket of attackers enters the bridge with guns pumping rounds into fleshy Armada targets. Gunshots pass into men and women on both sides, but numbers are three-fold on the side of evil. Only one Armada member remains alive on the bridge, but he is taking his final breath on the floor.

All looks to be lost for the vessel's future, but Armada members, soldiers, doctors, scientists, and civilians alike swarm, late to the fight, from the *Lifeboat*'s depths. They are in combat gear and armed with onium rifles.

Their suppressive fire is nonstop and overwhelms the invaders, forcing them to fall back or surrender their lives. Tide shifts to favor the Armada as they run. Hundreds of Uprisers die before fleeing the *Lifeboat* to Chimark's surface, desperate to take cover. Many are shot in the back before they exit the ship.

The battle pours over onto the launch deck as Armada members step over their dead oppressors' red-and-black bodies. Uprisers of old are falling fast in the open, unable to find cover after they annihilated the capital city's surface buildings. They have dug their graves.

Dolofónos with Butchers Two and Five overrun the *Dwarf* with precision and ease. While it is the vessel carrying Armada armaments, its loading process is complete, and there are few on board to put up a fight. They burn through the *Dwarf*'s defenses without breaking stride and send those on board to greet eternal darkness.

They move into positions after eradicating all life aboard the *Dwarf*. Their game plan is meticulous and steadfast. Some move into positions to shut the rear cargo entrance, five make their way to tactical stations on the warship, and others move to maintenance and piloting command centers.

Many Armada personnel are aboard the *Ark*, but most of them are wealthy civilians in Med Bay lines to have their DNA added to its archive. The resistance they offer is minimal at best. Gunshot after Upriser gunshot boots them from existence. Not a single Upriser intruder dies in the attack. Nine teks are all it takes for Dolofónos to claim the critical vessel.

PHASE ONE

"We have the *Ark*," says Dolofónos, stepping over a fallen man and woman in Armada scientists' cloaks. "I need a status update from my Butchers."

"*Dwarf* secured and ready to go," says Butcher Five.

"Then get these things fired up," says Dolofónos.

"You heard him," says Saddi.

The invaders move to their remaining predetermined positions and go to work.

"And the *Dwarf*?" asks Dolofónos.

"It's past final construction," answers Saddi. "They shouldn't be putting up much of a resistance."

"*Dwarf* Secured," answers Butcher Two over comms.

"Butcher One," says Saddi. "Status?"

"They're wiped," says Butcher Two. "I was in direct communications with Butcher One and lost him. They were retreating."

"Retreating?" asks Dolofónos.

"Retreating, sir," answers Butcher Two.

"Then they don't deserve to come with us," says Dolofónos. "Fire up, pull out, and get rid of the *Lifeboat* on your way up."

The *Ark* and *Dwarf*'s external rocket propulsion engines power up and rotate to point skyward before spitting flames onto the Grid 9 staging pad. They take off for the brown on a slow rise to orbit where external engines will eject and freefall back to Kep Four.

18-5
No Man Left Behind

The *Ark* lifts skyward under reverse gravity propulsion near orbit with the *Dwarf* rising to follow. It discharges rail guns mounted at the warship's top, bottom, left, and right sides.

With each shot, a laser leads a tiny solid steel projectile into its target at near light speeds. It only takes a few bursts before the *Lifeboat* explodes and is officially off the grid.

"Initiate stage six," says Dolofónos.

"Are we a hundred percent sure about this one?" asks Butcher Five.

"Are you planning on coming back?" asks Dolofónos.

"Of course not."

"Then do it."

"Yes, sir," says Butcher Five. "Detonating Geo-Incinerator."

Butcher Five enters a few commands into his station. An explosion somewhere on the other side of the planet takes place that I cannot see. I know what it is. They have already said it. They have detonated a Geo-Incinerator—a devastating weapon forbidden by Armada law thousands of cycles ago that causes an unstoppable chain reaction. It burns from one airborne molecule to the next until it reaches the ozone layer to burn it all away, leaving an atmosphere with nothing to breathe in its wake.

Dolofónos and his Uprisers reach orbit in the skyjacked interstellar vessels as a wall of fire makes its way around Kep Four like heated wax flowing over a BlazeBall. Any left alive on the surface will soon burn to death. Those lucky enough to be inside will never have oxygen to purify and breathe again without artificially creating it indoors. Earthquakes, brown tsunamis, and a destroyed ecosphere will turn the planet into a cemetery.

Hope on Kep Four is deader than those living their ultimate moments through the cataclysm.

"Dr. Tangin," asks Dolofónos, "are we ready?"

"Retracing course and opening the bridge..." answers Dr. Tangin, "...now."

PHASE ONE

A cloud engulfs their stolen vessels. They rumble and are surrounded by fluctuating colors on the darker side of the spectrum. A portal two paces off the hull opens in front of them. Subtle vibrations turn into angry shakes.

"Power to one-hundred percent," says Dr. Tangin.

"Power to one-hundred," says Butcher Five.

"Power to one-hundred," says Butcher Two.

"Release artificial gravity well," says Dr. Tangin.

The *Ark* enters the wormhole. The *Dwarf* follows. They glow a brighter fluctuation of colors as they push into it. The *Ark* disappears into the Ein-Rosen bridge until its aft is gone, and the *Dwarf* moves in to follow. Kep Four's orbit grows quiet as the Geo-Incinerator's fire makes its final wrap around it.

CHAPTER 19
Incoming

A brilliant white light bullies my eyes into a squint. It hurts clear to the back of my head, but the illumination alone cannot cause this. It fades.

A scent of synthetic relon rubber fills my nostrils.

"Easy, Mason," says a voice.

A pressure in my head... A snake slithers through my sinuses, and I sneeze. I try to get up, but hands grab to hold me in place.

The room comes into focus. It is Doctors Klinroy and Sellers, and they are pulling a bio tube designed to release nanotech from my brain. The snaky sensation pulls from my head and out my nose until it is no longer in me, and the pressure behind my eyes subsides.

"Almost there," says Dr. Sellers.

Something pulls from my lungs. I clinch bed sheets at my hips to hold myself in place. A gag reflex... I almost puke onto the doctor's hands as the tube exits, leaving my nose to drip something slimy. An unsavory combination of infection and blood fills my mouth.

"Wha—"

I gag again.

"We were trying to get video feed while we had you sedated," says Dr. Klinroy. "Tried everything we could but couldn't get a feed, but I bet your head feels better."

I rub my hands over my head.

"It does, actually," I say, "but did you shave part of my head?"

"Old world," answers Dr. Klinroy, "I know, but we wanted direct contact without implanting anything under the skin or doing anything else remotely. We already had enough going on with REM extraction attempts and Sperprazidoneri along with high levels of Mizophile working to block receptors."

"Yeah," I say. "Thanks for trying to dumb it down for me, but I can handle a little scientific mumbo-jumbo, believe it or not."

Dr. Klinroy laughs.

"She's pretty savvy," says Dr. Sellers.

"I know she is," says Dr. Klinroy. "It's a habit. Can you stand for us? We canceled the Mizophile sedation. It should wear off now."

I stand with the help of Dr. Sellers, but I do not need it.

"Wow," I say. "I feel fine. No headache or anything."

"Good," says Dr. Klinroy. "I was starting to think I'd have to transfer to *Athanasios* just to take care of you, permanently."

"Snowfall has eased up," says Dr. Sellers. "But it's been storming the last few rotations. Quite the sight; flashes of lightning and snow, but it has made it difficult for all but drop pods going and coming from the planet."

"How long was I under?" I ask.

Dr. Sellers looks to Dr. Klinroy for a tik and back to me.

"Thirteen rotations," he answers.

"What?" I ask.

"Did you have any visions?" asks Dr. Klinroy. "We weren't able to extract them, if you did."

"A lot of them," I answer.

Athanasios goes black, and I see nothing. The room has all but disappeared.

"Looks like the final Armada vessels are about to come through," says Dr. Wright over comms. "Ein-Rosen is opening in..." he checks his overseer. "In four."

"They're here," I say.

"We know," says Dr. Wright. "The *Ark* and *Lifeboat* have been scheduled since—"

"It's not them," I interrupt.

Dr. Klinroy powers up a wrist light and moves to put it on, but I need it more than he does right now.

"I need that," I say, grabbing it from him and putting it on.

"Who's here, Mason?" asks Dr. Sellers.

"Dolofónos," I answer with a breaking voice. "Uprisers."

I rush from the Med Lab under a full sprint through *Athanasios*, barefooted and with my medical gown flapping behind me. It is a big ship, and I have a long run to the cockpit.

"Mason to Sergeant Bentley."

"You're up?" asks Sergeant Bentley. "How are you feeling?"

"The Uprisers are here," I say through labored breaths.

"Come again?" he asks.

"The Armada thinks it's the others coming from Kep Four," I answer, "but they've captured our ships."

He takes a few tiks to respond.

"Are you certain?" he asks.

"Set the airfield on fire," I say. "Scramble everything we've got."

I turn a corner and slam into the corridor wall as I continue.

"Now," I shout.

INCOMING

"I'll try to get them incoming," says Sergeant Bentley, "but I don't know if—"

"We're all dead if you don't," I interrupt. "Ending transmission."

I blaze into the forward. *Athanasios* powers back up as the wormhole opens. *Uno* is on the forward viewing pane with Dr. Wright and a few others at interface panels. I stop, frozen in awe at the chaos to come.

The wormhole forms right next to *Uno*.

"Captain Balter to—"

Uno's front half is sucked into the Ein-Rosen bridge. Air, gas, and people are pushed into space from its severed back half and sucked into the wormhole. The *Ark*'s nose is emerging when *Uno*'s front half collides with it in the Ein-Rosen.

Several explosions take out a small portion of the *Ark*'s bow.

"*Athanasios* to *Ark*," says Dr. Wright.

No response.

"*Athanasios* to *Ark*," says Dr. Wright. "Can you read me?"

The multispectral Ein-Rosen bridge stays open as the *Ark* makes its way out with Debris floating around it. Distress signals fill the airwaves with accompanying red and white flashing lights. I look around in horror.

"*Warning*," says *Athanasios*. "*Ark to Athanasios impact imminent.*"

"Dr. Wright to *Ark*," he continues. "We're going to need you to hold position when your aft is cleared."

"*Barrows* to *Ark*," says Captain Selk. "Initiate reverse propulsion."

No response.

"*Barrows* to *Flemlace*," continues Captain Selk. "Can you reach the *Ark*?"

"Negative," answers Captain Menjay. "Been trying to reach them on sub-channels, to no avail. You're going to have to reposition *Athanasios*."

"The Ein-Rosen opened too close to us," says Dr. Wright. "We're not protected like the others, and it put us down for a moment. We're rebooting now, but dead on propulsions for another two."

"Impact in five..." says *Athanasios*. *"four... three..."*

"Halt course, *Ark*," shouts Dr. Wright.

"Two... one..."

Athanasios sounds out with reverberations as a violent impact throws us to the floor. I stand in a personal brawl with balance to reach the cockpit and fall again. The ladder is right there. This is something I can do. I go for it and pull myself up, nearly falling a few times.

I enter the custom Beltric Class Six cockpit designed for *Athanasios* and strap myself in.

"Armada voice clearance," I say, "Mason, five, Sinote, one, four, McKayla, three, six, display all visual security feeds intercepting *Athanasios*."

My cockpit's six panes come to life with the usual 360-degree view around the ship's hull displayed. Armada auditory airwaves link to it.

"Armada voice clearance, Mason, five, Sinote, one, four, McKayla, three, six," I repeat. "Disengage cockpit from *Athanasios*."

"Cockpit disen—"

An explosion rolls *Athanasios* like a rejuvenation boat hit by a wave in the tainted Jade Sea on Kep Four. Chemical fires burn on my external viewing panes, driven by the mighty ship's oxygen. Its hull breaches one section at a time like small helium balloons tied together and lit on one end.

INCOMING

The lever throws, and I drop from *Athanasios*—my mother ship's—rolling belly in the Beltric Class Six.

19-2
Losing orbit

I need to get my bearings. Panes reveal stars, Wah'Lor, and my wounded mother ship, pummeled by an equally damaged *Ark,* both of which are plummeting toward the planet's surface at a gradual angle while losing orbit.

Drop pods launch from my mother ship in all directions as it tumbles toward the atmosphere below. Dozens head in different directions through space as it barrel rolls and flips. Some move straight toward Wah'Lor. Others eject into the black, correct their path, maneuver around the ship they departed from, and find a way to the surface.

"Mason to *Athanasios,*" I say.

"Stabilizers are..." says Dr. Wright. "I can't—"

An explosion echoes comms and cuts him off. I try to think of what to do or how to help. There is no way I can stop it from happening, not alone in the Beltric.

Armada comms fill with panicked voices calling out *TOCSIN* from different departments, not yet realizing we are under attack.

"Isolate surface comms and leave only recon squad one, *Athanasios,* and orbiting crafts," I say.

The signal declutters.

"I got Dr. Wright into a drop pod," says Dr. Sellers. "He's hurt. I'm right behind him."

"Excellent," says Sergeant Bentley. "What do we have up there, Mason?"

I look at the visual panes for an appropriate answer. Chaos left behind from the impact is all I see. Small fragments of the *Ark* and *Athanasios* catch light to flicker around a descending *Ark* and rolling *Athanasios* like metallic-glitter confetti celebrating the wrong event.

"The *Ark* just slammed into *Athanasios*," I say.

"Vessel status?" asks Sergeant Bentley with running, labored breaths shouting to someone in the backdrop. "Incoming!"

"Lost," I answer. "*Athanasios* is off the grid."

Sergeant Bentley does not respond. He is fighting. I will help as soon as possible, but there is too much going on up here to leave the black.

The *Ark*'s nose is concaved from the crash with *Athanasios*. Anyone in the forward is dead unless they ejected, but there are no signs of anyone trying to escape the seed-bearing vessel. If we lose it, we lose humanity and animal DNA along with a stockpile of seeds thousands of cycles old.

Athanasios spins through the black like a knife thrown in sidearm fashion while simultaneously rolling from port to starboard. The *Ark*'s nose went up upon impact to drag its aft along my mother ship's hull.

"They're going down," I say. "Both of them are going down."

"We're almost to you," says Sergeant Bentley. "Other squads are right behind us. Medical is scrambling to transports."

Athanasios's stabilization thrusters use multiple points to release a series of pops and small contained explosions to level out its trajectory. It is no longer rolling but is having difficulty stopping its spin with such a heavy mass. Maybe I can lend it a hand now that it is no longer tumbling.

"I'm going to try to stop *Athanasios*'s spin before it reaches orbit," I say.

INCOMING

Sergeant Bentley and the rest of my squad enter the black in Bomba Class 1 Fighter vessels. Readings tell me Bentley, Chubb, and Fister—who once never wanted to engage in combat with anyone besides his fallen brother—are in one, Bell and Sapp are in the second, and Delgado is in the third flying solo.

"Let's see if we can level her out," says Sergeant Bentley.

"Copy that," says Delgado.

"Right here with you," says Bell. "Nose and port are too damaged. Let's grab her at port aft."

"Agreed," says Sergeant Bentley. "Move in. We'll take bow port. Bell, position beside us. Fister, you take the rear."

"And me?" I ask.

"Don't let anyone leave the *Ark*," he answers.

I strafe alongside the spinning Ark. It is leveling itself out. Power comes back online for its passengers.

"I'm taking out its thrust ports," I say.

"Do what you have to do, Mason," says Sergeant Bentley, "but we need what's on the *Ark*."

"Understood," I say.

I continue my strafe around the mighty seed-bearing vessel intended to bring life.

"Armada voice clearance, Mason, five, Sinote, one, four, McKayla, three, six," I say. "Initiate combat type two dash nine."

My starfighter's nose opens to protrude 25 rotating barrels locked together.

"Override Armada combat safety protocols," I continue. "Target all energy export points on the *Ark*."

The barrels spin to release a never-ending stream of high impulse lasers at 22,000 bursts per tek. A wavy, puzzle-board patterned, corkscrew scar is burned around the *Ark* as I spiral around it, targeting thrusters and stabilization ports. I am at 25 gravitational forces and 1/8th a click off its hull to hold my pattern.

Engaging the *Ark*'s aft thrusters, I glance over my panes. My squad struggles to stabilize *Athanasios*. Their vessels are slowing it, but they are getting battered by its hull and bump repeatedly off it.

"I'm coming to assist with *Athanasios*," I say.

"I got it, Mason," says *Flemlace*'s Captain Menjay. "Stay on the *Ark*."

"We're coming to help," says Captain Selk. "But we're a quarter orbit from you."

I hit a micro-jump to come a 1/2-click from *Athanasios*. It was not necessary, but it is in my nature to push the threshold when flying. I cannot help myself.

19-3
Black Heaven

My squad's Bomba Class 1s push against the hull of *Athanasios* using extendable tungsten limbs with clamps at the end of them, designed for docking against larger vessels. A laser rail gun fires from an unseen cannon. I look to see the same Uprisers that destroyed the *Lifeboat* on Kep Four before departing.

"*Dwarf*," I say. "*Dwarf*."

"Break off!" shouts Sergeant Bentley.

My squad releases from the once-mighty *Athanasios* to escape. I look to my rear-viewing pain. The *Dwarf*'s laser rail gun blast rips through the front portion of *Athanasios*. A series of explosions dominoes toward my disengaging squad and other engaging vessels.

I hit another micro-jump to be at the attacking ship's top aft side. Dozens upon dozens of red-and-black attack vessels emerge from it, and I waste no time lacing into them with deadly rotating barrels of blue laser fire. The first to exit are annihilated with no chance to retaliate given.

"Get out of there, Mason," says Sergeant Bentley. "We're auto-targeting smaller vessels and engaging with scat-shots."

My eyes widen. I hit another micro-jump without hesitation. No way I can be in the path of that kind of firepower. Nothing beyond the *Dwarf* can handle it.

I stop a click out and above the *Dwarf* before turning to see them fire. Fifty-one balls of antimatter reconfigured to effect pre-programmed targets release from Bell and Sergeant Bentley's ships to punch across the black like a green horizontal rain seeking to do anything but make friends. Delgado's vessel fires last. I am sure it took her a moment longer without a secondary aboard to help her at the targeting station.

Upriser vessels are hit before they can engage and dissolve into nothing. Fire from the explosions are short-lived and fade from existence without oxygen in space, leaving pieces of them floating to cool in orbit around Wah'Lor.

Scat-shots are the most dangerous thing the Armada has ever created for a flight vessel. Rarely have they been used. Their existence is now justified.

The Flemlace opens fire on the warship, but a single laser rail-gun blast from the *Dwarf* pierces its bow, pushes through its body, and exits its aft. It is more than a formidable shot. It is a fatal one. The concussion expands Captain Menjay's *Flemlace* from front to back like a long, skinny, inflating balloon. The following explosion is a grand one that knocks The *Dwarf* to an angle and sends my squad mates' vessels tumbling through the black like rocks thrown in zero gravity.

"Stabilize," shouts Bell.

"Leveling out," says Sergeant Bentley.

"Same," says Bell. "Delgado?"

"Trying," says Delgado. "You got that thing under control, Sergeant Major? Because I'm having it handed to me right now."

Her vessel is dead in the black and tumbling toward the upper atmosphere.

"Heavy damage from debris," she says. "I'm going down. Planet side."

The spherical cloud of *Flemlace*'s debris continues to grow around us as dozens of Armada vessels break into orbit. Over 30 red-and-black ships emerge from the *Dwarf*'s rear to engage them in combat. Crafts on both sides are damaged in the initial exchange. A few are destroyed. Flashes fill my panes.

A half-dozen Uprisers take into the lower atmosphere. It is unplanned anarchy. There was no time for formations or strategy. This is combat with only the instinct to survive at our disposal.

"Protect the planet," calls the Planetary Sovereign over all channels. "Protect Wah'Lor."

I have had all I can take. That ship is going down. I hit several micro-jumps and fire at different portions of the *Dwarf*. Between each shot it takes at me, I dive against its hull to lose its weapons' line of site and come off in an arch that pushes my starfighter to gravitational forces I can barely handle—which is far more than any other pilot—and I fear breaking my craft. The controls shake in my hands as it attempts to keep pace with me. Blood pressure in my legs burns as I flex the lower muscles throughout my body to keep oxygen in my head.

"I don't think I'm doing anything here," I say with a struggle through the immense G's.

INCOMING

"We have nothing for that thing," says Sergeant Bentley. "Break off. We're going after Delgado."

I pull away and hit another micro-jump two clicks into the black and take back into my high G's vortex as it traces me with multiple guns and periodic laser rail gun blasts. They are going to find their mark if this keeps up. I make another jump from the *Dwarf*, 50 clicks out to leave them wondering where I am, needing its sensors to drop me as a target. It proves to be a decision not in favor of those on the surface of Wah'Lor.

The *Dwarf* ignores me and aims at Armada signatures on the planet to rain destruction upon them. It obliterates many of the vessels we have on Wah'Lor. Tracer rounds leave its underbelly and pierce clouds to ignite small flashes planet-side where they meet their mark. Lives are no doubt being lost. But I am unaware of the numbers. Casualties must be high.

I make another micro-jump and stop a half-click under the *Dwarf* for a shot at its underside. A lower panel 10% the width of the vessel slides back, and a telescoping stem with a bulb lowers from it to open like a wilting flower hanging toward Wah'Lor. Energy builds up at its tip. I must move.

"Thermo-pulses incoming!" I shout.

It fires. The blast lights up my visual feed panes white. They clear up to reveal…

"Sergent Major," I shout. "There's—"

HU-1 is hit at its aft. A continuous wave of energy burns down it longways with a series of thermogenic bombs traveling though it. The beam melts HU-1's top as the explosives enter what has become a home to families. A series of explosions cascade through it with people trying to escape until it is no more—thousands of voices silenced in a single strike from a black heaven above.

My eyes water. Blood boils with an urge to fight.

"I'm killing this glezlock," I say.

I angle up with rotating barrels drilling the *Dwarf*'s black-to-surface weapon. It rips from its stem and falls through the upper atmosphere. I move in and take aim into the open panel on its underside and fire, but it closes when my weapon reaches it. A small explosion tells me a few rounds made it in to cause some internal damage, but the panel closed before I could deal a crippling blow.

"Readjust audio to sync all Armada airborne vessels," I say.

"Comms linked with Armada vessels," says A.I.

"I need everything we have in the black," I say. "We've got to stop the *Dwarf*."

"Sky squads are tied up, Mason," responds Kuzio. "I have three partials heading your way."

Three Armada sky squads from Kuzio's fleet are with me on my six as I pass the *Dwarf* for its topside. There are normally five or more vessels to a squad, but there are two sets of three here to help me. The other only has two ships in it. That is all I am getting for help.

"TOCSIN," shouts Delgado over comms. "TOCSIN."

She is in trouble. Someone will help her. I cannot.

Airborne Armada squads joining me engage the warship from underneath it and move to its topside while opening fire. The *Dwarf* stops moving. Six rotating barrels like my starfighter wields emerge from the attacking ship: one on each of its top, bottom, bow, aft, port, and starboard sides. It opens fire.

Silent explosions with few flames and lots of sparks fill the spots where Kuzio's squads moved in. All but a few of the vessels he sent are gone. I could only stick around as long as I did because of the Beltric and my ability to handle its advanced flight mobility. They did not stand a chance.

INCOMING

"Fall back," I call out over Delgado's shouts of *TOCSIN*.

It is too late. There are only three vessels left of those that came to stand with me against the *Dwarf*.

"Everyone, clear out," says Captain Selk of *Barrows*. "We're ramming this thing out of the black."

"Negative," I say.

"There's only forty-six of us on board," continues Captain Selk. "The rest have ejected in drop pods or left in transports. We've made our decision. Clear out."

Barrows comes full tilt over the planet's horizon with what used to be *Athanasios*'s and the *Ark*'s debris burning up as its pieces hit the friction of Wah'Lor's upper winter atmosphere. Several clicks off them to the left and down is Delgado. She plunges through the upper atmosphere with my squad going after her. The sky, both black and blue, is filled with misery.

Dozens of munition cubes and 50 drop pods release from the *Dwarf*'s underbelly as it takes out the last two vessels from the squadron of fighters that joined me in battle. *Barrows* comes into view, but the *Dwarf* turns its cannon into position to fire.

"Their initiating auto-locks," I say.

I hit another micro-jump and stop, offset between its laser rail guns, cannons, and the incoming *Barrows*. My heart is pounding when I come out of it to draw fire, knowing I have but a fraction of a tik to engage. Its cannon targets me.

I barely get another jump off as the blast sears vertical flight blades on the rear of my starfighter. A tik later, and I look at my rear panes. *Barrows* hits the *Dwarf* at full velocity and pushes partly through it in the process. They crumple together for an instant before releasing an explosive shockwave as they are both instantaneously destroyed.

It is between Wah'Lor and my starfighter, leaving me no choice but to dart farther away from Delgado and the others to avoid the blast. The explosion is massive. Its expanding, disk-like shockwave did not hit Wah'Lor. It did, however, go vertical to create a giant area keeping me at bay from it.

"All visual feed panes to recon squad one's feeds," I say. "All ships. All feeds. Segment if needed."

19-4
Plummet

Delgado's shuttle is lighting up against the upper atmosphere. An approaching Upriser vessel fires an electrostatic blast that clips the backside of her vessel. It holds for a few tiks, then thunders off its hull. Smoke pours from her ship as it falls hard left.

The Upriser's vessel explodes. A Beltric Class Six starfighter emerges from the fiery result.

"Reaper," I say.

"Got him," says Kuzio. "Reengaging."

Kuzio banks down upon four Upriser vessels tailing two Armada transports. The man fires and takes one out while the other three break off. He follows them from sight at a high rate.

A Proximity Alarm sounds out in Delgado's shuttle. Fister looks to his right. She is barreling toward him. He snatches the controls aggressively as her shuttle's smoke and fire engulf their windows.

Fister looks the ship's way as the lesser shuttle passes by.

"Delgado's going down hard," says Fister.

"Delgado," says Sergeant Bentley. "Try to get your—"

Delgado comes into view for a split-tik.

INCOMING

Bentley glances her direction and flinches away. The impact rocks his crew and knocks them to an odd descent angle. Their exposed side-paneling glows hot from atmospheric friction. Alarms go off with red and white lights flashing as Sergeant Bentley panics to regain control of the shuttle. Fister holds tight to his harness.

"*Warning,*" says A.I. "*Fire in transport bay.*"

"Somebody get that," says Sergeant Bentley.

"On it," says Chubb.

"*Damage to panel seven,*" says A.I. "*Warning.*"

Chubb unbuckles. Centrifugal forces toss him to thud his helmet against the wall. It takes a tek to regain his composure and pull himself along the ship's interior.

Delgado struggles. Clouds, warring aircraft, and Wah'Lor spins across her windshield with glimpses of *the Ark* nearing a distant horizon on its freefall from space.

"Code gray," calls Delgado. "Code gray."

Sparks fly from the control panels and knock Chubb across a back section of their vessel as flames erupt.

"Mason," says Sergeant Bentley, "can you access Delgado's primary controls and find out why she doesn't have power?"

"Can't," I answer. "Its systems are fried, and I got a few more tiks before this shockwave dissipates enough for me to assist."

Heat bleeds from my squad's shuttles when they break through the upper atmosphere. They are no longer engulfed in flames, but Delgado's vessel is still smoking under a slow spin.

Bentley regains control of the larger ship, but alarms are still going off.

"Can someone get to Delgado and pair with her descent?" he asks.

"*Warning,*" says A.I. "*Fire in transport bay.*"

"How's it going with that fire?" asks Sergeant Bentley.
"Damage to—"
Sergeant Bentley cuts the vessel's warning audio.

Chubb is fighting with a fire that is growing out of control. The damaged panel is bent outward toward the atmosphere.

"I'm going to need a little help here," says Chubb.

The panel next to Chubb tears loose from Sergeant Bentley's ship. The vacuum puts out the fire but sucks Chubb from the vessel. He curls himself up and shoves his arms and legs out into an 'X' pattern, activating his X-wing suit. He disappears from sight.

Delgado battles to stabilize her descent.

"You're going to have to eject, Delgado," says Sergeant Bentley.

"The door's jammed," shouts Delgado, kicking at the exit.

"Bell," says Sergeant Bentley, "slow her descent."

"Already on my way, Sergeant Major," says Bell.

Bell re-angles to follow Delgado down.

"Locate Chubb," says Bell. "So, I don't hit him."

"Corporal Chubb is no longer onboard the vessel," says A.I.

"Location?" asks Bell.

"Approaching Specialist Delgado," says A.I.

Sergeant Bentley and the other crew members look out their windows. Chubb comes into view and gives a thumbs-up as thrusters on his suit guide his descent for a slower, more controlled free-fall. He points to his mouth and holds his hand up to his helmet, signaling he cannot communicate.

"Can you hear?" asks Sergeant Bentley.

Chubb gives a thumbs up.

"Chubb," says Sergeant Bentley with a sincere tone. "Get Delgado."

Chubb nods his head with equal concern before turning from sight.

Bell's trying to position his shuttle under Delgado's, but it bumps away from him. Chubb comes in hot. His helmet slams into the side of the shuttle door. He barely hangs on to its handle after the blow, but shakes his head and pulls himself to it. An impact like that would have knocked me out.

"Do me a favor, Mason," says Chubb.

"What's that?" I ask.

"Shoot another Upriser or two for me on your way in from the black," he answers.

Delgado steps back and uses her robust mechanized legs to kick the door as Chubb lowers down to examine the bent portion of the frame on its exterior. The ship's hull is dented. Delgado kicks the door again. It almost breaks free. Chubb pulls a rigid piece of equipment from his suit, sticks it in the doorjamb, braces his knees against the hull, and pulls as Delgado steps back to deliver another powerful kick.

Chubb pries hard as the kick lands. The door flies open. It bashes him on the head, and he falls unconscious from the shuttle with the door. My heart sinks as he bounces off its aft wing.

"Chubb" I say.

Bentley sees it happen from the cockpit.

"Sapp," he says.

"On my way," says Sapp.

Sapp leaps from his and Bell's shuttle and activates his X-wing suit. The wind catches him and snatches him away. Delgado stands in the doorway and looks toward Chubb and Sapp for a moment with worried eyes before she jumps.

A pair of parachutes fire from the hips of her mechanical legs at a 45-degree angle. A third chute lunches out from the center of her back and straight into the air. They come together to work as one, compensating for the weight of her robotic legs.

An Upriser patrol vessel passes Delgado with an Armada vessel of the same make chasing it with guns firing. She closes her eyes and turns away but is not hit. Her parachutes spin her around a few times, and she levels out, looking back to see the Armada patrol vessel shoot down the Upriser it was chasing.

Sapp approaches an unconscious Chubb and reels him in after a subtle impact sends them circling around each other. He pulls a cable from his back and clicks it to Chubb's ripcord before easing away from him. Sapp snatches the line on Chubb's parachute and his own simultaneously, launching their chutes to guide Chubb to safety.

"Reroute visual input feeds to this vessel," I say.

The *Dwarf* and *Barrows*' shockwave has dissipated enough. I make my way through it and to the planet. Distant smoke from somewhere over the horizon sheds light on the direction the *Ark* went down. I want to jump over there and confirm, but I am too worried about Chubb. Planet side, that is where I am going. My only fear is seeing the destruction Dolofónos and his Uprisers dished out upon the innocent when I get there.

19-5
Stragglers

I enter the atmosphere and push low. Kuzio is in a five on one battle with a limping starfighter. Below him, the Armada is locked in a skirmish with Uprisers on foot. Shots streak across my panes in all directions: east to west, north to south, and surface-to-air. It is a litter of lights, flashes, and explosions.

INCOMING

"Coming in hot, Kuzio," I say. "Break up."

Kuzio pulls up without hesitation as I open fire. Two Upriser vessels are hit and go down in flames toward a remote snow-covered forest. The reaper air-brakes and drops behind the last airborne enemy as he is hit but gets a shot off from his crippled starfighter before ejecting. We are far from Lesdelop ti'it renasa, and my starfighter only seats one.

"Lieutenant Commander Kuzio's dead in the water," I say. "He had to eject. Noting location now."

His descent is slow. I hover near him to see where he lands. The wind is high, but I do not want to lose him.

"Mason to Kuzio," I say.

No response. He cannot see me. This cockpit adaptation version of the Beltric Class Six is without windows.

Kuzio turns his chute away from thicker areas of trees, but the gusts at higher altitudes are formidable. His arms go limp at his side. His head drops. The wind blows him over the chilled forest below, and blood is running down his lower back, buttock, and legs. Kuzio is in trouble, unconscious, and possibly bleeding out.

An Upriser patrol vessel is approaching from his left to finish the job. I rush to set jump parameters:

```
Duration: 0.1 tiks
Power output: 2.15%
```

My Beltric jumps and comes out of warp between the incoming patrol vessel and Kuzio. A blast rips into the side of my Beltric. It spins.

"*Warning,*" says A.I. "*Power fluctuating in energy bays one and thr—*"

"Silence warning," I say.

The approaching patrol vessel is still targeting Kuzio. It must be. It is not facing me.

The enemy vessel rotates repeatedly from right to left across my viewing panes in brief glimpses as I twist through the air. My shot needs to be timed perfectly. I count the passes in my head as dots for a rhythm.

"Dot," I say, awaiting but a few tics for the next pass. "Dot. Dot."

I fire. There is smoke passing across my panes now, but the patrol vessel is nowhere in sight. I look over the manual flight controls and at the radiant H.U.D. Controls show a few things of concern:

> Altitude—1.31 and falling.
> Click Speed—1cps, erratic.
> Engine field temperature—3,309 kelvin, overheating.

"Purge power bays one and three," I say.

"Power bay one and three purged," says A.I.

I take control of the Beltric and level out. The Upriser patrol vessel went down somewhere in the snow-capped forest about two point three clicks from here with a trail of smoke leading to where it crashed. Flames rise from the point of impact with no sign of parachute deployment. The pilot probably did not survive.

"Kuzio," I say. "Mason to Kuzio. Do you read me?"

I coast the overheating Beltric Class Six above nearby trees in search of him.

"Scan for surface life signs," I say. "My size or larger."

"Unable to scan," says A.I. *"Systems are—"*

"Forget it," I say, looking back at my H.U.D.

Engine temperatures continue to climb. I must get this thing into the black or into the snow soon.

"We need you back here, Mason," says Sergeant Bentley. "Check for stragglers. We're pushing back the rest of the birds now."

"Kuzio's down," I say. I lost him.

"And his location?" he asks.

"General," I answer. "And I need to cool the Beltric five teks ago."

A few shots echo over his comms.

"Remember the area," says Sergeant Bentley, "and get back here now."

I must return to the scene of battle with doubts low on Kuzio's health. A fleeting moment passes as I look into the area I last saw him.

"Good luck, Reaper," I say, turning my Starfighter back toward Lesdelop ti'it renasa.

19-6
Cooldown

A few Upriser vessels are in the area when I return, but they are retreating. The skies over Lesdelop are clear of enemy crafts. Small firefights are still going heavy near HU-2 and the smoldering fragments of what used to be HU-1. It is about to be over.

I study a group of four Armada soldiers and a civilian with a rifle in hand. They are taking cover behind a tipped medical transport. Across from them are three Uprisers firing behind an out-of-commission patrol unit on our makeshift airfield with a slew of other decimated vessels ablaze. A second skirmish is underway on the other side of the field, but I will handle this first.

I move in on them and open fire while passing overhead. Anyone not in Armada or Kla'Wah attire's bodies rip apart as I coast over their heads. It does not feel good to kill even scum, but ending three could save hundreds or more.

A U-turn leads me back for a second pass over the other skirmish. I take small arms fire until I reach them. It clanks and ricochets off my vessel. Another volley of shots for the two enemy squads and the rest of our attackers make a run for the tree line, only to be mowed down by Armada gunfire—shot in the back like the scum they are.

"I'm double-checking the skies," I say. "But I think they retreated for now."

"For now," says Sergeant Bentley. "Head to the black and check low orbit for a bit to cool off that starfighter."

"Yes, Sergeant Major," I say.

"Sergeant Major," says Dr. Sellers. "I'm going to reach out to some of the other squads and housing units to get a casualty count. We're going to need everyone with medical training we can get."

I pull up high and search the clouds for hiding Uprisers. Several teks pass.

"Nothing in the clouds that I can see," I say. "Dropping to check closer to ground level one last time."

There are no other vessels in the air that I can see during my return path toward the surface of Wah'Lor, but they are not trackable. I cannot tell where or what directions they took off to. They have a game plan. Of that, I am sure, but I do not know how many Uprisers made it to the surface or which ones were on the ships we destroyed.

"Mason," says Dr. Wright. "Check high orbit before you return. I don't want any more surprises."

"Yes, sir," I say. "Just confirmed that with Sergeant Bentley."

"Apologies, Mason. Comms were down here. Dr. Wright out."

INCOMING

I turn back toward the black. It is littered with small fragments of once large interstellar crafts. *Barrows, Flemlace*, the *Dwarf,* and *Athanasios* are no more. What remains of their larger sections is now in the distance and breaching the upper atmosphere, just as the *Ark* did. They will land somewhere far from here. Perhaps they will reach the oceans before they settle down.

"Local orbit clear," I say. "Powering down all but life support for a temperature drop."

"Head back when you can, Mason," says Sergeant Bentley. "We're going to need all the hands we can get down here."

I sit in thought while powering down everything but what I need to keep me alive. A small light barely illuminates the cockpit enough for me to see the manual controls and a few switches that mean nothing to me right now. My thoughts are with those on the surface.

CHAPTER 20
Aftermath

It is time for me to return and see what lies in the wake of this horrific attack. The fight took thousands of lives in the unfolding black battle. I do not know how bad it is at ground level yet. Nor do I know if any of the Dah'Sel were caught up in our misfortune.

I lower the starfighter cockpit delicately through Wah'Lor's upper atmosphere, not wanting to see what I am about to. We lost orbiting vessels along with any crew members onboard. I swallow hard, think about it, and worry about those I care for.

Pillowy clouds offering no comfort disappear from around me as I dive cautiously through them. Dolofónos has left a terrible visual for me to gaze upon while drifting to the surface: HU-1 is off the grid and no longer exists beyond fragments strewn amongst a once snow-covered field now melting in response to the fiery debris and hot metallics littering it. HU-2 is 75 percent intact. Dark smoke rises from its demolished aft.

Bodies… So many of them. A civilian family wearing what used to be matching blues and browns of high-end fashion tells me they were wealthy financial donators to the Armada cause. Their prosperity got them here and killed them. A family of five: a mother, father, two girls, and a boy; all dead sooner than they would have been if they had remained on Kep Four.

Armada soldiers and Uprisers are motionless in the field as far as the eye can see between damaged and undamaged tele-tents, amid them and Lesdelop, strewn around what used to be HU-1, and spread across the field like random splashes of paint flicked from a brush wielded by the blind. Cooked... Shot... Some are in pieces and unrecognizable. An arm sits by itself a few paces ahead of me as I walk.

People are crying, but I cannot focus on any one person. My senses and emotions are overwhelmed. The smell of burning metal, flesh, wood, and trees mix in my nostrils.

Salty water builds up to burn my eyes. I close them and try not to cry with the others while wiping away fragments of tears that made their way out to join another horrible example of humanity that will join our historical archives. Finding the strength to help is a challenge. I must overcome it. I bite my bottom lip before turning my attention to Lesdelop ti'it renasa.

Dah'Sel and humans running across the open area near Lesdelop come into view like specs of dust that get larger as I descend. Dah'Sel mothers run from the structure to snatch curious and upset children inside.

"*Vula,*" shouts a Dah'Sel mother, dragging two of her youth inside. "*Vula rot. Rot!*"

Dah'Sel fathers emerge to help and make their way across the battlefield when their little ones are out of sight. They rush onto the field with the bravery and calm demeanors I am looking for. Two of them stop to help wounded Armada soldiers near Lesdelop while dozens of others press across the field. Uprisers are passed up and left to die where they lie.

What few medical transport vessels there are have teamed up with standard transports to rush wounded from devastation to a patch of land still covered with snow. There are so many bodies. Too many to count. People are walking the fields and checking the wrists and necks of the downed for pulses, chests for breathing, and bodies for any signs of life.

The Dah'Sel had never seen technology before our arrival. They know now what it is capable of in the hands of a toxic race, like humans. They may not forgive us for this. It is our fault as a whole; it happened because we came here.

We will forever be our downfall.

I pray to no one for our species and not just those living through this. I long for a promising future. No matter how advanced we have become as the cycles pass, over time, nothing has changed. We are always going to have people in our populace who think violence is the answer. Personally, I have never taken a life until moments ago in the black defending Wah'Lor, but I do not consider it murder. I am saddened my actions were necessary. This rotation will haunt me for the rest of my life.

"Locate Corporal Chubb and set course," I say.

"Corporal Chubb not found," says A.I.

"Locate Sergeant Bentley and set course," I say.

A mapped trajectory plots a waypoint on my H.U.D. I bank right to land beside them. My squad is only one click away. I could not get there fast enough if I wanted to.

20-2
Fallen

I set the starfighter down 20 paces from my squad. Chubb lies in the snow with Dr. Sellers over him. I cannot tell if he is breathing or not.

"Is he okay?" I ask.

My approach is frantic with shaky steps. Dr. Sellers turns to me, and I know the answer. They do not have to speak to tell me. I almost wish they would not, but the question has already been asked.

"He..." answers Delgado, with watering eyes. "He didn't make it."

"But I thought you guys got him," I say. "I saw Sapp ... he was..."

"His spinal cord was severed at the base of his skull when he hit the back of the Bomba Class," says Dr. Sellers. "If we still had *Athanasios*, maybe we could have saved him. I don't know. There's nothing we can do now."

I turn my back to them and place the palms of my hands over my eyes. It takes a moment to gather myself. It is hard to process. So much happened so fast.

"Mason," says Sergeant Bentley.

I do not respond.

"Dr. Wright didn't make it either," continues Sergeant Bentley. "His drop pod, along with several others, were damaged by ejecting debris from *Athanasios* or hit during the exchange of fire in the black. We don't know how many yet, but, without a functioning link to *Athanasios*, some never slowed before impacting the planet."

My eyes water as I open them to run my fingers through my hair. The visual before me cannot be unseen: HU-1 is fragmented and smoldering. Dah'Sel and humans alike are being dragged across the field. Parents and children on both sides are crying and wandering around aimlessly, calling out for missing loved ones. The only glimmer of hope I see through these watering eyes is the fact that none of the Dah'Sel structures were damaged. I do not think they are going to see humanity the same after this.

"Where's Pru'Cet?" I ask.

"We haven't seen him," answers Sergeant Bentley. "We haven't left Chubb's side yet, but we need to. We have to help the others."

Even the calm panic. I do not know if he is hiding it or not, but Sergeant Bentley remains steadfast, logical, and right. We must help all we can. It is the only thing we can do.

I walk across the field toward pandemonium with a core-sinking feeling farther than my feet in the snow. Nothing is right about this. Serenity has fallen.

20-3
Choosing Lives

Damage before me overwhelms my thoughts as I approach it. My pulse races to keep up with the panic in my steps. It is hard to focus.

There are so many wounded, dead, and still smoldering in the snow. The smell of burning flesh, paint, relon, and who knows what else is mixing in the air for an emotionally and physically painful eye-watering sensation. It is the smell of suffering.

I break into a jog when the wrecked, unfinished Armada edu-center comes into view. An impact on my left sends me spinning to the snow. Someone runs into me. I look to see who it is. The person who bumped me lands close by in scorched Armada attire. It is a new transplant from Kep Four.

"I'm sorry," I say.

He is severely burned and face down in the snow with hair seared from his head. I stand and help him up but snatch my hands back upon touching his sides.

"Ah," I shout in pain.

He picks himself up. A charred child is pushed into the snow under where he landed. The man's clothes are still smoldering and hot to the touch as he leans down to grab his kid. I step back, trembling with worry as he pulls the toddler he was carrying from the snow.

"Is your baby..." I ask. "We need to get you guys to—"

He stands and turns to face me. It is a woman. The child's mother, I assume. Her upper body was so charred ... I could not tell she was female. She makes eye contact with me for an instant and takes off with her child again.

My principles tell me I should pursue them, but I am frozen here. Overwhelmed would be an underestimation of what is happening within and around me. Neither life nor the Armada has prepared me for such a calamitous event.

A far-off Dah'Sel catches my attention, weeping several paces beyond the edu-center I was heading to. My steps quicken. I recognize him. It is Wat'Uza. He is cradling someone in his arms.

I cannot accept it as I grow closer. I must be mistaken.

"Wat'Uza," I call as smoke rolls past me.

Burning, dry eyes stop me in my tracks. It enters my lungs. I cough until I hit my knees and move my nose and mouth close to the snow, dig a small hole to get under the smoke, and lower my head into it. The smoke rolls over me until the wind takes it in another direction. A few deep breaths, and I open my eyes to stand.

"*Wat'Uza, ka ama jelq?*" I ask.

He does not respond. I get closer to realize he is holding Wete'Uza in his arms. My steps come to a fast halt. My breathing shifts to nearly nothing as I cover my mouth and turn away, unable to see the Dah'Sel leader cradling the empty vessel once carrying the love of his life.

"Pru'Cet?" I call out. "Tila'Cet?" I dodge an Argos rolling my direction toward HU-2 and run across the field toward Lesdelop ti'it renasa. "Nala'Cet? Bah'Cet?"

I reach their home structure. Its guards wave me in.

"Pru…" I call out again, looking into the main hall.

Dah'Sel women and children are crying in the main corridor. I investigate the small room to my left, where I stayed the other rotation. It is full of the same, all hiding from the madness outside.

I ease further into Lesdelop. A room to my right has wounded Dah'Sel inside. They are being cared for by other members of their sect. Their wounds do not look severe compared to what lies in the surrounding fields: an adult male's broken arm is being wrapped in a splint—light blood on the hair of a young female from a minor cut. They glance my way for but a tik before looking away from me.

I am hit with a wave of fearful eyes as I move from the corridor to the open area. Sixty-plus people have gathered here to escape maltreatment from the Uprisers. I do not want to push through them toward the back of the structure in search of the 'Cets and decide to look for them outside.

I exit Lesdelop ti'it renasa and make my way across the field. Dozens of vessels once airborne are piled into a smaller region near the airfield where youth often gather. I head in that direction. A female Armada member with an open gash the size of my palm bleeding on the top of her head grabs me by the arm.

"Where's Marku?" she asks. "Have you seen Marku?"

"I don't know a Marku," I answer. "Where did you see him last?"

"Please tell me where he is," she continues. "I can't find him in this place. Where am I?"

"I'm sorry," I say, pulling away from her. "I'm so sorry."

The hairless patch of red with skin folded back on the top of her head, mixed with her words, tells me she has brain damage, temporary or not. I have my own people to find. At

AFTERMATH

least, that is what I tell myself, to shake the guilt of leaving her hemorrhaging in the snow.

I am a quarter-click from the edge of the airfield and step gingerly through sharp metal fragments of what used to be vessels. Armada personnel and Dah'Sel lie pulseless in upriser-delivered grief. Several from Kep Four and Wah'Lor cry under broken steps in search of family and friends. My face crinkles with their suffering. Further tears flow as I turn to look behind me, unsure of where to go. There is nobody I can help here, and I am becoming overpowered by it all.

"Mason," calls Sapp, "in here."

I follow him into HU-2. It was 300 paces wide and 1,400 paces long before the attack. I cannot tell if I am in the forward or aft section of what used to be a ship. Bodies lie in some areas. Other sections are disintegrated to the point potential survivors or victims in them will no longer have a place to stay.

Melted metallic objects with sharp edges line every step. Small bouts of sparks and electrical currents periodically show themselves as a warning not to touch. Sapp leads me to what I can only assume is the forward. It is hard to tell; I am turned around, and stepping over this charred body is far from helping me concentrate.

Sergeant Bentley steps over debris with a small woman slumped over his shoulder that is missing a leg. She is not bleeding. Whatever took it from her cauterized the wound.

"There are more," says Sergeant Bentley. "We're getting everybody into the field in case what's left of this section collapses."

I nod as he passes. He is right. We must get everybody into the field before this thing decides to go up in some unknown chemical reaction.

"Mason," says Sapp.

I did not realize I had stopped walking.

"Yeah," I say and follow him again.

Shock must be setting in. Mental, not physical. Fight or flight mode is kicking in, and I know of nothing I can do other than avoid flight mode and save some lives. I must focus on helping people.

"Here," says Sapp. "In the foreword."

We enter what used to be a forward on a magnificent vessel to see dozens injured or worse. Bell is trying to get a few onto his shoulders and carry them out. Fister is helping a large, wounded man across the battered floor over wreckage.

I approach the only person light enough for me to pick up—a small child with a badly-broken broken leg, crying over what I think is her parents. I lift her. She struggles against me to stay with them, but I cannot allow it. If she does not come with me for a Mizophile injection soon, infection in her protruding tibia will set in.

"I'm sorry, honey," I say as she screams in pain. "I know. I know. I know. I'm sorry."

I wrestle her into me until she submits to embrace me with sobs.

"Mommy," she cries in my arms. "Mommy ... Daddy"

Her pleas continue as I carry her, tripping over something I did not see before rounding the corner of a waist-tall piece of flayed metal protruding from HU-2's floor that used to be a wall. Cries for her parents ... they are blatant screams from a broken child lost in a world she can no longer understand. My chest heaves with weeping, bonding with her pain as I rescue a child who would rather stay with her parents and die than leave them.

AFTERMATH

20-4
Field of Emotion

I carry her across melted regions of snow until I am in a portion of the field that is knee-deep with it. Adrenaline has given my body the strength to continue carrying her but has not fortified my sentiments. She is holding me now and no longer fighting back. Even for a child, acceptance is an unavoidable destination during a journey with no veils to cover the truth.

So many wounded... So many weeping... So many lost...

Hundreds of people are laid out here with black thermal-cloth wraps around them that warm when in contact with anything cold. Dr. Sellers and a few others are taking readings as fast as possible to dose them properly. They cannot keep up with the inflow of injured. There are Dah'Sel here as well, but their fatality numbers are much less.

The watery image hits hard through dripping eyes as I near them. I am wounded, though nobody can see it. An unseen knife targeting empathy pierces my spirit. I try to remain strong but turn away when several sections of the *Dwarf* and *Flemlace* reach the planet's surface in my peripheral, sending snow-covered fragments from a faraway mountaintop into the air. I look up. A meteor shower of technology flows through the sky in the far distance behind Lesdelop ti'it renasa.

I am shaking. My arms are getting tired. I do not know why I am so weak.

The child I carry cries out in pain again. I stop and check on her 200 paces from Dr. Sellers. Mental strength leaves me as I reposition her in my arms.

I lay my back on a bank of snow. It is deeper than both of our torsos are in thickness from front to back once laid down. I keep the child on my chest to keep her from freezing. Somebody will notice us offset from the rest of the wounded and come to our aid soon.

For now, I lay with a cold planet pressing into the medical gown my doctors had me in while I was in a medically induced coma. I had not noticed it until just now, the cold, that is. Shock has worn off. Reality sets in.

My feet and hands burn from icy surroundings. A watery-eyed blank stare over a quivering bottom lip is the best I can do to fake strength for this little girl until they reach us. The least I can do is keep her warm.

Dr. Wright is gone, Chubb is gone, and our population continues to dwindle with this attack. The Dah'Sel leader has lost his union partner, and I have not seen the 'Cets yet. I only know this child needs me. I will watch the sky turn black before I leave her, be this our final resting place or not.

Time passes to drag on the cries of others. I am no longer shaking, but I know what that means. Breaths are shallow—the first stages of hyperthermia.

"I got her," says Sergeant Bentley, hoisting the little girl from me. "Get Mason to her tele-tent and changed."

Delgado pulls me from the ground with an Armada transplant I do not know but am happy to see. They carry me toward my tele-tent as I watch the little girl that I saved in Sergeant Bentley's arms with Dr. Sellers approaching them. She is asleep from either the cold, trauma, or both.

CHAPTER 21
Bereavement

Uprisers have thrown a globe of peace into turmoil while its inhabitants suffer. Something along those lines should be the human motto in general, but they have ensured we will never escape such phrasing.

"Over here," calls someone in the Armada. "Over here."

I cannot see them from where I am.

"Position indicated," calls another Armada member.

My hands, now gloved but still cold, dig into the snow. What started as a foot revealed a leg, hips, and torso. Whoever he was, I do not think he is alive buried in this mound of ice piled upon him after an Upriser craft slid to its last resting place.

His wrist comes into view as I dig, and I remove my right glove to check his pulse. Nothing.

I stand, slide my glove back on, and pull a small red flag attached to a thin metal rod from a pouch on my side and stick it into the white.

"Position indicated," I call out.

Sweat builds inside my clothes as I wipe it from my forehead in the frigged weather. I need to work slower. The building dampness between my skin and garments could lead to hyperthermia or frostbite when I stop moving if I cannot get to a warm place. Better safe than sorry.

I move to my ... I do not know ... twentieth body in the field? Black flakes of skin are peeling away to reveal pink flesh beneath it. He is burned and has three gunshot wounds in his torso. There is no way he is alive, but I remove my glove, step in, and check his pulse.

My hand to his wrist. Two fingers feel ... nothing.

"Position indicated," I call, sticking another red flag into the ground.

"Position indicated," call three others in the field.

I step over a piece of an unknown transport, possibly an aircraft, and walk around another. It might be something from the housing unit.

HU-1 is unrecognizable. All inside the construct died a quick death. At least, that is what I keep telling myself.

Engineers and electricians are at the back and sides of it working to shut down its power cores for safe entry. No one can enter yet. Electricity circulating it and a rise in thorium levels. It will need a full purge before being swept for non-existent survivors. Half of it is still up in flames.

Several areas of Wah'Lor's forest regions are ablaze near downed fighter vessels. The fires are not spreading quickly with the snow being thicker out there. Trees here are resilient, but we must address it soon. The Armada labor force is low and focused on saving lives at the moment, and the Dah'Sel have left us to clean up our enemies' mess.

Another body comes into view. Female. Several gunshot wounds speckle her legs, and there is a piece of shrapnel lodged under her lower left floating ribs.

I move to check her vitals and...

"Help," she says. "Please help me."

"I got one," I shout, rushing to her side.

BEREAVEMENT

I push a signal stick into the snow with its wick up and pinch its glass tip between my fingers. It breaks, and a green billow rises from it.

"You're going to be okay," I say. "Help's on the way."

I remove a thermal cloth wrap from the pouch on my other hip and lift her left side to snug it under her, then repeat the process on her right side.

"I'm..." she says as her eyes roll back and close.

"Stay with me," I say. "What's your name?"

She does not respond. I shake her shoulders.

"Hey," I say.

I cannot feel a pulse and scan the field of snow. A male Armada medic is jogging toward us.

"I need a revival kit," I say.

The medic turns back to look behind him, placing his hands on his cheeks to amplify his voice.

"Revival kit," shouts the Medic.

He reaches us and pulls a telescopic field gurney from the top of his backpack. Two shorter rods connect the ends of two longer ones at their tips. A relon sheet connects them in the middle. He pulls the two longer rods to expand them, and they click into position. The telescopic field gurney extends on its own until it is large enough to haul a human on.

"Give me a hand," he says.

I grab her legs while he grabs her torso from under her armpits.

"And..." he says. "Go."

We hoist her from the snow and place her on the field gurney.

"Alright," he continues, turning his back to her, squatting down, and grabbing the handles. "Let's pick her up ... and go."

I squat and lift with my legs. He takes sidesteps to his left with the gurney to line up with HU-2 and takes the lead. I follow.

An Armada patrol vessel flies overhead to ensure we do not get caught off-guard again. I study it for a tek but feel no reassurance. This is not a war for resources, a fight against classes, poverty, or territory. It is personal and will not end until one side of the equation is deleted.

"Revival kit," calls an approaching female medic.

"Here," I say.

We set the gurney into the snow.

The female medic runs up and drops to her knees with the kit—a small box that automatically targets the nearest lifeform without a pulse for resuscitation once activated. She unbuckles its clasp and slides back the lid.

"Clear," she says, turning a dial and pressing a button to activate it.

The revival kit powers on. Small relon-coated arms with metallic pads at the ends telescope out and over the lady on the gurney and press to her chest. It beeps, reads her vitals, and sends a visible electrical current through her clothing. The lady's chest and lower back jump from the shock. She gasps as the telescopic arms retract.

Her chest rises and falls with deep breaths. Her eyes open. She panics.

"My name's Fielding," says the male medic. "Med. Fielding. I'm here to help you."

The lady passes out.

"Let's move," says Med. Fielding.

We lift her and head toward HU-2 again.

"Revival kit," calls someone from an unknown location.

The female medic grabs the revival kit and runs toward to next victim.

BEREAVEMENT

"We're almost there," I say.

We enter the undamaged side of HU-2. The smell of smoke and burning electrical wires is thick in the air. A battered, dirty, and bleeding father and mother at the far right of the entrance hold a lifeless little boy in their arms with hollow expressions.

"I need any available surgeon," calls Med. Fielding.

A nurse coordinating trauma injury approaches.

"They're all in surgery right now," she says. "How bad is she?"

Fielding pulls back the thermal cloth wrap to reveal the lady's wounds.

"Severe," he answers. "We already lost her once."

"How much training do you have?" she asks.

"Basic field surgery," answers Med. Fielding. "Nothing more."

"This way," she says.

We follow her past the wounded and dying, more dead than alive, and into an empty room. Blood lines an operating table with a crude operating light tied with a rope to hang above it. The nurse wipes down the table.

"Put her here," she says.

We set the gurney on the table and slide it out from under her.

"Are you qualified to assist?" asks the nurse.

I shake my head.

"No."

"Can someone else take care of influx?" she calls across HU-2.

No response. She looks at the male medic.

"Okay," she says. "You lead. I'll assist."

"I can't do this," says Med. Fielding. "I've only—"

"You're doing it," interrupts the nurse, turning her attention to me. "Mason, is it? Go assist the geo-protection units. You'll be more help there."

I watch for a tik. She pulls a cart of surgical tools next to the table as Med. Fielding cuts back the lady's clothes. The nurse eyes me and points toward the entrance.

"Go," she says.

I turn and exit. Steps are slow. Thoughts are high.

The little girl I rescued is on a gurney with 20 or more injured, recovering, or dying in an open area of HU-2 around her. I did not notice them on the way in. Her leg is missing and bandaged. They must have amputated it.

A tall, lean doctor with fresh stitches in his ear wheels out a patient whose head is wrapped in its entirety. His assistant locks the bed's wheels as the doctor moves to check on the little girl.

"Excuse me," I say. "Doctor?"

He stops.

"It's Dr. Lasor," he says. "Can I help you?"

"Is that little girl going to make it?" I ask.

"She'll make it," he answers, walking to his next patient.

He is too busy to talk, which is a hint that I should be as well.

I exit what remains of HU-2 and move across a heartbroken field to its backside. The forest starts half a click from here. Flames have most likely spread since earlier.

21-2
Cold Embers

I enter the forest edge and move under aganite trees. A downed Upriser's vessel too busted to tell its make is on fire 40 paces out. Aganites around me are burned but never

BEREAVEMENT

caught fire. Their amber-colored timber's concentration of iron is high enough that they are unaffected by standard fire.

Planetary Protection Units are not fighting the craft's flames. Their mission is to perform controlled burns around disabled aircraft and ground transports in wooded areas. I do not know how to help them, but I will try.

"Mason," says Fister. "You're with me on this."

Fister, as defined by Commander Helmwoke before we made the jump to Wah'Lor, is a self-proclaimed firebug with an addiction to incinerating devices. I bet he finds solace from the mortality in the fields here and is comfortable in the bright orange fire protective suit he has on.

"Take this," he says, handing me a shovel. "Dig a line six paces out from the fire like they're doing over there."

He points to an area of fire with no fallen vessels around it. Three men are digging the top layer of vegetation from an area around the fire. It is not what I expected to do here.

This is hard work in frozen ground. I do not have the bodyweight needed and jump on the shovel's step with both feet several times to get its spade tip into the soil. The scoop is heavy, but I toss it over my left shoulder into a snowless patch.

Fister has a mid-sized fuel tank on his back with a line running to a tubular rod with a homemade trigger behind a small flame. He squeezes the trigger and sprays the ground with fire.

"That doesn't look like an Armada-issued thrower," I say.

"It's not," says Fister. "Made it myself. You like?"

"Looks dangerous," I answer. "Do I get assistance like the group over there, or am I digging all this myself?"

He studies the other group of workers and grabs a fire deterrent canister from a stack next to a tree behind him.

"I have these," he says.

They are foot-length, green, cylindrical canisters of highly compressed mixtures designed to put out fires and cool surfaces so objects can be handled immediately after. Fire deterrent canisters can spray from their top nozzle or be set to pop after five tiks with the pull of a pin. Handy when needed, but heavy to tote around.

"Then why do you need me?" I ask.

"Need is a strong word," he answers, setting down the canister. "But I could tell you wanted to be here instead of in the field."

"Thoughtful," I say, placing my hands on my hips to eye him. "Why don't you give me that and you take the shovel?"

"Not a—"

The tank portion of Fister's improvised flame thrower pops. A hiss follows. He unstraps, strips the canister from his back, tosses it into the woods, and grabs a fire deterrent canister.

"Ruuuun!" he shouts.

He does not have to tell me a second time before I take off. A few tiks later, I hear the boom and hit the snow. The sound of crinkling leaves fills the air.

"You guys, okay?" asks one of the other workers.

Fister looks at me for confirmation. I give him a nod, still unsure what happened.

"We're good over here," answers Fister, holding up the fire deterrent canister.

The others go back to work. As crazy as Fister can get, he is trusted around fire.

"What was that?" I ask, pulling myself from the snow.

"Let's just say I'm not salvaging scraps to make things anymore," he answers. "Unless I can test their structural integrity." He pulls the fire deterrent canister's pin. "Popping it."

I take a few steps back.

BEREAVEMENT

"Four," he continues. "Three. Two."

Fister tosses it over the fire he started. It pops to spray a glistening mist over the area and settles slowly. The fire dies down quickly and goes away. Steam rises into the treetops above.

"Are we done here yet?" I ask.

I watch him, unsure how I feel about working around his self-replicated tools of destruction.

"Still have four more fires to go," answers Fister. "Counting this one."

He grabs another canister from the ground, pulls the pin, and tosses it over a second set of flames to smother them.

"Why aren't they using them instead of digging?" I ask, motioning to the other workers.

"They're conserving resources," he answers.

"And you?" I ask.

Fister looks through the trees toward the field.

"Grieving," he answers. "You go ahead. I'll go pop these on the rest."

"And you're sure you don't need me?" I ask.

He raises his brows and gives me a stare.

"Alright," I say. "I'm out."

I turn to leave the scene and head back into fields of dread. It is easy to understand why he is out here. Nobody wants to be in the fields right now, but it must be done.

The trees clear my line of sight, and I push onto the field. There are only a few things left to do: search for bodies in hopes of finding another survivor, clean up the wreckage, or count bodies as they are hauled in and identified.

None of those are calling to me. It will be over soon. That is what I force myself to believe.

21-3
The Missing Reaper

Armada members haul bodies and drag pieces of HU-1, airfield wreckage, and general scrap to a large pile east of HU-2. Remnants of fire loom in the form of smoke that refuses to stop rising from hot embers. It will all have to be recycled, eventually.

I drag a long, thin piece of a Bomba Class 1 fighter to the pile. It is heavy. My breaths are labored—arms tired, thighs burning—but I cannot not yield. An attack could come at any time, so we must prepare for battle.

Sergeant Bentley is carrying half of the steering helm to an A.A.T.V.. His back arches as he walks with the heavy object. Delgado has a tow strap tied around the hip area of her lower robotics. She leans forward to drag a bulky sled full of metal behind her. Sapp carries something I cannot make out beside her as they walk.

I drop my haul against the rest of the rubbish and place my hands on top of my head for a few deep lungs full of needed air, thinking about someone who still needs me. There is no way to tell if he is alive or not, but I need to know. The thought of him dying alone in the cold or being eaten alive by some animal is getting to me.

"Sergeant Major," I say.

He drops the steering helm into the pile. It lands with a hard clank.

"Go ahead, Mason," he says.

"Has anyone heard from Kuzio?" I ask.

"I'm afraid not," he answers. "From what you told me, he didn't make it."

"Sir," I say, pausing in thought. "I need to find out."

He eyes me for a moment. I can feel his connection to what I am going through. He understands why I want this. He nods.

"Confirmed, Mason," he says. "Take Delgado with you in a Plegma Nine if we have one left. EMP drive only. Full mask. If you can't find him visually, come back. No scans. Nothing that can be traced, detected, of pinged. Is that clear?"

"Yes, Sergeant Major," I answer. "And thank you."

"Delgado," he says, "You're with Mason. She'll explain. Me and Sapp will unload this for you."

She unhooks from the sled and drops the towrope in the snow.

"This way," I say.

She moves to my side and walks with me to the shattered airfield.

21-4
Plegma Nine

Chatter from both languages fills the air like unwanted whispers as we walk. Delgado has spoken exactly zero words. Her eyes are colder than the ground beneath my terra boots—her expression numb as I explain what we are about to do. She has shut everything out. I envy that.

The airfield is empty compared to what was there before the attack. Vessels are still patrolling the overhead sky as guardians of our clouds. Of the five or six that remain on the ground, three are damaged.

Workers are towing vessels broken beyond repair to the scrap pile. Dragging the vessels has carved long trenches into the ground. A worker approaches us as we near the Plegma Nine.

"This area is off limits until we get it sorted out," says the worker. "Going to have to ask you to turn tail on this one."

"We're here on orders directly from Sergeant Major Bentley," says Delgado. "We're going to find Kuzio. So, step aside, or I'll step you aside."

The worker looks from her to me and back.

"Go ahead," says the worker.

The worker moves to another vessel to examine it and turns back as we enter the Plegma Nine.

"Ladies," says the worker. "The steering grid on the Plegma is finicky. Took a shot from the blue during an Upriser fly over."

I walk to the other side of the vessel. There is a long crack along its underbelly, but it looks flyable.

"It'll have to do," I say.

We climb into the Plegma and power it up. There are no input codes or commands needed. Those were wiped when the vessels arrived here, unaware we would ever see the face of evil again.

21-5
S & R

That worker was right. The steering on this thing is inaccurate. It is a constant struggle to fly in a straight line. This is a problem, especially with the importance of time management during a search and rescue. Precision is key, and my flight of path is true. Yet, our Plegma Nine's nose points left at a 45-degree angle. I am constantly counter-correcting to the right—an odd sensation for a seasoned pilot, but I can handle it.

We near the crisp treetops where I last saw Kuzio.

"Stopping here," I say, easing our Plegma Nine to a halt over the trees to look around.

Kuzio must be here somewhere unless nature has claimed him.

"Is this the area?" asks Delgado.

"Yeah," I answer, "but I'm not sure how far the wind took him. I was in a locked in combat when he went down."

A tiny cloud of smoke is almost unnoticeable far to my left.

"You see that?" I ask, pointing to it.

"What?" asks Delgado. "Is that where Kuzio crashed?"

"No," I answer. "That's the Upriser vessel that fired on him when he parachuted down. I took it out, but Kuzio was unconscious from my vantage."

I guide the Plegma forward and lower it close to the treetops.

"Kuzio was headed this way last I saw him," I say. "Keep an eye out."

She looks directly through the translucent floor, past the cracked underbelly that looks like broken glass, and into the trees. I do the same through manual flight controls. Everything is under mask. We are not visible to the outside world.

"I hope he isn't looking for us," says Delgado. "He won't be able to see or hear us if he is."

"I can lower the mask for a tek," I say.

"Wasn't Bentleys orders," she says, "and it could get us killed. We don't know who's down there."

She is correct. It would leave us vulnerable. We are not formidable in a Plegma Nine.

I continue forward and low, barely missing the flora below. We search in a grid pattern for nearly two taks, and power reserves are running low on the Plegma. I hope we find him soon.

"Stop," says Delgado. "I think I saw something. Back up."

I reverse our vessel. Time ticks.

"There!" she shouts, pointing to the other side of a grouping of trees. "I see him. Squeeze us in there."

The fit is tight. Our Plegma brushes the white powder from bending leaves as we lower down, then I see it. A parachute is entangled in lower branches.

His body hangs lifelessly from his harness. His feet are only a half pace from the ground.

"You think he's...?" I ask.

"Don't speculate," says Delgado. "We don't know yet."

The vessel touches down. We open the doors and exit. There he is, less than a few paces away. Delgado approaches him and reaches up to check his pulse. My breathing halts in anticipation.

"I think he has a pulse," she says, "but it's weak. Let's get him down."

She pulls a T-blade from her robotic legs and cuts him down while I hold him up. He is too heavy for me and falls. Delgado catches him by the torso. His body hangs limp in her arms.

"Kuzio," I say. "Kuzio, can you hear me?"

He does not respond. Kuzio's head flops over Delgado's arm. His face comes into view with closed eyes and pale skin approaching a light blue in color.

"Hurry," says Delgado. "He's cold. Let's get him into the Plegma and back to HU-2 medical."

We lay him on the translucent sphere we call a Plegma Nine's floor and take off. Time is not on his side. He saved lives during the attack and risked his own to protect us. It is people like him I aspire to be like. All I can do now is fly.

BEREAVEMENT

21-6
Burial

We flew in with bodies speckling the ground under us. Medics met us near HU-2 when we touched down and took Kuzio straight in to treat him. His condition is unknown.

Our numbers were just over 30,000 before the attack, with hundreds of thousands still to come. Now, we are down to 673 with few soldiers, scientists, or doctors remaining. Almost everyone was in HU-1 when that monster came through the wormhole. We have no exact count of the dead yet. The *Dwarf* incinerated many, but there are 24,000 lying in the quarter-click trench dug for their bodies.

The air is ripe with the smell of cooling flesh. I pretend it is not in the air, but no one can hide from it. This is the cost of war.

Two Class 'A' Excavation Units—like the one that crushed Father's left leg—extracted significant amounts of soil and rocks for relocation in a swift amount of time. All I could think about watching their robotic arms telescope from each of their three sides to grab and break up roots and rocks, was Father. I am glad they finished and powered down.

All 673 of us gather in a half-oval circle around the mass grave. Most are women and children, maybe as much as 80 percent. Families were in the depths of HU-1 while Armada workers and fathers hauled supplies in and out of it. Some were working the hard winter ground with Dah'Sel like Din'Mos when the attack broke out. No one saw it coming but me, and I warned no one. There was no time. I did the best I could, but still feel I failed them. This is my fault.

The half-oval circle is full of faces I will not make eye contact with today. There is no...

A gunshot interrupts my train of thought, fired into the air by an Armada soldier in full uniform at the far left of us. I jump along with others as the gun salute starts. Children bury their faces in the bosoms of crying mothers. A second gunshot from a soldier a few people to his right rings out. A third soldier down the line fires after him. The process continues until the shots reach a machine gun's rate of fire. Repeating in reverse fashion from the far right of the half-oval, the salute of shots travels back down the line until it slows.

The last five soldiers to fire take forever. Time slows mentally. Let this be over.

Sergeant Bentley stands front and center with his back to the tomb and faces the onlookers.

"This tragedy," he says. "It is something that we will overcome. We lost all our former leaders from Kep Four. Most didn't make it here, but we lost the Sovereign today. We lost loved ones... families... partners... kids... friends. This is not over, but we delt a crippling blow to the Uprisers when they came. Who they have left is no more formidable than ourselves, but we have friends here as well."

He motions his arm over our heads and behind us. The entire line of humanity turns to look back. The Dah'Sel sect, at 812 strong, has been here supporting everyone in silence while giving us space to say goodbye.

"I want all of you to go home," continues Sergeant Bentley. "You've already been assigned who to buddy up with for living arrangements. The Dah'Sel, despite everything, are helping us organize accommodations. Let the excavators auto-bury them, their final moments in peace. You can come back to this place any time you'd like to. We all can. Be strong and move on, Armada."

BEREAVEMENT

We dissipate. The Dah'Sel walk ahead of us with the 'Cets grouped in front of me. None look back. They continue into Lesdelop ti'it renasa, and we are alone with our memories.

CHAPTER 22
Recovery

A few rotations have passed since the burial, three of them. Maybe four. I doubt anybody has been keeping track of 96 of the Kep Four transplants succumbing to their injuries—bringing our numbers down to 577. I feared such a thing would happen.

Our interplanetary jump ships run a highly modified form of ECB (Escherichia Coli Bacteria) to process information. It did not take long for it to get into some of those with exposed wounds. A single Med Lab is all that remains for treatment. It is not enough. Most of our medical equipment is worthless now. There was no saving them.

The Dah'Sel lost 46 members of their sect, bringing their numbers to 766, and they are mourning. It would have been higher, but some were hidden from sight in underground tunnel systems where I have not been yet. The Dah'Sel avoided Armada housing units the way new arrivals respected their wishes for privacy within Lesdelop. Even though they received invitations to HU-1 and HU-2, they appreciated humanity's need for personal boundaries. Turns out it was for the best.

While we lost Dr. Wright, who is the reason we could make the jump to Wah'Lor in the first place, Dr. Klinroy escaped *Athanasios* before its demise. His drop pod landed safely, and he went without hesitation to those in need. He is a good doctor and an even better example of what others should be. He inspires.

Dr. Klinroy has my and Dr. Sellers's mentality on life, along with Dr. Utley's abilities as a scientist. Sergeant Bentley took him up on his offer to fill the gap Dr. Wright left behind. I am glad. We need him like Dolofónos needs a trip into the black without a helmet for a permanent nap.

Mother's memory files were on *Athanasios* when the attack started. There will never be another way for me to walk into her home, talk with her, or deliver a final goodbye kiss to her forehead. I am troubled by the thought—one I need to avoid as much as possible. There is enough depression on Wah'Lor without it.

Algash is here in my tele-tent with me. I check his pulse and stand after confirming he still has functioning lungs. He is not about to die. I am checking on instinct after how many times I have done it to so many still in the field since the attack.

"Pulse," I say. "94 beats a tek."

He is fine but lost his father in the attack, along with his left limb and hand from the forearm down. None are sure exactly how it happened because consciousness has not found him yet, not with his Mizophile dose being what it is. He should wake up soon.

This is not a situation I prefer to be in, but bunking up with somebody is unavoidable now. Everybody is doing it. Those currently without wounded staying with them are bunking up four and five deep in these little tele-tents.

NIVEOUS WAR

22-2
Confirmation

I exit to brilliant binary suns and squint my eyes. The clouds have cleared. They are brighter than normal against the snow. I pull my sunbans from my pocket and put them on.

My nose crinkles. The dirty, ugly, brown jacket and pants I am wearing over cotton-textured undergarments the Dah'Sel gave me stink. I have not showered or taken them off since Sergeant Bentley took that little girl from my arms and ordered me to my tele-tent to get dressed, which I was lucky enough to have intact.

I still do not know her name but am haunted by the memory of her crying as I carried her barefooted across the snow. Something about it reminds me of the little girl my brother Comilo and I played with when we were young. I did not know her name either.

"Mason," says Delgado. "I was coming to see if you were up, but it looks like I have my answer."

I look at her robotic legs in the white powder beneath us.

"I'm quieter in the snow, huh?" she asks.

"A little," I answer. "I was distracted when you walked up. What were you coming for again?"

"You're talking to everyone outside of Lesdelop this rotation. Remember?"

"That's right," I answer. "How long until it starts?"

"They're gathering now," she says, "but I'm not sure if everyone's ready."

"Okay," I say, forcing a partial smile. "I'll be there."

Delgado walks away. I am jealous that she does not have to worry about her feet getting cold in the snow. Her legs are naturally warm while encased in robotic prosthetics. I would, however, have to say it is funny seeing her in winter garments only from the waist up. Not that I will mention it to her. She is still beautiful.

I turn to scan the undergoing recovery efforts. Newly recruited medical assistants without training are busy in the field helping Armada doctors. They are at workstations mixing what compounds we have left together in a desperate attempt to heal our wounded when requested. Doctors periodically move from one tele-tent to the next while their poorly schooled assistants run supplies to them as needed.

I pass them in thought about how nice it was for the Dah'Sel to construct a few dozen of the square, teepee-like structures they call bengas for us. Their generosity surprised Armada personnel, especially after the drama humanity has brought upon them thus far. I was not.

The Dah'Sel have great ethics and cherish the flora and fauna on their planet. It is what separates them from the humanity of the past. While we discovered that we all evolved from the same DNA shortly after our arrival, they evolved differently.

We are products of our environment, but those of us who descend from Ancient Earth have repeatedly chosen destructive routes toward each other and the planets sustaining our lives. The Armada better be taking notes for the next generation. Not that they would listen.

My squad comes into view amongst other humans. Dah'Sel stand in wait. I will be at their side in a few more paces. I am both dreading it and longing to make things right.

"Mason," says Fister. "Glad you could make it."

He is every bit as upset as the rest of us but hides it behind a stone face. Whether he wants to admit it is irrelevant. It is in his nature to suppress things since he lost Rhigas, and that is okay. We all cope differently.

I study him for a tek as the others gather. He looks away from the group and into the sky.

"You okay, Fister?" I ask.

"Sorry," he says. "What was that?"

"I asked if you were okay."

"I'm fine. Just thinking about my sister, Bo. Never heard from her. She was supposed to come on the *Lifeboat*. The recent Upriser attack reminded me of the BlazeBall bombing at the arena. She almost died. Now she might be..."

He looks back to the sky again.

"I'm sorry," I say.

He says nothing. I swallow empathy and look toward the snow to shake it. His pain is something I am familiar with.

Wat'Uza approaches with Pru'Cet's mother, Nala'Cet, and uncle Bah'Cet. I have not seen Tila'Cet or Pru'Cet. I wonder where they are, but will not ask. The last thing I want is to appear unfocused.

"McKayla," asks Wat'Uza. "*Mabab dit ama matao a elo blazee plup?*"

My crew and the others look to me for translation.

"He asked where I saw the sky bird fall," I say before answering Wat'Uza. "*Mabab e blagrah lekde ot ma ulta ne e heeza-zis jokata.*" I turn to my squad, repeating my answer. "Where the white snow is no more, and the suns rise."

"Tell us everything afterward," says Sergeant Bentley.

"*E Plako Helkla,*" says Wat'Uza. "*Ama cre jesen, lab po cre azata e fusite.*"

He shows his teeth and releases a grunt before turning his back to me and walking away. He is understandably upset over humanity's actions. I cannot place blame on him.

There is no evil amongst the Kla'Wah. Though they have differences in opinion, the Vee'Sal and Dah'Sel have always found an avenue for peace. We are still alien to them as a species. My squad and I believe we are all he holds trust in anymore.

"*Blight uptru eo ama,*" says Bah'Cet.

Nala'Cet lowers her forehead to him. They raise their arms overhead for their palms to come together. A moment passes as we watch.

"I got some of it," says Sergeant Bentley. "But ... for clarity, what all was said?"

"Wat'Uza said the area they landed in..." I say with a pause.

I do not want to say it. We were told it was off-limits when we arrived here, but these are dire rotations.

"What?" asks Sergeant Bentley. "Where is it?"

"It's near E Plako Helkla," I answer. "The forbidden area. He said we could go if we're going to end the war, but he wasn't happy about it. Bah'Cet said he's taking us there."

Bah'Cet pats Sergeant Bentley on the back. "*Blight uptru eo ama.*"

"Thanks," says Sergeant Bentley.

22-3
Prepping

Bah'Cet steps away from Lesdelop ti'it renasa. Something is on his mind. I follow him.

"*Wabuki ama polasa-zim ti'it Pru'Cet nacas Tila'Cet?*" I ask.

"*Saisay jesen-zim ti'it polasa bea e Vee'Sal,*" answers. Bah'Cet. "*Zamba-zim jappa e fusite lats-zim. Wat'Uza wena-zim siwbe.*"

"Why?" I ask. "*Wazme?*"

"Mason," calls Sergeant Bentley. "We have to go."

I jog to his side. Our squad is leaving without us. I take a worry-eyed look at Bah'Cet and hurry to join them.

"What was that about?" asks Sergeant Bentley.

"I was trying to find Pru' and Tila'," I answer.

"Any luck?"

"Kind of," I answer. "They went to Lesdelop ti'it ratim-zis."

"Isn't that where—"

"Yes," I say. "Wat'Uza sent them to talk with the Vee'Sal when the Uprisers attacked."

"This is going to get interesting," says Sergeant Bentley, turning to the squad. "Bell, Sapp, I need the two of you together in an Argos. Make sure it's equipped with a mask and armed. Pilfer artillery if need be. Delgado and Mason, you're with me."

"You want me with Fister?" asks Dr. Sellers.

"Yes, but that can't happen. There're people here that need you."

Dr. Sellers looks to the field of tele-tents converted into temporary emergency rooms.

"Of course," he says. "Understood."

"Fister," continues Sergeant Bentley. "You're with Delgado and me. Change of plans for you, Mason. Have an engineer double-check your starfighter and make sure it'll still operate under mask for extended durations if necessary. Everyone clear on that?"

We acknowledge and part ways.

I spend a good tak in search of an engineer I trust and do not find one. Most were stationed in HU-2 and made it out alive. All is not lost.

Algash is exiting my tele-tent with sleepy eyes.

"Algash," I say, making my way to him. "I could use your help right about now."

He looks around the snowy field of misery. "How many died? Where's Dolofónos and the Uprisers?"

"I don't know," I answer. "That's partly why I need your help."

RECOVERY

"What can I do?" he asks through a yawn. "Sorry. Still waking here, and a little drugged."

He looks at his mangled left stump in a sling.

"Not sure I'm going to be of much help," he says.

"Follow me," I say.

He cradles the makeshift sling holding his wounded arm in place and follows me to my Beltric Class Six starfighter. It takes a moment to help him into the cockpit when we reach it.

"What am I doing here exactly?" he asks.

"I need a full spectrum system check from someone more competent than myself," I answer.

He raises a brow.

"You realize," he says. "I still had a cycle left in the training program before being qualified by the Armada, right?"

"That's five more cycles of engineering than I have," I say. "Seriously. This is important, and we need that check as quickly as possible."

He shakes his head and throws me a long stare.

"Are you going to do something crazy again?" he asks.

"Most likely," I sigh. "But nothing like you're probably thinking. Recon squad one is leaving to locate the *Ark*. We need to know if there are any survivors and if there's anything worth salvaging."

"Any other squad's going with you?" he asks.

"Maybe one," I answer. "I'm not sure if there're any full squads left to go with us anymore. One might have to be pieced together."

He nods and gets to work. I watch him for a tek before turning to take in what humanity has brought to Wah'Lor, and I cannot stop wondering why Pru'Cet and his sister are going to meet with the Vee'Sal about. My biggest fear is that the Dah'Sel no longer accept us, but another side of me knows they are naturally forgiving.

I recognize they are going because they believe it is for the best. What they tell them is beyond my control, but I doubt they will be as understanding as the Dah'Sel. We have heard the stories. They do not want us here. After they hear about the vicious onslaught Dolofónos waged upon us, there is no way the Vee'Sal are going to change their minds about the human presence on Wah'Lor.

"Took me a little longer to input everything and run scans with one hand," says Algash. "But all systems are fine. You're golden here."

"Thanks," I say, helping him down. "You can get some rest now. Sorry to bother you."

"You're fine, Mason, but I do think I'll lie back down." He walks from the starfighter toward my tele-tent. "Thanks for letting me take over your place, by the way."

It is time for me to get together with Sergeant Bentley and anybody that joins us. We must locate the *Ark*, find out if there are any survivors, and retrieve its life-giving seeds. We hope to get back to the Dah'Sel and ensure we can survive with possible starvation in the cycles to come. Those seeds could help feed us once planted, excluding what may be invasive to the Wah'Lor ecosystem.

CHAPTER 23
Searching for The *Ark*

We have run every scan we can think of attempting to pinpoint the *Ark*'s location. Nothing has proven fruitful. Dolofónos must have the seed-bearing vessel's mask activated, which is the most effective of all ships. It had to be better than the rest; its contents were too valuable to risk running into an unknown, advanced, and possibly hostile species and losing its contents to them.

Sergeant Bentley has teamed up with two other fragmented squads agreeing to go on the hunt with us, neither of which has their original members. The Armada only brought enough crafts on the first ships to form four small, eight-member squads consisting of five vessels each during the first phase of interplanetary jumps. It better be enough to get us through looming chaos.

The bulk of armament was on the *Dwarf*, which shattered into a million pieces and scattered who knows where across thousands of clicks on the planet's surface. Who we have joining us is all that's left after the *Dwarf* attacked. One squad did not make it at all.

"How much longer?" I ask.

"We're waiting for one more," answers Sergeant Bentley.

I nod and take a deep breath to exhale my nerves. Sure, we are scouting nine vessels strong for the *Ark* with my squad and others, but it does not relax my concerns. There is no telling what we will run into once we reach E Plako Helkla.

We wait patiently in the debris-littered area between HU-2 and the torn-up airfield. A gust of wind hits me. I shiver it away.

A Beltric Class Six like mine lands several paces from my vessel on the other side of Bah'Cet; only it is not nearly as beat up. I watch in curiosity for someone to emerge. A moment passes before its door opens.

"I thought the other Beltric was destroyed," I say.

"This is the last one," says Fister, stepping from its interior.

I look around in confusion. A man who looks just like him from the back is talking to a flight member from the other squads. I point to him.

"I thought that was you," I say.

"You thought wrong," says Fister.

The guy I mistook for him turns around. He is young, as in second cycle apprenticeship young.

"Guess your foresight isn't with you anymore," says Delgado.

"Yeah," I say. "One can only hope."

"All right, everyone," says Sergeant Bentley. "Listen up."

Full attention from all nearby goes to Sergeant Bentley.

"Right now," he continues. "I want what remains of my original squad with me, squad-A on my left, and squad-B on my right, where we can all see each other."

The group does as ordered.

"Mason will be piloting the Beltric in our squad," he says. "We'll be Squad C, but I'm moving my second-in-command to squad-A because they're light on personnel."

Sapp walks to join Squad-A.

"I'm also moving Delgado to pilot the other Beltric," continues Sergeant Bentley. "This will leave us with four small squads. I know it's a little light, but it's the best we can do for now."

"Sergeant Major," says the guy who looked like Fister from behind.

"Go ahead, Barsa," says Sergeant Bentley.

"Don't you think I should pilot the other Beltric in your squad?" asks Barsa.

"Negative. Mason has that one."

"But, Sergeant Major—"

"How old are you?" asks Sergeant Bentley.

"Seventeen cycles," answers Barsa.

"First cycle with the Armada?"

"Second."

"And you think you can fly it better than her?"

Barsa looks me over and answers with a nod.

"Then you haven't researched your teammates," says Sergeant Bentley. "She flies full combat at over a hundred sustained G's without a flight suit ... and she does it manually." He turns to the others. "All three teams will have an Argos and a Bomba. Treat them well. There are only four total Bombas left. We have three of them here. Squad-B will have the Plegma. You're flying it, Barsa."

"But—"

"We've equipped it with a mask," continues Sergeant Bentley. "I want you to roll out ahead of everybody else. No vessel here, masked or not, is quieter than the Plegma Nine."

The kid smiles. I remember being young and Gung-ho. It will wear off in time.

"You," says Sergeant Bentley, addressing an unfamiliar face. "What's your name?"

"Fielding," the man answers. "Med. Fielding."

"You're the one that helped me in the field," I say. "You saved that woman."

"I remember," says Med. Fielding.

"How long have you been a medic?" asks Sergeant Bentley.

"Nine cycles," answers Med. Fielding.

"You're with me in this Bomba," says Sergeant Bentley. "You too Bah'Cet. Load up. We're moving out and staying low with this skeleton crew. Keep turrets on auto but locked in safety. There's a lot of wildlife out here that they've not been programmed to register yet. We don't need any blunders. Everyone got that?"

Bah'Cet and the squads acknowledge, and we move into position. I study the two new guys for a moment. Barsa is normal looking as far as young Armada males go: short military haircut kept high and tight, a chiseled clean-cut face, and an unbreakable serious attitude with no sense of humor displayed so far.

Med. Fielding is my height, but rail thin. I may even have a few pounds on him. He appears to me malnourished like the many I grew up with on Kep Four, but it could just be the way he has always been. Either way, the man looks seven-doors-from-ruin tired and has dark bags under his eyes to prove it. He did not look this rough in the field. I bet he has not slept. We are all lacking rest. It will not sharpen us.

I move to my Beltric and sigh at its dented and scarred appearance. They say it is a miracle the *Dwarf* did not shoot me dead in the black. Whatever it was that kept me alive, I will take it.

I climb in and close the cockpit door, curious if there was any reason for Sergeant Bentley to reorder the squads. He might have done it on impulse. Does not matter. We are about to fly shortly.

"Armada voice clearance," I say. "Mason, five, Sinote, one, four, McKayla, three, six. Engage power for manual flight."

23-2
Lassabax

We head across a clearing. The Argos units under me are bouncing lightly on the terrain.

"In a hurry?" I ask from my Beltric over comms.

"No," answers Sergeant Bentley from his Bomba. "Why?"

I glance at the H.U.D. to see how fast we're going:

Speed—60cps

"Just asking," I answer. "We're at sixty clicks per sequence."

He does not respond.

Communication over comms reminds me of pilot training courses in the Armada. Almost all is white as we proceed. Distant blez'nez trees break up the landscape with blue leaves, patches of spider-webbed flowers with above-ground root systems, and snow-free surroundings due to their warm temperature.

"*Gwana,*" says Bah'Cet. "*E gwampa-zic lassabax.*"

It did not take long to reach the first landmark he tells us we would encounter.

"That's it," I say.

"Turn left and follow it until we reach the second mountain on our right," says Sergeant Bentley.

We turn left with the river to make our way down crystal clear waters teeming with large aquatic lifeforms I have never seen in historical files. I am unsure what they are called, but they are beautiful. At least, I think they are charming as far as aquatics are concerned: brilliant yellow, long, thick bodies, and green fins that reach half a pace out before turning into what appears to be tentacles.

We continue upstream as the blue water tints with traces of pink shifting further red. Swimming vertebrates grow in size with the changing water and shift colors by the click to match it.

"That's odd," says Sapp from squad-A's Bomba.

"Have you ever seen a river before?" asks Bell.

"Not in person," answers Sapp.

"Maybe it's something rivers do," says Bell.

A few clicks later, the river is too red to see through. Aquatic animals blend in with it. They have almost doubled in size as well. It is fascinating and leaves me wondering what is causing the changes until the answer comes into view.

Large red plants stand firm to hold their positions at the base of the river's flow. Two pace-long leaves wave as if made of silk in the stream. Color comes off them and pollutes everything downstream red for 10 clicks.

"Scan those plants," says Sergeant Bentley from his Bomba.

"Scans say the aqua plants are dense with nutrients," says Fister. "Aquatic life here are larger because the plants are saturating the water."

"Sellers would have a field day with this," says Sergeant Bentley.

"That he would," says Delgado from the other Beltric.

"There it is, boys and girls," says Sapp from the other squad's Argos.

To our right stands the mountain with a passageway carved through it. Stones seal its entrance.

"The sooner, the better," says Sergeant Bentley. "Let's cross the water and do this."

All airborne transports, Beltric Class Six fighters, Bombas, and the Plegma Nine hover over the river. We make our way to the makeshift tunnel and wait. All three Argos ground transport vessels turn side-by-side and ease their tracks into the moving water. They cross upstream from the plants to avoid damaging the ecosystem. The water submerges them after their turrets lower. An overhead door closes behind them for an air-tight seal.

"Doing okay under there?" asks Sergeant Bentley.

"Great," answers Fister. "Besides the fact that the current here isn't as kind to me as it is to the aquatic life."

They will not be under long. The click-wide water flow's end is in sight for them. They emerge off course after the powerful current bullies them. The Argos's tracks spin in place for a moment on all three vessels before making it to a solid surface.

"Okay," says Fister, "That was fun. What's next?"

23-3
Carved Mountain

It will not take long to remove the rocks blocking the tunnel with a trio of Argos vessels. Their forward clamps are powerful enough to move them easily, and it takes less than five teks to clear the way. Part of me wishes it would have taken longer. I am not looking forward to the possibility of running into Uprisers.

"Squad-B," says Sergeant Bentley. "Move in after us and squad-A. We'll not stop until we're on the other side of it."

We fall into position and enter the passageway one at a time. It is a tight fit for Argos transport vessels but widens inside. The hand-carved segue cut through this mountain's base is stunning, to say the least.

"Wow," I say.

"That about sums it up," says Bell.

Its inside is laden with clear, orange-colored crystals reaching from a hand-width wide to over a pace long and a quarter pace wide. They catch the lights from our vessels like a prism to release it back into the tunnel, one piece of the continuum at a time. It beams around us.

"Diamond, quartz, and something else we don't have on file," says Delgado.

It takes 50 teks to make our way through the tunnel. Tiny flyers with long sharp teeth overhanging their bottom jaws cling to the cave's ceiling and sides as we go. They blend in with its brown, stone-carved walls. I believe they are the cave-dwelling pemptes Din'Mos spoke of.

"The other end is probably blocked as well," I say.

"Clearly not," says Barsa. "As soon as you round the corner ahead, you'll see what I see."

We press on until we reach the corner Barsa mentioned. The end of the tunnel comes into view with a lush world on the other side of it. Patches of snow and dozens of warm-blooded trees fill the scene in a florescent rainbow pattern spanning the spectrum. The colors fade to white further toward the region called E Plako Helkla's outer edges at our distant right. It is off limits.

"I love this place," says Barsa.

It gets brighter as we near the exit. The tunnel illuminates under its light. It will not be long until we are close enough to be concerned about our search for Dolofónos and his band of hooligans.

I keep my fingers crossed that all goes well. We suffered heavy losses the last time we encountered his Uprisers. Thousands are missing, and we may join them soon.

CHAPTER 24
Investigation

Barsa eases out the Plegma Nine ahead of us and with the vessel under mask. We cannot see him without sensors, but we know where he is. I watch him with guilt that I have not bothered asking members' names of the rest in Squad-B.

Getting to know people on a personal level feels like it will only lead to heartache these rotations. I am already having a hard enough time dealing with losing people I grew close to. Worrying about what Pru'Cet and Tila'Cet are up to over in the Vee'Sal sect is troubling enough. I do not need more on my plate.

"Squad-B," says Sergeant Bentley, "keep your Argos and Bomba Classes here near the tunnel while we press forward. We don't need anyone seeing us."

He is right. Both those vessels currently have nonfunctioning mask systems after taking heavy damage in the initial attack and have experienced minor technological failure. Gashed hulls, dark burns, and bubbled electro stenciling from heat reflect the war against Uprisers. If they had come with us and our enemies survived their crash landing, Uprisers would have spotted the Argos or Bomba class.

"Everyone else," continues Sergeant Bentley, "spread out for a ten-click sweep. Let's go."

"I'm taking center?" asks Barsa.

"Affirmative," answers Sergeant Bentley. "We're establishing V-formation a quarter click back for each line. A click back if you're first in line behind the Plegma Nine. My squad will fly right side. Squad-A, you got the Plegma's left. Sapp and I will tail him with the Bombas. Delgado and Mason, you sweep outside of us with the Beltrics. Fister and Fielding, outside formations in the Argos units, but hold an extra two clicks back in case anything happens."

We acknowledge his orders and press forward with Barsa at point. Hopefully, it does not take too long to find the *Ark*. The suns will set soon. We are in unfamiliar territory and there could be anything out here waiting to make things difficult for us.

24-2
Visual

We slink silently past the blue line of fluorescent flora that ends with a dreaded brown. The immensity of the trees is something I did not appreciate a few clicks back. They reach nearly 300 paces in height and range between 15 and 20 paces wide at their base. I do not know if they will grow taller with the passing of time.

Faint signs of dwindling smoke in the distance catch my attention.

"I think we found them," says Barsa.

"Confirmed on that," says Sergeant Bentley.

"I don't think we're going to be able to go much farther on our side," says Fister.

"Agreed," says Bell. "Let's stop here."

"Trees got you held up?" asks Sergeant Bentley.

INVESTIGATION

"Yes, Sarg," says Bell. "They're thick. Might not be able to push through them."

"Fielding?" asks Sergeant Bentley.

"Yes, Sergeant Major?" answers Med. Fielding.

"How are you and your buddy looking down there?"

"Same in half a click," he answers.

"All right," says Sergeant Bentley, "you guys hold position. Maintain open comms and scans."

"Not a problem," says Bell.

"Speak for yourself," says Fister. "I want to see what happened over there."

"Same," says Fielding. "Argos is too wide to make it here."

"I'll route my visual feeds to you," I say, "if you'd like."

"Sounds good," says Fister.

"That'll have to do," says Med. Fielding. "I guess."

"Would you rather sit there and be bored?" asks Fister.

"Not really."

"Raise your altitude," says Sergeant Bentley. "No sense in staying low."

"You've already raised my altitude," says Delgado, pulling into the air.

"Cut the chitchat and focus," says Sergeant Bentley, following Delgado into the sky.

"I got something," says Barsa.

"I see it," says Delgado. "Looks like munition holds ... and they've been opened."

"That's not good," I say.

"My thoughts exactly," says Sergeant Bentley.

We pass over them, and I can only assume the others are as worried and disappointed as I am. They do not open by themselves. Dolofónos and his Uprisers must have emptied them. They have the *Ark*'s DNA surplus, seed supply, and everything else brought that is intended to help those seeds grow, purify ground soil, and support life for us here.

"Delgado," says Sergeant Bentley, "didn't you help with the initial selection process in deciding what would be coming on the *Dwarf*?"

"That's correct, Sergeant Major," answers Delgado.

"Would you mind filling me in on the details?"

"You don't want to know," she answers.

"Tell me anyway," says Sergeant Bentley.

"Five Bomba Class fighters," answers Delgado. "Five Beltrics, Five Argos ground transports, and one War Stopper." She pauses. "Plus a legion of ground troop armaments."

"Why did you have to tell me there was a War Stopper?"

"Said to tell you."

"Next time ... don't listen to me."

We continue easing forward under mask until the *Ark* comes into view. It is partially buried in Wah'Lor's surface, banged up, cracked, and still venting its contents into the air. There is no way it will fly again.

Thousands in Upriser uniforms are hauling seeds from its interior, using Armada equipment to till several patches of ground, and attempting to grow food. Dozens of ships are patrolling the air and possibly other areas on the planet's surface. They survived, and they are planning on sticking around. I hold no doubts that Dolofónos plans to rule this planet through sheer military force by using the food source as a point of leverage against us.

What they do not know, however, is the fact we are learning how to live off summer and winter land. We also know of species dangerous beyond imagination. Eat the wrong things here; it could poison you. Walk too close to carnivorous plants, and they will eat you.

INVESTIGATION

"Let's move a little higher and watch them for a while," says Sergeant Bentley. "We can't go down there and meet that kind of resistance, but maybe we can figure out their game plan if we—"

"Code gray," shouts the Bomba Class pilot from the tunnel's entrance. "We're going down."

"What happened?" asks Sergeant Bentley.

"We just lost—"

"Uprisers," shouts the tunnel-side Argos team.

24-3
Skirmish

We can't get to them in time without breaking our masks, but Delgado and I waste no time in joining the fight.

"Armada voice clearance, Mason, five, Sinote, one, four, McKayla, three, six," I say. "Initiate combat type two dash nine."

"Hold for us, Mason," says Sergeant Bentley.

"Too late," I say.

A micro-jump later, I come out to see Squad-A's Bomba Class crashing into Wah'Lor. It is out of control, under heavy fire, and Sapp's men must have fired a scat shot out of desperation because it is—

"Oh boy," I say to myself.

I am spinning now as well. One clipped my starboard side high in the clouds. I pull toward the black under weakened power until my Beltric Class Six fails and free falls toward the terrain below. Delgado emerges from a micro-jump beneath me and half a click to my left.

"Mason," says Delgado, "Your Beltric's—"

"Disappearing," I interrupt. "I know."

The antimatter's slow burn from the rear of my ship to the front is erasing it from existence.

"Armada EM voice clearance, Mason, five, eject." It does not respond. "Great."

"They're not flickering when they fire," says Delgado. "I can't see them."

A high-impulse laser spits 22,000 bursts per tek from a cloud or somewhere. I cannot tell. The rounds are coming from nowhere. They miss Delgado's Beltric, but the stream of fire continues and closes in on her. She ejects only a fraction of a tik before it rips her vessel apart. Any later, and she would no longer be with us.

I reach between my legs with half my starfighter gone and pull the manual hatch release. It pops off the Beltric and flips into the air behind me. I get my bearings, unstrap, climb from the cockpit, and jump before the antimatter's disintegration process reaches my hands.

Delgado is freefalling with me in the distance. I pull my ripcords and watch her Beltric Class Six slam into the side of the mountain from which we emerged. The wind catches me. My starfighter disappears until nothing is left moments before it crashes into the tunnel entrance.

"Paint the skies until you hit something," shouts Sergeant Bentley. "Mind Delgado and Mason are up there. Watch your fire."

Turret's spray wildly into the air around us from both Argos ground units as they move in. Scat shots from the Bomba Classes Sapp and Sergeant Bentley are piloting rain the skies with antimatter. It is all around me. I close my eyes and wait my turn at death.

Two explosions take place. A scream escapes me without warning, like someone dumped a thousand meck-bugs from a rusted bucket over my head. My eyes open partially. The

INVESTIGATION

scat shots hit two targets, and the Argos-powered ground team targets them during their freefall. They are gone before they reach the ground.

"Holy Armada," says Delgado.

Sergeant Bentley and Sapp move into positions near us, open their rear docks, and go nose down for us to drift into them. Not a moment is wasted before Sergeant Bentley snagged Delgado and Sapp me. Their rear hatches close behind us.

"We've got to move," shouts Fister.

I take the gunner's seat next to Sapp. Multiple shots breeze past us. The Uprisers must be firing manually. They have to be. I doubt any of them have Armada voice clearance for auto-targeting.

"Let's get out of here," says Sapp.

"Already gone," says Sergeant Bentley.

Sapp and Sergeant Bentley spin the Bombas 180 degrees to face their six and reverse thrust toward the cave's entrance, releasing a series of scat shots along the way until they run dry. Three Upriser vessels unmask when they are shot from the blue and eject, but one pilot's parachute is hit with a scat round. The thin material disintegrates too fast for him to cut it loose and pull his reserve chute. Antimatter reaches his harness and moves across his body until he is no more.

Uprisers in red-and-black transports converted to hold small arms weapons come over the tops of taller trees in the area. Their side doors lift. The enemies inside open fire. We take out several as we near the tunnel and watch them plummet.

Fielding and Fister open fire from their Argos vessels with automated targeting. Their turrets turn to maintain locks on the enemy as they enter behind us. The tracked ground vehicles follow us into darkness and stop a few hundred paces in.

"Where are you, Barsa?" asks Sergeant Bentley.

No response.

"Bentley to Barsa?"

Nothing. Sergeant Bentley pauses for a tik to see Uprisers nearing. They open fire into the tunnel.

"Blow it," says Sergeant Bentley.

"Barsa's—"

"Now," says Sergeant Bentley.

We take off and open fire on the tunnel's interior walls. It collapses behind us as we go, nearly catching up with us. Small rocks bounce off Med. Fielding's Argos bringing up the rear.

24-4
Exit

We emerge from the tunnel without a moment to spare. Its collapse nearly snags Med. Fielding's Argos to the point of burying it, but he pulls free. I did not think he was going to make it.

"Couldn't have gotten much closer than that," says Fister.

"We should keep moving, guys," says Bell. "Look behind you."

The collapsing tunnel has destabilized a portion of the mountain. A massive landslide rushes toward us. Airborne units pull up as they cross the river. Those helming Argos vessels hit the water at full speed, skimming its top halfway across before submerging.

Sergeant Bentley stops us a half-click beyond the river, and we turn to see the landslide push into the water as the Argos vessels emerge.

INVESTIGATION

"Oh no," I say.

"What?" asks Bell. "We made it."

"E lassabax," I answer.

"What are you talking about, Mason?"

"The river," I repeat.

All turn to look. Silence follows. We have once more caused harm to this planet's natural developmental process.

E lassabax is blocked three-quarters of the way across it. Water is building up behind it, spreading out and flowing around the blockage. Everything turns brown downstream from where the landslide invaded the river. Dirt and sediment are no doubt smothering life from it in the area. I am sure it will clear up before this rotation is up, but along with everything else that has happened since our arrival, it is a stark reminder of our history of not caring for the planets we inhabit.

CHAPTER 25
Game Plan

It is terrible news for all when we reach the Armada base camp, but we must spark thoughts on how to deal with the situation instead of inciting panic. The Dah'Sel are my biggest concern. All they have done for us so far is sacrifice.

Their Lessdelop ti'it renasa structure comes into view as we near the fields leading us around tall, covering trees. It peaks higher than average over the surrounding nature because of our elevation while returning to our smoldering base camp. I watch and am lost in thought as we approach.

The view of its topside is excellent from here. I recall the moment Dah'Sel youth snatched ropes atop it to pivot flaps covering reflective obsidian tubes. *How could I forget?* It bled moonlight into the tubes beneath it to bounce off its reflective walls until it reached the Dah'Sel. I will never forget the first time I saw the Klaz'Dra transformation.

I thought we were going to die that rotation. The moonlight skirmish in the field was bad enough, but Rhigas... Fister still visits his place of rest daily and stays the night lying next to him in a black thermal cloth wrap.

"You all right over there, Mason?" asks Sapp.

"Yeah," I answer. "Just remembering the first time we saw the transformation."

"You, my friend, are not alone."

GAME PLAN

"You guys follow me," says Sergeant Bentley. "We need to figure out how to organize this meeting with the Armada."

"What about the Dah'Sel?" I ask.

"Them too," says Sergeant Bentley, "but with the Planetary Sovereign. Commander Helmwoke, and the rest of our leaders lost to that psychopath on Kep Four, and the majority of who were left in positions of power lost to the *Dwarf*, I don't know who's left that everyone'll be willing to follow."

"I know someone," says Delgado.

"Who?" asks Sergeant Bentley.

"You."

"No..." says Sergeant Bentley. "Not exactly my strong suit."

"And when were you an Armada leader to know that?" she asks.

"I agree," interjects Sapp. "You're the most respected leader of their military, notably more so after we launched on Expedition Anchor."

"I'm with Sapp and Delgado on this one," says Fister. "Bell?"

"Agreed as well," answers Bell.

"Mason?" asks Bell. "Your thoughts?"

"He'll do all right," I say.

"Thanks, Mason," says Sergeant Bentley. "We'll cross that bridge when we get to it. Humanity's still going to need structure when the dust settles. I'm not bringing it up."

"You won't have to," I say. "That's where we'll come in. Besides, the Dah'Sel would be in favor of it as well. They trust you. They trust us, and their opinion will carry weight amongst the Armada."

Sergeant Bentley sighs heavily over the comms.

"Delgado to Sergeant Major Bentley secure," says Delgado. "Bentley."

"Go ahead, Delgado," he says.

"You know you can do this," she says. "You need to be the one to do this. This world trusts you. Mason trusts and follows you. That alone is enough for the Dah'Sel. You're more than enough of a leader for the Armada."

"It's just…" says Sergeant Bentley. "I'll think about it."

Delgado is talking with him to ease his mind about it, but I do not think she intended to leave communication open between their vessel and the rest of us. She should have started comms with him as '*secure to Sergeant Major Bentley,*' not '*Delgado to…*' I should probably say something, but I am interested to hear more.

"You know how much you mean to me," she continues. "You mean a lot to everyone. They need you."

"I feel the same about you," says Sergeant Bentley.

"Holy Armada," interrupts Fister through an uncontrollable laugh. "We get it."

"Oh, my word," says Delgado. "I didn't know that. I thought we were … Haze."

The group giggles at her embarrassment. Delgado and Sergeant Bentley stop talking. They have most likely switched to properly secured communication and are talking about what just happened.

I would say the last leg of our journey home was a breath of fresh air. We got so caught up on giving Delgado and Sergeant Bentley a hard time that we momentarily forgot about what we had just gone through. My only concern now is Pru'Cet and Tila'Cet. It has been rotations since I have seen or heard from them.

GAME PLAN

25-2
The Talk

We have gathered the highest-ranking personnel willing to come to our meeting. Some were reluctant. Those who refused to join us believe the best course of action is to flee the area. This is something I am not okay with, and I refuse to leave the Dah'Sel in a vulnerable position.

Do not get me wrong. I understand the logic of shifting to a different part of Wah'Lor. It is a massive world, and it would be easy to lose Dolofónos in it—for a while, that is. He would find us sooner or later, be it in 10 rotations or a few cycles from now.

There are only 18 Dah'Sel with us at the meeting, and Sergeant Bentley decided it was best to hold our gathering in the surviving HU-2. It is a half-click away from the nearest person, but within eyesight to let everyone know we are putting together a strategy.

Sergeant Bentley declines to put himself into a situation to debate his decision with everyone, but will give this a shot. Those here accepted our suggestion to follow his leadership. There were few other choices.

Thanks to the additional influence from Wat'Uza, Nala'Cet, and Din'Mos, the Armada counsel we put together had little to no choice but to accept him as commander and chief. It is for the best. Sergeant Bentley knows the area better than newer arrivals, and the Dah'Sel hold him in high regard. He is also a veteran with a solid theory on how to combat Dolofónos and his Uprisers.

"We're in a bad position here," says Sergeant Bentley. "I'll admit that. The Uprisers are heavily armed and have greater numbers as far as those wielding weapons are concerned, but we have a better knowledge of the land than they do.

Together, with Wat'Uza and the Dah'Sel, we can figure out a way to use this world to our advantage."

Chatter fills the scene amongst the crowd when he pauses.

"*Zune tatam-zis ka ya e fenka sa plenta-zis,*" says Wat'Uza. "*Po uptru jo teedoe zindoc ti'it azata gwan seblak-zis.*"

Sergeant Bentley turns to me for clarity.

"He says," I say with a hard swallow, "the dangers at the forest of graves region of Wah'Lor will be deadly enough to end their attack."

"Forest of graves?" he asks.

"It's a first for me too," I answer, "but that's what he said."

"Lovely," says Sergeant Bentley. "Where exactly is that?"

"Where the scama grows," I answer.

"Those plants you told me eat people?"

"No," I answer. "They've only eaten a few Dah'Sel. They haven't eaten a human yet."

"Well, that's just—"

Four onium discharges resonate into the halls of HU-2. People outside scream fearful cries through its walls. I rush to the exit with my squad. Dozens of frantic people and Dah'Sel are in front of and behind us. This is probably the best position for me to be in. There is no idea what I will run into if I am first to exit. If I am last and we are under attack, the area will be targeted by the time I hit the white. Being in the middle will let me know which way to run and give me insight into what is happening, judging from the reaction of those exiting before me.

I bounce from left to right, trying to reach the edge of the ship. Everyone is bumping into me, or vice versa, in panic. Civilians of high standing are rushing back into HU-2. Parents drag their children in a frantic state. A small boy is knocked to the ground in front of me in tears.

"Daddy," he cries. "Daddy."

I reach for him, but another woman picks him up.

"I'll take him in," she says, scooping him up and running into HU-2 for cover.

Recent Upriser attacks have all on edge.

The exit is nearby. I move through it with the others. A crowd has gathered alongside the hull to my right. I squeeze my compact frame between the group of onlookers and emerge beneath the shoulders of two men.

Med. Fielding already has a man on the ground's leg secured in bio-wraps. I whip my head to the sky in search of attacking vessels and see nothing. I spin 360 degrees and scan for anything I can see to find nothing beyond confusion and worried people. There has not been an attack here. There has been an accident.

"Dr. Sellers," calls Sergeant Bentley, running to another location. "Come with me."

Dr. Sellers jogs after him. I run to catch up, but it takes a tek to reach my long-legged friends.

"What happened?" I ask when Dr. Sellers comes to a stop at another gathered crowd. "What is it?"

"I don't know," he answers.

"Sapp," says Dr. Sellers, "make sure someone has a trauma kit on the way."

Sapp eases away from the madness to call into his comm, but I cannot hear him from here.

Wat'Uza arrives and stops next to me.

"*Ulat iscafo?*" he asks.

"Yes," I answer. "Maybe? I'm sorry. I don't know." I pause to face him. "*Lipfa. Blight pes gingo grenas po ot pest baklee seblak. Blight grenas po ledad pest turahan.*"

I push into the gathering crowd of humans and Dah'Sel. An onium rifle lies next to a body—a gunshot wound into the heart with a clean exit.

"Holy Armada," I say, covering my face.

I know who this is—the lady carrying the burned child after the initial attack. She was charred. I thought she was a man. Her eyes... The way she looked at me after we knocked each other into the snow. She gazed helplessly at me with her child dying in her arms before running off. It plagues me.

Dr. Sellers approaches and stops when he sees her. His mouth opens, but he doesn't say anything before turning to Sapp.

"Cancel that trauma kit," says Dr. Seller.

Sapp looks down at her, steps aside, and makes the call.

"Did anyone see what happened?" asks Sergeant Bentley.

"I didn't realize she had it until it was too late," says an unknown male Armada soldier. "I only set it down for a tik to adjust my bootstrap. Just a tik. She shot that guy over there in the leg when he tried to stop her."

"Where's her toddler?" I ask.

"She lost her," answers another woman. "She passed away earlier this last rotation. It's all she was holding on for."

My eyes go back down to the woman in the melting snow at my feet. The onium rifle she stole from this careless Armada soldier next to me is lying at her side, though I should not blame him for it. These are chaotic times.

The blast she delivered to herself was point-blank. There are no burn wounds anywhere on her clothing. Just a hole. She could not handle losing her child and made it clear that some things can only be fixed by discharging a weapon into a once happy heart.

"Does she have family here?" asks Dr. Sellers.

"I don't think so," answers the other woman. "I met her three or four rotations ago. Her partner was supposed to be coming on the *Lifeboat*, but I don't think it ever came through."

"It didn't," I say. "It never made it off Kep Four."

Sergeant Bentley walks off.

"Get a cleanup crew on this," he says.

I cannot be around such a grim situation. Not now. I turn and walk across the field a few dozen paces, staring at distant mountains they say Tila'Cet and Pru'Cet headed toward last. A moment passes as I think about the times I played with Pru'Cet without worry and how I feel when I am around Tila'Cet.

"Ah, man," I say to myself. "Hopefully—"

A movement rising over distant treetops steals my attention. I turn to examine it. It looks like ... I am unsure. It is not a flyer. Wait...

"Sapp," I call. "Do we have an Argos drone out?"

"I don't think so," answers Sapp. "Why?"

I point. He turns and sees it, back-peddling toward his tele-tent.

"Incoming!" he shouts.

I whip back to see what startled him. Several drones are flying overhead from within outlying trees. The Uprisers have found us again.

CHAPTER 26
Flyby

Eleven unmanned enemy drones are approaching our position at high speeds over the far end of treetops at the snow-covered field's edge. Armada personnel and Dah'Sel alike look up and scurry for cover, unknowing what is to come. Uprisers are sure to follow.

I make a break for it with the others as the drones open fire. Shots are streaking around me. Snow and dirt eject from the ground and stick to my clothes and skin. I squint my eyes to keep from getting anything in them and run with limited vision with the group.

Two men ahead of me on my left are struck down and slide to a stop in the white powder. A lady to my left is hit and drops a few steps later. A full sprint will not outrun them, but there is nothing to do but try. Another is shot in front of me. He goes down hard. I jump over him, but my foot catches his leg as he tumbles.

A drone's blast sears the hair on my head and warms my scalp as I fall. It would have killed me had the man in front of me not fallen. Someone falls on top of me. I roll to push her off, only to realize she is dead. The shot that was supposed to end my life has ended hers.

Others are blazing past me. Cover is needed. I get to my feet and take off again with the sole focus of reaching shelter.

There will be no time to look around or check on others if they get injured—a selfish act to ensure my own survival.

I recognize the drones as they pass overhead. They are Slaka D Class models firing solid titanium rounds. They do not miss when running off A.I. If I am to help anyone, I need to first survive.

A terrified crowd nears me, and we merge in a sprint toward the Lesdelop ti'it renasa structure. It is the closest thing to us and our best hope for survival. It is also dusk, and part of me wishes we had not removed the Klaz'Dra transformation disease from the Dah'Sel's culture.

Are there 10 of us running? Twelve of us? Twenty? I do not know, but the group I am running in is...

"*Bleku,*" shouts a Dah'Sel guard at Lesdelop's entrance. "*Bleku, Ble—*"

Five titanium rounds rip through his torso. His body jerks and twists from the weapon's effect. He staggers back and falls into the main corridor. The aftermath of his wounds peppers my body. Part of me wants to cry. Another part wishes to scream. The logical side of me is running to the opening of...

Searing hot titanium tears through a Dah'Sel's chest a few paces in front of me, exits her torso, and rips into my outer left thigh, twisting me to the ground.

I shout in pain.

The others continue without me. Five are torn to shreds, but one of them has stopped to help me up. Had I not been shot and stayed with the crowd, I would most likely be dead myself. Fate is momentarily on my side.

"*Kuzsoec,*" says Din'Mos, struggling to hoist me. "*Kuzsoec tadak-zut.*"

I do as he says with a face wrinkled in pain and force myself up to follow with his help. A drone circles back around to square up with us. Its sleek, half-pace wide, darting design, and chrome finish outline the hallow-lead plate covering its visual input sensors. It is magnificent, deadly, and posed to kill us when the front half of it is ripped apart by an onium round and lands at my feet. I cut my head to see who fired it and catch a glimpse of Sergeant Bentley.

"Sergeant Major," I call.

"Run," he shouts.

I look his way for only a tik before hobbling toward Lesdelop ti'it renasa the best I can with Din'Mos's help. Sergeant Bentley saved our lives, but the drone tries to take off again and knocks me back to the ground with my helper. We must hurry before another targets us.

We are up and moving with my squad and other members of the Armada. They open fire on the nimble A.I. attackers. Some shots land and others miss the drones and their erratic movements.

This blood on my arm ... it is not mine. I scan Din'Mos as we enter the Lesdelop. His left arm has blood running from it. I cannot tell how badly he is hurt with the hair on his arms concealing the wound.

"You're bleeding," I say.

He cuts me but a glance and continues in for cover. Gunshots echo into the structure with us. I look back and move into the room they once let me stay the night in while rounding the first corner.

"Din'Mos," I say. "*Ama ka hakiya-zic. Ver pota ot woo.*"

"*Blight orsplap*," says Din'Mos. "*Ver letrow ot ipasag hakiya-zic.*"

"Yeah," I say. "My leg's bleeding too, but worry about your arm before dealing with me. Go get a doctor."

"*Polasa Kla'Wah*," he says, helping me down and cutting me a frustrated look. "*Polasa Kla'Wah.*"

He is right. I need to talk in their language. There is no time for me to translate or make time-costing mistakes. Not with Dah'Sel and Armada wounded still pouring in.

"I said…" I say, pointing at him as I speak. "*Blight polasap ti'it nery das ver yata.*"

"*Ama ka fejaz,*" says Din'Mos. "*Blight uptru jesen pilim pisip tom meva ti'it glenoda.*"

I look down at my leg. It is worse than I…

26-2
Transfusion

My surroundings take a tek to come into view as I awake in the same room in which I passed out. Delgado is sitting upright next to me. I get my elbow under me to sit upright, but it feels like gravity is 20 times that of normal. Something is making me lightheaded. The room spins.

"Hold up there, speedy," says Dr. Sellers.

Delgado pushes me gently back down.

"You've lost a lot of blood," she says.

Din'Mos smiles from the floor with his back against the wall.

"*Ohrap ka jelq rot,*" he says.

We are okay now. It is nice of him to say, but I doubt it. Things are going to get much worse before they get better. Dolofónos will make sure of that.

Dr. Sellers is wrapping my hairy rescuer's once-bleeding arm. He must have shut the wound for him. I am sure Din'Mos appreciates his skill set. Of all the cycles I have known Dr. Sellers, I have never seen him make a mistake on the medical side of things. I have, however, seen him get drunk enough to need detox before closing self-induced gashes.

"Feeling better?" asks Delgado.

"Yeah," I answer. "I'm a little lightheaded."

"Me too," she says.

I notice an I.V. running into Delgado's jugular close to her ear. She is not wearing her mechanized legs. There are no wounds on her; none that I can see. They must have been damaged in the attack.

"What happened to you?" I ask.

"You did," she answers.

I trace the line running from her I.V. and realize it is connected to a pressure monitoring exchange pump with another line heading toward me. I place my hand on the tube and let my fingertips slide over it. It runs over my legs, up my body, over my shoulder, and into my...

No. This cannot be right. I widen my eyes and part my lips when I feel it meeting and penetrating my flesh.

"Haze," I say, startled by the find. "This is plugged into my neck."

Delgado giggles.

"She's the best match for you here," says Dr. Sellers.

I look her over while she sits on the floor without her robotic legs. In all the cycles I have known or known of her, this is the first time since the accident involving her and Sergeant Bentley that I have seen her without them. Her legs are rail thin from the hips down from muscular atrophy and motionless.

She places her hands on the stone floor and scoots herself back to lean against the wall. Her legs slide with her across the flooring. I scan the room for her mechanized legs. They are nowhere to be found.

"Delgado," I say. "You're not in your—"

"Legs?" interrupts Delgado. "They're standing in the main hall. Wouldn't fit in your little suite here."

"I'm sorry," I say.

"Don't be," she says. "Got me a little buzz now. Besides, they need to charge for the coming week."

"How long have I been out?"

"Only about forty," answers Dr. Sellers. "I gave you something to wake you. Sergeant Bentley thinks the Uprisers will be back before the rotation is up. They're probably planning or staging now."

"What about the Dah'Sel?" I ask.

"We have a plan for them," answers Delgado. "A false retreat of sorts."

"I don't understand," I say, turning to Dr. Sellers. "Can we take this out yet?"

Dr. Sellers finishes up with Din'Mos and moves to the pressure pump.

"Sure can," he answers. "Let me get this unhooked for you."

He turns it off and works on removing the I.V. from Delgado as we talk.

"So," I say, averting my eyes as the I.V. is pulled from Delgado's neck. "About this so-called retreat?"

"The Dah'Sel have a series of underground networks here they hadn't yet told us about," she answers. "One of its entry points is in one of the back rooms right here in Lesdelop. It webs out to Dah'Sel points of interest for clicks under the land. Another access and exit point is in Vut Honna. They excavated it to pass under its forest and reach the other side without concerning themselves about dying trying to cross through it."

"Makes sense, but..." I say, pausing to hold my breath while Dr. Sellers pulls the I.V. from my neck. "Ouch. Thanks."

I rub my neck.

"Mason," says Dr. Sellers. "You'll be able to walk around now, but it's going to cause you some discomfort. And try not to overdo it. We hooked a few people up to you before you were stable. Your body is going to take time to balance out its blood levels."

"Even with the nano you put in me?" I ask.

"You lost over half of them," he answers, "but they should have you balanced out within ninety and feeling fine again ... sore but fine."

"So, I can stand?"

"You can."

I sit up and roll to my knees. Din'Mos moves to Dr. Sellers's side to assist in helping me up.

"I thought you said I could stand?" I ask.

"You can," answers Dr. Sellers, "but I didn't say it would feel good."

I get my feet under me and push through a bit more pain than expected to stand.

"Ah..." I mumble through a strain. "Yeah. This sucks."

"*Jo dwaloc*, McKayla," says Din'Mos. "*Jo dwaloc.*"

"I'll try," I say with a forced smile. "Does anybody know how many were hurt in the last attack?"

"Twenty-six," answers Dr. Sellers. "Twenty of them didn't make it off the field."

"Including Din'Mos and me?" I ask.

"Twenty-eight," he answers. "Dr. Klinroy has a team working on the other injured."

Twenty died. I hope the rest are lucky, like Din'Mos and me. From what I saw before I made it into the Lesdelop ti'it renasa structure, there were at least seven Dah'Sel wounded during the assault.

There has been less than a complete cycle of peace on Wah'Lor since our arrival. Sure, we cured the Dah'Sel of their disease, but we traded it for another—humanity. Despite how good our intentions are, we have always found a way to spread through whatever world is giving us life like an intelligent virus incapable of correcting its course of actions.

"I'm going to go see if I can help out there," I say.

"Good idea," says Dr. Sellers. "Don't run though. Take it easy for a few taks."

We make our way through the exit and into the hall.

"Hey?" asks Delgado. "Is someone going to take me back to my legs or what?"

Dr. Sellers and I stop to cut each other looks with raised brows. It was not polite of us to walk out, mainly after she assisted in saving my life, but I did not even think about it. I would never do such a thing intentionally.

I peek my head back in and feel like a dyogg turd about it.

"Sorry," I say.

Din'Mos is motioning his hands back and forth between Delgado and us. I guess smart alecks are not confined to Kep Four. It turns out that it is a universal trait.

"*Dada ama*, Din'Mos," I say. "*Ohrap orsplap.*"

"I can't carry you alone, Delgado," says Dr. Sellers. "At least, not in an efficient way, and I don't want these two trying to lift you yet. I'll get a few people to help you here in a tek."

26-3
Preparation

Twenty plus teks have passed. Dr. Sellers and Sapp are finally getting Delgado fitted back into her robotics. She is not upset about the wait. Nor am I. We understand the circumstances and have been waiting at the exit in small conversations with her about nothing important.

Sapp unhooks a small charging pack from the back left hamstring of her robotic legs and retracts the cord.

"You can go jogging for the next two weeks if you want," he says. "You're welcome, but I wouldn't recommend swimming."

"But that's my favorite pastime," says Delgado.

They share a smirk. Sapp exits Lesdelop with the charger as Delgado leans over to twist out a small cylinder on her outer left thigh. She slides it back into her robotics and twists it into a locked position.

A male connector at the back of her metal legs snaps into a female receiving port in her lower lumbar. The hip region of her mechanical legs manipulates into position to cover her hips and lower stomach before snuggling into her. She gives me a wink.

A set of yellow lights flash on each of her mechanized hips. Its knees straighten from a bent position and lock upright. She takes a few steps.

"Feel better?" I ask.

"I do, actually," she answers. "Now, let's join the others and find out what's going on out there."

We make our way across the clearing toward the Vut Honna forest region of the planet. We are not going all the way to it, but within a quarter click for sure. If Sergeant Bentley is planning what I think he is with the Dah'Sel, it makes perfect sense.

Something grabs me from behind. I scream and turn, with Delgado watching.

"Pru'Cet..." I say.

My arms wrap him without warning. He matches my action. Then he kisses my forehead, showing he has picked up some of our sweeter nuances. I love this guy, even though he is taller than me now, and enjoys pointing it out.

"Where's Tila'Cet?" I ask through a grimace.

"*Bea E Vee'Sal,*" answers Pru'Cet. "*Yama ot kuzsoec-zic bea siwbe su fesnop troqfel.*"

"Coming tonight is good," I say, "but we were just attacked again. The Uprisers, I'm sure they're planning something for later."

"I know," says Pru'Cet. "I send meggage."

"Meggage?" I say. "You mean message?"

"Vee'Sal be ready," he answers with a nod.

"That's what we want to hear," says Dr. Sellers. "No idea what it means, but it sounds good."

"When you say The Vee'Sal will be—"

Pru'Cet grabs my hand and pulls me toward the Vut Honna forest where the others are gathering.

"Ouch," I say with a heavy limp. "Easy."

"Sorry," he says.

Pru'Cet stops, gives me another hug, and continues again with slower strides.

Dr. Sellers shakes his head as he walks alongside us.

"I knew you two were going to be stuck to each other like logorgan paste the first time I saw the two of you in the science lab on *Athanasios*," he says.

I felt the same way about us, but I do not know about the logorgan paste. I have never tasted it, because that stuff stinks like a rotted gaznote egg. Maybe worse.

CHAPTER 27
Sub-Terrain

We arrive to find our entire squad with Pru'Cet's uncle Bah'Cet already here. They are murmuring amongst themselves with relaxed postures, but concern has flooded their faces. They know what is coming.

"Did you get her all patched up?" asks Sergeant Bentley.

"Sure did," answers Dr. Sellers. "She's as good as new."

"I wouldn't go that far," I say, "but I'm certainly in better shape than I was earlier this rotation."

"Better than nothing," says Sapp.

"Everyone here knows the game plan besides those of you that just showed up?" asks Sergeant Bentley.

Everyone chimes in with confirmation. A few nod as Nala'Cet approaches Pru'Cet and her brother, Bah'Cet. Their arms rise. They match her, and their palms meet as their foreheads touch for a moment. Then he hugs her—something I have made him accustomed to—before she lets him go to hug her brother.

"*Jo quamza,* Pru'Cet," says Nala'Cet.

"*Blight uptru,*" says Pru'Cet. "*Blight armona ama, rita.*"

"*Ne blight ama,*" says Nala'Cet with a worried smile and turns to her brother. "*Ama eo tanza sa soo.*"

"Pru'Cet," says Bah'Cet, "*cre eo tanza sa Pru'Cet. Tump blight o bea soo.*"

Nala'Cet smiles again to mask her concern and nods to the group before walking toward the Vut Honna forest. She is not good at hiding her emotions. I feel no different. Fear courses through my veins.

I watch her as she walks away and the others talk. Pru'Cet is doing the same, but for different reasons. We both hold worries for what is to come, but mine is over the forested region of Wah'Lor she will enter in a moment. They say the outer perimeter is not initially hostile, but it is supposed to get reasonably treacherous the farther one gets into it.

Trees in front form a high canopy, and the initial outskirts of the Vut Honna forest appear open and clear of flora but become dense with vegetation as you continue. The bark on trees here is smooth like glass yet maintains a knobby texture resembling traction ridges found on carbon convoy tires. It does not look safe.

A smell emanates from it, filling the partially melting field with hints of burning plastic. Though the area has no warm-blooded beta'bet trees to battle against the snow, its canopy maintains its purple and green swirled leaves stiff enough to house nearly a pace of white powder on top of them. I cannot see them from here, but we were warned scama plants are growing rampant beneath the white.

It is crazy to think that I cannot see any because they are supposedly bigger than me. Not that I have ever seen one. It is an area we have never had a need or desire to enter.

"Mason," says Sergeant Bentley.

I snap out of the thought.

"Sorry, Sergeant Major. I was..."

A noise above and to my right. My eyes stretch in their sockets. An empty Plegma Nine without a pilot is heading straight for me. Pru'Cet and his uncle tackle me a fraction before what would have been my end.

The Plegma Nine passes a distance less than the width of my hand over us and slams into the monolithic HU-2 housing unit. Another is on course. We run down the side of its target as it pushes through the wall.

"Mason?" repeats Sergeant Bentley. "You with us?"

"Yeah," I answer. "I'm fine. I'll try to focus."

There is no need to say I had another vision. Not now. We have bigger things to worry about than me seeing an empty Plegma Nine crashing with no further information to offer.

"Let's move out," says Sergeant Bentley.

Along with Pru'Cet, Bah'Cet, and Din'Mos, my squad and I make our way to an Argos parked near the tree line.

"She's ready to rock," says Bell, placing an integration jewel on his right temple.

I have been either too stuck in a vision or dreaming awake about everything Sergeant Bentley said. It will be fine either way. The game plan is apparent: they will post this Argos near the tree line, several of us will be armed at its edge, and when the Uprisers move in, we will open fire running into the Vut Honna forest. The others will most likely remain behind for a moment to deal damage before moving in after us. Hopefully, our enemies will follow.

27-2
Implementation

We wait for what feels like rotations. I am near the center of everyone lined up at the forest's edge. From my left to right are Sapp, Delgado, Bell, Din'Mos, myself, Pru'Cet, Bah'Cet, and Dr. Sellers. Sergeant Bentley would not let us engage without someone to tend our wounds. Fister and Sergeant Bentley are standing in front of us. All are in combat suits, even the Dah'Sel.

I think they have Din'Mos and me near the center due to our recent injuries. It makes sense. The entrance for the underground tunnel system the Dah'Sel built is nearest here, though I am unsure of how it looks. I assume it is just a hole in the ground.

"How long do—"

"There," says Fister, pointing to the Lesdelop ti'it renasa structure.

"Ready weapons," says Sergeant Bentley.

I study the solo red-and-black drone scouting the area, flying from the top of the structure to its side, and strafing in a spiral while scanning it until at its base. If I had to guess, I would say it is checking for life signs. It will not find any. Everyone—Dah'Sel and humans alike—are underground awaiting their moment to strike at dozens of entrances and exit points—all of which are sealed with a trapdoor. Atop those trapdoors are living plants that allow them to blend in flawlessly with their surroundings.

"Wait for it to see us," says Sergeant Bentley. "We need Dolofónos to think he's got the drop on us. In fact, put down your weapons."

"Come again," says Fister.

"Place them on the ground and take a step or two toward the person next to you. Act like you're talking. They have to think they're catching us off guard."

We do as he says. None of us has a reason to have anything less than trust for Sergeant Bentley. If the man has a plan, I believe in it.

A moment passes. The drone moves from the building and routes itself toward what little we have left as intact housing units. Sergeant Bentley walks toward our Argos in a blatant attempt to get nonchalantly noticed. It takes but a tik to work.

The drone spins to face him and locks onto his position, undoubtedly relaying visual feedback somewhere near Dolofónos. We act as if we have not seen it yet while Sergeant Bentley closes the Argos door and walks casually back to us.

"Well," I say, "I think that did it."

"Let it get a little bit closer and act like you just noticed it, Mason," says Sergeant Bentley.

I watch the drone from the corner of my eyes as it eases our way. A hundred more paces, give or take, and I will react. Three, two, one...

I turn casually, look at it, and point.

"Drone!"

The others react. Sergeant Bentley rushes back toward his weapon. I pick up my rifle, and three rounds go off. Fister, Sapp, and Bell have already opened fire. The drone's front side is riddled with shots, forcing it to power down and plummet to the ground—hot metal melts surrounding snow with newborn flames.

Hundreds, maybe a thousand, Uprisers rush from the trees beyond Lesdelop and charge in our direction while releasing a war cry. Dozens shoot as they run, but the shots are nowhere near us. I wait patiently behind the nearest dofabe tree for orders to return fire, but several airborne vessels matching the ones we encountered searching for the *Ark* blaze over distant trees and the heads of approaching Uprisers.

"Take them out," shouts Sergeant Bentley. "Target left to right."

We open fire on incoming targets in the order stated. It is a good call. There are two Bomba Classes on the left, followed by a Beltric Class Six and lesser vessels on the right. Onium from our rifles does everything from missing, penetrating, and bouncing off the Bomba furthest left to ricocheting back at us, into the sky, and through the forest behind us.

Bah'Cet, Dr. Sellers, Pru'Cet, and Din'Mos are not the best shots. Thankfully, the rest of my squad is. The turret atop Argos is feeding off the integration jewel tapped into Sapp's thoughts without missing a beat. He is ready to raise haze.

A concentration of fire decimates the first and second enemy Bomba Class fighters, but The Upriser Beltric Class Six pulls high. Sapp rips into a Plegma Nine with his rifle and Argos. Whatever is in his crosshairs, the integration jewel relays to the assisting turret.

A few rounds rip into our Argos, pothole the ground as impacting rounds pass it and make their way toward Bah'Cet. He is unleashing gunfire at his target and does not notice.

"Bah'Cet," I shout.

Din'Mos takes a few steps, grabs Bah'Cet's combat suit, and snatches him backward hard enough that they both fall to the ground. Incoming gunfire sends dirt, grass, snow, and small roots flipping into the air.

Sapp's eyes close as the integration jewel seeps further into his subconscious. It glows a bright gold on his temple, and the turret pauses for a brief tik and hums with a matching gold light at its base before reanimating as one with him. It locks from target to target and takes out the drones: one low, one high, three left, one right, and one enemy patrol vessel in the distance. What drones remain have no choice but to pull up and preserve their place in a future fight.

A single damaged drone flips and spins in multiple directions on an erratic flight path. It is out of control and falls from sight behind the trees. I sigh in relief as the others fly off.

"Are we clear to move?" asks Sergeant Bentley.

"Everything looks good from—"

The malfunctioning drone crashes through the treetops near us to break branches and send leaves drifting around us. We dive for cover. A heavy impact echoes the surroundings. I cover my head. Fragments of metal land around us.

I look over my shoulder from the ground and see impact burns and scrapes on the side of the Argos. It stops rocking.

"Sapp," I say, standing to rush to his side of the Argos and open its door. "Are you okay?"

Sapp is sideways in his seat.

Delgado and Sergeant Bentley reach the Argos. Sapp is shaking proverbial cobwebs from his head. A small trickle of blood drips from his integration jewel.

"I should have strapped in," says Sapp, removing the integration jewel from his temple.

He resets it and places it back to his temple while moving behind the Argos with Sergeant Bentley.

"I can still control it," he says, "but I've lost the deep link."

"Good enough," says Sergeant Bentley.

A StarBird, far into the blue, catches my attention. Red and black. Dolofónos and Saddi are the only ones I can imagine commanding it.

"Guys," I say.

The others turn to look. Uprisers on foot are over halfway across the field and running in our direction with inaccurate shots, but there are a lot of them. A blast hits the tree next to me and we take cover.

"End that stampede," calls Sergeant Bentley from behind the Argos.

We fire into the onrushing crowd. Several Uprisers drop to the cold surface they charge upon. Others take a knee for precision aim.

An onium round grazes the sleeve on my left arm. I take cover behind the tree. Bark splinters off it. Another shot knocks off a branch. Delgado dives from her cover to avoid being hit by it, and they open fire at her. She rolls back behind the tree next to her and returns fire in full auto as she pulls herself up with its trunk.

They are overwhelming us. There are too many of them and too much firepower is coming downfield for us to stand in front of it.

"Fall back," shouts Sergeant Bentley. "Into Vut Honna. Move. Move. Move."

We do as he says. I keep my back to the tree and run into the forest for cover behind another tree, and repeat. No visions of my own death yet, not that I am trying to trigger one thinking about dying here this rotation.

"Bring that Argos in behind us, Sapp," says Sergeant Bentley. "I want them to think it's being operated internally."

I drop in front of the Argos with the others. Its rear is taking heavy punishment. A loud clatter of metal flapping on metal resonates the forest with gunfire.

Branches, leaves, and snow continue falling from the trees as we push in with rounds clanking around us. I need to watch for patches of snow with green stems sticking out of them tipped with pink, feathery leaves. They are the scama plants. To touch their feathery leaves is said to be an inevitable loss of life.

Bah'Cet grabs me.

"*Azata,*" he says, pointing for my eyes to trace his finger. "*Scama.*"

Its stems are thin, hard to see, and much smaller than I thought they would be. I nearly ran into a series of them. They are almost transparent. I would have been plant food in a few more steps.

Bah'Cet pulls me around it and stops to give me a stern look with laser-focused eyes.

"*Icci qicea ti'it cea,* McKayla," he says. "*Tatam quo-tot-zis pisip.*"

I follow him to a large opening in the ground. Delgado, Pru'Cet, Sapp, and Fister are already entering. Wooded steps are near its entrance. I descend halfway down before noticing Din'Mos, Bah'Cet, and Sergeant Bentley are not following.

"Din'Mos," I call.

Sergeant Bentley stands his ground and fires for a moment before tossing a fog-spreader toward the field. The small black cube hits the ground, or maybe a tree for all I know from down here, and hums with a whoosh as it ignites to blanket the Vut Honna forest with a wide and almost instantaneous screen of smoke.

"Let's go," says Sergeant Bentley, entering the hole to descend its steps behind me.

Din'Mos and Bah'Cet move to the side of the hole, grab its upright lid, and pull it down far enough for it to close on its own. They jump in behind us to avoid the heavy closing door and tumble down the steps. They probably would have been hurt if it were not for their combat suits.

What sounds like thunder fills my ears as the ground shakes around me. The charging Uprisers have not slowed. Screams follow as scama plants tear into them nearly 1/2 click deep into the woods.

"*Saisay uptru gingo pilim yetia zamba sa Vut Honna jotap,*" says Bah'Cet.

"Let's hope not," I say.

Sergeant Bentley's cutting me the what the haze did he say look. Bah'Cet needs to work on our language more, but he is learning like the others.

"He said they won't make it out of Vut Honna alive," I answer.

I listen for a tek and almost feel bad for them. I cannot imagine being blinded by the disruptive and equipment-jamming cloud of smoke unleashed by Sergeant Bentley. Not only are they physically overwhelmed by it, but it is rendering visual aid from the H.U.D. in their suits inoperable.

Upriser screams match their horror. It is blood-curdling. I do not know how much more of it I can bear to hear. It could be worse, I guess. We could be the ones screaming.

Wat'Uza once told me the trees in Vut Honna are alive and capable of defending themselves, but are only triggered once the scama plants are disturbed. He said everything in this area of Wah'Lor is connected and works together—minus the sad-looking dofabe trees. He could not have convinced me such an intricate design of flora existed while I was living on Kep Four.

"Sounds like the screams are fading," says Bell.

"Yeah," I say. "I wish."

Echoes of creaking wood penetrate the cave ceiling as surrounding trees do whatever they are doing to protect their region of land, but it stops when Wah'Lor shakes. Explosive rounds are annihilating the forest above—another planetary segment destroyed by humanity.

"Dolofónos must've ordered a strike," says Sergeant Bentley.

"Probably thinks we're still up there taking them out under the Vut Honna canopy," says Sapp.

"*Ohrap licea jesen,*" says Pru'Cet, turning to the others. "We need leave."

I am not going to correct him on the word *must*. The time for such things is not in my favor. For the moment being, I will follow him with the others. I do not know where we are going. It is away from here. That alone is enough for me to follow. Hopefully, the other Dah'Sel and Armada members were as fortunate as we have been so far this rotation.

CHAPTER 28
Ushering

This underground tunnel system—built by the Dah'Sel and Vee'Sal before they separated to form their own sects—is nothing short of astounding. Hieroglyphs and all, it is very much in line with what adorns the inner walls at the Lesdelop ti'it renasa structure. It still bothers me that a language I cracked and literally wrote the Digi-book on was also found here, and I cannot read it.

"I really want to see the place they got the symbols from to create their written language," I say.

"I'd second you on that," says Dr. Sellers. "With a team accompanying you, of course."

We make our way through the tunnel system behind Pru'Cet, his uncle Bah'Cet, and Din'Mos with Sergeant Bentley walking at his side. It is nice to see that they have bonded so well. I hope nothing happens to either one of them over the rotations to come.

The interior walls are intensely reflective and made of obsidian—the same naturally occurring, sanded, and polished volcanic glass that is found in their home structure. It is like overhead lights project into the tunnels for us to see with everyone in fully activated combat suits.

We pass through an open area with obsidian benches and a few places to rest nested out in each corner. Maybe it is a place the Dah'Sel come when they need a break from socializing, or perhaps these are the areas where the Vee'Sal once stayed before their sects separated—not that I have ever seen any of them visit this part of Wah'Lor. I wonder if visits were commonplace before our arrival.

"We get close," says Pru'Cet.

A few hundred more paces down a descending tunnel with reflective steps carved beneath our feet, and we arrive at an area where thousands come into view: Armada military personnel, men, women, and children are there with a good portion of the Dah'Sel population. I do not know how many, but this is one of four areas where we are holding meetings before our next plan of action. How we are going to pull this off is beyond me.

I wish the Uprisers would just go away.

Sergeant Bentley walks to the center stage of the large opening. Those here are circling the empty floor in bleacher-style seating. Chatter amongst the waiting comes to a hush.

Sergeant Bentley turns back to us for a moment.

"This is incredible," he says, activating his comms. "Are all personnel channeled into my signal?"

Confirmation comes back from the other three gathering halls.

"Everyone's aware of what we're up against," continues Sergeant Bentley. "Those that initially doubted the severity of what Dolofónos and his hoard of trash that survived are capable of should no longer have doubts. We have already seen the first wave, and I can assure you they are formidable."

He paces and rubs his fingertips nervously together. I cannot blame him. I am nervous thinking about it while translating to Kla'Wah for those around us as he speaks.

"We're making our next move in forty," says Sergeant Bentley. "That should allow enough time for the Uprisers to settle and start coming up with their own game plan, now that they don't know where we are. We can't stay down here forever though. It's time to fight. Outnumbered and outgunned as we are, we're going to have to be crafty in our approach. In forty, we're coming up from each access area of the tunnels in even-numbered groups. A leader is in each group at the gathering halls of the Dah'Sel's tunnel system. That leader is to separate those around them capable of combat into four different groups and assign a sub-commander to each. I believe they've already been selected. If not, get on it. The next communication will be in five before we move. Bentley out."

28-2
Final Conversation

Sergeant Bentley's eyes dance in their sockets as he paces. He talks loudly so everyone around us can hear. His voice echoes with every word in the highly acoustic chamber.

"I want all children," he says, "as well as mothers of children under the age of ten, to step fifteen paces from the walls."

I move closer to Sergeant Bentley's side to translate for the Dah'Sel.

"*Blight hasta renasa ubido fit-zis ti'it kuzsoec qa'qu olov-zis kimit cea,*" I say.

Hundreds of women and children exit the obsidian bleachers and step 15 paces toward Sergeant Bentley and me.

"Anyone not able to fight can step forward as well," continues Sergeant Bentley.

"*Renasa gingo gona ti'it seblak cre olov kimit cea ki hamp,*" I say.

Hundreds more step forward. Some men, some women, all either elderly or crippled. Many were injured in the Upriser attacks humanity brought to Wah'Lor. Sergeant Bentley glances my way.

"Now," he says, "we need to get the drone operational." He turns to Fister. "How long until it's ready?"

"It's ready to fly now," answers Fister. "Just got the mask up and running again."

"Let's get it in the air then," says Sergeant Bentley. "I'll relay to the other four groups."

Fister moves to the control unit the Dah'Sel carried down for us before we went underground. It is a smaller version of the drone he pilots from within Argos transport units. He takes a seat, powers it up, puts on his accompanying headpiece and goggles, and activates the portable station's projector.

The Slaka F Class drone he is using resembles the Slaka D Class that attacked us earlier. Only it cannot be equipped with armaments of any type. It is roughly the size of a human head, capable of full mask, and often referred to as The Baby Slaka. Armada disapproved of this nickname, but it was used so much that they eventually accepted it.

28-3
Scouting

Fister pilots the drone back to the tunnel we entered. A three-dimensional image of everything it sees comes to life in a two-pace sphere in front of him. It is not long before the drone reaches the end of the tunnel where Armada personnel and Dah'Sel are lifting the hatch enough for it to squeeze through.

USHERING

Charred bodies, fallen and flaming trees, burned shrubs, and no signs of life come into view. The Uprisers have decimated the area, and not a sign of life remains. A combination of steam from the overly moist scama plants and smoke fills most of what is visible.

Fister takes the drone into the air and pauses its flight.

"Looks like this isn't going to be a walk in the Denta fields," he says.

He is right. Nothing about this is easy. It never will be again until this threat is eliminated.

What I see on the projection is the opposite: Uprisers in noncombative vehicles are flying over trees near and far in search of us. Thousands of them are on foot, moving in and out of HU-2. They are also moving into the Lesdelop ti'it renasa structure.

"We need to act now," says Sergeant Bentley, "before they figure out where the tunnel entrance is in the back of Lesdelop ti'it renasa." He activates his comms again. "Everyone, get ready; we're going in three."

My heart sinks when he says it. Before I know it, the first wave will emerge to engage the Uprisers; there is no way we can do it without losing someone. I will, however, keep my fingers crossed that the numbers are limited.

CHAPTER 29
Engagement

There is no sense in war. Sometimes you have no choice. It only takes one person or one side of the equation for there to be conflict. The only option is to fight when put in such situations, or else you find yourself lying back, not resisting the attack, and getting hurt or worse. This is our situation, like it or not.

We do not want to fight. We want peace, but the opposition will not allow it. They will kill us all if given a chance. I accept that.

Why does humanity have to be so flawed? Why is there always someone that wants to argue, fight, kill, or wage battles resulting in death, desperation, and suffering?

This is humanity's biggest flaw—the inability to accept others for who they are, even though those not accepted by others are harming no one. I do not attack people because they do not think the same way I do. Why everyone else does not reckon this way or hold back their verbal, political, and physical onslaughts and embrace a life of peace is beyond me.

No matter how right or wrong my thoughts on this are, we are about to commit an attack that will result in bloodshed. Both sides will feel the impact of Upriser hate, but

ENGAGEMENT

I think that is the greatest desire of Dolofónos. He wants suffering.

"Ready in ten," says Sergeant Bentley, with attackers ready to rush from the tunnels at twelve different exit points, "nine ... eight ... seven ... six ... five ... four ... three ... two ... one..."

The hatch nearest me flies open, allowing Armada and Dah'Sel in combat suits to surge from it. There is no war-cry. All I hear is my accelerating heartbeat. It is getting hard to breathe, and I am clutching Pru'Cet so he cannot leave.

"Wait," I say. "Let the others go first. They're more experienced."

"*Ma*," says Pru'Cet. "*Blight jesen.*"

"They're not fighting alone," says Sergeant Bentley. "We're going to be right behind them here in two, but we can't all go out at once."

Pru'Cet nods. I guess they are both learning the others' language better than I thought. At least, they are hearing and understanding more significant portions of it.

Sapp, Bell, Fister, Sergeant Bentley, Delgado, and even Dr. Sellers line up beside us as we ready our turn. Two more squads are in front of us. One is at our backs. If the same happens at all 12 tunnel exits, this will be a massive attack. Let us hope it is enough to end it quickly.

There is no snow around us. Along with all the Uprisers, plants, and wildlife, the area is a patchwork of smoldering embers and wet grass. Charred remains of life crunch beneath my feet as I jog under a full mask in a combat suit, trying to ignore the pain in my healing leg with the rest of my group.

The first two teams out charge to form a "V" pattern as they press forward, allowing us to go straight across the field.

Those emerging behind us hold until we are nearly a click away from them before they come out.

Snow deepens to be shin and knee-deep as we...

The War Stopper is heading in my direction, out of control, and coming in fast with large flyers attacking it. The ship comes to a rest upside down against a large boulder protruding from the ground 50 paces away. As an Upriser emerges from the war-vessel, winged creatures tear him apart, feasting on his flesh when he attempts to exit.

I am facing down in the snow and look up to see the unique, partially transparent aura surrounding my group's silhouettes, letting me know where they are while masked. Their names float above each of their heads for identification on my helmet's visor. Dr. Sellers and Pru'Cet are running back to me while the others carry on.

"What happened?" asks Dr. Sellers.

"I tripped," I answer, knowing he can see right through me.

"Another vision," he says, pulling me to my feet as the group to our left takes fire. "You'll have to tell me about it later."

"Agreed," I say.

Sergeant Bentley leads the others into HU-2 and opens fire. Another squad is pushing into the opposing end while a third enters a breached east wall. I will be in the mix with them soon, but am hesitant about shooting another human being with a rifle. It is going to feel personal compared to aerial combat.

I had never taken a life before coming to what some Armada personnel angrily refer to as the WolfStar of Andromeda. Some even wanted to label it as such on interstellar maps officially. To me, it is Wah'Lor and the first place I ever took the life of another in aerial combat. I have Dolofónos to thank for that and no desire to do it again with this rifle.

Pru'Cet enters ahead of Dr. Sellers and me. The area has become a war zone but already looked the part before we entered. I look back one last time to see a group of Dah'Sel emerging with high-V-sticks from a faraway tunnel near Lesdelop. They ambush nearby Uprisers engaged in conversation, heading to a red-and-black starfighter. If the enemy does not take off in that vessel soon, it will be mine.

"Move, Mason," shouts Bell.

"Coming," I say.

"No," says Bell, pointing as he runs. "Move!"

I turn to look. My eyes stretch in their sockets. An empty Plegma Nine without a pilot is heading straight for me. Pru'Cet and his uncle tackle me a fraction of a tik before what would have been my end.

The Plegma Nine passes a distance less than the width of my hand over us and slams into the monolithic housing unit. Another is on course. We run down the side of its target as it buries itself into the outer wall of HU-2.

Dolofónos once stated that a vessel without armament was nothing more than a Kamakazi. He must have meant what he said because the twisted man is using them as such.

"*Cakou*," shouts Bah'Cet.

We turn and run toward Lesdelop as the unmanned Plegma Nine rips into the front portion of HU-2. Pieces of the housing unit and the Plegma spring into the air and into the dirt around us. We dive for cover.

"State your name if you're still with me," says Sergeant Bentley over comms. "My suit's not reading anyone."

The team responds.

"Fister."

"Bell."
"Sapp."
"Sellers."
"Delgado."

We are almost to the structure when dozens of Uprisers exit.

"Mason," says Sergeant Bentley, "see if you can get to that starfighter next to Lesdelop."

"Busy, but here," I answer, firing a missed shot at a distant upriser while taking cover behind Plegma nine debris. "Pru' and Bah' are here with me. We got separated. We're—"

Bah'Cet opens fire on the Uprisers. Pru'Cet joins him. I watch, hoping they do not need me to help, but three more Uprisers exit and raise their rifles.

I hit the one on the far-right dead center of her chest after missing a shot or two. She goes down. My heart sinks as Pru'Cet and his uncle take out the rest. A lifetime promise I would never take a life on the ground has been broken more than once this rotation.

My feet pull me without warning toward the nearby starfighter. It is most likely the last one on the planet. I climb in and punch the dash several times with a scream to release tears of sorrow for my actions ... and stop. A wave of numbness hits me.

"Mason," calls Delgado. "We have airborne incoming."

More numbness. A lack of emotion or empathy like never before takes over me. This is going to end now.

"Armada voice clearance," I say. "Mason, five, Sinote, one, four, McKayla, three, six." The starfighter powers up. "Initiate combat type two dash nine. Override Armada combat safety protocols."

ENGAGEMENT

I look at the sky. Armada pilots are engaging the Uprisers with what little we can offer as aerial defense, but they are not faring well. The numbers are too great against us.

"Engaging now," I say.

I hit a micro-jump straight from the ground and join the battle. Every available aerial combat vessel in the Armada arsenal is in flight. Everything red-and-black is about to be under my aim.

"Time to burn the—"

A shot passes over the back of my starfighter and skims over my hatch. It would have been a direct hit if I had come out of the micro jump a few paces farther.

I bank right and push myself through as many G's as I can handle and look back to the vessel that took a shot at me. I fire. All 25 barrels rotate to release their payload. The vessel explodes when its core ruptures.

"That was for you, Chubb," I say.

The Armada is losing the sky and, from what I can tell up here, the ground battle as well. Tides need turning. I take out a few more airborne vessels to speed up the process, but my biggest fear appears in front of me: the War Stopper.

The War Stopper is the nastiest thing in the Armada arsenal. It houses two of the barrels possessed by the Beltric Class Six, Scat-Shots, EMP burst capabilities, masks itself between shots, and it has the toughest hide in our fleet next to the *Dwarf*... and I will have to engage it, but not yet.

I believe Dolofónos is using the StarBird as a relay station for their communication signals. It is a long shot, but unless he had Armada codes and voice clearance, he cannot communicate freely without rewiring it. That is one of many reasons capital leaders are all that have been allowed to ride in them. They were built for commanders and chiefs. I can separate their ability to communicate and doubt the Uprisers have enough training to maintain structure in battle.

I go nose up toward the StarBird's undercarriage as it shoots down two Armada transport vessels trying to take it out.

"Goodbye, Dolofónos," I say.

The StarBird's belly is converted to metal ribbons when I open fire. It banks back and to its left as it goes in for a crash landing. Several eject in drop pods. Dolofónos must be in one of them.

I bank down after them with an Armada vessel pulling in behind me to help.

"I'm on them," says James Algash.

"Good to—"

A series of shots shake my starfighter. I lose flight control.

"One down," says James Algash.

"Hey," I shout. "Algash? Any reason you just shot me? And where did you come from?"

"Mason?" he asks. "Why are you in a red-and-black Upriser—"

"Just take out those pods while I correct this," I interrupt.

He dips in pursuit of the drop pods and opens fire. I do not have time to watch and see if he gets them, nor can I help. Luckily, the scout ship he is piloting has nothing more than onium burst capability, though I have not regained control of my starfighter yet.

"Armada voice clearance," I say. "Mason, five, Sinote, one, four, McKayla, three, six, Purge electrical systems, flush, and reboot."

The H.U.D. is down and gives me nothing more than a series of dots:

ENGAGEMENT

....
....
....

I am free-falling, hoping this thing restarts before I must eject and let it crash into the surface. It is taking longer than expected. The windshield around me behind the H.U.D. leaves me wishing I was in the darkness of my Beltric with viewing panes not working. It would be better than watching my plunge.

"Well," I say, "looks like I'm out a starfighter."

I reach for the eject lever with the ground coming quickly. It powers back up. I grab the controls again, but it resists my piloting efforts. My small stature is no match against a helm while its systems are still rebooting. I pull with force against its noncooperative mechanical components. It is not enough.

"I..." I say with gritting teeth and straining arms. "I should have eje—"

The starfighter's underside smacks into the planet's surface. My head whips back and forth while it tumbles across a snowy field tarnished with the blood of the fallen. I wrap my arms around my head to stabilize it and...

CHAPTER 30
Calamity

I open my eyes to an aching head with fuzzy vision. The suns have set. Night is upon me with the blue moon rising over peaks of mountaintops.

Thousands of nails feel to be forming in the center of my brain and growing outward like an expanding iron star. To make things worse, it is dark, and if not for the backup power supply, I would be sitting with a perfect black control panel in front of me. Why the starfighter is wholly powered down is beyond me. Perhaps the War Stopper sent out an EMP that entangled my ship in its grasp after I crashed. I cannot think right now.

My flight controls come into focus as I place my hands to my head in an unsuccessful attempt to stop the proverbial star of nails from expanding. It is not working. I either have a concussion or brain damage. Then again, headaches could be returning because I bled out half the nanobots in my system implanted to suppress visions.

I lower my hands. They are wet with red. There is a reason they say to helmet up before flight.

It hurts when I close my eyes and pop my neck while listening for anything. The cracks are loud, and my left arm jumps from what they call a body jolt. It is a painful and frightening sensation.

CALAMITY

Upriser vessels litter the sky with the Armada engaging them in combat. Gunshots and minor explosions fill the air. I can hear more of it than I can see, though I do not know how it is going for us.

"Armada voice clearance," I say, closing my eyes tight to focus. "Mason, five, Sinote, one, four, McKayla, three, six. Purge—"

The red-and-black starfighter I stole interrupts me with a rough shake and stops. It is powerless. There are no visual feeds for me to see.

"Armada voice clearance," I repeat. "Mason, five, Sinote, one, four, McKayla, three, six. Purge secondary—"

The starfighter shakes again and powers back down. It is useless to keep trying. I am going to have to open the hatch manually.

I fumble for the release lever and pull with everything I have. It is barely moving. I might be too disoriented and weak from the crash or previous injuries to do this right now.

My shoulders slump back into the seat. I take a few heavy breaths.

"Come on, McKayla," I say. "They need you. You can do this."

I reach for the lever again and pull aggressively with both hands while propping my feet against the floor for leverage. It does not budge, but I continue straining. It clicks.

I relax for another moment.

"At least it's unlocked," I say with a heavy breath.

I muster the mental gall to stand in the cockpit and lift the hatch. My arms are shaking over a grimacing face. I do not remember it being this heavy. It cannot be, not when it is made from the lightest known materials.

The hatch finally lifts enough for mechanical hydraulics to take over and raise it skyward. A final blue sun is about to set and join its binary twin on the other side of Wah'Lor. Shooting stars and passing comets are streaking the night sky in a display of... No. Wait. They are not shooting stars or a meteor shower; it is from the battle waging above me.

I climb from the cockpit and suck air between my teeth when its hull burns me, then throw myself from it to escape the pain. My body tumbles into the wet ground where a half pace of snow once rested.

"Sheesh," I say. "That's hot."

I assume it is warm from being blasted with the EMP. At least, that would explain why its systems are down. I am thankful it did not overload the core enough to ignite the ship during my unconscious state.

People are fighting in the air and on Wah'Lor's surface in the distance. I see more red-and-black than I do the Armada's green and yellow. We are losing.

I do not know what to do, but I will not cross that field to join the battle unarmed. My rifle is still in the starfighter, and its hull is too hot to scale again. My only other option is to make my way to the nearest...

The starfighter hums to life.

"Wonderful," I say. "Now it wants to fire back up?"

I stand to ponder how I am going to climb back into the cockpit without burning myself. Then it powers down again.

"Perfect," I mumble.

I turn to cross the shortest section of the field toward the Vut Honna forest without thinking.

My dizzy-and-crooked-paced jog causes me to fall a few times while the one-sided battle wages in front of me, but I am not surrounded by it as I once thought. That is the only reason I am still alive. Crashing a click away from the heart of battle was an unintentional blessing.

This snow is hard to tread with weakened legs. Every step I take is a struggle.

"What the heck is that?" I ask, easing forward to investigate.

Snow covers the person's head on my side and much of the upper body. Only the legs remain free of powder.

"Please tell me that's not someone I know."

I approach with cautious steps. His face comes into view. It is Dr. Tangin.

At least Dolofónos lost his best doctor from my visions, not that I wished him dead. Luckily for me, there is a ... never mind. That is his other hand. The way it looks, lying severed in the snow next to him, led me to believe it was a sidearm of some kind I could snag to protect myself. No such luck here. Not this rotation.

My best bet is to move into the lower region of the Vut Honna forest. If I do not venture too far into it, I should be safe. I will keep my distance from its center. Stepping into the reach of a scama and becoming plant food is not on my list of things to do this rotation.

30-2
Edge of Vut Honna

I enter, turn right, and make my way through the outer perimeter of the tree line. The oncoming night sky to my right is full of smoke. Sporadic fires and mostly unrecognizably damaged vessels pockmark the snow beneath. One is a standard transport. Another is an A.A.T.V. The rest are disfigured beyond recognition and on fire.

I stop to watch for a moment with watering eyes.

The dofabe tree Rhigas, Dr. Wright, Morris, Dr. Utley, and Skedelski are buried beneath is burning. It looks like the Uprisers found the Dah'Sel's tunnel entrances. They are overrunning the Armada. We cannot win this. There are too many red-and-black-suited fiends with varying weapons and numbers. All are armed. Our civilians are not. There was not enough firepower to go around for all of us.

Vut Honna forest's edge is forgivingly guiding me under its cloak, but something just snared my attention: Armada and Dah'Sel combatants emerge from the unfound twelfth tunnel exit. It is a perfect flank. They unleash onium rifle blasts into the backs of our attackers.

I jump and clench my fists as they fire.

Something catches my eye. I turn for a closer look. The War Stopper is coming back over treetop horizons and reigning a heavy payload upon Armada and Dah'Sel resistance. Our ships are falling. Ground vessels are retreating and getting torn to shreds. We are not going to stop it. Not now. We do not have enough crafts in the sky.

Instincts kick in. I leave the forest and rush across the field to the only tunnel entrance not in it, but it is not close.

"Mason to Sergeant Bentley," I say.

No response.

"Mason to anyone."

Nothing. My comm must have been damaged in the crash, but I cannot take it apart to examine it without tools. I need to reach the tunnels and find someone to communicate with my squad.

"What the…?" I ask, stopping in a two-foot-deep patch of snow.

Nearly a hundred of the benvata flyers that destroyed our camp when we first arrived are emerging from an overhead patch of clouds. Their drop is that of a 45-degree angle heading straight toward the white battlefield. I backpedal, turn, run back toward the Vut Honna forest, and look over my shoulder to ensure they are not heading my way.

The benvata fliers are more significant in stature than I remember. It is hard to tell from here, but something is different about them. They impact and grab the red-and-black War Stopper repeatedly until they shroud it. It turns, spins, and roles to shake them—most of which do not let go. Those that shook free go right back to attacking it. Some are shot and fall lifeless to the planet's surface, with feathers lofting behind them.

The ship is heading in my direction, out of control, and coming in fast. I break right to get out of its path, looking back one last time to see the large flyers letting go of it before it hits the ground. I stumble and fall before reaching the forest edge again, looking to my right as it tumbles past me.

It comes to a rest, upside down against a large boulder protruding from the ground 50 paces away. The flyers have torn sensors and small attachments off that the Uprisers no doubt hooked up to bypass Armada coding. An Upriser is still alive within the War Stopper.

The wounded man slides through the side door holding his neck in pain and coughs as black smoke rushes out of the cockpit and rises for the clouds. He runs a few paces from it and drops to his knees in search of fresh air.

Benvata flyers smother him in attack. I cannot see him past their flapping wings and colorful feathers. Sharp talons and teeth must be tearing the red-and-black garments from his body. Shreds of it fly around them.

"Ahhhhh," screams the Upriser. "Ahhh!"

I take off toward the Vut Honna forest again. The Upriser's cries behind me stop. He has met his end. I do not want to be next. My pulse is rapid at the thought of being eaten alive and knowing it might happen. I need a good hiding spot. Ten more paces, and I will be…

A benvata lands near me. I scream and come to a halt. It is staring with a cocked head but not attacking. Not yet. I continue toward the forest, but it hops beside me and opens its wings to intimidate me. Moonlight catches its multicolored feathers as it stretches out its wings, opens a half-pace wide beak, and squawks an ear-piercing tone.

I cup my hands over my ears and stumble. That sound … it is disrupting my equilibrium. My body is not obeying me. I crawl. The best I can, I crawl.

It stops its squawk of death. This is my chance, now or never, and I am going with now on this one. This rotation is bad enough without me being mauled.

I barely make it to the tree line before realizing it is hopping after me. There is no way I can outrun it. I stop and turn to face it as slowly as possible. Its blue, red, and yellow eyes do not project a feeling of empathy toward me.

"Please don't eat me," I say.

A flyer larger than the benvata flies close into view and hovers in place with flapping wings. I peek my head over its side. A Vee'Sal is riding it and covered with the dried muddy mixture the Dah'Sel coated themselves with the first 30 rotations of our arrival before braving the moonlight.

This flyer he is on, its height is taller than what Skedelski was by half a pace. Turquoise feathers spot its black undercoat. Hundreds of tiny teeth and large, sharp talons let me know it is formidable, but the burgundy-colored saddle and reins looped around the outer portion of its circular horns protruding from its beak let me know someone tamed it. At least, it is tame to its rider.

"*Lep ne kook,*" he says. "*Ma ulat. Ohrap seblak-zim e lep ne kook.*"

CALAMITY

The large flyer looks back and forth between me and the Vee'Sal for a moment—while I try not to defecate myself—and takes flight. The Vee'Sal riding it cuts me an intensely piercing look and shakes his head. I am glad it is gone, but it leaves me wondering why he is so agitated with me. I could feel the negative tension in his gaze. Also, that was certainly not one of the benvata that destroyed our camp when we first arrived on Wah'Lor. Not a clue what these new flyers are, other than dangerous.

30-3
Hitching a Ride

I move from the Vut Honna forest and take across off the field again in what I think is my third attempt to cross it. An Armada medical transport vessel approaches me from my right, and it is coming in hot. The urge to jump out of its way fades as it slows and stops next to me. It is Dr. Lasor.

"Get in," he says.

I do not think twice before climbing in and shutting the door behind me.

"Are you okay?" asks Dr. Lasor.

"I think so," I answer.

"And you're sure about that?"

"Why?"

"I saw you limping," answers Dr. Lasor while piloting the medical transport vessel. "And your eyes aren't exactly tracking correctly. You have a heavy concussion."

"You can tell all that just by looking at me?" I ask.

He points to vital feeds overlaying the forward view pane.

"Completely forgot about those," I say. "It's worse than I thought, isn't it?"

"Your head?" asks Dr. Lasor. "No. The battle, I'm afraid, yes."

I look at the skies.

"What are those things attacking the Uprisers?" I ask.

"Not a single clue," answers Dr. Lasor. "I'm just glad they're not attacking us."

I watch them for a moment.

"You mean," I say, "not attacking us yet."

Dr. Lasor looks up for a moment.

"My fears exactly," he says.

We are an easy target in this medical vessel, but the Uprisers are too concerned with eliminating the remaining Armada and Dah'Sel to focus on us. We are not a threat to them right now. As soon as their task at hand is complete, they will surely kill us.

Ground battles come into view when we reach the peak of the field's highest ground. Bodies are everywhere. Both Armada and Upriser ground transports lie scattered and destroyed throughout the area amongst a few fallen airborne vessels.

We come to a stop near one of the tunnel entrances and exit. Dr. Lasor grabs his med kit and moves into the tunnel behind me. I stop, only long enough to shut it once he is inside.

30-4
Trauma

The tunnel feels longer than usual as we run through its large, open area. A lady in non-Armada military attire is weeping at the wall to my right. I pass her under the influence of Dr. Lasor's urgency, too hurried to stop and address her worries. She has probably lost a loved one, and I cannot help but wonder where the 'Cet family and my squad are upon seeing her fret.

My eyes widen with a gasp when we reach the meeting hall in the tunnel system. I know now why Dr. Lasor was in such a hurry to get here. This has become a place of triage.

"I'm going to need your help," says Dr. Lasor.

"I've got to find—"

"Now," interrupts Dr. Lasor. "Please. I just need you for a moment."

I look around for somebody else that could help him. There is no one. A broken arm here and a missing leg over there. All here are wounded. A woman is unconscious with her head heavily bandaged. No one is with her. I stare for a tik and realize she is not breathing. She is gone.

"Mason," says Dr. Lasor with a raised voice.

"Okay," I say, "but where's everybody?"

"Risking their lives in the fields to bring in more wounded," he answers.

"What do you need me to do?" I ask.

Dr. Lasor sets up his med kit and points to a man with an open wound on the left side of his chest cavity. His sternum and ribs are exposed but nothing appears broken. It is a weapon burn of some kind. Flesh drips from his body around the wound.

"Take the north corridor about a quarter of a click," answers Dr. Lasor. "There's an indentation in the wall on the left. Grab the life-rack from it and bring it to me. Make haste."

I take off. "I got it."

"Mason..."

I stop and turn back to face him.

"Have you ever operated a life-rack before?" he asks.

I shake my head.

"Its power switch is on its underside," says Dr. Lasor, "dead center between its legs. Power it on, hold the red button at the top center for five tiks, and it should be mobile."

I take off again. Tunnel walls fly by as I rush to save a life and get back to my squad. The life-rack comes into view before I know it.

It is nearly my height, full of unfamiliar instruments, and resting on four legs without wheels. I reach quickly to its underside and flip the switch he mentioned, then stand on my tippy toes to hold down the red button. Moments later, the legs telescope into themselves as it powers up and lowers half a pace to hover.

I can barely hear my footsteps over my thoughts while racing it back to him. They are random and all over the place. Unfocused.

"Mason," says Dr. Lasor.

I cut left and rush the life rack to his side as he flags me down. He takes it from me to do whatever he will do with it while pulling a few cables from it.

"That's all I needed," he says. "Go find another starfighter and show these Uprisers what a mistake they've made."

I take off without telling them there are no more starfighters to my knowledge. Casting further gloom upon him would be pointless and do nothing more than distract him from helping the injured. The man does not need to be looking over his shoulder, awaiting his turn to get shot while saving lives.

30-5
Desperation

I exit the next tunnel hatch into a field of rampage. Uprisers and humans alike are running low on ammo and energy reserves. A few are still firing. Many are locked in hand-to-hand combat with fists, blades, and High-V sticks. One swings an empty weapon like a club.

"Here," calls a nearby female Armada soldier.

I rush to her side behind an overturned Argos.

"What's the situ—"

The Argos we are hiding behind is impacted and rocks up and back to a single track for a tic before falling to its base again. With what, I do not know. We barely get out of the way in time before it crushes us and take cover behind it again.

"Screw it," she says, pulling a disorientation charge from her side.

It is a powerful, oval-shaped, grenade-like weapon that targets the equilibrium and central nervous system. Its effects last for five or more teks.

"You're not going to—"

"You'd better believe it," she interrupts.

She inputs her identification code to activate it and throws it as far as she can over the battered Argos protecting us. Not three tiks later, the night sky lights up with a white-hot flash. My vision narrows to nothing, and I collapse.

Cobwebs in my head thicken as I lie on the ground next to her. We struggle to stand but fall. I roll to my side to scan the field.

The Armada and Dah'Sel are retreating in vast numbers before she can throw it. Many are falling to the Upriser onslaught, but all within a three-click radius are on the ground. Even the fliers fall to the field, barely moving.

This lady lying next to me is a fighter. She set it for the highest yield and maximum range. It was a wise decision, per Armada tactics. If one is losing any given battle, they are to render both sides inactive on the field. Once motor functions return, the process is repeated by another, then again. Armada members do not stop this course of action until backup arrives and the skirmish returns to their favor. The problem now is that we do not have anyone coming to help. All we have are already engaged.

It is wearing off a little, but not much. My extremities are tingling the way a foot or hand does after falling asleep, but I only have enough strength to crawl on my elbows right now.

I clamber around the battered Argos as others stand and fall in attempts to be the first to fire again.

"Do you see that?" I ask.

She is too out of it to understand the question with only a single eye open. Her head wobbles and drops to the snow.

More Dah'Sel are coming on a large cart-like platform on wooden wheels. It is being pulled by ... I honestly do not know. The two pulling it have four muscular legs under an equally developed top and a head way too small for their frames. Large, curved horns protrude from their spines between their front shoulder blades and angle over their heads—facing forward like daggers.

Atop the cart they pull is a leather canopy. Tila'Cet is driving it with reins in her hands and hair blowing in the wind. Four Vee'Sal covered in mud wait in the safety of a cage beside her with green horns in hand.

"Tila'Cet," I shout.

She pulls closer and does not stop until reaching the center of the battlefield. Several Armada and Uprisers get to their feet and drop to a knee or fall while trying to grab their rifles again. They have not recovered from the disorientation charge.

"*Pilim aday,*" she shouts.

I repeat her call to *get back*, though most are already trying to create distance between themselves and her. It is a good thing most of the Armada know the simpler of

CALAMITY

Kla'Wah words. Those within earshot of me who did not understand her move as far away as they can. Others relay my cry to *get back* to those downfield.

"KLAZ'DRA!!!" I scream across moonlit darkness with a breaking voice.

Armada members take off, running as far from the incoming cart as possible. They know what is coming. We all do.

Tila'Cet grabs a rope, unhooks the four-legged creatures pulling the cart, and climbs atop one of them with the rope in hand. I am glad she is okay but continue running away with uncoordinated strides like the surrounding others without looking back. She waits for the first Upriser to grab a rifle, then pulls the rope while riding off on whatever they call that thing she is riding at full speed.

The rope gets taut fast and snatches her back before it pulls a canopy from the platform she was hauling. Dozens of Dah'Sel... No. Wait. White undercoats... It is the Vee'Sal. They are standing on the cart unprotected from the moonlight's shine.

Klaz'Dra transforms them into the beasts we once waged an unintentional war with. They tear immediately into the protective cage on the cart for the mud-covered Vee'Sal to no avail, then target Uprisers remaining on the battlefield ... decimating all without mercy. Limbs not being eaten fly through the air to splat the ground around them.

Each of the crazed beasts takes out five or six terrified red-and-black-suited enemies at a time. Another cart pulls in from the flank side and does the same. Twenty or thirty Klaz'Dra crazed Vee'Sal tear the Uprisers to ribbons. More body parts are flying... Entire sides of ribs are torn out with claws and tossed to the side as their torsos become bowls the transformed drink from.

Running out of Uprisers to share, they attack each other along with all around them. Nothing is safe. All is fair game during their sacred *Black Sky Transformation.*

Benvata fliers awaken in the field, take back to the air, and remove the last few Upriser vessels present. It does not last long once they get involved, but it is not pretty. Three flyers are snatched from the air by mutated, high-leaping Vee'Sal under the transformation. Feathers float around them as they drop back down to eat their flying snacks.

Vee'Sal covered in mud to protect themselves from the transformation open their protective cages and leap from the carts with curved wooden sticks that have a cloth attached to them and launch ceramic-looking balls at our enemies like slingshots. Their targets are drenched with liquid fire upon contact. Further Upriser screams ensue.

In less than a tek, they have the Uprisers wishing they had never come here and remained on Kep Four to accept their fate. There are only a few left by the time it is over, and they are surrendering without resistance. Some are still being maimed. One drops to his knees.

"Please," shouts the Upriser. "We give up."

A transformed beast lands behind him, tilts his body to the left, and bites into his shoulder and torso ... successfully removing the man's head and arm in a single bite as another one of the beasts attacks it. They fight and tumble over the man's body for dominance over who gets to eat the rest of him.

More Vee'Sal covered in mud storm the field with the same pale green horns. They stop and blow into them. I stop running to look back when I hear it.

The transformed creatures once Vee'Sal drop in pain and flop about the ground.

Mud-covered Vee'Sals move in and throw large blankets over them to shield the moonlight's shine, forcing a quick change back to their natural state before getting escorted away undercover. The rest of our saviors are binding the submitting Upriser's hands behind their backs with rope.

This points to Upriser heart and mentality because those in the Armada would have given their last breath in a battle like this. Such victories are mentioned in historical digibooks, but no Armada personnel has ever had a reason to engage in such a heated conflict until now. This was their chance to go down in history, and everyone, including myself, has earned their place immortalized in time.

CHAPTER 31
Parting Ways

It has been 12 rotations since the Vee'Sal leader I came to know as Kre'Lux spoke with Wat'Uza. Humans were not allowed to be present during their conversation. The Dah'Sel leader told us the Vee'Sal demanded we leave Wah'Lor before they left for Lesdelop ti'it ratim-zis with their captives.

Wat'Uza told him we are no longer capable of departure and that the Armada side of humanity is not inherently evil. Kre'Lux did not accept the retort. He stated if we are not the same as the Uprisers, we will let the Vee'Sal take the surrendered. As it turns out, they are planning on feeding them to the large fliers they somehow guided in their attack, as well as to other livestock. It is a horrifying thought.

The Vee'Sal stayed in the underground tunnels the night of that rotation until the moon's shine left the dark sky. Hundreds of surviving Uprisers were left unhappy in bindings with them when the suns rose. Something about it bothered me—not that I know what we would have done with them—but part of me is uneasy about sending the captured with the Vee'Sal. We would have done nothing more than further decimate our standing with the secretive sect if we stopped them from taking them.

Uprisers are scum. Albeit born into their nature or a choice some made of desperation, that is all they are. Still, none of us could bear telling them of their stomach-bound fates before the Vee'Sal left with their new livestock feed lined up and tied behind them. At least, I could not. Perhaps somebody else did. I am unsure; but the walk back to their sect will be 60 clicks on foot for our attackers. They will find out when the Vee'Sal's animals get hungry along the way.

The Vee'Sal never spoke a word to me or anyone else transplanted here. They never will. Their sect's hate runs deep for humanity. I would feel the same if I were in their position. We have turned a world of peace into one of heartache and violence. Wat'Uza has advised us to keep our distance from them.

I walk the fields near the burned dofabe trees where my comrades are buried. Their leaves will return to shelter those beneath them from the suns, snow, and rain. The same cannot be said for the hearts of us who lost children and loved ones. There is no shelter from sorrow.

"Sellers to Mason," calls Dr. Sellers over comms.

"I'm here," I say.

"You okay over there? You've been gone a while."

"Yeah," I answer while circling a dofabe tree with my palm on its bark. "I'll head back in a bit."

"Alright," he says. "Just checking on you. Sellers out."

Kuzio, the man who taught me how to fly, pulled through after Delgado and I found him. He is currently sharing my tele-tent with me. I avoid going into it unless sleep is needed. Doctors are in and out of there at all taks of the rotation and checking on him. It is a depressing reminder of all that has happened to sit and look at him.

The tree next to me has Skedelski beneath it. Fister is a click from here at the furthest edge of the field visiting

Rhigas. He is not as talkative as he used to be, but he still has his moments.

I look toward warming stars and take in a deep breath of them before heading back toward the Dah'Sel's Lesdelop. We will spend the next 10 or more rotations cleaning the fields and forest. It will be easier with the snow melting. We owe the Dah'Sel that, but my help will have to wait until after Dr. Klinroy reconstitutes my bloodstream with more nano to stop oncoming visions and headaches. I almost died on the table three rotations after the attack ended. He does not want to take any chances.

There is more debris to clear than I originally thought: pieces of vessels large and small, from Beltric Class Six's to the Armada *Ark* and more. We must dispose of their remains without damaging the planet. We also have a lot of begging for forgiveness to do.

As for Dolofónos and Saddi, we do not know where they and the two Butchers that came down in the drop pods are. They could have died on impact or still be out there somewhere in a melting region of Wah'Lor's winter trying to figure out their survival. There are few I have ever known in life that I wished dead. May the planet take them.

No one heard from that young pilot named Barsa after we went searching for the *Ark*. I feel he did not make it, but I have hope. *What would anybody's life be during a time of crisis without hope, but meaningless?*

I found out the large flyer that Vee'Sal was riding is called a swatel. I do not know how long it took to tame and fly them, but it would not bother me to never see one again. They terrify me.

We have another series of graves to dig now that we have broken down HU-1. I am tired of watching Armada diggers bury people. It was even harder to watch the Dah'Sel digging under dofabe trees to bury their own. If it never happened again, it would not be long enough.

Sunrises and sunsets are going to prove challenging in the future. Every rotation will be a test. Some Dah'Sel question our presence here since the Upriser invasion, though most still accept us. Our knowledge and technology have done a lot for them over the last 200 or so rotations. Their bond with me is one of the best things we have going for us. It must be protected.

I think everything will work out for the best, but there are no guarantees. What remains of humanity on Wah'Lor are good people. Some may not be the nicest or most talkative, but none of us wish negativity upon the Kla'Wah that live here.

My fingers are crossed again for the best, and I am looking forward to a life of serenity. I have my squad and the 'Cets—my intergalactic adoptive family—to care for, embrace, cry to, and laugh with if needed. My support will be theirs as theirs has been mine. I will not let Tila'Cet slip from my reach before letting her know how much I truly care for her. Our union will come to fruition soon, and this war has told me how much I desire someone like her next to me when I open my eyes to start a new rotation.

For now, we must clean up our mess. Less than a cycle here, and humanity has already hurt this planet along with its generously forgiving inhabitants. I do not think it is too late to find peace with the Vee'Sal, but that is a bridge we must cross when we get to it.

I believe most of humankind is good by default at birth. The vast majority of us oppose the use of violence or inflicting suffering upon others. We always sought ways to keep each other alive and in good health with what resources we had.

NIVEOUS WAR

The problem with humanity is that there are always people who will use the suffering of others as a stepping-stone to get where they want to end in life. We spent hundreds of generations systematically eliminating and breeding these people out of our populace. Still, those who do not believe in a unified race formed the Uprisers and mounted resistance to our cause. Over time, that resistance became an enemy of the Armada.

I think about the circumstances heavily while walking in this field of misery. It is time for the Armada to clean up our mess. We have thousands of cadavers to dispose of. There has not been a body count yet, but the number is high. Nobody in my squad died in the skirmish, nor did anybody I know personally within the Dah'Sel sect. They only lost a handful from their side this time around. While it is unacceptable, they know we did our best to fight our fight without drawing them into it.

We lost James Algash in battle. I do not know how it happened, but his body was amongst the fields with a few others. Regardless of how he went out, I know he did the best he could and gave his life in the name of humanity.

Sergeant Bentley is in critical condition, but doctors Lasor, Klinroy, and Sellers have all informed us about his overall outlook. He is expected to pull through. Delgado reported him wounded and unconscious, with our squad holding their position during the battle's final moments.

Fister took nasty onium rounds to the back to protect Sergent Bently after he went down, but is okay now. They should both fully recover within 30 rotations. None of us will be the same.

Din'Mos has been sitting bedside with Delgado awaiting Sergeant Bentley to awaken. Myself, my squad, and the 'Cets pay regular visits in the hope of being there when he opens his eyes. We have grown closer than ever, and I am more than thankful for it. I thought many of them were killed in the Upriser blitz. The tears I cried when I found out they were alive could have been enough to drown in.

Tila'Cet has proven herself beautiful, brave, and without equal. When the battle ended, our first embrace was that of legend. My heart sings fables of a future with her.

I believe that time is right around the corner. It is the reason I can still smile from time to time, and I am ready for it. I cannot wait to see what rotations to come will bring. Hopefully, the Vee'Sal will be more accepting of us in a cycle or five from now.

I am going to focus on showing the Dah'Sel we are dedicated to healing them and the planet they call Wah'Lor. The approaching summer will be a hot season. We arrived in fall, went to war in winter, and hope summer is picturesque in all ways. We will know soon, and I will approach it with love in my heart and a first night spent together in union that is right around the corner.

There is one thing I am curious about. Nala'Cet said there is another sect here on Wah'Lor. They still go by "Kla'Wah" and apparently live in the original settlement some 600 clicks from Lesdelop. Half of them wanted to leave the Kla'Wah region and spread themselves across the planet. They left eventually and settled on this side of Langaea and broke up to become what we know now as the Dah'Sel and Vee'Sal.

I hope we can meet them someday. For now, we will focus our efforts here with the Dah'Sel and repair the damage we have done. Anything beyond that is possible in time ... and time is something we have plenty of. We will use it wisely.

NIVEOUS WAR

I make my way across the field toward the tele-tents when an unexpected smile creeps onto my face. This is my home. It is all of ours. I still love it here and will make things right. Come haze or high water, I belong to Wah'Lor now.

LANGUAGE TRANSLATIONS
WolfStar Universe

Kla'Wah to English Translator— (Alphabetic order):

Abaz = Trouble/Problem
Aday = Back
Ama = You
Anag = Rest
Armona = Love
Aryan = Hand
Axta = Better
Azata = End/Stop
Banra = Lift
Bea = With
Beena = Sleep
Besta = Crazy
Bex = Separate
Baklee = Evil
Bela = Life
Benja = Apart
Bizmon = Demon
Blagrah = White
Blakabak = Announce
Blenya = Friend
Blenyas = Friendship
Blazee = Bird
Bleku = Hurry
Blight = I
Cakou = Run
Can = Tear/Rip
Caves = Else
Cea = Me
Chant = Best
Chasta = Since
Chit = Heaven
Conan = Place/Location

Cre = Can/Could
Crelo = Can't/Cannot
Crez = Our
Da = At
Dada = Thank
Dalasa = Catch
Dasa = Trust
Dase = About
Deadis = Ahead
Delt = Need
Dexlee = Please
Deyar = Ready
Dez = Nothing
Dind = Find
Disen = First
Dit = Did
Dita = Dad/Father
Diti = Hold
Dolpoz = Demand
Dotin = Next
Drost = World
Dubol = Ground
Dwaloc = Strong
E = The
Elo = Sky
En = My
Ena = From
Enlasa = Miss

Eo = Took/Take
Erif = Free
Ersee = Bye
Erude = Heart
Exes = Look
Fak = Rotation
Falsa = Bring
Fasna = Lot/Much
Fax = Lose
Faxi = Lost
Fejaz = Worse
Feld = Animal/Wildlife
Fenka = Forest
Fesnop = This
Fit = Child/Kid
Flazee = Head/Mind
Flis = Control
Flowcee = Drown
Fradus = Kill
Frat = Open
Fraza = Sad
Frex = Accept
Friveka = Beautiful/Pretty
Fusite = War
Ga = Eye
Gane = Part/Portion
Ganta = Proud
Gate = Off

WOLFSTAR UNIVERSE

Gav = Ask
Gazno = Last
Gecsapasa = Impossible
Gessah = Message
Gingo = Not
Glakef = Taste
Glenoda = Help
Glezlock = Bitch
Glotren = Scared
Gof = Meet
Golos = Hear
Gomee = Up
Gona = Able
Gopo = Write
Grag = Believe
Gratalua = Permission
Greh = School
Grenas = Think
Grinsapes = Tradition
Gwampa = Change/Switch
Gwan = Their
Gwana = There
Haka = Oath/Promise
Hakio = Blood
Hakiya = Bleed
Hama = Natural
Haman = Nature
Hamp = Well

Hasta = Want
Haza = Wall
Heeza = Sun/Star
Heg = Lay
Helkla = Area/Region/Zone
Heltno = Dream
Hempa = Sorry
Henkadi = Follow
Himan = Past
Hitto = Reach
Honna = Plant
Honkea = Different
Hue = Sister
Hueton = Here
Icci = Stay
Ikkida = Try
Illa = Odd
Inbem = Enter
Inhala = Smoke
Inots = Like
Intom = Least
Ipasag = Also
Irina = Become
Isacaz = Truth
Iscafo = Violence
Jambit = Leader
Janest = Gone
Jappa = When

NIVEOUS WAR

Jasros = Winter
Jesen = Go
Jazaxe = Then
Jelq = Okay
Jem = Win
Jezafe = Soul
Jipwa = Transformation
Jo = Be
Jokata = Rise
Jotap = Alive
Ka = Are
Kalps = Agree
Kav = Over
Kawen = Wake/Awaken
Kela = Word
Keleo = Magic
Kena = These
Ki = As
Kimit = Toward
Kipoa = Other
Kiskil = Bless
Kit = Should
Klava = Same
Klaz'Dra = Disease
Klis = Sick
Klota = Forward
Kook = Black
Kurka = Lucky
Kuzsoec = Come
Lab = If
Lassabax = River
Lazzaz = Foot
Ledad = Was
Ledasno = Return
Lekde = Snow
Langaea = Pangaea
Lats = Start
Ledram = Time
Lep = Red
Leprev = Under
Lessdelop = Home
Letrow = Leg
Licea = Must
Likiedasno = Bastard
Lilimensa = Sit
Lipfa = Yes
Loilcim = Breathe
Lokodee = Prepare
Loudac = Happy
Ma = No
Mabap = Where
Maner = Remain
Matao = See
Mecee = Every
Meceete = Everybody/Everyone

WOLFSTAR UNIVERSE

Meldu = Moment/Instant
Mesp = High
Meva = Doctor
Miga = Yesterday
Mola = Moon
Muto = Save
Nacas = Or
Nasig = Decide/Choose/Pick
Natroqfel = Tonight
Nax = Only
Ne = And
Nebes = Earn
Neeb = Been
Nemons = Crops
Nery = Worry/Concern
Nesplu = Understand
Nest = Soon
Niss = Wait
Nit = Chest/Torso
Nosaj = Secret
O = Am
Ofdrec = Might
Ohrap = We
Ola = Before
Oladi = Elder
Olov = Step
Olsa = Make
Opacha = Large

Onas = Long
Onast = Longer
Ooves = Clouds
Orsplap = Know
Ot = Is
Ox = Extremely/Very
Ozalt = Check
Pacala = Keep
Pac = Another
Pasho = Reflection
Peelota = Flower
Peca = Thing
Pegnada = Dance
Pes = Do
Pilim = Get
Pisip = Us
Pizta = Use
Plafoh = Visit
Plako = Forbid/Forbidden
Plama = Let
Plenta = Grave
Plett = Because
Plup = Fall
Po = It
Polasa = Speak/Talk/Say
Polasap = Said
Pota = Arm
Prajet = Pass

Prakan = Starve	**Sawez** = New
Prakanto = Starvation	**Seblak** = Attack
Qala = Between	**Sexti** = Alone
Qicea = Close	**Seza** = Join
Quotot = Surround	**Siju** = Field/Clearing
Qua = Almost	**Sinol** = Baby/Infant
Quipa = Amazing	**Siwbe** = Them
Quamza = Careful	**Skarm** = Fight
Quena = Water	**Smetlac** = Happen
Ralaha = Correct	**Soo** = He/Him
Rarge = Union	**Sopet** = Drink
Ratim = Generation	**Specap** = Hello
Reema = For	**Staog** = Tree
Refet = Still	**Stafor** = Represent
Relee = Brother	**Su** = On
Renasa = All	**Suetrow** = Body
Pest = An	**Swil** = Mouth
Retsu = Were	**T** = Share
Ricath = Honor	**Tacab** = Just
Rilc = Hair	**Tadak** = Fast/Quick/Rapid
Rita = Mom/Mother	**Takiep** = Sect
Rolt = Harvest/Gather	**Tanza** = Care
Roser = Done	**Tar** = Fear
Rot = Now	**Tata** = Door/Entrance
Sa = Of	**Tatam** = Danger
Saca = Has	**Taxag** = Right
Saftic = Those	**Taxat** = Left
Saisay = They	**Teed** = Dead

WOLFSTAR UNIVERSE

Teedoe = Deadly
Teefa = Death
Teeza = Die
Teilis = Silence/Quiet
Tese = Set
Tigeth = Together
Ti'it = To
Tirqesa = Relax
Tom = A
Topcal = That
Tos = Dirt
Tralama = Good
Tralea = Monsoon
Trampt = Younger
Trang = Plus
Trensapa = Nobody
Trestaluk = Welcome
Tret'tret = How
Tribeka = Translate
Troqfall = Tomorrow
Troqfel = Night
Tump = But
Turahan = Accident
Lekda = Snow
Ubido = Small/Tiny
Ulapra = Finish/Complete
Ulat = More
Ulaula = Approach
Uneger = Finger
Unel = Tool
Unsha = Hunt
Uptru = Will
Utlu = What
Vasa = Wrong
Vasika = Touch
Vel = Game
Vemp = Who
Ver = Your
Verall = Arrive
Verallto = Arrival
Volna = Remember
Vula = Inside
Vulat = Outside
Vut = Hungry
Wab = Give
Wabuki = Have
Wagthra = Peace
Wams = After
Waq = Scale/Size
Watt = Aside
Wazme = Why
Wazo = Drunk
Wella = Light
Wena = Send
Whattka = Family
Whaul = Break/Shatter

Wist = Never
Woo = Hurt
Wubeno = Damn
Ya = In
Yama = Her/She
Yamag = Mad/Angry
Yapo = Excite
Yata = Self
Yataat = Man
Yaw = Feel
Yelta = Name
Yetia = Out

Yilp = Safe
Yirit = Banish/Exile
Yom = Way
Yop = Had
Zama = Walk
Zamba = Leave
Zasta = Heal
Zenta = Hi
Zindoc = Enough
Zotka = Push
Zune = Many
Zibot = Grass

MODIFIERS:

-**Zap** = less (as in useless)
-**Zal** = 's (Possessive)
-**Zeg** = un (as in unnecessary)
-**Zel** = ment (movement)
-**Zic** = (Present tense - ing)
-**Zim** = (Past-tense)

-**Zis** = (Plural)
-**Zõk** = Re (As in replay)
-**Zut** = ly (as in accidentally)

NUMBERS (CONSTANT INITIAL SEQUENCES)

Toop = 0
Qa = 1
Qe = 2
Qi = 3
Qo = 4
Qu = 5
Za = 6
Zi = 7
Zo = 8
Zu = 9

Tens have singles rotating to the front of word, as in 10-20 below:

Qa-toop = 10
Qa-Qa = 11
Qa-Qe = 12
Qa-Qi = 13
Qa-Qo = 14
Qa-Qu = 15

Qa-Za = 16
Qa-Zi = 17
Qa-Zo = 18
Qa-Zu = 19
Qe-toop = 20
Qe-Qa = 21
Qe-Qe = 22
Qe-Qi = 23
Qe-Qo = 24
Qe-Qu = 25
Qe-Za = 26
Qe-Zi = 27
Qe-Zo = 28
Qe-Zu = 29
And so forth…

Numbers (100+ initial sequences):

Toopa = 100 - (Hundreds)
Toope = 1,000 - (Thousands)
Toopi = 10,000 - (Ten-thousands)
Toopo = 100,000 - (Hundred-thousands)
Toopu = 1,000,000 - (Millions)

TIME MEASUREMENT:

Aionas = 100 cycles
Cycles = Years
Dekatee = Decade
Rotations = Days
Taks: = Hours
Teks: = Minutes
Tiks = Seconds

BOOK CLUB QUESTIONS

1. How many trials and tribulations do you think the Dah'Sel can or will take from humanity before they have had enough and decide to alter their standing with them?

2. How much more medication and how many more visions do you think McKayla Mason's body can handle before she dies and suffers permanent brain or psychological damage?

3. Will Dolofónos keep his Upriser's motivated enough to stand and fight at his side with all that has happened without them turning on him, and do you think anyone from The Armada would take them in if they sought asylum?

4. Will humanity ever stop destroying their environments or worlds they may live on in the future? If yes, how? If not, why?

5. If Sergeant Bentley's critical wounds leave him crippled, will it affect his ability to lead?

6. What is the outlook on Mason and Tila'Cet's future with all that is happening between the Dah'Sel and Vee'Sal's strained relationship and Uprisers looming on the horizon?

7. As Pru'Cet continues aging, what role do you think he will assume in the Dah'Sel hierarchy, and how could it affect the Vee'Sal relationship if Mason officially becomes family?

8. What do you think was the tipping point in Wat'Uza's mind that led him to reach out for the Vee'Sal's help to save a race they already disdained?

9. How will Wat'Uza deal with the loss of Wete'Uza?

10. How do you think the previously unknown third Kla'Wah sect, 600 clicks from Lesdelop, will play into the WolfStar world?

11. Would you rather live on a world like Wah'Lor before the Armada arrived with your family and loved ones, or the one you live on right now—known as Ancient Earth in WolfStar?

AUTHOR BIOS

Jason Diamond and C R Buchanan:

Combined, Jason Diamond and C. R. Buchanan have a long history of writing, with a friendship that spans over a dozen years. With the conclusion of wrapping the first book and mapping out the complete WolfStar story, they realized the epic was going to consume years of their lives and buckled down. Between the WolfStar saga and writing feature films, they will never stop putting pen to paper.

C. R. BUCHANAN
C. R. Buchanan's website: www.crbuchanan.com
JASON DIAMOND
Jason Diamond's website: www.vondiamondink.com

Discover more at
4HorsemenPublications.com

10% off using HORSEMEN10

www.ingramcontent.com/pod-product-compliance
Lightning Source LLC
LaVergne TN
LVHW041744060526
838201LV00046B/903